THE FINEST YEARS AND ME

Mark Woodburn was born in Edinburgh, 1968, and grew up in Scotland, Canada and South Africa. His colourful employment history includes work in forestry, pet food, ladies' fashion, risk analysis and as a part-time soldier in the Royal Corps of Transport.

He currently lives in West Lothian, with his wife and daughter, and is a season ticket holder at Heart of Midlothian Football Club. His first novel, *Winston and Me*, was published by Valley Press in 2012.

The Finest Years and Me

M A R K W O O D B U R N

Valley Press

First published in 2015 by Valley Press
Woodend, The Crescent, Scarborough, YO11 2PW
www.valleypressuk.com

First edition, first printing (October 2015)

ISBN 978-1-908853-56-1
Cat. no. VP0073

The publisher and author would like to thank Jo Brandon for her
editorial assistance during the preparation of this novel for publication.

The verse on page 315 is from 'At Bladon', written for Churchill's
funeral by Avril Andersen, a *nom de plume* for Lily Avril Crabtree.

Printed and bound in the EU by Pulsio, Paris.

www.valleypressuk.com/authors/markwoodburn

This book is dedicated in memory of my father,
William Woodburn

London, February 1942

THE YOUNG MAN *poured from the brandy decanter and handed the glass to his father, who sat slumped despondently in his chair. The son then returned to the sofa, reclining next to the room's other occupant, his mother.*

'Bollocks, Pop!' the young man announced angrily after draining his glass in one swallow. 'No way can that spineless bunch get rid of you! Christ, the very thought!'

'And should I care? Should I? Who has led the country to this moment! Oh, the shame of it! The shame!' The old man appeared to sink deeper into his seat, the glass grasped in both hands, his head down.

'It isn't your fault, darling. You can't be blamed.' The soothing words from his wife elicited no response from her husband.

There followed a momentary but strained silence. Winston Churchill then slowly lifted his eyes and blearily stared ahead. They sat in the small living room of the No.10 Annexe, the reinforced flat near the Prime Minister's official residence in Downing Street. They had moved in shortly after Churchill took office, as the historic address was deemed too fragile to protect during German bombing raids.

All the old man could view in his mind's eye were thousands of his soldiers being taken away to God knows what fate at the hands of a barbarous enemy; many of whom had been led off newly arrived troop ships to be marched straight into captivity. Some of the early reports coming in were still sketchy, but that one above all tormented him profoundly.

Youngsters; laddies ... what would he tell their parents?

'It was not supposed to happen. Wavell assured me it wouldn't happen...' he moaned almost inaudibly.

'Wavell couldn't find his arse with both hands and a compass!' his son, Randolph, cursed.

'No, no, my boy, it's more than that,' his father attempted to explain. 'It's something that has plagued us long before this war began. A malady, a particular British malaise of complacency, of arrogance and of sheer slothfulness. Oh, if I had the chance all over again!'

'Well, it can't be undone now,' his son commiserated. 'But Pop, more immediately, what about Cripps? And Max? Those two bastards are as dangerous as the Japs! You have to smash 'em, both!' Randolph slammed his glass on the wooden arm of the couch for effect.

'Randolph, really!' his mother, Clementine pleaded.

But the old man had returned to painful musing. 'All those men, gone to some unimaginable fate…'

'Papa! Wake up for Christ's sake! You're in trouble! The wolves are gathering! You can't just sit there and drink and whine! We have to do something!' Home on leave from his unit based in North Africa, Randolph was infamous for his fiery temper, intolerant views and notorious drinking and gambling. He was the apple of his father's eye, but was also indulged too greatly; Winston's own lack of fatherly affection perhaps playing a large part in that failing. But for all his bombast, Randolph was entirely devoted to his father and also incredibly loyal and generous to his friends, which bred deep affection as well as exasperation in those who knew him best.

His mother, outraged at this hectoring of her stricken husband, rose to her feet. 'Enough! Let him alone! I demand that you stop bullying your father or I must ask you to leave this house at once!'

The old man who was Prime Minister rose wearily from his chair. 'Excuse me, but I have to visit the loo.'

As he left, Clementine sat down again. She was a highly strung woman who found it difficult to contain her often raging emotions. She had on many occasions resorted to days and sometimes weeks away on her own, to recharge herself, at friends' houses or on cruises abroad, when the highs and lows of her husband's career impinged

8

on her disposition. But she was also tough, and could give out as much as she took. Her husband desperately needed her now, for she believed him to be at his lowest ebb since the war began.

The conflict had not been going well. The latest blow was the recently announced capitulation of Singapore to the army of Japan, a new enemy in the war that had now been raging for over two years. The Asian bastion of the British Empire had been deemed an impregnable fortress, its massive guns pointing out to sea acting as a warning to any foolish naval force that attempted to loiter too close. But the Japanese had not come by sea. They had invaded from the north, by land through Malaya, in tanks and on bicycles; a feat dismissed as impossible by military experts.

They had cut through the numerically superior British, Australian and Indian forces, and only belatedly had Britain sent its most experienced fighting General, Archibald Wavell, east in a vain attempt to retrieve the situation. Wavell was an aggressive and hardened soldier who did his best, though it was believed that the man was exhausted from earlier battles in the western desert and Greece, and years of neglect, complacency and imperial arrogance in Singapore had extinguished any lingering hope. Thus an army of 100,000 men surrendered to a smaller army of 30,000, who were nearly out of food and ammunition and had resorted to a bluff in demanding surrender of their numerically superior – though morally bankrupted – enemy, in order to gain a remarkable victory.

The previous day, the Prime Minister had made a radio broadcast to the nation. It contained the usual fine words and Churchillian flourishes, but this time it had not gone down well with his people. They wanted good news, and all the news had been bad for a considerable period. They demanded action; victories. They no longer wanted platitudes and calls to arms; they were tiring and the end was nowhere near in sight. The time for talking big was over.

Closer to home were concerns over his very position itself. There would be a vote of confidence in the House of Commons which the Prime Minister would win overwhelmingly. But recently, his erstwhile friend and colleague Max Aitken, better known as Lord Beaverbrook, had resigned on grounds of ill-health from his position as Minister of Production. It was disputable how truly "ill" he was, and the whispers in Parliamentary corridors had it that the Canadian newspaper baron was positioning himself as Winston's replacement.

Another potential rival was the recent ambassador to the Soviet Union, Sir Stafford Cripps. The tall, ascetic and socialist Sir Stafford had been making a name for himself with some insightful radio broadcasts, and was seen as an up-and-coming man. Winston, sensing a threat, offered him Beaverbrook's old post, but Cripps refused. He was then offered Leader of the House, effectively number three man in government after Churchill and Clement Attlee, the Labour leader in the wartime coalition. Astute enough to realise he would have to take the position, Cripps accepted – but after a bright start would soon find himself out of his depth and floundering.

This was all in the future but at the present moment, the Prime Minister faced dangers everywhere. The most worrying emanated from the man himself. He had been voicing concerns lately of his tiredness and lack of desire to continue in his mighty task. Clementine, astute as always, recognised this as the most worrying threat. She knew only she could solve that problem, and it was essential that he regain his strength in order to round on his enemies and respond to threats with his customary vigour. But what exactly could she do?

'He's just so alone. That's my worry,' Clementine thought out loud. 'He's surrounded by soldiers or civil servants. He has his doctor, his bodyguard and valet; but they're not his friends. And his health ... how he was in Washington. The thought of that happening again.'

On a recent visit to the United States, the Prime Minister had taken unwell and the truth had not been revealed as to the magnitude of that illness. Clementine knew, and it had added to her worries considerably.

'Well? Who else is there? And what can friends do anyway?' Randolph growled harshly. 'He hasn't had a real friend since F.E. died. The rest, Bracken, the Prof ... bunch of oddballs and nutters!'

Clementine spoke carefully. 'He needs someone that cares for but isn't frightened of him. Who can tell him when to stop! Someone who can remain behind the scenery but has the personality and will to impose himself when it matters. Someone who can inspire and help bring him out of his Black Dogs...'

'A bloody saint, you mean!' Randolph scoffed. 'Mama, there's no-one. He drives everyone mad!'

'...someone who wants nothing or needs nothing from him,' Clementine continued, measuring her words. 'But who has affection for him and understanding. Most of all, understanding!' She smiled suddenly.

'What is it?' Randolph asked, mystified. 'Why the big grin?'

'I know who that someone is,' she replied artfully.

Her son, his thoughts now exactly in tune with his mother's, stared at her directly over his glass, silently mouthing a name.

There was no time to waste. Clementine rose to her feet. 'Randolph, we have to make a telephone call concerning an old friend.'

Chapter One

I HEARD THE knock at the door and got up from my newspaper to answer. I was alone on a Saturday afternoon. Vera, the wife of one of our trawler men, who cleaned and washed two days a week had just left. The girls were out, terrorising North Yorkshire.

I opened the door and the individual standing before me resembled a character straight out of *The Beano*. I'd always taught my daughters not to make judgements based on first impressions; that principle had tested me on the first occasion I'd been introduced to the fellow now standing before me, and I confess to being found wanting. Not a great example of prescience on my part, admittedly, but believe me – if you'd met him, you'd have sympathised with my plight.

'Hello, Brendan!' I declared, though my genuine surprise at seeing him was tempered by caution.

'Jamie! How are you?' A curious accent somewhere between Ireland, Australia and the East End greeted me. I was once told he fancied himself as Errol Flynn, regarding his speech. He thought himself similar to the *Tasmanian devil* in other ways, too.

I welcomed Brendan Bracken, Minister of Information in Churchill's wartime cabinet into my home and helped him remove his overcoat. The winter that year had been a harsh one, particularly in Scotland and here in the north of England, but fortunately Scarborough had missed the worst of the snowfall. Nevertheless my coal fire was blazing away heartily as Brendan went over to it and rubbed his hands.

'How's your driver?' I asked, concerned.

'Oh, don't worry, Jamie. He's driven up further before, so

he tells me,' Brendan replied cheerily.

'What, you've come all the way from London?' I recoiled in some alarm. 'Brendan, you should have called first! What if I was out?'

'Typical, Jamie! What a worrier! Come on, get the tea ready, I'm freezing. Oh, take me back to sunny Adelaide!'

The hills of Tipperary, more like, I thought. I waited till he settled down before I went out to prepare the tea. Loading up with what goodies I could spare with the rationing, I returned with a tray through to the sitting room.

On my re-entrance, as if in recall, Brendan smacked his forehead and roared, 'Christ, I almost forgot!' and dashed out of the room making his way to the front door. He returned from the motorcar moments later, carrying a large hamper which he dropped to the floor before me.

'There you are, Jamie, my boy! Get "tore" into that lot, as you Scotties say!' he declared, breathing heavily while lighting a cigarette.

Bending down and lifting the lid, I found myself gazing in astonishment at luxuries unseen since before the war. American cigars, peanut butter, jam, tinned fruit, sweets and two bottles of whisky: Haig and White Horse.

'Brendan Bracken, you rascal! Marvellous! Let's forget the tea and have a wee dram, eh?' His infectious good humour along with the sight of the Scotch had momentarily removed my earlier reservations.

'No, I'll just have the tea, if you don't mind. It's business first, Jamie.' I was afraid of that and poured the tea, but added a drop of Haig to my cup.

'How long did it take you to drive up here?' I asked, as I retook my seat while folding away the newspaper.

'Oh, forever. I booked a room at The Grand.'

I pulled a face. 'Come on, Brendan. I could have put you up here.'

'What, and frighten the girls? No, I like The Grand and anyway, I'm only here for a day.'

"Frighten" was a highly appropriate term to use. Brendan Bracken was many things in his own mind, but a beauty he certainly wasn't. He was tall and had a face that was open and friendly enough, but he had the worst set of teeth I think I ever saw. For all his wealth, he refused to have them fixed. Added to that were big round spectacles, and a hairstyle that could only be described as looking like someone had dumped a load of ginger candyfloss on his head and left it there. My daughters always giggled when they met him, even on the most solemn occasion of their young lives – though I was grateful for anything that lightened the mood that day.

Brendan was a mover, a fixer, and a complete mystery. No one knew the real truth about his origins. Regarded as something of a fantasist, he was ironically said to be 'so false, even his hair is real.' He latched onto Winston in the early 1920s when he was young, but in time built up an empire in the news industry, and was now very well off. He became a Tory MP, stuck loyally to Mr Churchill throughout the appeasement crisis of the 1930s, and received his reward when war broke out with cabinet postings, eventually being made Minister of Information – or the "British Goebbels", as I heard one wag describe him.

Now he was sitting in my house and something was brewing. And it wasn't just the tea.

'Right,' he said. 'First of all, I have to ask you – how are things and how are the girls?'

I told him, somewhat guardedly, that things were fine. My eldest daughter, Joanne, was in London working at the War Office.

'And she sends her regards,' Brendan replied, with a knowing smile.

Somewhat surprised, I responded a little too quickly. 'You've seen her?'

'Yes, and I've found her a better job with me if she wants it. Smart girl. Just like her old Dad, eh?'

'Well, I'm grateful, Brendan. I worry like hell with the bombing and all that. I just want her to be safe.'

'And she is, Jamie, she is,' Bracken assured softly. He sipped his tea, looking over at me pointedly. 'My more immediate concern is that of a mutual chum of ours.'

Now we were at the nub of our meeting. I knew who he meant and awaited the details. He stubbed out his cigarette.

'Winston's in trouble, Jamie.'

'Aye, the news of Singapore was terrible. I heard his speech.'

'It's a bit closer to home than that. The Indians are circling the wagon that is Winston Churchill. They smell blood – the swine.'

'Who?'

'And do you know the worst of it, Jamie?' He went on. 'Who the *real* enemy is? Where the direst threat comes from? Winston Leonard Spencer Churchill, that's who. Your old colonel. The lad you used to know.'

'And you want my help.'

He grinned widely. 'That's why I was right to tell her, to tell Clemmie. I said, "Get Jamie Melville down here fast, Mrs C. He's the boy to sort it out!" They wouldn't listen at first, but I brought them round, sure enough.'

'Rubbish, Brendan,' I scoffed. 'It was Clemmie who thought of it. Remember, I've known her over twenty-five years. She's like an old Auntie to me. It was her, not you.'

He slapped his thigh and roared with infectious laughter. 'It's true; you can't cheat an honest man! Jamie, you got me. But here it is on a plate. The old man is in bother. I'll tell you now a few things that maybe three or four people in the world know. I'm one of them and now you're going to know, too. That's how important you are. But first pour me another cuppa. That's a right grand drop of tea you've scalded the pot with.'

I grabbed the handle and poured. He took a sip and leaned back.

'Jamie, the old man had a heart attack.' My eyes widened. 'Alright, alright,' he placated, with one hand raised.

'When?' I replied sharply.

'In the States, back in December when he was meeting the President. It was kept quiet – and thank God he lived – but it gave us a fright, I can tell you. Only Clemmie and one other knows and that's his doctor. If you can call that old rogue a physician.' This would have been Charles Wilson. The opinion was unfair and I thought afterwards that it was typical of Brendan. He was jealous of anyone who got close to Winston.

The true state of Winston's health was so closely guarded a secret that not even he, or the President, were ever made aware of the Prime Minister's seizure. Winston had been told he'd suffered a mild angina attack. The truth would come out years later; but in a state of shock after the revelation, I did not think it untypical that Brendan was in the know. He wasn't Minister of Information for nothing; the problem was he could never quite keep his mouth shut.

He sipped again from his cup and then continued. 'The worry now is that the old boy has got a lot of serious negotiations to do with the Yanks over the Second Front. And I happen to know there isn't gonna *be* a Second Front. Not this year or the next. He has to tell them this, and our pal Joe in Moscow, and that'll be difficult, no question. But he has to stick to his guns. If our boys are sent to France this year there'll be a massacre that would make Verdun look like a day out with the Methodists. Now the Yanks are fine lads, but they're new to this game and a bit over-eager. They need to be kept in line until the right moment. Winston can do that. Only, the old fella has to be breathing at the time.'

I listened, and in between the shock of hearing of Winston's health and the news of the Second Front, I felt my stomach start to churn ever so slightly. This was heady stuff for Jamie Melville from Gorgie Road.

'Alright, Brendan. But how does this affect me? What can *I* do?'

'Wait yourself. There's more.' He bit on a biscuit. Some crumbs rolled down his front and he brushed them aside. He then lit up another cigarette.

'Winston, as you know, doesn't like being told what to do. His latest hobby is to fly out to Moscow or anywhere else that suits his fancy. I can't tell you enough how dangerous that is. He's an old man; he was fit as a butcher's dog in 1940 but not now. If the plane flies above a certain height it could kill him. And usually planes have to fly very high to avoid fighters and flak. He just won't take no for an answer.' He sniffed. 'But by the by, he won't be flying for a wee while yet.'

'Brendan, I *asked* you; how does this concern me?'

He flicked ash into the tray. 'Happy with your lot, Jamie? Enjoy the fishing trade?'

I shrugged. 'It's tough at the moment with the war. We're only allowed two boats. And keeping *them* is a struggle. But you know all about that anyway, no doubt.'

'Yes, and I also happen to know that your inheritance a wee while back meant the fishing doesn't really matter now, does it?'

'For God's sake, Brendan! Just tell me what you want, eh?' My temper was flaring.

He recognised the signs. 'Whoa! Steady! I certainly don't want to be at the end of a "skelp" from James Melville! Alright, here's the proposition. We, that is Clemmie and I, want you to come down to London and keep an eye on Winston. You were his batman once and you know him as well as anyone.'

'I was just a wee lad in those days, Brendan. It can't be like that anymore.'

'And that's where you're wrong, Jamie, my dear. He misses you badly. He always has.' He then leaned forward and tapped my knee. 'I'll tell you a wee secret: I don't like other people to get close to him. Yes, I want him to myself. Does that surprise you?'

It didn't. Every once in a while Brendan would reveal a

small piece of the truth about himself. I had long wondered if such disclosures were for genuine reasons, or if – with all the lies and fantasies – these revelations were proffered for effect. I never found out the answer.

'I suppose we all care about him,' I replied, carefully. 'He was like a father to me. I've known him most of my life and I'd be nothing today if not for him.'

'And he'd be dead today if not for you.' Brendan was alluding to the episode back in the trenches, where I crawled out into no-man's land and rescued the then Colonel Churchill after he got caught under the wire.

'*You*, I don't mind sharing him with,' he then confessed, chummily. 'Do you know why? Because you want nothing from him. You never did. You left him when he could have made you eminent. It's hard for me to understand anyone doing that. That's why he loves you so. Me, he just likes. But I love him, too. Never forget that.'

There was a moment of silence whilst I gathered my thoughts.

'I don't really know what I can do. I mean, I'm no-one important. You want me to keep an eye on him whilst all these politicians, generals and Yanks try to get him to do what they want? How can I be of influence? Unless you make me a government minister or Field Marshal – and even then. I used to give him a telling off back in the day for his smoking and drinking and scruffy habits, but he rarely listened. He just found it amusing. Have you spoken to Winston about this?'

'Again, that's typical of you, Jamie. Too modest. You had more influence than you know. But it's gone way beyond that – it's not just Clemmie and me, there's important people I can't name that have concerns also. All I can say is, you'll be given full access to Winston and the word will be sent out. There's talk that you can be given the rank of Lieutenant Colonel in the regiment of your choice. But it's up to you; you may think you can be more effective out of uniform rather than in it. Personally, I think you're better off in a suit.

Whitehall's filled with mystery men. You'll be another. But it's your decision.'

I now had my head in my hands. 'Brendan, I've got two wee girls to look out for.'

Stubbing out his latest fag, he came over and sat next to me on the settee.

'From what I'm hearing, your brother looks after them well enough when you're away on business. And Tom's off the boats now, isn't he? The firm can run itself with him keeping an eye on things. Oh, and can I say,' he winked, 'I think I can chuck one or two contracts at you, just to see you right.'

I paused and took a breath. The day had come as I knew it would. Only, I could never have imagined it would be like this. I still didn't understand everything and was not sure what good it would do, but one thing I was certain of: the old Jamie Melville had to come back. He'd been away too long.

'I won't do it for that,' I said, finally. 'I owe that man everything. He once told me that I would be needed by him one day for some special reason. I was just young then, but I believed him, and I believed that the day would come, too. Now it has. Tell Clemmie, yes. I want to be at his side again.'

I did not feel as confident as I must have sounded to Brendan. But I would do it. Whatever "it" really was. After all, I had to do something – I didn't have a choice. I left Brendan to chat away, but didn't listen much. I was somewhere else, as I stole glances away from the speaker over to the hot, bright coals from the fire; igniting long-suppressed memories of what had passed, while providing tantalising glimpses of what I hoped and dreaded was about to come.

Chapter Two

You may think it odd that in wartime I was willing to head off into the unknown, leaving two young children so readily. I was able to explain to them years later why; it didn't remove the hurt, though it did at least provide some form of closure.

But to tell my story properly, I have to return to when I left London and Winston behind over twenty years before.

Gemma, my fiancé and I had moved north to Scarborough to live with my brothers and their adopted parents who owned a business there. It had been the biggest decision of my life but if I had any doubts, I didn't have time to dwell on them. I threw myself immediately into learning the fishing trade and gaining an accountancy qualification through a correspondence course.

The Humphries Fishing Company had five trawlers in their fleet at the war's end. One was based at Scarborough, on which my brother Tom was a crew member, and the other four sailed out of Hull. I had to learn the basics first and went out on Tom's boat a number of times, which was enough to put me off fish for life.

In between spewing my insides out from the moment the boat left the harbour, I was supposedly there to learn basic shipboard duties. But due to my weak disposition I usually ended up being told to "fook off" and ordered to stay out of everyone's way. I also took my turn in 'gutting' the catch in order for it to be ready for display at the harbour, prior to merchants transporting it onwards to Hull, Grimsby and later as far as Scotland. The smell used to cling to my fingers and arms for days despite repeated washings.

I learnt skeining, flithing, and baiting from the herring girls and women, usually wives and family members of the crewmen, and suffered ribald and raucous comments over my ineptitude at the tasks. Believe me; it's true what they say about fishwives.

But give or take a few bad moments, I relished it all, mainly because I knew it was only temporary as I had been taken on for my brains, not my seamanship.

I gained my qualification and started to learn the financial side of the business, and soon found areas where I could make changes for the better. Ted, the accountant who I replaced, was an old but hardly trusted employee living in a previous century, who refused to use a telephone and kept a system known only to himself regarding the company accounts. I was never sure if he was *at it*, but I believed he was happy just to keep things afloat, come in every day and have as quiet a life as possible. That can be just as much of a danger to a business as dishonesty.

After the war ended, herring stocks were discovered to have risen dramatically due to under-fishing and we quickly moved to take advantage. My step-father, who had recently married my widowed mother in Edinburgh, made enquiries on our behalf and soon wagons were rolling into the harbours of Hull and Scarborough and whisking herring, cod and haddock up north to lucrative markets in Leith and Fraserburgh.

Gemma and I married in 1921 at St Mary's Church in the town. My brother Tom was best man and Winston and his family were present (only weeks later his little daughter, Marigold, tragically died of diphtheria). Gemma's parents and her brother David deigned to appear, but throughout the ceremony old man Ashby, my 'beloved' father-in-law, looked and behaved as though a terrible smell had been caught under his nose. He regarded me as a jumped up peasant who had seduced his only daughter (if only he knew) and thoroughly detested Winston – a hated former school chum who had played an extremely dirty trick on him once that remained unavenged. Believe me, the bastard deserved it. I've never watched a rugby match after without smiling. The snobbish swine.

At least David and I had always had an easy relationship. He was a subaltern in the trenches but returned infused with new ideas about treating the lower classes a little better than serfs, which went down like a lead turd at home. Consequently, Ashby senior now regarded his only son as no better than a Bolshevik. Thank God I was living two hundred miles away.

We moved into a house near the Humphries at the Burniston end of the town, and laid a lump sum down which came out of the large cheque Gemma's grandmother had gifted us before we left London. Our first daughter, Joanne, was born the following year but as both the pregnancy and birth were traumatic, the medical advice we received was not to have any more children.

We soon had a cosy home and Gemma left her position as a nurse to bring up the wee one. We visited London regularly to show off Joanne to Gemma's family, and stayed with Winston at his new country home in Kent each summer.

Things got better, if you'll pardon my cynicism, when in the late 1920s Gemma's father dropped dead one morning of a stroke, outside Bow Street Magistrates Court. Gemma's grandmother, who held the purse-strings and who doted on her two grandchildren (and me) now rewrote her will and left not an inconsiderable estate to be divided equally between David and his sister. When I was told the sum involved I nearly fainted. Of course, I had no wish for Grandma to join her only child too readily, but it certainly removed a lot of financial pressure from us.

Around this time Mr Humphries informed us that he was leaving the business to me and Tom, as he wanted to realise his dream of opening an Antiquarian bookshop. He had a tremendous library at home and had always wished to become a historian, but his father had pooh-poohed the idea and forced him to carry on the fishing business he had started up.

Arnold now believed the time was right and after changing the business name to Humphries and Melville Fishing Company, he found small premises in Queen Street in the town and opened his bookshop. He brought in old Ted to look after it whilst he was off to York, Leeds and other places tracking down rare items for stock. The business managed to break even with the holiday trade and that was enough to keep him happy. I've never known such a contented soul.

But Gemma hankered for more children. It worried me and I never felt comfortable when she spoke about it. I kept saying maybe next year, and generally let my concern show, but eventually I said 'yes' and to my intense relief, our wee Alison appeared without any problems. Then before we knew it, Claire introduced herself and I was the happiest man alive with three poppets to cherish.

Then in 1936, Gemma's feisty, opinionated but wonderful grandmother passed away. There weren't many at the funeral in London but Winston attended; we stayed with him and afterwards took the family down to Chartwell. My memories of that visit are golden. Though I grieved for the old lady who meant so much to me, to be with Winston as he ranted about Baldwin and Hitler, gossiped about the King and his mistress and had guests such as Brendan Bracken, Evelyn Waugh and his son Randolph present, was as intense an experience of happiness as I've ever known.

My old colonel took my girls by the hand and showed them round the gardens and fish pools of Chartwell, and enthralled them with tall tales of mysterious creatures who lived in the nearby woods. I sat in the dining room at the table and looked out over his swimming pool, with a glass of champagne, on that brilliant summer's day; Gemma chatting to Winston's daughters Diana and young Mary, whilst Randolph delighted Waugh and me with card tricks.

It was a reminder of the life I had given up. I would be a liar if I said I had no regrets. But those few balmy and blissful days in late August 1936 were to be the last before the shadows gathered. For shortly after that, my happiness came to an end.

It began with Gemma complaining of soreness in her chest and then finding a cut on her breast that never appeared to heal properly. She had started doing some voluntary work at the Scarborough Hospital in the Admin block, with Vera looking after the girls one day a week to allow Gemma time away. That's what I told the girls. In fact, she went there for treatment.

I received a telephone call at the office from the hospital that Thursday morning, advising me that she had taken unwell at home and an ambulance had been sent for. Could I come quickly?

The young doctor in charge had taken a blood test and an X-Ray and told me that what he found wasn't good news. He said they may have to remove the breast and I immediately gave my permission for them to do whatever was necessary. Everything was now happening so fast I could hardly think clearly. I did have enough sense to telephone Tom, who calmed me down somewhat and arranged to collect the girls and take them round to his home.

I was sitting outside the operating room when the doors burst open, and just caught a glimpse of Gemma's face – which looked as it did when she lay asleep beside me in our bed at home – as she was whisked past me on a trolley after surgery. The doctor advised me to go home as she would be out for hours, but if there was any change in her condition I would be summoned. No one gave me the impression things were serious at that time and I thought it best to head to Tom's and see the girls. First I went round to collect some things of Gemma's: books and night clothing, when the telephone rang again.

It was the young doctor. Gemma, my adored wife, had passed away.

Chapter Three

RETURNING TO 1942, Brendan told me he would send a motorcar to bring me down to London, but I explained that I needed a few days to sort out my affairs and would take the train. He winced and asked was I sure. I said yes, as I needed the opportunity to think; wartime rail travel always provided you with plenty of opportunities to think.

I visited Tom and his wife Irene to talk it over. They told me I should go and not worry about the girls. Tom adored having the cheery chaos of young children around and they naturally gravitated towards him. He was a player of games, a practical joker and was really a big kid at heart, whereas of course I was a near cripple with a busted leg that was getting worse the older I became. I was also showing early signs of the arthritis that would plague me in later years. Consequently, I could never be the most active of parents. The girls were used to spending weekends at his place with his boys who were of a similar age, and there was always plenty room there for all. Irene seemed happy with the arrangements. It was all males in her household and she welcomed allies.

I visited the bank and arranged a monthly draft towards the girls' keep. I left it open because I knew I might be in for the long haul with Winston. I also left a retainer for Vera to keep an eye on the house whilst I was away, to blow off some of the cobwebs from time to time.

The draft for the girls included the fees for the small private school they attended near Whitby. I removed them from the local school after I was late one morning taking them there and had to leave them for an urgent business appointment.

Claire, then only six years old, came home that night behaving oddly. I asked what was wrong. She told me her teacher had caned her for being late. I said nothing.

The following day I left the girls with Vera, made my way to the school and asked to meet the teacher in question. He turned out be a short, bespectacled little squirt with a quiff in his mid-thirties. I stood before him and held my hand out.

'Pleased to meet you, Mr Melville. I've heard a lot about you,' he said.

'No. Don't shake my hand,' I answered coolly. 'Hit me with your cane, instead.'

He whitened and drew back as I moved towards him. I lost control and the next thing I knew I had him round the throat and my stick was up against the side of his face.

'Listen, you wee English prick, hurt my girl again and I'll belt you to within an inch of your life!'

Then I calmed down, threw him off me and set about enrolling my daughters in a charming little school run by two spinsters. The girls had to catch a bus each day, but it was an adventure for them and they soon settled in happily.

I recount this story because that was one of the few occasions where I showed any real sign of the old Jamie Melville after Gemma's death. I had lost much of myself but hid it for the children's sake as best I could. Tom and Irene were a Godsend as they took the girls every weekend, to leave me on my own for a short time, immediately after her passing.

As you'll have noted, I was never anything less than a positive type of person with abundant confidence in my abilities. But I was shattered by her loss. I feared for my girls should anything now happen to me, and felt a failure for not being more decisive with Gemma regarding her illness. But I could not have known the true extent, as I gradually began to suspect that she deliberately kept it hidden from me. She was a nurse, after all, and I now believed she knew she was doomed and kept up a brave front for all of us.

I was just floating along, directionless; uninterested in life.

I didn't bother much with the business. Not that I needed to. The inheritance set us up. There was property and investments which meant a lifetime of steady though not spectacular income. I also had my small war pension. The house belonged to me and I only had the household bills and the girls schooling to fork out. When the war started and the boats were taken away, I passed some of the time doing the books for a few small businesses in town as well as our own to occupy myself.

Tom looked after the company. But with only two boats, margins were tight and I no longer took payment, instead putting my share back into the business to help out. Fishing was becoming a deadly business, particularly in the early years of the war as many boats were sunk by U-Boats and aircraft. Tom had to judge things carefully whenever he went out to sea and that was always a source of worry to both Irene and me.

The Humphries both passed away early on during the war. Tom stayed at the house that had been left to us, so he had no real financial worries either, as we had also been left money by that wonderful old couple. The bookshop folded in the late thirties and it was just Tom, Irene and the kids now. We were still Scots and always would be; but the roots were now deep in Yorkshire. It was our home.

The two younger girls were now used to life without Mum. The oldest, Joanne, was away in her own life but we kept in touch with letters. She had been a rock when it happened. She was only fifteen but seemed to turn into a woman overnight. A particularly wise and mature one, too. Or maybe I just hadn't really noticed before. That added to my guilt and desolation.

But I had to get myself out from my listlessness. It had been five years since she died and I'd been treading water and not really living. I suffered from nightmares from the war, too. I had been able to contain them for long periods, but Gemma's death had brought them on with far greater frequency and severity than they had for years. I'd found the strength not to turn to the traditional refuge of drink, as I was haunted by my dead father who wasted his life away in the bottle. I always stopped short of reaching for it.

But I needed *something*. I couldn't go on like this. A jolt from somewhere. *Anything*. Now it had arrived, I hoped; maybe a little too fervently. I remembered what Winston had told me long ago, on that bench in St James's Park after my two dearest friends from the 6th, Davie Thom and Duncan Davidson had died in battle. He told me to remember the departed with love and never fail to recall them to mind. But he told me that I owed life to the living.

Those words came back to me on that crowded train heading south, amongst the cigarette haze and the servicemen. Wedged against a window seat, I looked out over grimy wartime Britain, my leg throbbing away damnably. Lately, Gemma's face would fade from my memory from time to time. But I could always recall clearly how she looked that day, long, long ago, when I told her that Winston had found me a job in London and I would not be leaving her after all. We were in a tea-shop at Kings Cross just before I boarded the train to head home to Edinburgh.

I remembered her gleeful look. Relief, affection, and love all together in that purely innocent, sweet face. And as I gazed out now over the Home Counties, through the dirty carriage window, I heard her clearly telling me to start living again. That I had no reason not to go on. She was always going to be there with me, everywhere I went, but I must keep going on, never give in, and live. Just *live*.

It was awkward with two suitcases and a stick, but I managed to make my way off the train onto the platform at Kings Cross. As wartime train journeys went, one and a half hours late wasn't bad. As I was just getting to grips with looking for the exit, a young man in civilian clothing appeared before me and grabbed one of my cases.

'Mr Melville, I've been sent to collect you.'

'Thanks, where are we headed?' I asked.

'The motor's just outside, sir.'

He was brisk and efficient and I wondered why he wasn't in uniform. I followed him out onto the main concourse, and as I helped with laying the cases into the boot of the car I noticed Brendan sitting in the back.

'I won't ask if it was a nice journey!' he grinned as I got in, and he grabbed my hand. 'You got a seat? I know it plays fair hell with your leg. But remember, I could have driven you down.'

'No, it was alright. I could do with a wash-up and a whisky, though!'

'I don't have a bath to hand, but I do have this nice wee drop of Jameson's if you don't mind a touch of the Irish.'

I didn't, and he poured into the cap from a hip flask, which I downed in one go.

'That's better! Now, where are we off to, Brendan?'

He took a quick slug from the flask and then screwed the lid back on. 'Oh, you're looking fine now, Jamie, my lad! I see the old juices flowing again! We'll soon be there, just you sit back now!'

He started babbling away, but the Jameson's, together with my desire to see London again, saw me turn my attention to the view from the window.

I was interested in seeing for myself the damage to the capital. I had only previously viewed it in the papers and newsreels. All around were roofless and defaced buildings, holes and craters filled or left as they were, trees caught in blasts lying where they had been blown apart, and windows depressingly covered with tape; at least the ones that had survived and weren't boarded up, or left empty and gaping at passers-by. I did note one that had a plant pot with a purple Geranium pronouncing the home-owner's defiance towards its attacker.

I passed thriving shops with "Business as Usual" signs

that had miraculously survived whilst their neighbours lay desolate. This seemed to me to provide an inspiring reminder that amidst this man-made devastation, like some small lonely flower growing solitary in a desert; life would always triumph.

London had become a scarred city. All around was evidence of that onslaught. Homes despoiled; private dwellings, their intimate contents laid bare for all to see. Religious edifices that had stood for centuries reduced to rubble. Some bombed sights had lain so long they were overgrown with weeds. Many would stay as such well into the 1960s. Scattered around every street and corner were unfinished repair jobs, coils of fire hose lying forgotten, temporary bus-stops, sandbagged doorways and that particular smell of burning, of dust, decay and dirt that – unlike the homely odour of the breweries in old Edinburgh – was a reminder to me of the alien onslaught that had assailed us. A year after the initial blitz, the inhabitants of the city were wary, though no longer constantly on edge; the automatic responses of experienced soldiers to danger were now mastered equally well by their formerly sheltered civilian counterparts.

Scarborough had not escaped the bombing, either. There had been a particularly heavy raid in March 1941 that brought a lot of destruction to parts of the old town. I became used to taking the girls to our designated shelter at Northstead Manor Drive, and on the sound of the all-clear chiding them for debating whether or not our house would still be standing.

It always was; apart from a couple of occasions where shrapnel had knocked off some roof tiles and smashed a window pane. This caused widespread shrieks and squeals of horror from the girls, which usually resulted in a soft tap around the lugs to quieten them.

We turned off Euston Road onto Tottenham Court Road, and past the shops onwards through Cambridge Circus which was still blocked in places with rubble and debris.

Temporary diversion signs, still visible a year after the original blitz, directed disorientated locals and visitors alike in the aftermath of the conflagration. "Danger" signs pointed to partly-filled craters and warnings of bombs left unexploded and now removed. This last seemed to me to symbolise the still defiantly *humane* concern of the attacked, that at least morally vanquished the perpetrator of the barbarism wreaked from the air.

I could barely recognise it at first, as we passed Denmark Street; where I remembered faces from times long past. It was there that Eddie Marsh and I would meet a painter friend of his who later took his own life. I recalled Isaac Rosenberg and his strange but pitiful manner. I smiled in memory of the little education Eddie gave me. His was amongst the kindest of souls I ever encountered and I immediately promised to look him up now I was back.

We turned into Shaftesbury Avenue, past a potholed and bumpy Piccadilly, through Regent Street and then caught sight of St James's Park, which I knew well from days gone by. We drove on past Horse Guards turning into Great George Street, which I would soon come to know intimately, until the car eventually came to a halt outside a house in North Street.

'Here we are!' Brendan leapt from the motor and as the driver collected my luggage, Bracken handed me a key, and we both walked to the main entrance.

'I've been here before!' I suddenly recognised the house that had been a hive of perfidy before the war. For it was here in the street soon to be known as *Lord* North Street, where Brendan lived, that he had held parties for disaffected anti-appeasers amongst others, and it was rumoured that secret servicemen spied on its coming and goings. On a trip to visit Winston with the girls, shortly before the war began, I'd met Ronald Cartland there. Soon after, he would make his famous speech where he accused the Prime Minister, Neville Chamberlain of running a dictatorship.

'This is your gaff until you get settled, Jamie,' Brendan informed me. 'There's a nice wee basement room I've kitted out. It's safer when the bombers come but there are shelters around as you can see, too.' I noted there were signs stencilled on a couple of houses pointing to safety areas.

'There's someone here to meet you first, so don't hurry yourself unpacking.' He took the key back from me and let us into the house. The driver dropped the bags off in the hallway and returned to the motorcar.

Brendan led us through to the dining area of the flat, where a gentleman was sitting down at a table.

'Mr Melville, it's so nice to meet you.' He must have been in his sixties, with a military-looking moustache and – despite the vestige of a smile around the lips – a cold set of blue eyes that weighed me up behind his spectacles. He looked like a brawler; and someone not to be messed with despite his age. I shook his hand firmly and was not surprised that he had tried to squeeze mine, which I detest, and sat down opposite him. He did not tell me his name.

Brendan sat next to me, clasped his hands and looked down.

'I trust the trip down wasn't too dull?' the gent began.

'As journeys go, it was alright.'

'Forgive me if I haven't told you my name. But I certainly know yours and you've come with the highest recommendation. I gather Mr Bracken has provided you with some rough details about why you are here?'

I'm not an idiot, and I could tell this bloke held Brendan in disdain. Most people did.

'I'm needed to help the colonel … Mr Churchill.' I still thought of him as that and always would. I called him Winston also from time to time when we visited him, but colonel always felt easier and it was more personal to me.

'Ah, yes, your service in the Royal Scots Fusiliers. Do you know, I've yet to hear of anyone who has a bad word for their old commanding officer in the 6th. A fine battalion.

And you were also held in high esteem, I believe.'

'I was just a wee boy, but yes, I loved my time there, though it ended badly. It was a good battalion. It was made easy for the colonel because all the officers were top-rank. All of them.' I detected a slightly superior sneer in his voice. Maybe he had been a guards officer or something. Regardless of whoever or whatever he was, no way was I allowing anyone to slag off my old regiment.

'And I believe you were instrumental in once saving the colonel's very life, were you not?'

'I happened to be the right shape and size required for the task at the time.'

He smiled but without humour. 'He needs you again, Jamie – do you mind if I call you that?' I indicated that it was fine. 'He is in as much danger now as he was that night at Plugstreet when he was fixed to the wire. Only, the dangers now cannot be removed by a brave young man with a pair of wire-cutters who had forgotten to take a pair of gloves with him.' I was astonished that he knew these facts.

Brendan lit a cigarette. He still had not spoken.

'Jamie, I represent an important department of the government,' he continued. 'A major part of our remit is to locate and remove risks from both within and without our country. Every day we are working very hard to ensure that enemy agents are found and their networks are rolled up and that any leak of secret information is plugged. These are really our bread and butter operations. But even we cannot be everywhere. Thus, we rely on specially selected, hand-picked operatives with particular skills, who are able to report to us anything that is suspicious and of possible threat to the well-being of our citizens. In addition, we employ the services of individuals with *superior* talents in high areas of government to carry out certain tasks that, due to their very nature, require uniquely placed persons. You are one of them.'

I was almost falling asleep. 'Sir, you'll have to tell me what you want. Mr Bracken told me something about the Second

Front and the Prime Minister's health.'

Brendan choked and coughed out loudly. 'Excuse me, for a moment,' he garbled and got up and left the room.

Only when he had closed the door behind him did the man continue. 'Mr Bracken is correct. These are very serious matters and very few are aware of them. I am not party to everything but I ask you to keep these facts close and divulge them to no-one.'

He reached down to his side, to a leather briefcase, and took out an official-looking document and a pen.

'There is something that while you are with us you must view and append signature to. This is the Secrecy Act. I believe it has been amended since last you signed it. Please look it over, confirm and then sign your name.'

I could have used a cup of tea, and his intensity really wasn't what I needed, as I looked wearily over the papers he'd brought with him.

'If that's all, now, I'd appreciate it if you could allow me time to unpack,' I said after passing the signed document back to him. 'I'm knackered and my leg is walloping. I was his batman once and also an assistant at his Ministry. I know him as well as any man and I'll do anything to keep him safe. But right now, if you don't mind, I'm going to fill a bath and soothe away that train journey and after that you can take me to our leader.'

Something resembling a smile appeared on his face.

'Yes, of course. I've been thoughtless.' He then lifted a small piece of paper from inside his suit and handed it to me.

'Can you look at these?' he asked. There were a set of numerals which looked like a London telephone number. 'Will you read them out to me?'

I did as he asked. He then leaned over and took the paper from my fingers and put it back in his pocket.

'Please call that number anytime you feel the need. If you see or hear *anything* that you are uncomfortable with whilst you are with the Prime Minister do not hesitate to ring, no matter how trivial. Even the smallest detail can be vital.'

He stood up.

'I've enjoyed our chat, Jamie. I don't get the chance to meet a real war-hero very often and the Prime Minister never stops talking about you. He thinks very highly of you indeed. I've also spoken to the Air Minister, Mr Sinclair, who also holds you in the utmost regard. Please remember that number.'

I rose and shook his hand. 'If I have to ring the number who should I ask to speak to?'

He looked directly at me. 'Just ask for Uncle Claude.'

Chapter Four

I GAVE MY new acquaintance no more thought and ran a bath whilst proceeding to unpack. After completing my ablutions and enjoying another drink, we were driven to meet my old commanding officer.

The motorcar made its way along Abingdon Street, through Parliament Square into Whitehall, past more damaged buildings and further evidence of destruction – but it all now seemed normal. We had been at war two years. Nothing was novel any longer.

As we pulled into Downing Street, however, I was slightly taken aback to see the sole figure of a policeman standing vigil outside the country's most famous front door. There were no protective measures such as sandbag emplacements which I expected at the very least. Nor were there guard posts with mounted sentries, apart from the checkpoint at the entrance to the thoroughfare off Parliament Street where we had to show our passes. On leaving Brendan's home he had handed me a special War Office issue identification card.

What with the mysterious 'Uncle Claude' and the ID, I had already begun to suspect that my life was now no longer my own. But as we made our way into Number 10 I was able to pause for a moment to reflect on Jamie Melville's journey from Wardlaw Place to the residence of the Prime Minister of the greatest empire the world has ever known. And the thoughts that came to me were those of my poor father and how I wished he were alive to share in this moment.

A more tangible feeling was the knot of excitement and expectancy in my stomach that I would experience whenever the occasion arose where I would meet *that* man. As far back as the occasion when he strode into the office where I worked in Whitehall as a young lad and asked me to tag along to the House to support him in the Nation debate, I had revelled in the thrill of just *being* with him.

I was entering my forties now, but the sensation remained and always would. I still believed I was right to leave him when I did all those years before; but I would never stop missing him.

I hadn't seen him much since Gemma's funeral. In a moment alone I'd sobbed on his shoulder whilst Clemmie held my hand. Randolph had stood look-out at the bedroom door before we left for the church in order to assure us of privacy. It had been my only show of emotion to anyone throughout that awful period. Winston shed tears along with me. He was the only person I could share such moments with as he'd known me man and boy. I had no secrets from him.

On being passed into the building we were left waiting momentarily in a large hallway. Then, striding before me was the Prime Minister himself. He was wearing a charcoal pinstripe suit, a waistcoat and a bowtie that flopped about like a butterfly trying to avoid a net. He appeared as energy-filled and ebullient as ever.

'Salvation is at hand, at last! Gorgie Road's finest son has arrived!'

Winston grabbed both my arms and shook me powerfully. My stick fell out of my hands and as I tried to release myself from his grip, he bent down and picked it up.

'Ah! Thompson!' he thundered, as a naval-uniformed officer appeared at his side. This was Commander "Tommy" Thompson, one of his senior aides and a complete pain in the arse as I would soon discover in the coming days.

'Discard this old piece of rubbish!' Winston ordered theatrically while handing my trusty walking stick over to the aide.

'Wait a minute, Colonel! I need that you know!' It may have been the centre of government and the leader of the nation himself standing before me, but I wasn't being buggered around by anyone.

'Hang about, Jamie!' pleaded Brendan with a desperate grin.

I turned to dispute with him when I noticed that Thompson had returned and passed an item to Winston.

'Oh, that temper! It shall yet be your downfall, James!' he laughed.

With both arms stretched towards me he passed over a beautiful gold-embossed walking cane with a highly polished black hardwood shaft.

'Please read the inscription.'

I took the cane in my hand and looked at the gold engraved plate on the side of the handle.

'To my dearest friend James Melville, from W. L. S. Churchill'

I couldn't speak; admittedly an unusual occurrence in the Jamie Melville Winston knew so well. There was a respectful pause before Brendan made his farewell, whilst Thompson scurried off.

Winston then ushered me alone down the passageway of the building and up a stairway. Passing an aged grandfather clock, we entered the famous address's holiest of holies, the Cabinet Room, through two sets of doors, one of which was sound-proofed. There was a long table surrounded by leather-backed chairs with silver candlesticks, a decanter of whisky and cut glasses nestled on it, amongst scattered items of stationery such as his famous red "Action This Day" labels. The room's large windows looked over the garden wall of 10 Downing Street, out over Horse Guards Parade and St James's Park.

'Please sit, James,' he commanded easily as he took his chair, which I noted was the only one in the room that had armrests. Behind his seat was a fireplace, above which hung the room's only adornment, a painting of Sir Robert Walpole. Well-stocked bookcases and a map of the world covered the remaining walls.

'That's to let the buggers know who's the boss!' he exclaimed, indicating his armrests as I took a chair and leant over onto the table. I sat on his right as he reached over and filled a glass half full and handed it to me.

'Tommy!' he roared, turning to the door. 'Where's the bloody ice? There is a whisky drinker here and I won't have him waiting to be served!'

Thompson appeared with an ice bucket and the Prime Minister dropped a couple of lumps into my glass. Winston knew how I liked it and I can't say I wasn't thrilled by this personal treatment from a man notorious for his thoughtlessness towards others.

Winston poured himself his usual very weak whisky smothered in soda and ice and took a huge gulp.

'Ah! James, I can't tell you how pleased Mrs Churchill and I are that you are with us again! It shall be like old times! You will curse me for my many faults and disgusting habits, and I shall guide you along the path to greatness! What finer combination has there been in the annals? *Bruce and Douglas*? *Boswell and Johnson*? No! Churchill and Melville!'

'I'm really glad to see you again, Colonel,' I replied happily. 'Thanks so much for the cane! I can't wait to show it to the girls!'

'And how are my lovelies?' he enquired.

We chatted for a short while and both of us unwound a little; only later would I understand how those precious few moments mattered to us. Normally he detested small talk and this was another bow to yours truly. The years rolled back and I remembered sitting with him and Eddie Marsh late at night at the Munitions office, gassing away over drinks and snacks. It was as it had been in happier times and all my cares dropped away. For a short while, at least.

We spoke of Joanne and Winston informed me that Brendan had found her a good job at his Ministry. We discussed his children and he talked about Randolph, who was serving with a Commando unit in North Africa. Mary had broken off her engagement to Eric Duncannon and Diana, who had always been Gemma's pal, was also in town. He never mentioned Sarah. Her marriage to the music hall comedian, Vic Oliver, was a sore point but I had always liked her, regardless of her marital choice. I liked all his children.

The conversation stopped for a moment as Winston refilled our glasses. Then I asked the question foremost in my mind.

'Winston, why am I here? I mean, don't misunderstand me, I want to do my bit. All Brendan told me was that he was worried about you. So is Clemmie. He said I was needed. But for what?'

'To watch my back as you always have!' he boomed heartily. Then he became serious. 'James, these are testing times, indeed. Our great saviour, the United States of America has arrived; belatedly, in all admission, but they are here. It is now only a matter of how and when the war shall be won. But there are great issues at stake and we are only at the countdown towards the *beginning* of the end. I foresee that I will have to undertake great voyages to meet our allies and will require trusted aides to assist me. Remember when we spoke all those years ago?' I nodded.

He was referring to the last conversation I had with him in his office back in 1918. I went with my knees trembling to tell him I was leaving him and London to go up to Yorkshire with Gemma to live. He accepted my decision but made a prediction on the subject of his personal destiny. A destiny which would also involve me one day.

'I already have Inspector Thompson, who you know is my bodyguard. I have Sawyers, my valet, a *blackguard*, who moans and complains worse than Jamie Melville on a day when the Hearts lose! And I have that old washerwoman, Tommy Thompson, who fawns, toad-eats and grovels in quite the most revolting manner. But all these are *servants*! That is why you are required; I need someone who is a *friend*. Someone unafraid to shout back at me and deal effectively with my tyrannical and bullying ways!' He winked conspiratorially at this last.

I laughed but was somewhat embarrassed at his candour, while remaining only half-convinced by his explanation for my new-found eminence. He then swallowed what was left of his whisky and soda.

'Now, James, I believe Brendan introduced you to a gentleman at his home today.'

'Yes.' I leant forward.

'That individual is an extremely important official and the fact that he has asked to meet you is highly significant.'

'He told me he worked for the security service.'

'He is a high functionary of state, yes. And the reason he spoke to you and requested your services was because of your unique background and history as a close confidant of myself.'

He continued. 'James, there will be occasions in the months ahead when you will be made aware of many important matters. This may place you in grave danger but at the same time it will place you in a position of opportunity. There are to be great discussions between ourselves and our new allies, the Americans. We have another ally, the Soviet Union. However, even as we speak and with the situation so critical on the Russian front, we have cause to be concerned by the actions of our erstwhile comrades and their ultimate aims.'

I knew his feelings towards Russia, but like the rest of the country I was in thrall of the brave Red Army which seemed to be the only force capable of killing Germans. I had a regard for their leader Joseph Stalin, as everyone else did, and saw him as a lovable old bear fighting away bravely, alone. But at that time there were real concerns that Stalin would ask for a negotiated settlement with Hitler to avoid total defeat.

'Is that not the old colonel and his anti-Bolshevik opinions showing though?' I asked, only a little ironically.

'If only it were, James, if only. But you may well ask, "what will *I* do?" You will do many things. I believe you have been offered a commission?'

I moved in my seat. 'Winston, I'm not sure about that ... Brendan said I had the choice but he thought me remaining a civilian was more practical.'

He pulled a face. 'It is a sad day when a Lance-Corporal refuses the offer of a Colonelcy!' He then laughed. 'I would dearly love to see my former batman in the splendid dress of a senior officer of the Royal Scots Fusiliers! But we will have a think on it and not rush to a decision.' He reached over and refilled my glass again before his own. We drank silently for a while, comfortable in each other's presence. I asked a few questions about the room we sat in, which he answered expertly.

'My boy, how have *you* been?' he then asked quietly.

I paused and looked down. These were the quiet moments we had shared in the past, as far back as the days in the 6th when he used to paint and I'd watch, whilst he asked me about myself and my dreams. I understood years later that that was the moment he decided to do something for me. That through my words and childish innocence he saw someone of worth; who would never have got anywhere in that hidebound, class-ridden age because of where he had come from. Nowhere without a helping hand, freely given without equivocation.

And now he was asking me for assistance but at the same time, *helping* me again. For he understood the pain of loss in someone young. His own father; his adored child, Marigold, the *duckadilly*, who died as an infant.

Controlling myself but having to hide my eyes with my hand, I tried to speak. He reached over and gently removed my hand from my face.

'It has been a trying day, James. We will talk no more of these matters for the present. Clementine is at the Annexe and she awaits you. Let us leave here now and go to her!'

'Colonel,' I gathered myself together. 'I want to try and

get on with my life again. I'm so grateful that you've sent for me. I'm ready now, to do my part. Like we talked about, years ago.'

'Then let us proceed, James. *Together*.' He took my arm and led me out of the room.

Chapter Five

AMONG MANY OTHER faults, Winston was criticised over the company he kept. The view in the main being that he attracted eccentrics and imposters who acted as supplicants to him and indulged his every whim, in order to receive favour from a man considered brilliant by some but reckless by others.

I became acquainted with most of them throughout the inter-war years. There was Brendan Bracken of course. Desmond Morton acted as his unofficial intelligence chief during the period in the thirties when he was a voice in the wilderness railing against appeasement. Duncan Sandys, his son-in-law who was generally regarded as being inept and difficult to work under, would find his way into the war-time cabinet.

All three exhibited a worrying tendency towards indiscretion and this provided ammunition for Winston's critics. Another close friend was Fred Lindemann, later Lord Cherwell, known as the "Prof." I found him to be the most unctuous snob both socially and intellectually, but he was someone who was (almost) running on the same brain-power as the Prime Minister. He was usually civil to me but nothing more. I believed this was because he thought of me as no better than a servant and therefore of no consequence.

By far the most troublesome of Winston's inner circle was also an old acquaintance of mine, Max Aitken. Lord Beaverbrook as he was better known had been Minister of Aircraft Production and oversaw the remarkable increase of fighter construction activity of 1940 that played a significant role in winning the Battle of Britain.

But the miracle of 1940 came at a cost and figures would later prove that actual production of aircraft began to increase significantly well before Aitken took charge. Max caused a lot of bother in an on-going feud with the Air Ministry run by my old comrade from the 6th, Archibald Sinclair, Secretary of State for the Air. He was now one of the most senior ministers in cabinet and leader of the Liberal Party.

Beaverbrook continually impinged on Archie's domain while completely failing to understand that his sole requirement was to build aircraft and then pass them onto the men who would fly them. His real desire was to swallow up piece by piece what was a separate Ministry thus increasing his power base. There were those that mistrusted his motives to the extent that they believed him to be a future rival to the Prime Minister. To Winston's discredit he appeared to take Max's side in the continual squabbles; Archie was nearly worn though by it all and considered resigning.

Aitken himself would constantly threaten resignation unless he got his way until in 1941, Winston by now tiring of Max's histrionics, called his bluff and accepted it. The position then fell to John Moore-Brabazon who went on to have a far better relationship with Mr Sinclair.

Now in 1942, Beaverbrook had been persuaded to return to government as Minister of Production, but had resigned a week into the job through what he described as "ill-health." He did suffer from asthma and was a man in his mid-sixties but many remained unconvinced.

Some months before he had made a much publicised trip to Russia and had returned adulating Marshal Stalin and demanding that Britain step up her aid to her new ally. This whilst in North Africa our army was involved in a death struggle with Rommel and the Afrika Korps. Before the war, Beaverbrook had sung the praises of Von Ribbentrop and had met Hitler himself.

Worse, he had started publicly calling for a second front, an invasion of mainland Europe by the British in order to relieve pressure on the hard-pressed Soviet army. No way was the country prepared for that and the last thing Winston needed was someone agitating for it through his own newspapers.

Beaverbrook was a man who didn't like taking orders and it was questionable whether he should have been brought back into the fold. But Winston's thinking was, better having him on the inside where he could be watched than on the outside creating mischief. Knowing Max, who was incapable of *not* indulging in meddling and plotting, I believe this was another failing on Winston's part.

The Prime Minister was exposed at that time. The Russians had been our allies for over a year and the Yanks were in now, too. But we ourselves were still suffering defeats: the infamous channel dash had recently occurred. Perversely, that had a greater effect on the morale of the country than Singapore's fall.

Winston was vulnerable; no doubt about it. And someone like Beaverbrook, who always harboured ambitions for the top job, was a distraction my old colonel certainly didn't need. The man just couldn't be trusted. It was said that if Aitken became Prime Minister in 1940 he would have become the British Laval.

A few days after arriving in London I was tasked to speak to Max on the Prime Minister's behalf. This arose from a discussion held at the Annexe, the reinforced flat above the underground War Rooms near 10 Downing Street where Winston and Clementine lived in the main during those years.

Winston, Brendan Bracken and Randolph – the Prime Minister's son, recently returned from the Western Desert – were present. I was starting to become used to another in the PM's retinue, Inspector Walter Thompson, Mr Churchill's bodyguard. He was a very tall and well-built man in his fifties who said little but gave off an air of complete confidence, and as time went by I would come to be grateful for his presence.

Randolph of course I had known since he was a child. In many ways he was more difficult than his father but I always got on well with him. Once on a visit to Chartwell a guest asked him 'who is the cripple with the stick?' referring of course, to me. Randolph nearly threw the swine into Winston's swimming pool.

The gist of the conversation was Max Aitken and what to do with him. It was soon becoming apparent that I was to be involved in the solution and I didn't know whether to be flattered or insulted. The terms and conditions of my new role, which saw me added to the Civil Service list earning the princely sum of £8 10s 8d a week, remained undefined. Winston had wanted me in uniform but I had an ally in Randolph who agreed with Brendan that I would be more effective as some sort of *éminence grise* prowling around in the background. I admit on hearing this I grew a little alarmed. Wide-eyed, I pleaded to Winston:

'Colonel, who'll take *me* seriously?'

Winston looked up in surprise from his chair at me.

'Whomever I order you to deal with on my behalf, of course. You are James Melville; if they don't take you bloody well seriously I'll have their balls on a plate.'

I was driven the following morning to the *Evening Standard* building in Shoe Lane, just off Fleet Street. It was near the site of the incident recalled vividly in Leonard Rosoman's famous painting, of a collapsing wall crashing down on two firemen during the Blitz in 1940.

Max had taken residence there in a flat on the first floor, as he lived a peripatetic lifestyle, preferring hotels to his home at Cherkley Court. His enemies however believed he spent *too much* time at his country home, especially whenever there was a threat of bombing in the City.

The cabinet office had telephoned to inform him that a messenger from the Prime Minister was being sent over to see him urgently. I made my way into the building and knocked on the door which was opened by a male servant.

'Send him through, Nocks!' I heard his dulcet Scots-Canadian tones order.

I was led into a small study by his valet, Nockels, where – gnome-like behind a desk – sat old *moccasin mouth* himself.

'Christ! Jamie, well I'll be damned! How are you, kid!' he declared in genuine surprise and strode round the desk to pump my hand. 'Nocks, break out the cookie jar! Scotland's sweetest tooth has arrived!' The valet left us as Max led me into his sitting room. He opened up a drinks cabinet and poured me a glass full of Canadian Club whisky, which he knew was my favourite tipple after Scotch.

'Heck! I expected some chinless wonder and here I have my old pal! I heard you were back in town! It's good to see ya, buddy!'

'Good to see you again, Max!' I took a sip from my drink and stressed, 'but I am on here on business.' Nockels brought through a tray of cakes and I reached for one and sat back in my chair.

'Yaas! He never says "no" this fella!' Max winked at the servant and signalled him to close the door on his way out.

We chatted for a while about Scarborough and the girls. I then told him I had just come down a few days before.

'And you only looked me up because of Winston? I'm hurt, Jamie!' he jested, only half serious.

'No, I would have come anyway.' I put down my drink. 'I've got a message for you. He wants you back.'

'Does he?' the mischievous grin remained, tempered now by a steeliness I knew only too well.

'Aye, he does. But I'm to warn you that though he wants you back, he can't go on *taking* you back.'

He stood up. 'He misses you, Max,' I continued, 'but he wants a stop to the prima donna behaviour. The man's tired. He's enough on his plate. But he wants you to know how much he values you.'

'Values me enough to make that clown Atlee Deputy

Prime Minister? Keep that aristocratic idiot Sinclair as Air Minister?'

I bristled at this last. My diplomatic skills weren't honed enough just yet.

'From what I hear, he was always very sympathetic to you regarding Archie. But this is a coalition government. Mr Atlee stays.'

'And the second front? Or is that outside your remit?'

'Stop going on about it. You know we're not up to it right now. You should have been more circumspect about what you said to Stalin.'

'I don't have to take that from Winston's batman.' He caught himself and smiled apologetically as he retook his seat. 'Damnit, I'm sorry. Believe me, the last thing I need is a fat lip from Jamie Melville!'

Trying to remain indifferent to his insult, I continued. 'I'm here to tell you as an old acquaintance, Max. He respects you too much to send anyone else round.'

'Sure, sure, I believe it. He wants someone to do his dirty work but no one else has the guts, so he sends Jamie. Well I'll tell you, rather from *you* than anyone else. The English, ha!' he gesticulated and rose to his feet again. 'Always get someone else to fight their battles! Luckily for them they have us Scots who can beat the crap out of anyone. The English? They'll offer you a cup of tea with one hand whilst they stick the butter knife in with the other.'

I had a certain sympathy for this point of view but not on the grounds of nationality. What Max was really talking about was the British class system. A son of the Manse, he had fought against it since he arrived from Canada before the Great War. He'd been one step ahead of a major financial scandal at home that had made him a fortune, and believed London was rich for further pickings.

He made a good marriage, then became a Tory MP and played a major role in the ousting of the Asquith government in 1916. He helped create the coalition under Lloyd

George and received a seat in the Lords as reward. But he was never trusted; the insults about his background would always rankle and he rarely forgot a slight. He got his revenge by making the *Daily Express* the biggest paper in the world; gleefully picking over the foibles of the upper classes to sell copies to the so-called lower orders, who devoured them in their millions.

I knew what he was like and could imagine how difficult he could be as a subordinate. Winston had given him a pretty loose lead; and that was yet another mistake on the Prime Minister's part.

His rant over, Max then sat down again. His face seemed to change completely. The angry imp was gone, replaced by something more melancholy in nature.

'I'm so sorry about Gemma.'

He hadn't been to the funeral but had sent up a very expensive wreath. He always remembered the girls at Christmas and posted me a case of whisky every year on my birthday. He was an enigma.

Some considered him evil; but I didn't. He was always telling stories and there was one he would always repeat, how back in New Brunswick when he was growing up he was going out for a date, and had a hole in the only pair of trousers he owned. He was eighteen at the time but had left home and was living in a boarding house. He'd asked his landlady to sew the hole but she asked for fifty cents to do it. He hadn't enough and on looking around noticed a fifty cents piece lying on a table near where the landlady sat, and when she wasn't around he pinched it and then handed it to her saying, 'here is the fifty cents, now can you mend my pants?'

He'd stolen his fair share of fifty cents over the years; it was this type of quick thinking that made his fortune and made him despised. He was also a notorious womanizer. He was said to have carried a flame for Lady Diana Cooper and had countless affairs with young ingénues and actresses.

He lavished money and gifts on the more impecunious

members of the aristocracy he loved to be seen with. His generosity was legendary but many questioned it. The suspicion was either he was buying his way in or enjoyed the hold his money afforded him. His wife Gladys, by all accounts a lovely woman, had lived apart from him. His children grew to loathe him and he had few real friends.

But I knew he wasn't all bad. There was another story which he never told but I knew to be true. He was once asked to visit a hospital that needed funds to build another wing. Whilst there he left the party showing him around and came to a small canteen and found a table. An old lady who ran the restaurant and had no idea who he was told him that a cup of tea and a bun were only a penny each but if he couldn't afford them, she would give him them for nothing.

Max then went home and wrote out a huge cheque to pay for the building of the new extension. That was who he was, too. But I still never cared for him much and certainly did not trust him.

'I was truly in shock when I heard. It must have been awful, just awful for those little girls. I know, remember, *I know*,' he commiserated.

His wife had died suddenly, fairly young. It was said he truly loved her, for all his infidelities, though it was also said his behaviour contributed to cutting her life short.

'Thanks, Max, I'll never forget your kindness,' I replied in return. I still didn't know where we had arrived as to our conversation. I tried to get back on track.

'So, what do I tell Winston?'

'Tell him I'll think it over. But I won't work with Atlee or any other of them sons of bitches. They hate me. They think I'm a sort of traitor. The Tories think I'm a peasant. We're not like them, Jamie. You and me, we're alike. Poor boys made good. But no matter what we achieve they'll always hate us.'

I wasn't in the mood for his self-pity and got to my feet. 'Max, that's not an answer. It's not enough to take back to Winston.'

'Jamie, you sit down and I'll tell you something for once.' I remained on my feet and reached for my cane.

He continued to speak. 'Winston Churchill? That great man you so admire? Let me tell you, that man will always put *Winston Churchill* first. I saved him once and when I needed his help after that bastard Lloyd George ran me out of the government, Winston said and did nothing. You know why? Because he had his use out of me and now he didn't need me any longer. And he does that with everyone.'

'This is nonsense, Max,' I said as I put on my coat.

'No it ain't, sonny. You've a rosy-tinged view of him. Alright, you were just a kid and thought he was the bees knees but I'll tell you. You hurt him when you left. He had high hopes for you. He wept; he *wept* in front of me!'

'Look, Max…'

'He said you were like a son. But I said, Winston, you leave that kid be. He's not like us. You told me yourself that he was nothing like you, that Jamie always thought of others first before himself. Hell, even when he stole from the stores, it was always for his pals, he never took anything for himself.'

'Max…'

But he was in full flow now. 'If he stayed with you, you'd bring that boy down. An MP? No way. He wouldn't last five minutes before those snobs tore his heart out. No, he was better off away from you. Because if there's one thing about Winston Churchill that's as sure as the sun rising in the east, it's that sooner or later he'll make you do something you'll regret or *he'll* do something that's so terrible that there's no going back from it. Then you'll have to live with it. And once your use to him is over, he'll cast you aside as if he never even knew you to begin with.'

It was bitterness from the very depths of his soul. His ugliness and well-known vindictiveness were spewing out in a torrent of bile. He was only five-foot-seven but he seemed to dominate me. I steeled myself as the sympathy I had felt momentarily was replaced by something else that had been stewing within me.

Brendan had told me that my daughter Joanne had attended a reception at his Ministry, having been invited along by a friend who worked there. Max Aitken had also been present and was seen to disappear for a short time with her.

I made for the door, brushing past him.

'You tell Winston I got his warning. How I deal with it is my concern,' he finished.

I reached for the handle as he followed me along the hallway. I opened it and turned to him. He was only a step or two behind me.

'Max. My daughter, Joanne,' I said, coldly. 'Stay away from her. That's *my* warning to you.'

Chapter Six

My meeting with Beaverbrook was deemed to be a success by Winston after I related the sanitised version of it to him. He congratulated me and told me I was worth more to him than the entire diplomatic corps. This was said in the presence of Sir Alexander Cadogan, the patrician permanent secretary for Foreign Affairs and coincidentally, Winston's main link to the Secret Service of which, as earlier described, I'd become acquainted.

Cadogan had said nothing and no doubt stored it away for another caustic entry in his famous diary, but all this praise left me very uneasy. The old feelings had resurfaced again from my youth when I used to mix with the great and the good. Though older and supposedly wiser, it still discomfited me to know I was mistrusted for my close association with Winston and sneered at for my lowly origins. And I was never able to fully develop a thick enough skin to be able to absorb such behaviour and let it pass over me.

But if I was to be any use in my new-found position I couldn't go around reacting to perceived slights, because if I did, I wouldn't last long. In truth, I rather enjoyed the fact that I was deemed competent enough to visit the home of a powerful man in order to deliver a warning from a much greater one. Especially when it was a man I didn't like.

Officially, I now came under the wing of the Prime Minister's senior secretary, John Martin, and my experience of running my own business was soon put to good use in the day to day jobs of wartime government.

I usually sat at a desk in Downing Street or in the War Rooms, the underground bunker in Great George Street.

It was a government of all talents and times were changing. The exigencies of war meant it didn't matter where you came from as long as you were productive and efficient at the tasks you were assigned.

I suspected that in those early days the idea was for me to be seen around the place, rather than for my value as a glorified clerk. I quickly gained the impression people thought I'd been planted there to keep an eye on things. This reminded me of the words of Brendan's odd house guest the day I arrived in the city.

My head was down at a desk most days. But I could come and go as I pleased, the work was fascinating more often than not and there were plenty of attractive female typists around to lighten the atmosphere. I soon found myself in demand.

That I was mixing with the world again seemed to have a positive effect to an extent, though I still felt guilty at leaving the girls behind in Scarborough. But I had no interest in forming any romantic attachments with any of my new colleagues, or the friends they wanted to introduce me to, however pretty (and available) they were. In such a small group there would be gossip of course and my circumstances would have been discussed. I couldn't do much about that. Instead I would duck out of most of the socialising that went on, citing work commitments, while engendering a faint air of mystery.

The only problem with that strategy was that it made me a greater subject of interest.

Around that time, April 1942, the Yanks well and truly were coming and in increasingly large numbers to our shores. One day I was told that Harry Hopkins, the special envoy of President Roosevelt and part of FDR's famous "Brain Trust" was in town. I was further informed that the American ambassador, Gil Winant and Averell Harriman, a senior diplomat were accompanying him that very day on a visit to Downing Street.

I was introduced to these gentlemen and found them all extremely affable and forthcoming. Later Harry invited me to lunch at the Savoy Grill where an interesting conversation ensued. I was apparently the subject of discussion back in Washington and he wanted to get to know me. Hopkins was a tall, skeletal, chain-smoking Iowan, around fifty years of age.

Charming, acidic, profane and generous, my granny would have described him as a 'puir looking soul.' He started his working life as a social worker in the slums of New York, and moved upwards into various positions before coming to the attention of the then Governor Franklin D. Roosevelt. He was given a senior position in the State Relief programme (the depression was at its height) and made such an impression on the Governor that when Roosevelt became President in 1933, he chose Hopkins to play an even bigger role, providing aid as one of the architects of the New Deal.

He helped create the Civil Works Administration that found employment for four million people in its first month alone. It made Hopkins powerful enemies however, including big business, unions, Republicans, and even unsympathetic elements within the ruling Democrats. He was accused of bringing socialist ideas to America and of running roughshod over labour laws when legislation was passed on minimum wages.

Large scale public programmes he created were mocked as "leaf-raking." Another term was used to describe the more fanciful schemes he created to provide work: "boondoggling." Elements of the press loved to dig up the more exotic programmes, such as ladies hairpin manufacturing and the printing of dictionaries in rare languages.

Despite this criticism, Hopkins pressed on and was seen as the coming man in Washington. There was talk about him running for President in 1940. He was made Secretary of Commerce, but just as the war began in Europe, his health broke down. Years earlier, he underwent an operation to remove cancerous growths, which had resulted in him being given a clean bill of health as to that disease; but the operation was botched in other ways that left him severely weakened. He'd been days away from death before the President put him in the hands of military doctors, who thankfully brought about a recovery.

He could no longer carry out duties as a cabinet member, but Roosevelt was loathe to losing Hopkins, so gave him an unofficial posting of indeterminate title, and moved him into the White House permanently. His second wife had died a few years before and he had a young daughter, who became the charge of Mrs Roosevelt.

The new position he found himself in created even more enemies, as he was seen as an *éminence grise*. I knew how he felt. But as a roving reporter for the President, he served a vital purpose. He was completely loyal to Roosevelt and wholly trusted. Indeed, the saying was that he was the eyes, ears and voice of the President: the conductor of his will.

As we were served our food, I noted his plate contained only a sparse amount of vegetables and nothing more.

'My body can't break down proteins or fats,' he explained. 'So I'm stuck with this shit!' He sipped only water throughout the meal.

The Second Front was the main topic of discussion, which we arrived at in a roundabout fashion. It was a priority in the eyes of the Yanks. They are an impatient people, I would discover. They wanted the war ended, fast. They were a nation of improvisers and inventors. Nothing was deemed a challenge that couldn't be overcome with good old American know-how and "get up and go."

'I really love it here, Jamie,' Harry said over a cigarette. He smoked endlessly. He barely touched his food, whilst I had scoffed mine.

'I've never been one of those anti-British types. There are a lot of them and you know what? They're usually called Norman, Harold or Edward!'

'Aye, the British colonial's a strange sort!' I retorted over my dessert.

'You know what it was? That little family squabble we had back in 1776? The children wanted to leave home, but Daddy wouldn't let them go. Hell, it was all about a bunch of Free-masons who had the highest standard of living on earth and objected to having to pay a little bit back for the privilege!'

'Here! Mind what you say about the Craft!' I mocked chirpily.

'Oh, God, Jamie! You're not one, too? Well! My boss is one. Hell, so is yours! If you can't beat them, join them!'

He then gossiped about Washington. He loved FDR, that was undeniable, but he then told me something that piqued my curiosity as to why.

'No one really *likes* him.' He meant the President. 'You know, he'll meet someone, say a crippled child and her family, gush all over them and then when they leave, say to me or an aide: "those people are so rough, and did you see what the mother was wearing?"'

I felt uncomfortable on hearing this, as I knew that to be the same snobbish attitude I engendered among many who inhabited the environment I had chosen to be part of again.

He then stopped and crushed out his cigarette.

'Oh, I'm sorry, Jamie, I can see you squirming!' But he mistook the true reason for my discomfort.

He then started talking about General George Marshall, the senior American soldier and Chief of Staff, presently in London.

'He's quite a character! You know, FDR once called him "George" and Marshall looked him in the eye and said "Mr President, I think it's better that you address me as General!"'

'Yes, we've someone like that too – old Brookie.'

The outwardly austere General Brooke was dominating the early discussions on Allied strategy and the Yanks were unable to deal with him. For the present. Of course, I wasn't party to these talks but I heard Winston go on about them. How the Americans were impatient and wanted a cross-channel assault that year. It was out of the question from a British point of view, as the Yanks appeared to have no conception of the problems a sea-borne invasion involved. Thus the early discussions had reached a standstill, with neither side budging nor offering compromise.

'Of course we totally respect Brooke's views. After all, he was one of the last men out of Dunkirk. He understands the hazards involved,' Harry conceded generously.

'I'd say he was pretty competent, is Brookie,' I stated. 'He's about the only man that I know who can shout back at Winston!' I wasn't sure that I should be telling this to an emissary from a foreign power, albeit an ally. Probably the wine and the decent grub were having an effect. Though I think the inherent charm of my luncheon partner was working the most on my system.

'How does Winston feel about it?'

I felt uncomfortable now and tried to deflect the question. 'He wants to win the war, Harry.'

It was no little wonder Winston labelled him Lord Root of the Matter. Sensing now that he had pushed as far as I would go, he then veered off the subject and spoke about the differences between London and Washington. After lunch, we went our separate ways as I returned to my desk at Downing Street.

That lunch taught me a valuable lesson and I would not repeat the mistake. I was beginning to understand now that I was deemed valuable property. I had Winston's ear. No-one truly knew, especially myself, who or what I was in the scheme of things but many believed I was party to secret knowledge and that made me a marked man.

I spent a lot of time at the War Rooms, the underground complex situated just off Great George Street that would become Britain's command centre during the war. I was given my own room, near Winston's, though he never stayed there overnight much.

It was a dank, smoky, troglodyte's world that rang with the sounds of typewriters, talk and scuttling about. Cream-coloured walls and yellow-painted ventilation pipes added an artificial chimera of brightness, but along with strip lighting fought a losing battle against the murk. The weird sound from vacuum tubes delivering messages between offices reminded me of childhood memories of eerie tales of dead souls, their underworld slumbers disturbed by the importunate living, venting their wrath in a shrieking cacophony of outrage. With the stench from the Elsan chemical toilets combining with tobacco fumes, cookery odours and sweat from overworked and tired bodies, I was often left with headaches that fuelled my newly recurring nightmares from the last war.

It was the least restful place I could think of; though I would spend many a night there. I'd leave Downing Street late and if I couldn't be bothered walking to North Street or there was a raid on, I'd head round to my wee room that I had made habitable with photos of Gemma, the girls and some books.

On the plus side, I became friendly with the Royal Marine guards permanently on duty there. Early on, one of them had seen me talking with Winston and later approached me.

Standing rigidly to attention, he requested permission to speak.

'Sir, you're Jamie Melville, aren't you?' he asked as we stood in one of the few quiet corners of the complex.

I replied, yes.

'All the booties really admire you sir, and we wanted to ask you if you could do the honour of helping us lads out.'

What my new-found friend of His Majesty's Royal Marines wanted was for me to nick the cigars that Winston put out and quietly pass them over to the boys on permanent guard at the War Rooms, who were doing a roaring trade selling them on to Yanks and other gullibles.

I said I'd be happy to oblige. After all, we rankers have to look out for each other.

As for the on-going discussions, Winston's chief concern was that the United States would turn their full attention to the war against Japan if they were unable to get their way in Europe. A careful balancing act ensued in the often acrimonious negotiations.

Of course, these days, it's easy to look back and say we won the war, so what the hell? But it was very different back then. For one thing, no-one believed the Soviets would hold out, and plans were discussed for us and the Yanks to launch a small scale but in all probability suicidal invasion of France, to try and ease the pressure if the Russian forces collapsed. Winston even had a plan to invade northern Norway, which he wouldn't let go as he believed that if we could knock the Germans out there it would allow more of our convoys to get through and provide increased aid for Stalin. The Americans were totally against the idea.

They weren't interested in sideshows; they wanted to deliver the knock-out blow in the only place they believed mattered, through the front door of France that led into Germany. But they had to be convinced that though we also shared this ultimate goal, it had to be done when conditions were right. Winston's secret weapon in these negotiations was his newly appointed Chief of the Imperial General Staff, General Sir Alan Brooke.

And James Melville, Lance-Corporal. Formerly of Wardlaw Place, Edinburgh.

He's been forgotten now. Ask someone who Montgomery was, everyone knows. General Eisenhower? Patton? MacArthur? All are remembered. General Brooke probably played a bigger part in the winning of the war than all of them, but because he was someone who preferred to stay out of the spotlight, is now overlooked by history. Unfairly, I'd say.

The story I have to tell now is of my part during this crucial period of the war. It's all true, and Jamie Melville and his native Edinburgh wits played a small but significant role. It's hard to believe now, but things could have turned out a lot differently. The Yanks might have packed up, headed east and dealt with the Japs first, the Russians could have made it to the channel, and the world would have been a very different place today.

Chapter Seven

I HAD BEEN in London for just over a month. So far, I had given Beaverbrook a telling off, typed up a few memos and undergone shooting practice at a range with Inspector Thompson in order to re-acquaint myself with the use of a pistol. Winston told me I had to re-hone my skills as he still worried about invasion by the Germans; but in reality he wanted me to sharpen up my latent musketry (I was also allowed to use other weapons) for purposes I would discover later.

I was now regarded with suspicion by a few of his staff. The aforementioned Commander Thompson took an instinctive dislike to me. He was a snob, jealous of my close proximity to – and former intimacy with – Winston. I told him to *eff off* early on, after a minor altercation, in order to warn him that I wouldn't tolerate any of his nonsense. Consequently, he formed a frosty attitude towards me. This led to me being regarded as a hero by the younger staff that suffered him and couldn't speak out.

I found the class distinction as bad now as I had twenty-five years earlier. But at least back then, I was only a lad and people made allowances. I'd met eminent figures like Lloyd George and Mr Asquith from the world of politics who'd been perfectly kind to me. Then there was of course dear Eddie Marsh and his artistic friends (though as many of them were plainly queer as coots – I'd had to watch myself).

I'd once been to a small party held at Eddie's home in Gray's Inn where two of the great beauties of the age, Lady Diana Manners and Winston's old flame, Pamela Plowden, Lady Lytton were present. The man himself became momentarily tongue-tied when the latter appeared; a sight to behold indeed, but she soon put him at ease, along with myself.

I admit to being transfixed when I saw her and absolutely petrified when she approached me and handed me her glass of champagne. I wasn't sure I was allowed to drink with the grown-ups but she passed her glass to me regardless in order to try a sip. It was sheer flirtation on her part of course. As for me, I knew my way around bubbly well enough from my days at the 6th serving Winston and visiting dignitaries and played the part of the innocent to perfection. The rim was tainted with her lipstick and I felt a terrific thrill at the sensation as my lips tasted it. I had indeed tried champagne before but never like this. Though she was in fact a few months older than Winston and would have been in her early forties at the time, I regarded her as the most beautiful woman I'd ever seen in my life. I still do.

I can hardly remember what we spoke of as she was so incredibly alluring; her delicate heart-shaped face with lightly-rouged cheeks and a skin that seemed to glow, the tiny lines at the edge of her eyes the only indication of her true age. She looked at me directly as we chatted and I found it difficult (I always did with gorgeous women) to look at her in return through terrible shyness, at least at first. But by the end of the evening, Pamela and Lady Diana (who was stunningly beautiful too, though much younger) joined in with me arm in arm as we raucously sang 'Champagne Charlie' together – Winston having related to the gathering in hilarious terms the famous incident where I nearly took his head off with a bottle of Pol Roger back at Plugstreet.

Both ladies insisted I call on them with Gemma, as I had gone down a hit. Lady Diana was working as a nurse herself at the time, caring for children. Afterwards, I remember lying in bed that night in a delightful, slightly alcoholic daze, happily recalling the faces of both ravishing beauties, unable (and unwilling) to remove them from my mind.

They had treated me with true *class* and I felt their chat and laughter had been genuine and unassuming. My experience is that the real snobs in life are never those who you instinctively *believe* must be snobs. Usually, the higher people are the more sincere they are. It's the jumped up little nobodies, struggling to get to the top; they are life's real pain in the arses.

With regards to my new work colleagues and acquaintances, as I've mentioned I did the rounds; mainly with typists and junior secretaries to a few clubs and pubs, early on, to get to know people. But after the first few weeks I cried off, offering excuses that I was needed elsewhere, winking enigmatically. This was probably the only time I used my notoriety for effect. I just felt some things were happening too quickly. Being made a fuss of by a lot of very dolly young ladies may be most blokes' idea of heaven, but it wasn't for me just then.

The Cabinet Secretaries themselves were all highly-educated, ambitious types who initially barely gave me the time of day. Amongst the military men, I did receive a smile and a hello here and there.

There was one extremely austere-looking officer the juniors referred to as "Colonel Shrapnel", who I observed darting around the War Rooms and Downing Street like an angry wasp. He wore thick, horned-rimmed spectacles, was slightly stooped and had a face like a mad bullfinch – which was apropos as I later learned he was a bird-watcher and expert in ornithological photography.

I'd spent the night in the underground bunker, and as I opened the door of my room still bleary eyed that morning who should bump into me but this fellow. He profusely apologised but I was surprised to hear him address me as 'Jamie.' He then scurried off. I thought nothing of it until I ran into him later at breakfast, where I found him sitting alone with a book.

After showing my pass at the entrance, I grabbed a cup of tea and a plate of the ghastly excuse for porridge that they served and decided to sit across from him. He had been pretty civil to me earlier and I thought there might be an opportunity for a little conversation with someone.

I reached over for the salt and he looked up from his reading.

'Ah, I have to admit, I prefer sugar,' he stated sadly, as he had noted my pouring salt on my porridge. Sugar, of course, was rationed.

'When I was a wee lad,' I replied, 'we didn't have sugar, but my dad always told me a true Scot only uses salt on his *parritch*, anyway!'

'Quite right! Quite right!' He spoke very rapidly, but it wasn't unpleasant and I could sense kindness in him.

'What's the book?' I asked.

It was about birds and he showed it to me. It had beautiful illustrations and the colours and drawings captivated me as I looked through the pages. He was leaning forward with his hands clasped, expectantly.

'These are lovely! I wish I could draw like that!' I exclaimed.

'Do you like birds?' he asked.

'I don't really know much about them. Oh, I know sparrows and there was always a wee Robin Redbreast perched near our tenement. We used to get lots of seagulls in Edinburgh! And starlings, I hated them! They were wee bullies!'

He rocked back and laughed happily. The old Melville charm was indeed irresistible.

'I see you know your birds! There are many fascinating species to be found in the cities. Why, did you know that birds from North America frequently get lost and end up in this country? Amazing!'

He then started a conversation that reminded me of Winston when off on one of his reveries. I could not have cared less about avian species ten minutes before, but he proceeded to absolutely captivate me in his love of his subject. By the end, he had virtually talked me into going bird watching with him the next opportunity that presented itself.

'Oh, I haven't introduced myself,' he suddenly remembered.

'I'm Jamie Melville,' I began and reached out my hand, 'but you already know that?'

'Oh, yes, I know who *you* are! My name's Alan Brooke. I'm very pleased to make your acquaintance! You and I have one thing in common. A very *big* thing in common! Mr Churchill!'

I laughed. 'Oh, *him*! Well, I used to be his batman and general dogsbody. I was a wee laddie back then, but he saw me right, though we did get into some scrapes!'

He laughed merrily again. He seemed so full of life and good cheer that it came as a surprise to me later when his manner changed to the forceful and often highly aggressive soldier that he was, particularly during the negotiations with the Americans. It was the awful stress, of course. But I like to think I was able to work the magic and bring a little light relief. What I was experiencing now was the attractive side of his personality, and it was utterly sincere.

'Yes, Jamie, I think you need to be here to ensure he doesn't get into any more scrapes! Just keep doing what you are doing! Oh, I know you think it may not be much but just keep on being Jamie Melville. That's the best way you can serve him. And all of us!' he chortled.

With this final remark, he rose from the table.

'I'm very pleased we've introduced ourselves properly. We'll be seeing a lot of each other over the coming months. Any time you feel the need to chat, please do not hesitate to approach me. Who knows! There may be times where I feel the need to chat to you. After all, no one knows him better than you do! That makes you extremely valuable. Good day, old chap.'

With that he gathered up his book and left the canteen, and I finished off my now-cold porridge.

A few weeks later, at the end of May, I made the acquaintance of another character who would loom large in events ahead. I should really say re-acquaintance, for the individual concerned was my brother, Arthur.

You'll note that I haven't made much mention of him. I hadn't heard from him in over a decade. Nearly fifteen years before, he had come to the house late one night asking me to lend him some money. He was working in the Grand Hotel in Scarborough as a junior manager and had got himself into some "trouble". He had to leave for reasons unspecified, but needed cash as he had a friend in London who was willing to put him up.

I said I would give him what I had, but he asked if I could write out a cheque for £50. He pleaded with me not to ask why. But I had strong suspicions anyway. I believed he was being blackmailed.

Arthur was homosexual. In those days, either you disowned a relative who was that way inclined or you tried to deal with it the best you could. He had never got on with his adoptive father, Arnold, and I never was able to find out why as Arthur was secretive and I never pressed him. I had grown more tolerant of him out of guilt as I grew older, because I have to confess I'd never been as close to him as I was to Tom when we were kids.

It was strange, twins are supposed to be inseparable but those two were as different as two people could be. Tom was open and generous, Arthur was secretive and hard to get to know; Tom and I had been far closer in nature. But when I realised what Arthur was I tried to show more understanding, which was difficult because he never gave much in return. He never asked me for anything and never came to visit us. I always had to make the first move and he appeared to have no friends that I was aware of.

I had been initiated into Freemasonry in a Lodge in London and after heading down to receive my degrees (I stopped off at Winston's when in London) I regularly visited a Lodge in Scarborough to meet people and soon made a few chums.

I eventually stopped attending because English Lodges were too business-minded, unlike Scottish Lodges where fellowship, camaraderie and charitable works are of greater importance. I also discovered a fiddle going on with bar receipts and threatened to go to the police.

The problem with that was the Chief Constable of the area was a Brother and he had a quiet word with me and asked me to drop the matter. I then threatened to contact Grand Lodge and mentioned a few eminent Masons I knew in London. His eyes nearly popped out his head when he heard the names and I told him if he tried to threaten me again he would be in serious trouble. I then told him he could stick the Lodge up his arse.

He then told me that my brother's proclivities were known to the force and inferred they may become common knowledge unless I kept quiet about the scandal in the Lodge. I then told him to stick the Lodge doubly up his rectum and stormed out, never to return.

(I was able to affiliate to my dad's Lodge, Roman Eagle No. CVX in Edinburgh, through contacts with his old Brothers and I attended a few meetings there when up in Scotland. The difference between Scotland and England is remarkable; if you ever want to experience the true essence of Freemasonry, head for old Scotia.)

So, when Arthur came to see me that night begging for a serious sum of cash, I could guess the reason. He had to be in big trouble to come to me, because he never concerned himself with any of us. But it goes to show that when needs must, blood's thicker than water, as they say.

I pressed him but he would only confirm that a policeman was blackmailing him. The bastard was a Brother, too and wanted payment up front or he would arrest him. Arthur had been caught soliciting and had the squeeze put on.

I suspected there was more because it all sounded too pat. He knew I had trouble at the Lodge and for a time my opinion of the local Bobbies was lower than whale shit. But

I didn't give him the cheque he asked for. I'm not dumb and the last thing I wanted was something with my bank details and signature floating around the circles I now strongly suspected he was moving in.

He started an argument and woke Joanne and Gemma; I had to shove him against a door to shut him up. But I gave him what I had in the house and told him to give me the address of the friend in London so I would know where he was. This was an error, understandable on my behalf, and he said he wouldn't give it to me as the police would come to me first looking for him. I said of course, he was right but to keep in touch, for Mum's sake at least. Mum being Ida, Mrs Humphries, who doted on him.

And then he was gone. I'd had a few sleepless nights over the years worrying about what had become of him. Tom, too. At one point I'd asked Winston, whilst he was Chancellor, to do some checking at the Home Office on my behalf and discovered that Arthur Melville had been imprisoned for three years for the offence of sodomy in the late twenties. He'd got involved with a group of upper class brown-hatters and had to carry the can after a raid on a house in London, whilst the sons of the gentry involved were let off with a quiet word.

I visited him at the Scrubs. He barely spoke to me and looked completely defeated by his present circumstances. He begged me not to tell Mum but didn't make it clear which "Mum" he referred to. I brought him some books and food which the Guards at first wouldn't allow, as homosexuals in those days were treated very badly indeed. But I dropped a name or two and they relented.

Naturally, on the way down on the train to London, I'd thought of him. I don't suppose he ever thought of me much. I did find out that whilst he was with this group that had led him to prison, he'd bragged about being Winston Churchill's valet during the Great War. He'd used the stories I'd told him and Tom and twisted them to look "big" in the circles he was moving in. Which of course was very sad but not unusual behaviour amongst such types, I'm told.

Anyway, that day at the end of May, I was at Downing Street when Inspector Thompson approached me. Walter was a very nice bloke who I got on well with. Later, he would confide in me when his son died in action and also when he was having personal problems of his own, usually involving ladies.

'Jamie, have you got a moment?'

John Martin had asked me to review some notes on food production and shipping losses, which I was currently wading through, and was glad of the respite. Walter led me out the front door and we stood outside. The rails had been removed for the war effort and we stood on the pavement, Walter leading me away out of earshot of the police guard at the door.

'Jamie, I've received word about your brother, Arthur. A pal tipped me off that he heard you were in town and wanted to meet you.'

This to me was very strange, but I told him to pass my address on to Arthur.

'He knows where you live, apparently. He went there and you weren't in. But we can't have him coming round here, of course.'

Walter then handed me a sheet of folded note-paper.

'Keep him away from Winston, Jamie. I know he's your brother but I trust your discretion.'

I thanked him and he walked off. I looked at the piece of paper and wondered why Arthur would want to see me. It was out of character and my first assumption was that he was in bother again. But how did he know I was in London? I couldn't imagine him contacting Tom and anyway, Tom would have let me know if he had. And what pal of Walter's? A policeman, no doubt.

I re-folded the paper, placing it in my wallet, and returned to my task at the office.

That late May evening, though the season was turning, I wrapped up warm. I've always been susceptible to cold and also wearing an overcoat provided me with some form of anonymity. In those days going without one was deemed a sign of poverty.

The bombing had started to tail off as the Germans now concentrated their attentions on killing as many Russians as possible. It made a pleasant change from snuffing out Londoners. The sky had yet to fully darken even though a 'Bomber's Moon' was out, that dread symbol to all of the city's populace, as I made my way on foot to Regent Street and the Budapest.

It was very popular pre-war and still did good trade amongst the upper-crust clinging on to memories of what it had once been. Now, refugee musicians would play their zithers or whatever it was that made those awful, depressing tunes, whilst customers dined from a menu the owners would not have offered to beggars before 1939. I'd telephoned earlier and arranged to meet Arthur as he knocked off at nine o'clock. He was assistant head-waiter there.

I arrived early – I had pre-booked a table through a bit of name-dropping – so sat back, lit up a cigar and ordered a drink. Winston was always receiving free smokes from admirers, which had to be tested for potential poison. Literally thousands of them ended up being destroyed, usually unnecessarily, to his great chagrin. As he didn't like the smaller Tom Thumb type I'm partial to, he passed some of them on to me, once they had been deemed free from toxic substances.

I sat about fifteen minutes before Arthur appeared.

'Jamie?'

I looked up and saw a pleasant-faced, still youthful-looking man in his early forties. His blond hair was receding drastically, but his features were still relatively unlined, soft and perfectly smooth even at this hour. He wore a light grey fifty-shilling suit with a neat collar and tie, but no overcoat, and as he sat down I automatically reached out my hand.

He seemed to momentarily catch himself, as if undecided what to do, but then put his hand out and slid it into mine. It was soft, there was little grip, and as I pulled away I caught a scent of some sort of cream as I took my cigar from my lips.

'Good to see you again, laddie! How have you been?'

He seemed to recoil into his seat somewhat.

'Oh! Do you want a drink or something?' I'd forgotten my manners momentarily.

'Can we go elsewhere to chat?' he replied, cagily. 'I know a quiet little place not far from here.'

I grabbed my coat and stick and he led me out of the restaurant, after I'd paid the bill. We wandered up towards Piccadilly, turned into a side street and walked along a few yards, till we came to a doorway with a sign above, with 'The Cherub' in faded black lettering lit in sickly yellow lighting. Arthur stopped and knocked at the sealed metal door. A few seconds later, what I thought at first was the letter box opened from within; then the door opened and he ushered me inside.

We walked up a flight of stairs and then entered into a surprisingly large and welcoming room with a bar and seating, with purple rococo lampshades on set tables. There were a few couples seated – and by couples, you'll have gathered by now what type I refer to.

The room looked straight out of *Le Belle Époque* and ordinarily I would have expected to see Can-Can girls and short-arsed painters floating around. But I was more likely to bump into Lord Alfred Douglas than Toulouse Lautrec and one of his supple dancers. It was a sort of Café Royal for fairies.

There were paintings of boys and young men in marble reliefs in the classical style, and I noted that the lampshades stood on little statuettes of Eros himself. I observed that the thing he was holding in his hand certainly wasn't his bow.

Arthur led me to a table, went off and brought back a whisky for me and what I assumed was lemonade or something soft for him. He neither smoked nor drank; at least he never did as long as I knew him. As he sipped from his glass I remembered my old grandmother who used to tell me that a man had to have some vices, and she would never fancy or trust one who neither imbibed nor liked a puff.

'So, how have you been?' I started things off.

He shrugged. 'Could be worse.'

'Where are you living?'

'I've a room in Camden.' He lived in Argyle Gardens, near Kings Cross station. I thought that living so close might have made him desire jumping on a train once in a while and heading home, but of course that was wishful thinking on my part.

He was being his usual uncommunicative self. But I was long past the stage in my life when I felt I had to go easy with him. The last time I saw him was in jail. I caught myself and tried to at least give him one more chance.

'Arthur, you wanted to see *me*, remember? That's unusual. For you, I mean.'

'Well, I'm not looking for a hand-out,' he declared pettily. 'Not this time. I'm doing alright. I just wanted you to know.'

I took a slug from my glass. It was decent stuff. Dimple, I thought, and certainly not watered down.

'And I'm not here to give you a lecture. I'm past all that now. I could mention that the Humphries passed away. My wife died and Joanne is in London, but would any of that mean anything to you?'

I *was* trying not to be angry. Common decency would have been for him to ask about me.

Then I felt someone approach me from behind.

'Are you alright, Alastair?'

I looked around for the source of the voice and also who "Alastair" might be.

'No, I'm fine. Really, Dilly, this is family,' Arthur answered.

'Oh, that's what it looks like? Wouldn't know myself.' It was the doorman, who then sidled off as quietly as he'd appeared.

I didn't want to know either any more. I drained my glass and got up.

'Where are you going, the loo? It's over there.' Arthur pointed.

'To get another drink, then I'm off. *Alastair*.'

I went to the bar and shook my glass at the barman who poured from a bottle of Dewar's. I'd gotten that wrong along with the rest of the evening. I brought the drink back to the table.

'Can we start again?' he asked as I retook my seat.

'Sure. Say your piece.'

'I'm sorry about Gemma. She was lovely and very kind to me. I really didn't know. I'm sorry about Ida, but as for Arnold, he can burn in hell. A queer hater; pure and simple.' He was as animated as I'd heard him, but it was the anger of a bitter, beaten man. It was as if he had long put aside the memories that inspired his rage and, now resurfaced, they were renewed in painful recall.

'I don't know what you're on about,' I said. 'He was a decent man who took in two children and did a wonderful job with them.'

'Christ!' It was an aside more than an oath. 'How little you know!'

My mood grew testy. 'Listen, mate, I don't want to hear any of your fantasies. And as for you going around telling everyone that you were Churchill's batman, leave it out!'

'Going to "skelp" me, Jamie?' Suddenly he was pure Gorgie Road. 'Gonnae wallop me? It would be you all over. You and that foul temper of yours!'

I got up. 'That's it. I'm off. The only good that'll come out of this evening is that I'll let Mum know you're well. You know, your *real* mother? Aye. She's still alive but a widow again. I'll also tell Tom, that other brother you have and the only other living being on this earth that worries about you. And it's nothing to do with you being queer. Tom and I never bothered about that. The fact is you're a dead bloody loss. Always have been.'

I felt bad immediately about the last bit but he always brought out unpleasant feelings in me. Some people are like that. He was one. By accident of biology we came from the same womb, but in truth were we not from the same life. I was better off not knowing him, but cursed to still worry about his welfare and in doing so, question myself.

He remained sat at the table but I had now calmed somewhat. 'Look, I'm sorry. Better leave it for tonight. I'll know where to find you and evidently you know where you can look me up. Do you need some cash?' He merely shrugged and stared at his glass.

'Thanks for the drink,' I said. He may have responded but I was too busy putting on my overcoat to notice or care.

I made for the door where Dilly opened it for me.

I stopped and turned to him. 'Just one thing, dear.'

'What is it, love?'

'Not having family must save you a fortune at Christmas. You could at least buy a decent suit.'

Chapter Eight

I LEFT THE club and wandered back towards Whitehall. I didn't fancy the War Rooms or being alone in North Street. Winston had told me that I could visit him at the Annexe whenever I wanted. I confess I needed his company that night. I'd left Arthur feeling down.

I was lonely. It was a novel experience for me as I'd never had cause to suffer from it in my life before. I was away at fifteen to the army and then after the blast and my injury, whisked away to my new life in London. I'd met Gemma almost immediately and then there was Eddie Marsh and Winston and a few pals I'd made at the office where I worked. I never had reason to feel solitary.

Married life followed, and building the business with three kids to raise. When Gemma died I had the girls to concentrate on and when left to myself in the days after, I was too numbed to feel anything, least of all loneliness.

But as I tramped through the darkened streets, past entrances to shelters, side-stepping the remaining detritus from the aerial cataclysm a year before, I realised that this was the life left to me unless I changed. But could I? After all, not only did I owe it to the girls, I owed it to Gemma and myself to move on from the past.

I'd been approached by one of the typists at Downing Street, Enid, and asked out for a drink in a roundabout but undeniable fashion. She was extremely pretty, a good few years younger than me and very much available. But in a very un-Jamie Melville-like fashion I mumbled something incoherent that sounded rather like a "no" and lost the moment.

Gemma had been the only girl I'd ever known. When I was a kid in Gorgie, I'd played kissing games with the local wee *hairies* as all the boys did, and that was as far as anything went with females for most of us in those days. Gemma had been my one and only woman and I'd been entirely content. She was beautiful, she was intelligent and she loved me and all that for any man should be enough.

I'd been assailed by the depressing state of loneliness that perpetually hung about Arthur. It was his fault really, I tried to convince myself. But it was self-delusion. His life, was it any different now from mine? God knows what he'd been through. And when I saw him in that club, I realised that he didn't even seem to fit in with *that* life. Or was I still deceiving myself, this time over my own brother?

I arrived at the Annexe but Winston wasn't there. He was in the Bunker having another late-night meeting with senior military men. I walked over to Great George Street, the entrance to the War Rooms, and was allowed entry after showing my pass. I made my way through the labyrinth of corridors after being informed he was in the Map Room, but that the main meeting was over and I could enter.

The Map Room, the heart of the war effort, was manned continually, night and day. You had to be on a special list in order to be allowed entry and I was one of the privileged few. It portrayed vividly the state of the World War through giant maps embedded with symbols of ships on the blue of its oceans and arrows and little flags in various colours denoting the mass of armies on land.

'Here he is! This is the laddie who shall deal with Herr Hitler!' Winston strode over and led me to a chair next to his. A creature of the night, he looked lively and remarkably fresh except for a line of sweat along his forehead. He was in shirtsleeves and his bowtie was in a disgraceful state. The occupants of the room were clearing their desks and I acknowledged General Brooke and "Pug" Ismay, the Prime Minister's Chief of Staff and a true gentleman, who winked over at me.

'It is only because Mr Melville has entered the building that I now allow these *paladins* the opportunity to slink off to their beds early!' Winston declared with a jaunty air. 'For I know that the ear-bashing I would receive from the Lance-Corporal for keeping these gentlemen from their slumbers would be more than my life's worth to bear!'

I immediately felt my spirits rise, and reflected that a potentially very late session listening to Winston gassing away was a small price to pay to help the war effort by ensuring the long-suffering officers got a much-sought-after early night.

We were momentarily left alone. There was a room just along the corridor that had been turned into a drinking den for staff, and it had become custom for them to congregate there after an evening session in the Map Room. It was by war-time standards remarkably well-stocked, and the place to be in that gloomy subterranean domain.

Winston passed me a cigar and from somewhere a bottle of brandy appeared. He knew that spirit gave me headaches and poured me a small one only. He filled his own glass to the brim.

'What kind of an evening have you had, my boy?' he asked after a slurp from his drink.

Behind us, the great map of the world gazed over the desks where the top men of the three services normally sat. I picked up a pencil that had been left and toyed with it.

'Colonel, can you ever truly give up on someone?' I asked.

'It depends on who that someone is.'

'A brother?'

'One cannot ever give up on one's blood, James. Or where would we be?'

I could always speak to him on any subject. I used to pour my heart out to him back at the 6th and also on occasions such as when I once suspected my Gemma of two-timing me. I was just a child then. But if so, why did I feel it necessary and more, easy, to speak to him now in a similar vein?

'And on a dead wife?'

He patted my hand. 'That lovely girl! How I remember her! How could one not? She loved you dearly. She surpassed all of the rules of this age; of *class*, of moribund *dullness*!' He then declared angrily, 'Those *snobs*!', took out a handkerchief and dabbed his wet eyes.

I was startled by the strength of his invective. But I shouldn't have been. After all, he was simply declaring his fury at those who had mocked his boy.

He recovered and then asked, 'Are you lonely, Jamie?' The question was now put and possibly a moment had arrived. But was I ready to let go?

I chickened out and asked him how the meeting had gone.

'Oh ... we are preparing a subterfuge, sadly. We must convince our American friends that we intend crossing the channel this year or at the very least the next, but in fact have to find a way of diverting such an attack elsewhere. It is no easy matter and it breaks my heart, for the Americans are a kind and generous people, if a little naïve.'

He then went on about the need to visit President Roosevelt and stress his case. He was off to America to discuss great plans. He then hit me with it.

'Would you like to accompany me?'

My heart started hammering. It was a dream come true and I could hardly believe it. 'To America? But what would I do? I'm not important.'

His fist slammed the table but his face broke into a smile. 'Oh, James! When will you *ever* learn that you are so loved and admired! Really, this Edinburgh modesty at times is quite beyond the pale!' The room began to fill again with the night staff. He stood and led me out along the dank, sometimes rat-infested walkway towards the exit and blessed fresh air.

'I confess it has its uses!' he continued cheerily as we strolled past secretaries furiously typing away at their desks, messengers darting between rooms and uniforms striding around carrying folders. 'But my boy, you owe yourself a little happiness!' He knew well my fascination for America. 'I absolutely insist ... no! *Order* as Prime Minister, that you, James Melville, accompany me to the Wild West.'

It was of course top-secret, and very few knew, but a meeting had been arranged in Washington to discuss allied strategy with President Roosevelt. They needed to iron out differences, but at no time then did I realise how serious those differences were.

I swallowed my initial concerns over sailing. When he had first met the President at Placentia Bay in Canada in late 1941, Winston had sailed on the ill-fated battleship *Prince of Wales*. That ship had been sunk later along with the *Repulse* by Japanese bombers in what he himself described as the worst shock he'd suffered during the war.

He'd sent them out against advice to show the flag and scare off any potential aggressor. But it was a gesture thirty years out of date. The episode again brought his judgement into question and hundreds of men paid the price. It was said he suffered nightmares from it, hearing the screams of drowning sailors and on occasions afterwards he was heard to stop and say to himself '*those men, those poor men!*'

I soon discovered that on this occasion he would be flying to his rendezvous. My relief at avoiding a week of seasickness was tempered by the thought of air-travel. I'd never flown on an aircraft before, the very idea terrified me and I seriously considered whether it was worth the risk. Three young girls might be orphaned so Daddy could go on a free trip to the United States.

I decided to travel back up to Scarborough to see the family for a few days before I flew off into the blue, still not entirely convinced it was advisable for a father of motherless children, particularly in wartime.

The trip home proved joyful after a somewhat strained

beginning. It was clear the girls had found my absence difficult and at first the youngest, Claire, was a bit stand-offish. But when I described in detail the damage the bombing had done to London, she soon went into raptures. She was a blood-thirsty wee devil and a bit of a tom-boy, even at nine. Allison clung to me, following me around all the time I was back, and it was all I could do to contain my emotion. She was due to start Secondary school in Scarborough, which meant Claire was left on her own at the private school. It would only be for another two years and she liked it there as the old ladies never used any form of physical punishment. From what I could gather she was a bit of teachers' sneak, forever dobbing in her school chums, which must have made her popular.

I filled in Tom about Arthur and gave him a potted version of what I'd been up to. Of course I couldn't say anything about America, even to him.

The "contracts" Brendan Bracken had alluded to when he originally invited me down to London included our being returned two of our boats from the Naval Reserve list with their crews intact. All our catch was to be sold to the government for the armed forces.

I made my farewells, ensuring the concerns about my trip were hidden and returned south.

On the way down I decided the next time I had the chance I would visit my mother and sisters in Edinburgh. We kept in touch by letter and I'd become particularly attached to the oldest girl, Maggie. She'd never married, preferring to see out life working in the same library in Gorgie Road that I'd spent so much time in as a child. It was one of life's ironies that one old spinster, Miss Primrose, who had looked after the place before, was being replaced by a younger version.

I worried about Margaret. She was still young and attractive but never would marry. Who knows what goes on inside another human heart?

On my return to London and after dropping off my bag, I left immediately for Bloomsbury and the offices of the Ministry of Information to meet up with my oldest daughter, Joanne.

Along with nearby Holborn, Bloomsbury had been hit hard by the Blitz. As I made my way on foot I noted to myself where every public shelter and entrance to the underground subway were located. I wanted to assure myself that Joanne would know where to go if the sirens went off.

The art deco building that was the head office of the Ministry always reminded me of one of those skyscrapers at the end of *King Kong*. The Senate University was one of the tallest buildings in London; its imposing entrance swallowed me up as I showed my pass and was led up to Brendan Bracken's office.

He was at his desk leaning over it with another bloke, going over a design for a new public information poster. The Ministry employed some of the best artistic minds in the country. At one time, John Betjeman and Graham Greene worked there. Brendan had dragged the Ministry out of the mire after a poor start under the tutelage of Sir John Reith, who Winston detested, and my old pal Lady Diana Manners' husband, that arch but lovable lecher Duff Cooper (though how any man would want to cheat on Diana is beyond me).

After sending the chap on his way, Brendan and I chatted for a while. He knew about America; he knew *everything*. He was notoriously leaky and there was always the likelihood of a public gaffe. But he was indispensable to Winston and was one of those types who excels no matter what they turn their acute minds to.

We then got around to Joanne. She shared a flat with two other girls in Muswell Hill. At the Ministry she worked in the department that dealt with notices to newspapers about bombing casualties. This was to ensure that the Germans didn't get to know how successful or not they'd been in raids. It called for tact and imagination, which Joanne had in abundance. I looked forward to seeing her again.

Brendan led me down to her office. On entering it I immediately drew breath, as in the room before me was a middle-aged man bent over a desk, his backside in the air, tinkering with the hair of the young lady sitting behind it who very evidently wasn't keen on the attention.

'Here, you! Heid the ba'! Get yer mitts aff fae her!' The Gorgie boy had been unleashed by the sight of this libidinous sod pawing his wee girl.

The man in question leapt around in surprise. One look at his pencil-thin moustache and Ronald Colman sliminess nearly had me swinging at him.

Brendan grabbed my arm. 'Hold it, Jamie! Freddie, buzz off and have a cup of tea will you, or I won't be responsible!'

Joanne took the opportunity to stretch over the desk and aim a smack that caught Freddie on the arm. He then proceeded to slink off to his office, slamming the door behind him.

'What's goin' on here, then? Is that bugger annoyin' you?' I remained incensed despite Brendan's intervention.

'Oh, Daddy! Trust you! I'll never live this down! I work here, you know!'

'Listen to me, my lady! Ye're no' working beside a leery swine like that nae mair, ye're no'!'

Brendan, who was undoubtedly considering consulting an interpreter, retrieved the situation somewhat.

'Steady, Jamie, I'll have a wee word with her boss! It seems he doesn't know who you are ... but he does now, I'm thinking! Now, calm yourself and go and have a natter somewhere safe with your little lassie.'

I shook myself down but felt not in the least embarrassed to have seen off that lecherous rogue. Young girls in offices in those days had no end of bother with fellows who couldn't keep it in their pants, who saw them as fair game – the filthy brutes. Whilst I was around it had better stay buttoned-up, or I'd have it kicked up inside his stomach.

'You just tell him tae bugger aff, my girl!' I said, my temper now abating somewhat. 'Dinnae gie his type any encouragement! Why, if your mother…'

'Oh, Daddy, be quiet and give me a kiss!' I did just that and we both burst out laughing as we embraced, happy to be reacquainted.

'Daddy, it's so nice to see you *smile!*' she said happily, but with some intensity of feeling.

We left Brendan and the office for a little British Restaurant nearby. We ordered an execrable lunch and chatted about Scarborough. I told her how the girls were getting on. Then I asked how she was doing.

Joanne liked her job and Freddie wasn't all that bad, but she'd been told by Brendan she'd be moving up soon and had to put up with Valentino a little while longer. It was seen as a rite of passage for secretaries in the building and most of the time she found him plain amusing. He wasn't at all a bad boss. He just liked the ladies.

She prattled on about her work, I tried to listen but after a pause I came out with what had been nagging me for a while.

'I heard you were talking to Max Aitken?'

'The pilot?' She asked with some surprise.

'No, his daddy.'

'Oh, *him.*' She pulled a face.

'Don't worry, I told him to stay away from you.'

She pulled another. 'What do you mean?'

I looked at her. 'Brendan told me you were chatting to him at a party.'

'Daddy, I had to tell him to get lost!'

I sighed. 'Beauty has its price, I suppose!'

Beautiful she certainly was. I saw Gemma in her but Joanne was taller, possibly taking after her Uncle David, Gemma's brother – but I had learned long before that she wasn't really like either of us in looks or manner, as she had her own particular style. Others saw similarities, but to me she was just Joanne. Unique; and along with Tom and Winston, my best friend.

'Just be careful,' I added automatically.

She knew I'd say it and would have expected my reaction to Freddie's advances. I was always a "hands on" father and took no nonsense from anyone. It could be a trial to them on occasion.

One similarity Joanne shared with Gemma was her coolness and unflustered manner in dealing with life. I adored her for that and would often ask her advice on matters, knowing I'd get a sensible and thoughtful response. She'd had to step forward at an early age, and I just hoped that it hadn't marked her too deeply.

'No one will come near me now that they know you're around! Do you know how famous you are?' she asked over her fork.

'What? Rubbish!' I replied dismissively.

'Daddy! You're *Jamie Melville*! Surely you know people talk about you?'

'One of the great mysteries of my life is why that name seems to provoke a response! I've no idea why, I'm just an ordinary bloke. Really, Joanne, don't tell me you buy into that nonsense!'

She beamed. 'That's why I love you so much! And Mummy did, too. You're the sweetest man alive!'

She then stopped and looked at me. 'Dad?'

The way she spoke gave me pause. It reminded me of when she was young and asking me endless questions about everything. They were serious concerns to her, so she always addressed me as 'Dad', deeming that more appropriate and grown up in order to capture my attention.

'When are you going to find a lady friend?'

'What?' I wasn't expecting that.

'Daddy, you're still young and still very good-looking! You've got all … *most* of your hair and you're lovely and slim. I heard chat Mr Churchill's secretaries are after you!'

It was my turn to be embarrassed. I must have blushed and looked down, but her hand came out and she put it under my chin.

'Really, Daddy, I don't want you to be alone any more. Mummy wouldn't either.'

It's quite something when you don't know what to say to your own daughter, but I admit to being stuck for words. I've always believed that if others are thinking what you're thinking then you can't always be wrong. Maybe I wanted her blessing. Her approval. But the impenetrable barrier of Gemma was still between us and though the possibility of new love felt exciting, it remained an uncomfortable subject to me.

'Thanks, darling, I needed that. I suppose it'll take time. I can't wear the hair-shirt forever, even though I don't feel it's like that. I only had one girl in my life and she was irreplaceable.'

'Yes, but you have to carry on, too. You deserve happiness. It's not a crime. The crime is to be lonely when you don't have to be. And that eats up so much of life.'

I took her hand. 'Sweetie-heart, I'm going away for a while. I can't tell you where but I have to go. I *need* to go. It's very important; that's all I can say. But I'll think about what you've said.'

We finished lunch and I saw her back to the office. Freddie had left for the day.

Chapter Nine

THE EVENING BEFORE I joined up with Winston on the special train that would take us north to Stranraer, where we would begin our flight, I was visited by my new chum from the Secret Service. I'd forgotten all about him and when the door went at North Street that evening, I didn't recognise him at first.

'Mr Melville? How are you?'

I stood and gawped, momentarily at a loss, then recognised him and showed him into the sitting room. I noted there was no motorcar or taxi waiting. He was alone.

I invited him to sit down. 'No. No, thank you,' he replied, all business. 'I won't be long. I understand you've a long day ahead and it's vital you get an early night!' He remained standing as I took a chair. I had a whisky balanced on the wooden arm. He declined my offer of one.

'Jamie, may I be candid?' I nodded. 'The reason you're accompanying the Prime Minister is not just a whim on Mr Churchill's part. My service believes that whilst in America there may be threats on his life.'

'I would have thought that was the case anywhere he went.'

'True, but we feel your presence at his side will alleviate those concerns somewhat.'

'What about Inspector Thompson? I can't see him appreciating me getting in the way of his doing his job.'

'Mr Thompson is an excellent officer and we have every confidence in him. But you are known of as more than just Mr Churchill's *shadow*. The facts of life are that anyone can be killed regardless of whatever measures are taken. We at the Service believe that as the Prime Minister is only taking the minimum of staff with him, we would feel more comfortable if there was someone close whose loyalty and devotion are beyond question.'

I didn't think much of this. In fact, I thought it was tosh. There had to be something more but in retrospect, it was difficult to argue with his logic. Winston was a man apart. Later on in the war, Walter Thompson would have a nervous breakdown and leave the Prime Minister's service for a period. Officially it was due to the fact he had suffered personal loss but it was undeniable that Winston's antics drove him to the edge on a number of occasions. This of course I didn't yet know, but looking back now, I see the sense in what the man was saying. I was the one person who would have done anything for Winston, and I also had my well-known way of handling him.

'Look, Claude or whatever your name is. Frank Sawyers can do as good a job as me of watching the Old Man. And I'd bet everything I have that he would step in front of a bullet for him. Winston's like that. You can't help caring for him.'

'Sawyers is his valet. And a *homosexual*.' He spoke the word as if describing a particularly loathsome disease.

I didn't like his tone. 'And my dad was a fitter from the Southside!' I retorted angrily. 'Take your worthless opinions and shove them, pal! Frank Sawyers is worth two of you any day!'

His eyes were as lifeless as a shark's as he gathered himself. He replied quietly but with no trace of remorse. 'I do apologise, Jamie. That was unfair, of course.'

'Alright,' I countered, somewhat wearily. 'Alright, it seems I'm hot property. I often wonder, as I'm so important, why the war was two years old before I received the call. You want me to watch Winston. I do that anyway. It's my job. Though I still don't know what my official role is. Court jester, I think.' I took a drink from my glass.

What passed for a smile appeared around his slit-like

mouth. He then reached inside his coat and drew out a pistol. It was a British officer's Webley Mark IV revolver. Very black, and very nasty.

He handed it over with a small box of ammunition. 'I believe you have proficiency in firearms. Please take this with you. It's a very fine pistol and I always believe that carrying a weapon automatically dispels the requirement of ever having to use it.'

'A good luck charm?' I sneered ironically.

'Yes, something like that.' The excuse for a smile re-appeared momentarily. 'I'll be off now, but please be careful and do keep your eyes and ears open. I know that's probably useless advice as you'll do that as a matter of course. Enjoy your trip. Washington is a remarkable city I'm told and of course, there are relatively few restrictions there.'

'Want me to bring you back a bottle of Bourbon?'

The death's head grin flashed again and I rose to show him to the door. When he left I poured myself another drink while weighing the pistol in my other hand.

The fellow gave me the shudders.

The Prime Minister's train departed from Euston just after 12pm the following day. The entire party travelling to America was aboard, but General Brooke and Winston went off alone to finalise their plans and I shared a car with the delightful Pug Ismay and Doctor Wilson, the Prime Minister's personal physician. By late afternoon Brookie and Winston returned and we then had dinner. It was a pleasant repast, Winston in fine form as he related tales about his journeys to the United States when he was young. By around ten o'clock that evening we pulled into Stranraer.

We were to board a seaplane for the journey, and as we hung about the jetty awaiting transportation, Winston broke into song and I joined in as 'Why are we waiting?' rang out – to the amusement of some, and embarrassment of the other humourless sods in our group. Then a motor launch finally arrived and we were taken to the aircraft. Luckily the distance between the jetty and the plane was not great and I was able to keep hold of the contents of my stomach.

Unfortunately, the odious Commander Thompson was travelling with us. By now he and I were mortal enemies. A career naval officer, he'd been beached after running his submarine aground in the early thirties. By brown-nosing (his only talent) he eventually came to the attention of senior naval staff as flag Lieutenant to an Admiral, and then found his way into Winston's entourage.

Clementine called him 'Goosey-Goosey' because like the baby goslings at Chartwell, wherever their leader went, there followed Tommy. He was universally detested, for among other things he always ensured he got the best accommodation on trips and never bothered to oversee others' requirements. This caused many a row though this was his job, the lazy, useless bastard.

Winston seemed to think him indispensable and saw no reason to sack him, though the complaints about him were legion. Knowing my man, the simian-faced Tommy was nothing but a go-fer to my old colonel. It undoubtedly amused him to see someone grovel in his presence, whilst the rest of us were sickened by his behaviour. I was determined that I wasn't going to bunk up anywhere near him on the flight and the feeling was undoubtedly mutual.

But there was also some good company to look forward to. General Ismay was the Prime Minister's Chief of Staff and had legendary charm and diplomatic skills that were vital in keeping a lid on the large egos amongst the general staff. He was remarkably good-natured, very informal and was nicknamed 'Pug' for his cheerful likeness to that breed of canine.

Dr Wilson appeared lofty and distant but by the journey's end I was fascinated to listen to him discourse on a number of subjects, which he described in a most interesting fashion. But he seemed to have an opinion on everything and regard for no one. I would find this a touch wearing after a while. God knows what he thought of me.

Winston brought with him two secretaries, John Martin and Patrick Kinna, to handle the administrative tasks. And there was Frank Sawyers, Winston's 'Man Friday', one of the funniest men I've ever known.

Along with Walter Thompson that was the happy crew that boarded the *Bristol*, the remarkable Boeing Clipper seaplane that was to fly us to America. It was the first aircraft designed to cross oceans and was the height of luxury for its day. There were staterooms that could bunk up to six people, a kitchen, toilet, a lounge and a bridal suite. The food was sumptuous and a rare treat during wartime.

I bunked with Pug and Brookie. I believe the latter had a quiet word and ensured Tommy slept on his own as the General despised him. Walter and Dr Wilson were quartered near Winston who was alone in the bridal suite.

There was an amusing moment as I was heading through the gangway for the loo and Tommy was walking towards me. I must have bumped into him 'accidentally' when the plane hit an air pocket, and I heard him snarl 'guttersnipe!' under his breath. I let him walk on then turned and shoved him in the back a little too hard and he lurched forward through the doorway, losing his footing and falling flat on his ape-like mug. Behind me I heard Brookie chuckle, 'not found your sea legs, yet, Thompson?' and felt a pat on my shoulder.

We dined that evening on the most dreamed-about food and drink. A shrimp cocktail followed by filet mignon with fresh potatoes and vegetables. The dessert, a most delicious baked Alaska. Winston, knowing my love of sweets, demanded I be served a second helping, and everyone was greatly amused as they watched me eyeing the waiter greedily as he brought it through. There was champagne and every type of liqueur imaginable, and at the meal's end there was a very happy and contented group of travellers.

Winston and Dr Wilson stayed up, but the others went off to their kip after night caps. I admit I was still in a state of excitement over the events of the day. It was my first flight and it was exhilarating to look out the window, though by now it was pitch black. Winston sat by me as we gazed at the stars, my former fears now forgotten.

'Well, Jamie my boy, we have come a long way since you shamed yourself on parade before your colonel all those years ago!'

I was also fairly tanked up with Drambuie, and many memories were recalled that remarkable evening.

'Why, Charles, do you know what this laddie did?' Winston said, turning to Dr Wilson. 'A boy of fifteen! Left his family to serve his country and sent home all his pay to his poor mother! And when he received a terrible letter informing him, wrongly I may add, that she had died he took off alone in an attempt to get home to his poor little sisters in order to care for them.'

I wasn't the only one feeling the glow of alcohol. But in all the years of knowing Winston, I was never completely sure if he ever was *drunk*. At least, not how I would rationalise inebriation based on painful memories of my own father. Drink revealed his unhappiness and the duality of his nature. Away from alcohol, Dad was a cheery, kind-natured soul. Though as I got older I suspected that he was a more complex individual than I had previously thought. He was someone who felt trapped within his predicament. He was fairly clever but intellectually slothful, thus frustrated with his place in life.

I knew nothing of his early background except his own father deserted him when he was a child and was last heard of living in the English midland town of Rugby, where he remarried. Dad's own mother died young of drink. Alcoholism is in the blood they say, though I for one have never believed that is an excuse. In my own opinion it's an old wives' tale.

My father was brought up by his grandmother in Forbes Street, in the less-than-affluent Southside area of Edinburgh. His father turned up at my parents' wedding out of the blue and offered Dad some money. My father told him to piss off and that was the last he ever saw him.

Unlike in my father's case, where it led to bitterness and violence, I always believed drink lubricated Winston, like engine oil; it never *drove* him. His intellect, his incredible spark carried him. Drink eased him and provided a happy travelling companion. When he was in his *dog*, I noted that he never drank.

'Yes, Winston,' replied Dr Wilson after further anecdotes were related of our early relationship. 'A remarkable story of devotion.'

'What I cannot understand is why the boys today are not like him! They cannot fight!' Winston angrily slammed his glass down on the small deal table. 'Why is that? Are they molly-coddled, cossetted and idle? And as for their officers! Huh! My lads at the 6th could beat the Huns without breaking sweat! The finest! To a man! Hakewill-Smith! McDavid! Sinclair!'

'And Sergeant Douglas,' I added, as a melancholy mood came over me. I had been cushioned by the warmth of the drink in my veins but now saw faces of friends long gone.

'Davie, Jock. Tommy Reid. And poor Duncan!' I rattled out their names.

Winston had stopped his reverie and looked at me, now concerned.

'Yes. Yes, son. Our friends, gone. And why? When only a few years later we are at it all over again?'

I took a deep drink of Scotch. Winston then reached over and removed the glass from my hand.

'There has to be change when this one's over,' I said. 'I don't want these boys today coming home to the poor-house.'

Our old comrade Sergeant Boab Douglas, amongst countless others, had fallen on hard times at the end of the war.

He'd been gassed and had a leg near shot away at Arras and ended up in penury in civilian life. But someone had written on his behalf to Winston and he'd arranged for Boab to be admitted to an old soldier's home in Lanark. He'd been fortunate.

'Listen, Winston,' I said forcefully, 'it can never happen again. All those men! You've got to ensure that it doesn't, because if you don't someone else will.'

'Jamie, what do you mean?' asked Dr Wilson.

'I mean that "touching the forelock" has ended. This generation are past that. They've been bombed, brutalised, killed and maimed and they're not going back to selling matches on street-corners, that's what I'm saying! So get ready for it. *My* girls aren't going to be treated like serfs any longer, either!'

'James! You're not a *socialist*?' Winston gasped in horror.

'Colonel, you're not a Tory but the days of upper class toffs calling themselves liberals are over. I'm offering you a warning, that's all.'

'My boy, I had no idea of your anger! But if what you say is true, then so be it. If the people decide they want change, they must have it. And why not? For as you say they are the ones who suffer for the mistakes of their so-called betters.'

'You're not wrong there,' I replied bitterly.

Doctor Wilson stepped out at this point, and we were alone.

'Colonel, I'm so sorry. I wasn't getting at you. But I saw their faces!' The dying glow of the alcohol had disappeared completely. All that was left now was clamminess and I felt myself shiver uncontrollably. I placed my hands around my stomach in an effort to control the spasms.

Winston sat down next to me on the couch.

'Visions?' he asked.

I nodded. He knew them very well himself. I'd learned that long ago one strange night in a British army headquarters in northern France.

He held my hand as I shook uncontrollably. That *smell* had appeared to me. Maybe it was the aircraft. The blowers from the air-conditioning, engine oil mingling with the atmosphere inside. But I was kidding myself. It was that stench that soldiers know and never leaves them. Death and decay, body parts, shit and filth.

'Oh, Colonel!' I was shaking all over as he now hugged me against him.

'Go away! Let him be!' Winston snapped furiously, to no one.

Doctor Wilson then returned and administered to me. He took my pulse and loosened my collar as Winston removed my jacket and tie.

'Palpitations. An *extremis*, no doubt brought on by war neurosis,' diagnosed Dr Wilson. 'Jamie, I don't want you to drink anymore. Just rest,' he ordered.

He stayed with us a while then left. My attack wore off slowly and I was left with that strange almost euphoric, late night feverishness, not entirely unpleasant.

Winston rubbed my hand, uttering kind, soothing words, like anyone's father would. Like I did when my own girls were ill.

'I'm better now, Winston. I feel a wee bit stupid!' I declared, somewhat embarrassed at my behaviour.

'Nonsense, my boy. Those feelings are with all of us. They are the price that warriors must pay from time to time. We can never tell when they will strike but there is no shame, *no* shame.'

I reached over for the bottle but put it back again. 'I drink more these days. Since I came to London.'

'James, you were never a drinker.'

'Colonel,' I confessed, 'I nicked a bottle of brandy from you once and gave it to Boab Douglas.'

'Did you?'

'Do you want to know why?'

'Tell me.'

'Because I thought you were a drunk. I was worried about you. I'd never seen anyone drink as much as you except my dad and was frightened that you'd end up like him. I thought you were wonderful. I was fearful that you'd fall down like him and bang your head and not get up again.'

Tears were streaming down his eyes. 'You ... were as dear as a son to me.'

I in turn squeezed his hand tenderly. 'I know. Dad was such a nice person but drink killed him. It wasn't his fault. But if he hadn't died I'd never have known you. That's what I have to live with.'

Though he would have been unlikely ever to have acknowledged it, I'd never been able to express my gratitude to Winston personally for all that he had done for me. I now wanted him to try to understand, with as much dignity and compassion as I could summon while struggling with illness and alcohol, that we both bore an equal share of the burden of guilt over the direction of my life. But now, though I wanted desperately to tell him he need no longer blame himself over an unfortunate and crippled child, I still could not find words adequate enough to express my feelings.

He composed himself. 'James, I insist that you enjoy yourself in Washington. I want you to see the capital and unwind. I know you were visited last night by someone. He is an *evil* man. But in war such men are required. I have known him forty years and he is rotten to the core. But he has his uses.'

This last enigmatic statement left resonance as I tried to relax back in my chair. I now felt afraid. Afraid for myself, afraid for Winston. Afraid for my darling girls. Something was going on. That nagging thought stuck to me as I was led off to my bunk. It stayed with me until I finally dropped off to sleep, very late and very far from home.

After a thirty-hour flight the plane splashed down on the Potomac river. I'd arrived in North America. We were met at Anacostia Naval Airbase and whisked off in great black motorcars to Massachusetts Avenue in the city, where we were to stay the night at the British embassy.

Lord Halifax, the British Ambassador welcomed us on arrival and we were ushered into the building. General Brooke was invited by Sir John Dill, his predecessor and now senior British Liaison Officer in Washington to stay at his home, and a couple of the others were driven away to their designated hotels.

Winston wanted me to remain with him that night as a lavish banquet was planned at the embassy. There was a moment of panic when I told him I hadn't brought proper evening wear but he waived my concerns away by telling me he would lend me one of his bow ties. If anyone said anything I was given permission to use Gorgie invective in response.

General Brooke had to rush back from his new lodgings and just made it in time. Dine magnificently we did, but I was completely exhausted by the end of the evening; after all, it was my first experience of jet lag. When alone on the plane, Winston and Dr Wilson had discussed this new phenomenon and provided me with fatherly advice in how to deal with it. I was to obey my natural body clock; that is, eat when I felt hungry and sleep when I was ready to.

Winston was off on one of his late night (or morning to us) sessions but on seeing me drooping, in an unprecedented moment in public, he ordered me to my bed. Halifax and Pug laughed to each other but I was more than happy to obey my Master's voice.

I was led to my room by Sawyers, who was ready to drop himself. Though it was a sticky Washington evening, I bedded down and went out like a light almost immediately – on this, my first night in the 'New World.'

Chapter Ten

THE FOLLOWING MORNING after a meeting with General Marshall, Winston was flown to Hyde Park, the President's country retreat for a private consultation with FDR before the main sessions began officially at the White House. Both Thompsons and one of the secretaries accompanied him. Before leaving, Winston visited me in my room for a few moments and informed me that I had his permission to take a couple of days off to acclimatise and take in the sights. He reminded me again that I was to worry about nothing and enjoy myself, and added rather excitingly that the President wanted to meet me.

Just after he'd left the room there was a knock on the door and Sawyers entered carrying a tray.

'There ye gaan, Mista' Melville! Jes' tak' a look at yon breakfast!' he announced.

'Bloody hell!' My response was entirely appropriate for a wartime British traveller to the United States. The tray held by Sawyers was piled up with kippers, bacon, eggs, hash browns, tomatoes and mushrooms. There was toast and croissant and a small bowl of jam. Yes, jam! There was another larger bowl of what looked like *real* porridge and one of cereal with cream. A jug of fresh orange completed the spread.

'It's coffee ye like?'

I was still lost in the wondrous vision before me. 'What did you say?'

'Coffee, Jamie!'

'Oh aye, Frank. Sorry. Yes, coffee!'

'And sugar?'

I couldn't take any more. 'Christ, Frankie boy, we're in heaven!'

Having eaten, enjoyed the sensuous thrill of a hot shower and shaved, I was left pondering on what was to happen next. Hanging around the lobby of the embassy gassing with some officials, I heard a female American voice call out:

'Mr James Melville?'

I turned and before me stood what would be described in Scotland as a *smashin' wee doll*. In her late twenties, she must have stood around five-foot-two and wore a short-sleeved red dress with white trim, and a black belt tightened round her waist which provided a perfect hourglass figure. The pleats of the skirts hung with a swish just below her knees, my eyes catching the rest of those legs down to the patent red-heeled shoes. Her hair was a work of art, all curls and pins, those not tied in place dropping just above her shoulders, complimented by neat but tiny pearl drop earrings. Around her very white throat was a tasteful string of more jewels from the sea.

She had China-blue eyes, made maddeningly alluring by the combination of her flaming hair and redhead complexion, and a little button of a nose which was irresistibly spotted with freckles above very kissable blood-red lips. She even had me beat for long eyelashes, which I was certain were her own. Overall, the outside was near as damnit to perfection as far as Jamie Melville was concerned. Her only blemish being the well-known overlarge mouth Yankee woman are prone to.

'Yes, I'm Jamie,' I replied, hoping she hadn't thought I was staring.

'Oh, yes! *Jamie*! So cute and *so* Scottish!' She pronounced it 'Scarrish' but I forgave her. She held out her hand. 'I'm Meredith Macaulay.'

I caught the scent of something expensive and extremely attractive. 'Hello, Meredith!' I took her fingers and squeezed slightly, ensuring I let them go immediately.

'I'm from the State Department. I'm to show you to your hotel and liaise with you whilst you're in Washington.'

'Oh ... yes. I was wondering what was going to happen to me!'

She laughed. 'We haven't forgotten you! Our cab is outside. Are you packed?' I nodded. 'Then if you're ready?'

We got into the taxi and made our way across town to Pennsylvania Avenue. When I saw the street sign, I asked: 'Is this where the White House is?'

'Yes, the hotel's not far from there. You can stroll, real easy!'

I saw to my left the famous equestrian statue of Andrew Jackson tipping his hat as we came to Lafayette Square, and in between the trees I caught sight of the north façade of the building we burnt to a crisp in 1814. The taxi took a left into Madison Place and after another turn we pulled up to our stop.

The trees surrounding the entrance were beautiful as their blossoms sparkled in the morning sunlight. Grabbing my bag and stick, we entered the Hay-Adams Hotel.

'We'll just check in and then decide what to do next, okay?' Meredith announced as I nodded my assent, and then flashed the identification card issued to me at the embassy at the desk.

'I'll catch the elevator,' Meredith said and took off as I signed the register. For the life of me I didn't know what she was talking about. After completing registration and being handed my key I looked around and to my consternation, couldn't find her anywhere.

Like an idiot, I wandered around the lobby area for a while until I felt my sleeve being tugged.

'What kept you? I thought you decided to walk!'

I couldn't help laughing. 'I've now just worked out what an "elevator" is! We call it the lift!'

She looked at me blankly and for a moment I believed she hadn't understood a word I'd said.

'Well, come on then!' she ordered briskly. 'We'll catch the next one.'

She led me over to the lift and we got in and headed for one of the top floors where, looking at my key number, we found the door to my room. We entered and I was just able to prevent myself from gasping aloud at the size and luxury of the interior; but then I spotted the view from the window. The home of the President, with the top of the needle-shaped Washington Monument behind it, greeted me as I drew breath.

'Looks good, huh?' said Meredith, noting my pleasure at the scene.

'Aye! Not bad! Almost as good a sight as Edinburgh Castle!'

She smiled, showing brilliant white teeth. 'How I'd love to go to England! It must be so beautiful there.'

'England's not bad, but Scotland's the best, believe me!' From her expression my attempt to carry the conversation evidently fell flat.

There was an awkward pause. I tried not to pay much attention to the bed, but lifted my case and rested it on top of a chair.

'Do you want to leave your bag and go for a stroll?' she asked.

I couldn't think of anything better and grabbed my stick as we headed back down to the ground floor. Leaving the building, we turned back towards Lafayette Square.

'First time in the States, right?' she asked as we sauntered along.

'First time anywhere! Except France and Belgium.'

'Yes, you were in the war? I've been told something about that.'

'The *last* war. I was just a wee lad. It was all very exciting at first. I met Winston and had a rare old time.'

'But then you got hurt, right?'

'Yes. But it probably saved my life. Most of my pals died and others were left crippled. Like me.'

'You're not crippled.' It was the first crack in formality. I did note it but my mind also raced back to when Gemma told me the same thing all those years ago, in bed with her in her grandmother's home. It woke me from the little fantasy I'd momentarily played out over the short interlude but somehow now, there was a hopeful rather than empty and desolate feeling within me. It may have been the hot Washington sun; but it was more likely to be the hot little number walking beside me.

'Thanks. Oh, and that's a lovely name, Meredith. Unusual, but it suits you, really.'

She grinned very widely as she lifted her head; I noted her delightful freckles and thought *slow down, Jamie. Leave the locals be.*

'You British! It's true what they say! An *absolute* gentleman! You could sure show American fellas a thing or two when it comes to charming a girl!'

We both laughed. We walked on quietly and then she slowed. 'Oh, Jamie, I forgot your injury. Do you want to stop some place and have a drink?'

'Thanks, I'm alright but I would love a drink of something nice if you have anywhere in mind.' I was feeling the June heat but my leg was fine.

'It's just here.' It was a pavement-type café and we ordered coffee, as I'd adored what I had been offered at the embassy and wanted to make the most of all such opportunities.

'Meredith, do you mind if I have a smoke?' I asked as we settled down at a table.

'Of course not. Go ahead.'

I lit a Tom Thumb and caught a glimpse of her side profile as she closed her eyes against the glare.

'D.C.! Phew! I'm from New York but god, it sure stinks here in summer-time!'

I knew of the city's infamous sewerage problems, which were exacerbated by the humidity and the large number of outdoor privies that still prevailed throughout the capital.

She then told me she had lived in Washington previously in the 1930s, as her husband served in the Navy and been based there. It was now overcrowded to such an extent that even some ground around the Mall and the Reflecting Pool was being taken up with temporary accommodation to house the influx of war-workers. Clearly, it wasn't her favourite place to be. This resonated with me and I tried not to catch her eye too closely.

Instead I puffed away, ensuring none of the smoke blew in her direction.

'Have you any children?' I asked.

'No. You have, though?'

She seemed to know a lot but I wasn't too concerned. If she worked in the State Department she would have been party to information.

'Three girls.'

'And your wife died. I'm so sorry.'

I wasn't sure if this was part of the act. Her entire manner seemed to subtly alter. The sassiness was gone. She breathed out noticeably, which I thought odd. I realised then she wasn't a very good actress.

'Thanks,' I replied.

There was quiet as I smoked and watched the people and city go by. She opened her bag and took out a pair of dark sunglasses and a packet of cigarettes. I noted that her hands shook, but she managed to get the lighter to work first time.

'Are you alright, dear?' I asked softly, leaning over to her.

'Sure. Thanks, Jamie. I guess I'm maybe not what you think I am.'

'What is it that you believe I think you are?'

'Oh, someone always in control. Always one step ahead.'

'I've only just met you. You're doing fine, believe me. I'm having a good time. Please don't worry. If it makes you more comfortable we can leave it here. I can walk back myself.'

A slight smile re-appeared. 'That's ... really sweet. No, it's alright. I apologise.'

I was at a loss and starting to feel a little uncomfortable. There was a growing suspicion that she was here to do a job on me for some reason. Maybe the Yanks wanted a hotline to what Winston was thinking. Who knows? Only, they'd sent the wrong girl. She was no whore, I was pretty sure of that. And if she was, she wasn't very convincing.

Then again, maybe I was just imagining things.

'Meredith, I really don't know what to say except you've been lovely. Please believe me. I'm only here for a few days and you've been very nice. Let's have a good time together. Just be my wee pal, eh?'

She drew deeply on her cigarette.

'So,' she gathered herself. 'Where would you like to visit?'

I was an American Civil War aficionado and told her I'd like to see Arlington, and Robert E. Lee's home.

She seemed to perk up. 'I'd love to do that, too.'

Taking a beautiful girl to a graveyard may not be your usual idea of a first date, but she hadn't been before and I was pretty certain she enjoyed herself. Riding in the taxi across town I was able to view sights along Constitution Avenue such as the Federal Reserve Building, the Gardens and the famous Reflecting Pool, then on past the Lincoln Memorial as we drove over the Arlington Memorial Bridge.

We spent a couple of hours there and I tried not to stop at too many of the graves to read the inscriptions. We then had a look over Robert E. Lee's old spread. I discussed the visit later with General Brooke, who had also availed himself of the opportunity to visit the old Confederate hero's abode whilst in the Capitol.

We left early afternoon and she dropped me off at the hotel, as she headed back to her own office at the State Department, in Foggy Bottom.

I returned to my room to change my shirt before dining. I'd brought a fair sum of cash with me in order to purchase as many necessities from the 'home of the brave' as I could.

On the following day, which was a Saturday, I planned to do some shopping and buy clothing for myself, the girls and my nephews. The coupon rationing back home meant you had to make do with what you had till it dropped off you. I also planned to stock up with as much chocolate and sweeties as possible.

I then went out for another stroll, as I was captivated by my new surroundings. The warm breezes and scents from the tree-lined terraces and boulevards were as far away from drab and battered Britain as one could be. There were Quonset huts, posters advertising war bonds and other sights similar to those in England, but these to me were the only visible signs of there being a war on. Night lighting had been dulled to save on electricity, and I would read in the local newspaper of complaints about shortages and rationing which included alcohol. But compared to old Blighty it was a land of plenty.

As I walked, my mind was in a swirl – and not just over the sight of well-stocked shops. Meredith had surprised me somewhat, but I rationalised with myself that she was just a guide whilst in a foreign land and nothing more. My thoughts began to return to more serious matters, in particular that piece of cold steel hidden deep in my suitcase. What on earth had that meeting the night before I left been all about? And what was Winston trying to tell me on the seaplane?

And why was I here anyway? I wasn't Harry Hopkins. He was a low-paid skivvy who bunked up at the White House, had no official position but was to all intents and purposes the President of the United States' Lord High Chamberlain. He had as many enemies as admirers, as he was seen as an interloper with no legal right to be where he was. Did people see me as someone like that?

For a time there were scurrilous rumours doing the rounds in London that Brendan Bracken was Winston's illegitimate son. It was nonsense of course, but Brendan had done nothing to dispel such ridiculous gossip. It had earned him the enmity of Clementine, who'd banned him from the house for a period. As far as I knew, no similar tales existed concerning me – but then, my story was well known, whereas Brendan was generally considered to be a fantasist and a pathological liar.

I was starting to think that after two months back in London, unless a firm, definable role was found for me I should seriously consider packing up and heading home. I didn't want to be seen as some hanger-on, or as Randolph called me, an *éminence grise*.

But in truth I had enjoyed most of the last few weeks. Mixing with people again had revitalised my former confidence, and I was enough of a realist to know you must take the rough with the smooth. If the odd remark from Tommy and sneer from a secretary got me down, there was still enough of the old Jamie Melville around that I could deal with any of it.

After all, I was now swanning round the streets of the capital of the United States. I was being put up in one of the city's top hotels at government expense, and had been told the President himself expressed a desire to meet me.

Scarborough had its charms, but nothing like this.

Next morning I was breakfasting and looking over the *Washington Post* when I caught sight of a figure heading towards my table.

'Did you sleep well?'

It was Meredith. Yesterday she had been smartly dressed and business-like. Today she wore a plain dress and her hair was loose and hanging down in beautiful red curls. If anything, she looked even better.

'I'm not used to the heat, yet! I left for a jaunt and came back and sat and had a drink till late.'

'On your own, I hope!' she teased.

'Of course! There's only one lassie in town for me!'

'I hope so!' she smiled, happily. 'Anyway, as for today, I wondered if you'd like to visit Georgetown? It's not far.'

I put down the paper. 'I wanted to do a bit of shopping. I need to buy some things to take back home.'

'Oh, that's my speciality! I could help you there!'

I tried to keep the grin on my face under control. 'Thanks! I hate shopping usually, Gemma...' I stopped, feeling awkward.

She looked at me. 'That's okay, please don't feel you have to say sorry.'

'Can we start again?' I asked.

She smiled, looking directly into my eyes. 'I'd love to take you shopping.'

After returning later from Georgetown and its famous Wisconsin Avenue, where we, or rather Meredith, picked out suitable attire for myself and the girls, I invited her out for dinner. She took me to a small and intimate restaurant she knew in the Penn Quarter. I'd noticed she was a big eater earlier, when she had guzzled a huge hotdog in Georgetown whilst I barely had a bite of mine. She had then disappeared and returned moments later with another!

If that was a surprise, what she ordered now and how she demolished it provided me with an unexpected insight into young American womanhood.

A starter of clam chowder was followed by the biggest piece of T-bone steak I'd ever seen. Not only that but piled on her plate was mashed *and* roast potatoes, parsnips, carrots, chick-peas and gravy. The "plate" I might add would have been called a serving platter back home. All this was polished off using only a fork, and then for dessert she ordered a huge piece of a type of cake I'd never seen before. It had what looked like an oaten base with a huge triangular slab of what resembled frozen ice cream on top. She called this a "cheesecake."

Then to round the meal off, real cheese and biscuits arrived served on an actual platter which was nearly the size of the penalty area at Tynecastle Park. She helped herself to a large chunk of Brie and carved huge portions over tiny Ritz crackers and popped them lovingly into her mouth.

I observed this exhibition trying desperately not to break out into laughter on several occasions. At one point I had to leave the table for the loo in order to control my mirth. She was some girl.

She *was* some girl, but in her culinary habits as I'm sure you are aware, not unusual. Americans eat like starving rhinos, especially the women, and it is one of life's great mysteries how so many of the truly beautiful ones like Meredith remain that way.

'You know, in America, "Jamie" is a girl's name,' she said after the meal over drinks.

'So I hear! But then again there are quite a few differences between us. Bourbon and whisky…'

'Tomatoes and…'

'Yes, yes, I've heard it!' We both laughed.

She then stopped and dipped into her bag for a cigarette. The carefreeness had been much in evidence but it was as if now she had to compose herself suddenly – as if she was at work, laughing with her colleagues and all of a sudden the boss had appeared. Unconsciously, I found myself looking around the restaurant for an interloper. Of course there was no one.

'Are you alright?' I asked.

She lit up and blew out smoke. 'I'm not used to that.'

'Used to what?' I asked, mystified.

'Being asked if I'm alright.'

'It's the normal thing to do.'

'Where you come from.'

She knew how to pour over cold water. It was disconcerting. The day before it had been interesting, but now I decided to prod her a little. My thoughts the night before, which I'd happily put aside as I'd enjoyed the day so much, had returned to me.

'Meredith, I have to ask you. What's going on?'

Drawing on her cigarette, she looked away.

'I've been through a bad time. I'm trying to put it behind me but every so often something happens to remind me. You know what that's like? We talked about shopping today.'

'Yes. I know what you mean.'

'You're only here a few days. It's been nice. *You're* nice. No really, I mean that.'

I couldn't live my life as something I wasn't. Maybe she was what she said she was, but I hated the fact that I couldn't allow myself to just enjoy being with her. I fancied her. Of course I did. I was still a young man whose wife had been dead five years, and for the first time had allowed myself to *feel* again. But I wasn't going to use her.

Or let her use me.

'Look, Meredith, I don't really know what you've read or heard about me. I'm just an ordinary person. I've had a strange life admittedly but a wonderful one, at least up till a few years ago. I sense you're troubled by something. You're sweet and happy-go-lucky one moment and sad the next. I know how that feels. Trust me, I know. I don't have to know your secrets. Or you, mine, though I don't really have any. But whatever it is it'll pass, believe me. It always does.'

She sat quietly. Her cigarette burned itself out; she noticed and stubbed into the ashtray.

'Can you excuse me for a moment?'

I rose as she left the table, then sat down and lit a Tom Thumb. I puffed away looking round the restaurant. She then returned and sat down.

'Everything alright? Do you just want to go home?' I asked.

'I'm alright. I'm enjoying myself, really.'

We had one more drink, but the chat was a little fraught and I thought it best to call it a night. We caught a taxi and dropped her off. She lived in a house on the corner of 34th and 35th Street which she shared with two girls from her office. There was an acute housing shortage in the capital, with an influx of workers due to the expansion of government departments and she was lucky to find it, she told me. She'd already told me the same thing earlier.

The cab then took me back to my hotel. Winston would be back tomorrow and I had a date with a President. Most of that night was spent restlessly thinking about Meredith. And finally when I dropped off, I dreamt of Gemma.

Chapter Eleven

ON THAT SUNDAY in June 1942, the entire course of the war would be changed. The British and American chiefs of staff had come to a tacit agreement between themselves that there would not be a cross-channel invasion that year. But on returning from their private talks together, the President and the Prime Minister were about to throw a grenade amongst them.

I wasn't present at those meetings, now known to history as the Second Washington Conference, of course. Instead I was shown around the White House and its grounds, and introduced to a number of staff officers.

I got into a discussion with a newly promoted Brigadier General named Dwight Eisenhower. He appeared to know a lot about me. He said we had something in common in that we had both suffered injuries that had affected our future participation in our relevant codes of football. He told me that a knee injury had meant he had to take up coaching rather than playing, and had at one point been offered a highly-paid job managing a top American football side. It would have meant leaving the army and though tempted, he declined the offer.

On returning to the White House from Hyde Park, FDR and Winston announced that there would be an invasion of North Africa that year. Brookie and General Marshall nearly fainted, there was a near run on the pound from what I heard later and feathers certainly flew. It was completely unexpected and the strong suspicion was that the Prime Minister had got to the President.

But there was also a political point to be made. Roosevelt

knew that he couldn't have hundreds of thousands of US soldiers based in Britain solely to chase local girls. A commitment had to be made to placate the hard-pressed Soviets. He was wise enough to accept what his military chiefs had failed to; that invading France in 1942 was a non-starter. He was well ahead of his own so-called experts on that score even without the influence of Winston. North Africa looked like the best option, though admittedly a hazardous one. FDR openly liked to admit that he was no military strategist. American knives were out for Winston as they felt the British had double-crossed them.

There was a more cynical view, expressed quietly, that as there were mid-term elections being held that year, the President had to be seen committing to action somewhere. The only realistic place for that was in the North African littoral.

It's difficult to believe now, after all we have learned about the Nazis and what they were doing to Europe, that there was a large block in the American military (and in the country) who still believed dealing with Japan was top priority. After all, the Japanese had attacked America. But what these types conveniently forgot was that Germans were sinking US ships and killing American sailors in the Atlantic long before the Japs sent the coded message to 'Climb Mount Niikata.'

The leading proponent of the Japan First lobby in the military was the senior Admiral, Ernest King. This man was notorious for his anti-British attitude and gruff manner towards virtually anyone who didn't share his views. It always surprised me when these types appeared on the scene. Like Harry Hopkins said, they were usually of Anglo stock – but back then we were still the big power. Today, the Yanks are the hated ones and have swapped roles with us. Now they know how we used to feel.

But King was a force to be reckoned with. He continually attempted to undermine all strategies towards defeating Germany first, which was the main aim of the President. It was strongly suspected that he deliberately siphoned off vital war material such as landing craft and switched it to the war on Japan.

Thankfully the Americans had General George Catlett Marshall as their Chief of Staff. He was fully supportive of the Germany first strategy and focused all his attention towards defeating Hitler. But he had as many battles to fight against his own side and us as he did against the Germans.

When the meeting broke up that Sunday, I was led back into the White House and sat alone with Winston in his bedroom for a short while. He was bouncing like an overgrown baby and told me he had won a tremendous victory, and that FDR was one of the truly great men of history.

'Well, my boy. The time has come,' he then said enigmatically.

'What do you mean?' I asked.

'For the laddie from Gorgie Road to meet a President.'

I was caught off-guard and became terrified. I could only gabble, 'Colonel, do I look alright?'

He stood before me and straightened my tie.

'James Melville is now ready,' he announced.

Winston Churchill then led a highly agitated but excited Jamie Melville down the stairway, through the corridor to the Oval Study. (It's called the Oval Office these days.) It hadn't been used much by previous occupants of the famous abode, but was chosen by President Roosevelt as it provided quick and easy access for a wheelchair. Many former Presidents had used rooms on the upper floors only. Still very nervous, I looked it over quickly.

The walls were painted in a workmanlike battleship grey, complimented by woodwork of a dazzling glossy white and decorated by vast arrays of paintings of a naval subject, with models of ships scattered around on every available surface. Mahogany bookcases, filled to bursting, contained pictures of FDR's wife, mother, sons and grandchildren, propped up unsteadily against volumes stacked on their sides.

I believe the main desk in that office nowadays is the

famous one carved from the timbers of HMS *Resolute*. The one in use that day was a large, fairly austere but practical object that had been presented to one of his predecessors by a furniture manufacturer in the mid-west. I quickly glanced over the desk, fascinated to note the items laid on it.

A small bust of a woman, which I was told was Mrs Roosevelt, rested next to a little wooden donkey, denoting the Democratic Party. There were other little toy-like figures of animals, a blue-shaded lamp and assorted knick-knacks like a nail-file, paperweights and some postage stamps laid out on a page of plain paper. He was a keen philatelist.

'Well, here's the fella I want to meet!' the voice of the President boomed out. He wheeled himself round and moved towards me. 'Mr Melville! Take a seat and pull one over for your old colonel, here!'

It's forgotten now, but back then the fact that the President of the United States was wheelchair-bound was still an open secret. Many Americans had no idea that their senior executive was paralysed from the waist down through polio. I had been tipped off earlier of course.

He was very big. He had a large head and broad shoulders and there was a sparkle in his eyes, as I arranged the worn but comfortable green and brown leather chairs around so that we were all sitting together. It felt odd, moving around furniture in the President's home.

He then gripped my hand. His butler, Fields appeared with a tray of glasses with a decanter and an ice bucket and laid the tray down on a small table before leaving the room.

'I know that Mr Melville drinks it like a true Scotsman!' declared Mr Roosevelt as he took charge of the whisky. He virtually filled my glass, popping a few ice cubes in before doing the same for Winston.

'Sorry Prime Minister, but there's no soda so you're just going to have to drink it like me and my pal, here!'

There weren't many people in the world who could dominate a room whilst Winston Churchill was present, and for the first (and only) time, I'd met one. I was swept up in the President's charm and had completely forgotten Harry Hopkins and our previous conversation.

'Jamie? Do you mind if I call you that?'

'Of course not, sir.'

He leaned over and patted my knee.

'My name's Franklin. I'm your *Brother*. No formalities here. We're meeting on the *level*.'

He then asked me about my Lodge. The man had that wonderful natural ability to make people feel at ease and I proudly told him it had been the one my father was a member of. He was fascinated to hear that the Lodge was sited so near to the castle.

'As all of *us* know, Jamie, the true heart of Freemasonry lies in Scotland,' he confided. He was very intimate and matey. 'One of my life's dreams is to see a Third degree performed in an Ayrshire lodge like Tarbolton, and stand where Robert Burns stood and recited lectures and teachings of our Order. I'd dearly love to visit Roslyn Chapel, too. And to view the field of Bannockburn where the great Mason, King Robert Bruce won his glorious victory over tyranny.'

'We'd be honoured to have you visit our Temple!' I replied fervently, my nerves evidently not yet quite under control.

He smiled benevolently. 'Brother Melville, there are many fascinating things I want you tell you about the city of Washington. Things that will resonate with anyone in the Craft.'

'I look forward to that, sir.'

Winston had remained silent throughout our discussion. I had been wrapped up in every word the President uttered and for a moment I felt a pang of sympathy for my old colonel. But he was still on a high after what he considered his triumph of earlier and was doubtless lost in his own thoughts.

Mr Roosevelt then began a fascinating discussion on the origins of Freemasonry in the United States, which I was beginning to lap up when suddenly the door burst open and in strode Generals Marshall and Brooke along with Pug Ismay.

Marshall handed a piece of paper to the President. He read it and his eyes closed, then opened slowly.

He then handed the note to Winston.

'Oh, God. No! No!' he cried after looking at it.

'Colonel! What's happened?' His face had drained completely of colour and for a dreadful moment I believed he would pass out and fall from his chair. I prepared myself to leap over to catch him, as my mind went back to Plugstreet all those years ago when I had fainted and he had caught me bodily before I'd hit the floor.

'Prime Minister, we must issue a response,' began General Brooke tentatively.

'It cannot be possible!' Winston moaned as he slowly gathered himself together.

'Colonel, what's *happened*?' I pleaded.

'Mr Melville,' explained General Marshall solemnly, 'Tobruk has fallen.'

Tobruk, the great symbol of defiance in North Africa, where the Australians had held out against formidable odds a year before and then handed over to the South African brigade, had now surrendered to the Afrika Korps and General Rommel.

Great quantities of stores had been captured and thousands of our men marched into captivity. The blame game soon started, particularly why the decision had been made to allow the inexperienced *Jappies* to take control of such an important position. But regardless of that, it could not have come at a worse or indeed more embarrassing moment for the Prime Minister. In his discussions with the Americans he had pointed to gains made in the desert in an attempt to allay American suspicions of British ineptitude, hoping the United States would pull us out of the mire in North Africa, instead of agreeing to what they desired: a full scale invasion of France.

I looked at Winston. The poor man appeared utterly defeated. I'd never seen him as lost. For something like that to happen *now* and happen *here* in this place, I could only imagine his desolation. Everyone in the room stared at him wordless. Those who knew him well, Brooke and I, were completely stunned to see him so bereft in this unimaginable humiliation. I could only walk over to him and stand by his side.

Then President Roosevelt, with just a few words, exhibited true greatness and Jamie Melville was there to witness it. It was something so simple and yet so profound. It encapsulated all that was good and kind and decent about the true spirit of America, to an extent that didn't register with me completely until later when I thought back on it.

The President of the United States, Franklin Delano Roosevelt, eased his wheelchair closer to where Winston sat in torment.

He reached out his hand and rested it on the Prime Minister's arm.

'What can *we* do to help?'

Winston said nothing. I then put a hand on each of his shoulders and shook him gently.

'Come on, Colonel! They can't beat *you*! They can't beat *us*! We'll show them!'

'Mr President, we have an armoured division that is fully equipped and ready. They would be honoured to serve alongside the 8th army,' General Marshall offered.

'Why, yes!' declared FDR. 'Winston! They're a fine bunch of boys and rarin' to go! They're yours!' Then he patted the Prime Minister's hand.

'Defeat is one thing,' Winston muttered, 'but disgrace is another! Thirty thousand men. How can it be possible?'

It was time for me to intervene. 'Never you mind, Colonel! The President's sending his lads! We'll get them! Don't you worry now! Gentlemen, if you don't mind, Mr Churchill and I are going for a wee walk.'

'Of course you should!' exclaimed the President. He wheeled himself over to the door and ushered out the Generals.

He then beckoned me over.

'Give him some air and bring him back. I'll talk to him, Jamie,' he whispered confidentially to me.

'I'll do that, Mr President. You just have the whisky ready!'

He winked at me to say 'sure' and I then went over to Winston and led him onto the terrace of the West Wing of the building, where I lit up a cigar for him. I took out one of my own and observed him warily as he wandered around aimlessly, speaking not a word.

After a short while he stopped and turned to me. 'Thank you, James. I am ready to return to the President now.'

'You have to be completely sure of yourself about what you have to say next,' I advised cautiously. I was gravely concerned over his state of mind at that moment.

He nodded without replying and then we returned to the office. After a few moments I left him alone with the President and wandered into the Cabinet Room where I observed Marshall and Brooke deep in discussion. I did an about-turn but then heard Brookie call out to me.

'Where is he now?'

'He's back with the President,' I answered.

General Marshall strode over and offered me his hand. 'Mr Melville, I would just like to say that you did your country a great service today. You handled things immaculately. It's been a trying day but thank you, sir. We intend having a dinner for the Prime Minister before his departure and would be honoured if you will attend.'

'I'd be glad to, General,' I replied, wondering what I'd done that was so important.

Harry Hopkins then appeared in the doorway. 'General, do you mind if I grab Mr Melville?'

After making my excuses to the Generals, Harry led me along the hallway up a flight of stairs onto the second floor of the building. Passing Winston's own room, the Rose Suite, he opened a door and we entered the Hopkins' living quarters.

I thought my daughters' bedrooms at home looked like bombsites, but this beat all. Formerly the study of Abraham Lincoln and originally two rooms, it had been divided when Harry moved in and a secretary had used the smaller one for a short time. Now, the larger had a four-poster bed and the smaller contained Harry's bath. There was a stunning view from the window towards the Washington Monument.

Whether the late President would have approved of the manner in which the room was being occupied presently was open to question. Scattered all around were items of suit clothing hanging from chairs, shirts and overcoats thrown with abandon over door hooks or lying fallen and forgotten along with the odd shoe on the floor. Various loose documents, folders, cardboard wallets and piles of papers tied with string sat precariously on, and in many cases over, the edge of any available flat surface. I had to manoeuvre myself carefully around volumes of books stacked sometimes knee-high on the carpet floor.

There were a number of half-empty cups of cold black coffee and ashtrays filled with butts that, along with the overpowering fug of tobacco which followed Hopkins around like an early warning card, bore testimony to the basic rootlessness and dangerously unhealthy lifestyle this remarkable man led. At that moment I felt curious feelings of protectiveness for him come over me, similar to those I'd felt for Winston over the years.

In the room was a fireplace with a plaque placed above it. In order to get a closer look, I was forced to lift some of the larger tomes from their resting places and dump them unceremoniously on to Harry's bed. I overcame the strong urge to begin tidying up the mess; once a batman always a batman, you'll be thinking. Instead I concentrated on reading the inscription on the plaque which stated that in this very room, President Abraham Lincoln had signed the Proclamation of Emancipation.

'Impressive company you're keeping these days,' I

declared ironically. 'I only wonder if Abe would recognise this pig-hole now!'

'Oh, that! I should charge a fee!' Harry laughed. 'Yeah, well, there is a system believe me. Working for Winston I thought you'd be kind of used to organised chaos! Sit down, will ya?' Harry made me a drink and then threw off his coat. I almost fell down on the chair that was offered and after loosening my tie lit a Tom Thumb. Harry poured himself a glass of water from a jug resting on a small cabinet at the side of his bed and then climbed up on to it, leaning back against the headboard.

'That's the nearest I've seen Winston to throwing in the towel,' I mused, worriedly.

'It was *bad*, Jamie,' Harry agreed sadly. 'It gives that son of a bitch King all he needs to make a real song and dance. That *bastard*!' he swore bitterly.

'I didn't realise the divisions amongst your own people.'

'Believe it. They're real. The Army and Navy *hate* each other. But I've every confidence in FDR to handle *him*. King. My worry is what the Admiral does when Franklin isn't around.'

'What do you mean?'

He got up and leaned forward, his glass grasped in both hands between his spindly legs. 'There's an agreement between your people and ours about intelligence gathering. We have our sources and you have yours. We let you see our stuff and the favour is returned. But our information comes from the Navy department and at any time King can turn off the source.'

'Surely not?' I replied, astonished by the latter comment.

'Like I said, you better believe it.' He then leaned back again. 'Oh, we have guys there who are friends of FDR who won't allow it if they can. He's a big Navy man remember, just like Winston. But King has his stooges, too.'

'Harry, what you're telling me is insane. We're all in this together. And you've seen London, what's been done to it.

Surely anyone can see that Germany has to be dealt with first.'

'Preaching to the converted, buddy. I know it, you know it and most importantly, Franklin Delano Roosevelt knows it. But there's going to be blood spilt first, believe me. We suspect but can't prove that King has been sending supplies to the Pacific that were ear-marked for Europe. But today FDR kicked his ass. No one knew about North Africa.'

'They'll think it was Winston who turned his head,' I pointed out.

'I can't help what they think. I only know that FDR has thought about it for a while himself. But I'll let you into a secret: it was Franklin's idea to invite Winston on his own to Hyde Park. What they discussed was pre-planned. He shares the Prime Minister's views that invading France this year is crazy and can't work. But he daren't tell the chiefs that.'

I remained unconvinced. 'But Winston will still get the blame and the chiefs, as you call them, will no longer trust the President. They'll believe Winston has him wrapped around his finger.'

Harry shrugged. 'It's all part of the way FDR operates. Jamie, I'll tell you something. Right now we're losing two ships to U-Boat attack for every one we're building. The real war is in the *Atlantic*. That should be the main priority. Meanwhile the Prez is fighting on every front and he's wasting too much energy having to keep a bunch of *prima donnas* happy in the military as well as in Congress. Christ! Do you know what King once said? "These logistics Marshall keeps bangin' on about, I don't know what the hell they are but I sure want plenty of 'em!"'

He lit another cigarette and took a long draw. 'Take it as gospel, Franklin wants that "Japan First" quasi-isolationist gang *crushed*.'

'How will he do that?'

'Oh, he has his ways,' he said enigmatically and sipped his drink.

Chapter Twelve

AFTER RETURNING TO my hotel room and pondering Harry's remarks, I decided to have an early night, but found myself unable to sleep through the evening humidity.

Warm air blew in through the open window. I got up from the bed and, leaning over the ledge, lit a cigar and gazed out at the night-time scenery. I felt far away at that moment. In those days, even though we had undergone a minor miracle in the seaplane, the world was still a large place. I felt again pangs of guilt that I'd flown over at great danger – though in luxury – when I should have been home with my girls. But the immediate and more personal source of guilt came from the beguiling Meredith.

I suppose it was the same thing a lot of men feel when they travel abroad unaccompanied. The temptations are there and many give in to them freely and with relish. In my own case the simple flirtations back in London with secretaries and typists (one of which went further than I'd anticipated) had reignited my enjoyment of female contact again. In the quiet hours after such moments I would feel the weight of reproach overwhelm me with renewed despair. But now my melancholy was tinged with something different: uncertainty.

How does anyone know when the time is right after great loss? Indeed, is a point reached where one becomes accepting of loneliness by retreating to the solace of its lack of ambition?

It wasn't Meredith; it was me. Could this trip to America become the tipping point? Could it be the moment where I ceased the scourging I'd given myself; five long years of assumed guilt for something I'd ultimately no control over?

And what about the girls? Were they not tired of the constantly unsmiling father they lived with? My temper admittedly was never an issue round them, apart from the mock anger with which I greeted their childish indiscretions. When Gemma was alive, I remember the trouble I had keeping a straight face when I scolded them and chased them screaming around the house in pretend anger. It always ended up with them hiding under the bed and me pulling them out and swinging them around like the wee giggling monkey's that they were. Which of course is what they had wanted all along. Those innocent times seemed so long ago, now.

No, I thought. Jamie, you owe it to *them* to change. And if I did, and brought another lady home one day, maybe I would receive a response from them that would surprise me.

After I finished my cigar, I went back to the bed and lay over the counterpane. We had a few days left before heading home. I would hang around the embassy and chip in with some paperwork to help out and pay my way. Winston was due to fly to South Carolina to view a military display, which I'd planned to give a miss as Sawyers and Inspector Thompson would accompany him. It wasn't a loss, as I've never been fond of parades.

I've experienced the results of marching to the tunes of glory.

The following day after breakfast I took a taxi to Massachusetts Avenue. As Winston had brought virtually no staff apart from that crumb Tommy and two secretaries, all the heavy work was carried out by embassy personnel.

Consequently, when I arrived, John Martin and Patrick Kinna were grateful to see me. I willingly took over some of the more mundane secretarial tasks such as typing up meeting notes and proof-reading documents. I was enjoying myself as my mind was taken off alluring red heads and screaming wee girls until who should appear but my old pal, Tommy Thompson.

'Mr Melville, I didn't know you were here. Can I help you?' he sniffed.

'Sod off, Thompson. Or better still, go away and empty the bins, that's all you're good for.' I made a sign with my thumb that signalled "hop it."

Thankfully, John Martin appeared at my desk. 'Jamie, here's some more notes to screen.' Sighing, I looked at the pile he dropped down before me. Immediately Thompson whipped them up in his hand.

'Mr Martin? Mr Melville; is he cleared to view such items?'

'Piss off, Tommy,' I snapped and, ignoring him, addressed Martin. 'John, it's been reported that the monkey house at Washington Zoo is missing one of their number. I heard the chimps there like eating bananas and hiding peanuts up their arses.' I looked at my watch and turned to Thompson. 'You should hurry back before they run out of both, or you'll go hungry while missing out on your only form of pleasure.'

His face contorted in rage and disgust. 'Filth! Such … filth! What one expects from low born riff-raff!' He then stormed off, whilst John had to rush after him to retrieve the notes.

Returning them to me he lamented, 'Jamie, you've done it now. Some little girl on the typing pool will pay for that!'

'If she does, send her to me. He's a shit. God knows what Winston sees in him. Throwing his weight around! Tell him any more of his lip and he'll get *thrown* alright. Straight out of the seaplane over Newfoundland!'

With such merry banter and a heavy but agreeable work-load, I passed a pleasant two days.

That Tuesday, the train that was to take Winston to Carolina broke down, and while a replacement was being arranged a meal was hurriedly laid on at the White House. I was invited and again felt a little inhibited, not having brought proper dress with me.

When I turned up, Mr Roosevelt wheeled himself over

and welcomed me personally. I profusely apologised for my apparel.

'Don't you worry about that!' he cried. He then removed his dinner jacket, showily. 'Heck, it's always too hot this time of the year anyway! And as far as I'm concerned, a friend of Winston's can come in his birthday suit to my place and I'd make him welcome!' He winked at Winston, who was hovering over the President's wheelchair.

'James Melville, like the Prime Minister himself, has nothing to hide from the President!' Winston was alluding to the embarrassing encounter where Mr Roosevelt had caught Winston swanning around his room in the bare buff after having a bath.

I relaxed and was led into the sumptuous State Dining Room. A splendid table was laid out, sparkling with silver and crystal, as my eye caught a portrait of Abraham Lincoln above the marble fireplace. Candles lit the scene and I could close my eyes and imagine great men – U.S. Grant, Teddy Roosevelt and Woodrow Wilson amongst others – who had all sat there. There were great men here on this night, too. Generals Marshall and Brooke, John Dill and Hastings Ismay.

On this occasion there was also what they call an "elephant" in the room, Admiral King, looking about as pleased as an Orangeman being force-fed communal wafers in the Vatican. With him was a younger man, in the uniform of a Commander in the United States Navy.

Harry Hopkins appeared and took a chair next to me, to my relief, as I didn't fancy being sat next to King. The table was too large for the numbers involved and we all sat around one end that looked out over the southern façade of the building.

Where I sat, I was looking directly at the officer with King. He would have been in his early thirties, immaculately turned-out in one of the smartest rigs on Earth; his hair parted to perfection above the bluest and most soulful of eyes, combined with the chiselled features of a flawlessly beautiful male matinee idol. I could imagine the little girls queuing up eagerly. He knew it too, I thought. His name was Howard.

Harry had warned me that the President served notoriously plain and unappetising fare at the White House. He wasn't kidding. Something of an effort had been made with the visit of its distinguished guest, but knowing Winston as well as I did, he would eat anything placed before him without complaint. Unfortunately this evening the so-called cook, who was of German origin and generally recognised as the worst in the history of the Presidency, was caught out in preparing for this hastily-arranged spread.

This individual, a Mrs Norbert, actually owned a restaurant of her own in town that did good trade. However, her idea of State cuisine was to dole out to the President cold gruel at breakfast, serve Brussels sprouts with everything, which Mr Roosevelt loathed (as do I), and specialise in a chicken salad in which a search party had to be sent out to hunt down anything resembling fowl whenever it was listed on the menu. And yet FDR couldn't bring himself to fire her, and indeed gave her a huge raise!

As for tonight, we were at least spared a potentially dubious starter. Instead, waiters piled through immediately after we were seated with platters of fish, which I was told was trout. The other choice was sliced Virginia ham. Fishing is my trade and hobby and I was curious to try out the American variety. I wish I'd stuck to old *Virginny*.

The waiter slapped my choice on to my plate, and I immediately noticed that it was decidedly burnt round the edges. This was fortunate as it was the only part of the delicacy that had anything resembling a flavour. The rest had been overcooked out of it. A few pathetic, hard-boiled tatties were plopped down to keep it company.

I knew it could be a long night, and though the quality of the food was negligible, I'd noted earlier that the President didn't scrimp on drink, recalling that huge glass of Scotch he'd poured me. With the likes of Winston around I knew I had to prepare in advance or risk early capitulation and ignominious retreat.

To my rescue appeared one of the waiters, holding a metal platter of what resembled an exotic type of salad. Catching me looking over at it, Harry warned in a whisper:

'Jesus, *don't!*'

The waiter stood to the shoulder of the President, who took a look and simply but firmly declined. Then he moved to Winston who requested an enormous dollop. As it landed on his plate he took a chunk in his chubby fingers and placed it into his mouth, chewing with gusto and obvious enjoyment.

The other American gentlemen passed on the treat, but us poor unsuspecting Britishers were too polite to decline such a generous offer. Brookie and Pug accepted small spoonfuls, but by the time the waiter reached me I knew I had to take a leaf out of my old colonel's book and either tuck in or starve.

'Lay it on, pal!' I cheerily told the waiter, idiot that I was.

It was a creamy, gelatinous, truly mysterious concoction, and at first I had difficulty matching the vegetables to any that I knew existed, even here in the United States. I took a mouthful of one decidedly square-shaped object, bit down, and coughed it out immediately back on to my plate. There's a time and a place for pineapple and it isn't with rainbow trout.

Harry nudged me. 'Told ya!'

I made do with the fish and spuds, and pushed the ghastly pile of mush across my plate. I noted Winston swallowing mouthfuls with relish and forced down my gorge in an attempt not to dry heave.

The ordeal that was the main course eventually came to an end. I was praying the dessert would be some good old stodgy but filling sponge pudding, covered in thick custard. Sadly, it turned out to be a form of apple crumble which looked like it had been cremated and the remainders reheated again just to make sure. A thin coat of glistening, amber liquid that resembled nothing that I knew of dripped depressingly down from it.

I forced down the first serving and, out of necessity, asked for another helping, declaring with a straight face that it had been "just delicious." The things I've had to do.

At the meal's end, the table was cleared and then drink flowed like water. To my surprise, I later heard that this was unusual in Mrs Roosevelt's spartan White House. It wasn't long before it had its effects, particularly on Admiral King. I did note that his boy Howard only sipped at his glass of wine, and marked him down as a watcher, there to keep an eye on the Admiral; someone both extremely efficient and highly ambitious, for King did not suffer fools in his entourage.

Admiral King was known for his monstrous rages. His own daughter described him as being "always angry." He was a tall, thin, dry and apparently colourless man in his early sixties. It was said that he only cared about one thing: the United States Navy. Two things he *didn't* care for were the United States Army and the British nation, as he was convinced the two were in collusion against him.

The chat was easy and good-humoured at first. Marshall and Brooke were discussing wildlife and Pug was reminiscing with Dill. Winston was gabbing away to FDR and Harry and I were chatting about his next visit to London.

King was sitting silently, playing with his glass, whilst his aide sat back in his seat watching and listening, offering no conversation. He reminded me of Tyrone Power, the actor. But whereas Power was pretty, this one had strong features that in no way could be described as girlish. And then I remembered one of my old grandmother's maxims: when someone is *too* good-looking, it usually means there's a flaw somewhere.

Talk flowed across the table. At one point, the President stated to Winston that he should have ensured some of the roast beef of old England was available in the kitchen, but alas. He would endeavour to make sure it was served the next time us folks came round to dinner. Winston turned to the President and uttered something in return that I didn't quite catch.

There was a roar of mock anger and pretend upset, followed by loud laughter from Mr Roosevelt.

'Oh, no! Winston! Please don't bring up that old chestnut!'

He then turned to General Marshall who sat to his left and spoke, but again I didn't make it out. The General shook with laughter and turned to Brookie. He in turn put his head in his hands and pretended to appear mortified.

'What is it?' I'd had three glasses of champagne and was starting to feel a little merry. 'Colonel!' I appealed.

'Oh, Jamie! Your Prime Minister must be removed immediately! Please see him out!' cried FDR.

I got up, walked around the table and stood between the two.

'Now, Colonel! What have you been up to?' I asked, joining in the fun. Winston, his face like a mirthful Buddha, was pleading innocence.

'Jamie, don't be fooled by his look of virtue!' The President laughed. 'This awful man has brought up the worst possible subject! And in the worst *place* imaginable!'

'What do you mean, Mr President?' I asked, mystified.

'I mean, James,' declared Winston, interrupting, 'that the last President to cook a roast in this room whilst British gentlemen were present nearly suffered the arse of his trousers burned!'

There was a huge eruption of laughter all around the table as Winston continued, 'Mr President, if I am indeed to be ejected, as the weather in the city has been very agreeable and warm of late, I pray you allow me time before leaving *to change my shirt!*'

There were loud groans, gasps of simulated upset and banging on the table. Looking at the jovial faces and failing to comprehend the meaning, I tried to shout over the uproar.

General Marshall, in control again, turned to me to explain. 'Mr Melville, certain countrymen of yours once had the effrontery to burn this building down to the ground. They then followed that with the torching of the city itself.'

'The War of 1812, Jamie,' offered Brookie, helpfully.

'But what does he mean about "changing his shirt?"' I asked, still at a loss.

As the banter went back and forth, Brookie tried to make himself heard. 'When the British officers arrived at the White House, everyone had vanished. But the former occupants left the dining table untouched. A meal had been prepared in celebration, in anticipation of what the Americans believed would be an easy victory when their army faced us earlier at Bladensburg, just outside the city.'

The room had quietened as he related the tale. Though others were still chatting, most were listening to the General.

'It had been a very hot day and the army had marched many miles. The British officers, before sitting down at the table to consume what the President had kindly left behind, went through each room in the building to look for a clean shirt to change into, as their own were by now filthy and drenched with sweat.'

'Oh, right!' I declared, then turned to Winston. 'Colonel, that's not a very nice thing to bring up! We're guests here! Honestly, Mr President, I don't know why this man is let out at night!'

There was another outbreak of horse laughs and guffaws when suddenly an angry, drunken growl emitted from across the table.

'Goddamn Limey sons-of-bitches!' Admiral King said, then repeated himself. 'I said, *goddamn* Limeys!'

General Marshall, across the table from the admiral, grew extremely taut and focused, the humour gone completely.

'*Admiral* King,' he said quietly, but with overwhelming conviction of authority.

'Go on. Tell us more,' continued the Admiral, ignoring the very pointed entreaty. 'Well, I can tell you something about *that* war. How the United States Navy kicked the shit out of the *Royal* Navy. How our privateers kept your miserable citizens quaking in their beds at night on that rotten little island. How Captain MacDonough beat the entire British fleet at Lake Champlain!'

He was drunk, bitter and angry after the shock of the day's news and he truly let rip. There was now a funereal silence in the room. Some looked away, smoking or raising a glass to their lips. Others stirred in their seats. No one spoke.

'If I may say so, Admiral, you are not *quite* correct,' Winston then retorted.

Anyone who tells me the man was an inebriate doesn't know a thing. That mind of his could turn on like a tap – and the pourings from it were usually golden. Tonight I would experience another example of them.

'Winston...' Mr Roosevelt had a hand on his arm. The room was deadly still. In the eerie quality of the candlelight, which set the scene beautifully, I knew that in a few moments all of the inhabitants were going to be taken back to another time.

'The battle of Lake Champlain,' began Winston, puffing away on his cigar, 'was a battle forced on the British Commander, Captain Downie, at the urgent behest of the military Governor, Sir George Prévost. His main ship, HMS *Confiance*, had not yet been properly fitted out. But as the battle opened up, that ship was able to do great damage to the USS *Saratoga*. However, misfortune occurred when the gallant Captain was killed. By this time there was a fierce action between HMS *Linnet* and the USS *Eagle* which forced the American ship to limp out of the fight. Unfortunately, of the four British ships engaged, only two were able to take any part and were thus soon outnumbered. Indeed, of the other two vessels the captain of one was subsequently accused of cowardice.

'It is a fact that the Americans did prevail and the British ships were forced to strike their colours. But it had only been an engagement between four ships on either side. And none of the British vessels could be described as *ships of the line*.' The last statement was made with an emphasis that was undeniable, and in such a manner as to leave no one in doubt who was master and who was subordinate. It was Winston's remarkably singular way of reproaching King for his unseemly behaviour.

'Humph!' King merely snorted.

'I seem to recall the USS *Constitution* overwhelming the HMS *Guerriere*?' Commander Howard had chosen this moment to speak. His voice was very well-bred East Coast. He was possibly deflecting attention away from his Admiral. At least, that's what I thought it was.

'Indeed.' Winston then pressed ahead. 'However *Old Ironsides* was a fifty-gun ship with a consequently far heavier broadside, and the smaller *Guerriere*, merely of thirty-eight, was seriously short of crew members as many had left the vessel to complement prizes.'

The Commander held up his glass as if to apologise for this unfair match-up. For the briefest of moments, I almost liked him.

'There were others, too! *Macedonian*! *Java*!' King rolled in his chair and then sat side on, his chin defiant as if to say, *here I am, say what you goddamn will*.

'Yes,' Winston agreed.

The atmosphere had settled somewhat, but there was still a palpable air of tension as the President attempted to lighten matters further.

'Come now, Admiral! There were successes for our cousins, too! It wasn't all one-sided!' Mr Roosevelt was an expert on naval warfare. He'd been Secretary of the Navy in a previous life and adored that service to the depths of his soul.

Taking the President's lead, Winston announced, 'I must then relate the engagement between HMS *Shannon* commanded by Captain Philip Vere Broke and the USS *Chesapeake* under Captain James Lawrence.'

The manner, the almost complete *recall* with which Winston spoke would have had you believe he had been there that day in Boston Harbour. The way the room stilled as everyone hung on each word (well, most of us) reminded me sharply of bygone days back with the battalion at Plugstreet, when I used to listen to him late at night (usually when I was supposed to be in my bed). As he stood there on this remarkable occasion, possibly through the drink but more likely through complete adoration, there was a tear in my eye of gratitude that I knew this man. And I still felt completely safe around him as I had as a child, though I was now a man of middle-age.

Part of me burned in anger at the intemperance of King. But unlike the boy who would have sought revenge in some childish manner, I knew that my old colonel had more than enough in his formidable armoury to deal with this situation. I sat back, relaxed and prepared for the fun.

Winston drained his glass and laid down his cigar. He had loosened his tie and his coat was unbuttoned. He pushed his chair back and stood with his thumbs inside his waistcoat. This was the stance he adopted when he spoke in the House, or on hustings.

'That day,' he began, 'Captain Broke had sent a note to Lawrence in Boston challenging him to a duel, declaring that they fight "ship to ship, to try the fortunes of our respective flags." The Captain of the *Chesapeake* accepted the challenge. Both ships met, and though at first the Yankee vessel had more sea room and consequently a better position, as she tried to come across the *Shannon* Captain Broke turned to starboard, thus bringing both ships parallel. Then the *Shannon* fired all her cannon into the *Chesapeake*. Although the *Shannon* carried fewer guns, through superior seamanship and gunnery after only fifteen minutes she had battered *Chesapeake* to such an extent that with the American ship's wheel shattered, she crashed into the *Shannon* uncontrollably, a boarding party putting an end to further resistance by the American. And despite the brave pleas of the dying

Captain Lawrence, "don't give up the ship!" she did indeed strike her colours and was towed into the harbour.'

'There you go!' the President said jauntily. 'One for old *John Bull*!'

'Thank you *Brother Jonathan*.' Winston acknowledged. 'And might I add if you'll permit me, there was a fine song written about the action that was sung in England's schools for many years after!'

'Let's hear it, Colonel!' I roared.

Then he sang, in that deep and ghastly bellow of his I knew so well:

Everyone flinched from the gun
Which at first they thought to use so neat and handy O!
Brave Broke he waved his sword, crying no, my lads aboard!
And we'll stop their playing Yankee Doodle-Dandy oh!

Polite applause broke out, Commander Howard clapping his hands with the others. Admiral King gave a testy salute and grudgingly raised his glass. He then reached over and refilled it. Looking around the room carefully, I could still sense deep discomfort and unease. It was as if there was a dreadful cloud hanging over us ready to burst at any moment. Or more likely, a sword ready to cut open and lay bare the growing discord that lay at the heart of the new partnership. Brooke in particular looked strained, and seemed to be trying to make his mind up about something.

'Why, that's just fine!' said the President, trying to remain upbeat. 'Now, who else will join in the harmony?'

Brookie, pushing his chair back, rose to his feet. I thought he was going to sound off but to my amazement he began to sing:

A British Tar is a soaring soul, as free as a mountain bird
His energetic fist should be ready to resist a dictatorial word
His nose should pant and his lips should curl

His cheeks should flame and his brow should furl
His bosom should heave and his heart should glow
And his fist be ever ready for a knockdown blow!

'Bravo! Bravo!' cried the President, amongst a little heartier applause. 'But who'll respond on behalf of the United States?'

There were no takers at first. Then General Marshall stood. I was fascinated to hear what he was going to say. I thought he was going to announce an apology. But he surprised me, too.

'Mr Prime Minister, Mr Melville, gentlemen all, in honour of your presence here this evening, there's a dear tune I am fond of that was written by the great poet, Robert Burns. If you'll allow me.' He then cleared his throat and sang in a not unpleasant voice:

Is there for honest poverty that hangs his head and all that?
The coward-slave, we pass him by, we dare be poor for all that!
For all that and all that, our toils obscure and all that
The rank is but the Guinea stamp
The man's the good for all that!

As he began the second verse, I joined in the great Masonic anthem and we both sang heartily together. As we finished we retook our seats to now far lustier acclaim.

'The British response?' declared Winston.

'Me now!' I cried and jumped out of my seat for a second time. I'd gulped down a further glass of the bubbly and though there were still the dying embers of an atmosphere in the room, I'd already decided on a riposte enough to bring the roof in.

I stood and started to sing:

We are merry Masons, oh!
We are merry Masons, oh!

The King, the Craft, the Mystic Eye!
Merry are we Masons oh!

We are merry Masons oh!
We are merry Masons oh!
The Level, the Square, the Winding Stair!
Merry are we Masons oh!

I carried out the actions; knocks and taps after each verse along with other assorted comic japes and turns, learned years before.

Then Winston rose and continued the song in his own particular style, banging on the table with the end of his fork. I had taught him the words, which he was able to recall perfectly. In the spirit of things, the President, catching on, roared out the words as best he could and slammed the table with his huge fists whilst taking his cue from me.

Pug and Brookie started hammering and stamping their feet in time to the song, as the others whooped and hollered. God knows what the White House staff must have thought, as I'm pretty sure that raucous Linlithgowshire Masonic ditty had never been heard in those parts before. They must have thought the bloody British had returned; their thoughts turning to yet another white paint job.

Catching the reaction of the Admiral out of the corner of my eye, I saw to my pleasure him voice his approval and join in heartily when the shout of 'Hurrah rah rah rah!' roared out between verses. He fairly slapped the edge of the table in time with the words.

At last the song ended, with me standing on the table panting and fair gasping for liquid refreshment. Hands grabbed me as I was helped off, heroically ignoring the ache in my leg as a price worth paying to maintain Allied solidarity. Handshakes and pats on the back were received from everyone. Winston handed me a glass of champagne and I downed it in one go. Thirsty work it certainly was.

The atmosphere in the room was now hearty and filled with jolly fellowship. But then an official-looking fellow entered and spoke to the President.

'Gentlemen,' FDR announced. 'I'm afraid we have to part from the *Square*! The train has arrived to carry Mr Churchill south and he must take his leave immediately.'

A coach had finally been found to transport Winston and General Brooke to Carolina to view the army exercises. The dinner party slowly broke up, with more back-slapping and good heart all around.

Before he left, Winston pulled me over to a corner.

'God bless you, my boy! You have turned a potential disaster into a triumph! If only you knew how serious things have been. But you have saved the day!' He patted my arm. 'Now, off you to your bed! I want you to enjoy the remainder of our visit. I do believe you have spent time in the company of a pretty lady? Continue to do so! And I shall see you on my return.'

The President grabbed my arm before I left and insisted on going over the words of my song, and took notes, as he was a great scholar of Freemasonry. He then handed me a signed picture of himself in his apron. Charging me to convey warm fraternal greetings from himself personally on my return to my Lodge's Master, Office Bearers and Brethren, we made our farewells.

As I was about to leave the room, I turned and before me stood Admiral King. In the dim light, he looked cadaverous and somewhat alarming.

'Mr Melville. I'd just like to offer my apologies for my behaviour this evening,' He seemed to falter momentarily, but then found himself. 'My father came from Scotland. And I kind of forgot that John Paul Jones was a Scotsman, too.'

'And a *Mason*,' I returned pointedly.

'Yes.' He began to turn away but then as if forgetting himself, reached out his hand and gripped mine. He then sidled off, remarkably steadily since his eyes resembled the proverbial piss-holes in the snow. I suppose these old sailors become constant as the stars that guide them.

We were now making our way to the entrance, with me leaning heavily on my stick. My leg was throbbing as I put on my coat and thought about the hot bath I'd have to run as soon as I returned to the hotel, if I wanted to sleep that night.

'I just don't know how you do it!' Harry Hopkins whispered in my ear, as he ushered me out of the building towards the waiting taxi.

'Do what?' I asked.

'Now you've even won old King's stony heart! You're the walking eighth wonder, Jamie! Come on, how did you nail him? And what did he say when he came up to you? God, I can't imagine!'

'Oh, that! Well, you have to *know* about these things, Harry. It helps also if you do your homework, too.'

Mystified, he looked at me.

'What do you mean?'

'Did you see what he had on his finger?'

He gaped at me. 'What do you *mean*? That big old Navy ring?'

'That wasn't the only one he was wearing. Goodnight, Harry.'

Chapter Thirteen

I AWOKE THE following morning not feeling too hungover, just a little heavy-eyed. After making my ablutions I made my way through another fabulous Washington breakfast.

After eating, I decided to view some more of the city and, armed with a guide-map, found my way onto 23rd Street, heading for The Mall and the Lincoln Memorial. But like many tourists from across the water, I misjudged the heat and humidity and was fairly puggled by the time I reached my destination. It was not too far a walk, but I arrived down to waistcoat and short sleeve order, jacket over my shoulder and in something of a sweat.

My British Worsted was certainly no match for a Washington June; I regretted not putting on the new lightweight suit Meredith had picked out for me. To cool myself down I stopped to buy a cold drink, a *root beer*, with the mid-day sun growing hotter and the shirt now sticking unpleasantly to my back.

Making my way into the south chamber of the monument, I viewed the carving of the Gettysburg address on the sculpted walls. Then on into the main hall and the mighty statue of the man himself. I stood for a while contemplating it. He always looked like a soul in torment; I thought about the burden he shouldered. He was like my old colonel in that he felt deeply the pain of the ordinary man. And yet he interfered, like Winston, and cost men's lives when he tried to overrule his generals, usually with disastrous consequences. Was that the weight that seemed to be pushing down on him as he sat there? The pain of guilt?

'He was every bit as impressive as a man.'

Startled, I turned around to see who spoke. It was Commander Howard.

'Oh, hello! Fancy meeting you here! Have you been following me?'

'I confess I have, but only to thank you as I didn't get the opportunity last evening.'

'Thank me for what?'

'Do you want to take a seat?' he asked.

I looked around. 'Where?'

'Why out on the steps, of course.' We left the hall and took a seat looking over the Reflecting Pool.

'Pretty view, isn't it?' Howard remarked as we both gazed ahead towards the Washington Monument. I decided not to mention the pre-fabricated buildings that Meredith had spoken of.

'Yes, it is. There's a place in London called The Mall, just like here. Gemma and I celebrated the end of the Great War there,' I recalled.

'I've never been. I would so like to,' he said wistfully.

I looked over at him. He *was* extraordinarily good-looking. But there was a vulnerability about him that I hadn't seen the night before. I felt a momentary pang of sympathy and some liking for him.

'It's not much to look at right now. Bombed to hell. But it always was lovely in summer. I spent some time there years ago,' I continued to reminisce.

'Yes, you've lead a fascinating life.' He turned to look at me inquiringly. 'Can I ask you something?'

'Certainly.'

'Do you think we'll win this war?'

I didn't have to think, but I knew he'd fired his first shot. 'Yes, if we get our priorities right.'

'And they are?'

'Germany first.'

'But many people in America believe that Japan is the real enemy.'

'Yes,' I countered. 'You do have a sizeable German element in your population.'

'We have our Japanese, too.'

I stood up. 'Commander, I don't know what you want from me. You look like a sensible bloke. I can hardly believe that with all we're hearing about going on in Europe – the rumours of mass murders, deportations, the disappearing Jews – you think we should turn a blind eye.'

He looked up at me. I admit at that moment the magnetism of his charm and striking good looks nearly threw me. He seemed melancholy and I felt a tinge of guilt.

'Mr Melville, have you heard of Nanking?' he asked quietly.

I sighed. 'Yes, I've heard of it. I know what happened there. But Berlin is a little nearer London than Tokyo. Can I ask *you* a question?' He nodded. 'Have you ever been bombed?'

He smiled, charmingly. 'I can't argue the case with that one! No. I've never been shot at, bombed or torpedoed. But I'd love to be able to try and make you see our point of view.'

I started to walk down the steps. He stood up and followed me.

'You really think I have some sway over Winston? You're mad. You and your boss. No, it's not like that, Commander.' I laughed out loud at the absurdity.

We stopped at the foot of the steps. 'In that case, all that's left for me to say is how grateful the Admiral is for your gracious conduct last evening. You may not believe it, but he can be very sociable under the right circumstances.'

'Oh? When he's dreaming of the Battle of New Orleans, you mean?'

He laughed once more and reached out his hand. 'Mr Melville, again, thank you and have a safe journey home. It's been a pleasure, believe me. You're everything they say you are. Good-day, sir.' With that he walked off leaving me standing alone.

In future I promised myself to be more circumspect during my sightseeing trips.

Wandering back through Constitution Gardens, I developed a headache and my leg began to throb badly. I took a seat on a bench for a short rest, but then decided to catch a taxi back to the hotel and have a lie down. I was suffering a little dehydration. With the drinks the night before, the longish walk I'd set out on and being new to the humidity, I'd overdone things a little.

On returning to the Hay-Adams, I asked for something at the desk and was given some aspirin. I took a cool bath, placing a damp sponge over my forehead. Afterwards, lying on top of the bed, I tried to put the whirlwind of events from the last few days out of my mind and grab a snooze, for a good kip is often the best remedy for an aching bonce.

I awoke and, noticing the clock, saw to my surprise that it was nearly five p.m. At home if I ever had a lie-down in the afternoon, I only stayed asleep for at most an hour. Here, I'd been out cold for the best part of five. I put it down to all the excitement catching up with me.

My head had settled and as I'd missed lunch, I was starting to feel some pleasant rumblings. I decided to spruce up and shave for the evening meal in the very plush dining room of the hotel. As I stood over the mirror I heard a small tap at the door. Thinking it must be a messenger from the embassy, I walked over and opened it.

There stood Meredith.

'Oh! Wrong moment!' she said. I was bare-chested and had a face covered in cream, but I don't know which of us received the biggest surprise.

'Meredith! Hello, come in! Just give me a wee minute!'

I made my way back to the bathroom and finished up as quickly as I could. I then remembered my shirt was lying on the bed and cursed to myself.

'Meredith,' I said as I stuck my head round the door. 'Can you pass me my shirt?' She picked it up and handed it over to me.

'Thanks!' I put it on and came out the bathroom.

'All through?' she asked.

'Yes! It could have been worse though!' I laughed and she gave a chuckle. She then stood up from the bed.

'I heard you were leaving the day after tomorrow. I just wanted to say my goodbyes.'

I stood and looked at her as I put on my tie.

'I … I was lucky you were here!' she continued hesitantly.

'I'm afraid I got a little bit of the sun today and had to come back for a wee lie down! We Scots are not so good in the heat, you know!'

She smiled and looked around the room. Again, she looked elegant, as she had that first day. Her hair this time was tied back in a large bun and she wore a short, black velvet coat with a large collar, a light frilly blouse, and a skirt with a wide split which revealed the inside of one very white thigh.

I knew I had to act and seize the moment. I was making a mess of the tie as my initial bonhomie was wearing off to be replaced by that shyness, the kind I'd felt as a young lad when meeting beauties like Pamela Plowden. At that moment, I was afraid and began to tremble. I prayed she wouldn't notice.

'Jamie, you're having trouble…'

She stepped over and took the tie from my hands. She was wearing heels and her eyes were just below mine as she concentrated on her task. She looked up at me then back down again. A hot flash of heat burst within, and the overpowering desire to kiss her came over me.

I resisted it, of course. But God knows how. The USS *Constitution* wasn't the only *Old Ironsides*, you'll be thinking. But at that moment what stopped me was the longing I had for her, to have her *entirely*. Not just a sneaked kiss that may have blown the entire chance and cheapened everything. But still … her eyes, her perfume, her alone with me in the room…

Aye, you're some man, James Melville.

'There,' she said as she finished. Did I hear a slight catch in her voice? I ignored the suspicion and turned away to look for my coat.

Putting it on I asked, 'Have you had dinner?' She hadn't.

'Why don't we dine downstairs together? It'll taste better knowing it's on the US government!'

'That would be real nice.'

We made our way to the door, I opened it and we both stepped outside. 'Oh!' I remembered.

'What is it?'

'My cane.' I'd forgotten it in my flustered state.

'It'll be alright. It's only downstairs, you said?'

'Yes.'

'Then don't worry,' she said and took my arm. 'Just leave it. I'll keep you on your toes!'

As we sat down at our table, Meredith dashed off to a booth to buy cigarettes. She was gone some time and on returning apologised profusely. She smoked heavily I'd noted. I was unused to that in a woman as Gemma abstained from the habit.

Dinner was pleasant but the Meredith Macaulay show didn't materialise again. Instead, she ate daintily. I thought it may have been because she had eaten earlier, and was just being sociable in agreeing to dine with me. But though she consumed her food slowly, she still made her way through all the courses on offer. The cheese and biscuits weren't neglected either.

When we were finished, she sipped from her glass of wine. She placed it back on the table and rubbed her finger around the stem.

'I have to apologise about something.'

'What about?' I asked.

'I made a pig of myself the other night. I forgot you British are going through rationing. And it has to be said, us Americans are big eaters!' She scowled. 'I must have looked *absurd.*'

I strongly suspected that her mood was about to change. And this time I couldn't just jump up on the table and extol the virtues of the Craft...

'Please, Meredith. To tell you the truth, I found it hilarious! Do you know I had to go the lavatory at one point because I thought I was going to burst from laughing? You were terrific!'

Thank God, it worked. 'Did you?' she gasped, then put her hand over her mouth.

'Aye! You're a wee lassie, but you can sure pack it away!'

She chuckled aloud, happily. It was a very sweet and child like giggle rather than a full-on laugh of a grown woman, which I found unbearably attractive.

'Well, I never say no to a good feed!'

'Quite right! Why not, eh? Enjoy yourself, that's what it's all about!'

I then began relating amusing anecdotes about the lengths some housewives would go to back home to feed their families. The black market, the scams, the fiddles; all the gossip that the wives of our trawler men would tell me in the most lurid detail.

She was plainly fascinated and there were many laugh-out-loud moments. She seemed to be enjoying herself and there was no visible sign of her returning to her sombre mood.

I was having fun, too. I was slightly disconcerted that she still hadn't revealed much about herself. All I knew was that she was from New York, she was separated with no children, her husband had been in the Navy and she worked in the State Department. I was even unsure of her age. At first meeting I took her for someone in their middle to late twenties, but I had since revised that opinion, now believing she was at least thirty. I wanted to know more but felt if I pushed there would be a negative response to my prodding. People were like that back then, so it was not that unusual.

But when the person in question is a beautiful girl that you long for desperately, it can be frustrating.

It was getting late. I didn't want our dinner to end because I didn't want to say goodbye. But I consoled myself that I was saying farewell at the end of a very nice evening. I'd got through it all, hopefully to at least leave her with a good impression.

Afterward, we stood outside together waiting for the taxi.

'Jamie, that was really lovely. I'm so grateful. You've been...' She stopped and then started to rake in her bag.

At that moment I *thought* I understood her at last. She was like me all along. Terrified of doing the wrong thing. I stood with her, wanting desperately to kiss her goodbye, but in agony over whether it was appropriate.

'You've been wonderful, Meredith,' I wanted to say her name as much as possible without it being obvious. 'I can't thank you enough for your kindness these last days.'

She didn't find what she wanted in her bag. She then looked at me. 'Oh, yes, it was a pleasure, really. I ... enjoyed your company, too.'

We both stopped. There was a pause. I looked around and saw the taxi slow in its approach towards us.

'Well, if you're ever in Britain, look me up! You must know my address?'

Then I stopped and stood close to her.

'You know *all* there is to know about me.' She did not reply but her eyes stayed with mine for an instant.

'Here's the cab!' she broke off and declared, a little too hurriedly. She got in and waved to me as the car drove off. I watched it until it turned out of the street. Returning to the hotel, I made for the lift.

I've never liked travelling in them.

The following day, the last, was all about packing and tying up loose administrative ends at a final meeting of the British and U.S. staffs. Harry Hopkins invited me to lunch at The Willard where we were led to a quiet table. He informed me that everything had ended well, but there would be further talks in London in a month or two amongst the various chiefs.

'There'll be an invasion this year. No doubt. It will be either Algeria or Morocco. We think Algeria is the best bet but we may have to go in under the Stars and Bars only. The President thinks there's less chance the Vichy Frogs will fire at Old Glory than Union Jack!'

Winston wouldn't have liked that, and I said so.

'He doesn't,' Harry agreed stridently. 'God, the French! To think it's thanks to them we beat you guys! They still hate you more than the Germans! And as for that DeGaulle – don't mention his name around FDR! It's mud!'

I'd heard rumblings myself about the Free French General and that Roosevelt despised him, despite the two men having never met. He was right to, although the Frenchman he would choose ahead of him as America's choice, Giraud, was even worse. But that was all in the future. Bloody Frogs, alright.

'I'm more concerned about how the President views me, after my exhibition the other night!' I joked.

Harry's shoulders shook with laughter. 'I tell you, Jamie! He told me the rest can go home but leave James Melville in Washington! He *likes* you, pally! He actually said so! Don't worry; he didn't mention how you dress. But he does like you, believe me. Which *is* kinda unusual.'

We then spoke about King.

'He's been kicked down. Momentarily. But it won't last. He's going to London next month with Marshall for one last push. But there are still too many voices in support of his views. It'll be tough but we have to plough on through.'

'Who is Commander Howard?'

He dragged on his cigarette. 'A young zealot. One of many who hover round the great man. He's a China hand. Brought up there. Wants it to be amongst the great nations of the world. Though he thinks Chiang Kai-shek is a slope-eyed Hitler! That's not a popular view.'

In those days the American obsession was bringing enlightenment to China. At the time that vast country was bedevilled by civil war and upheaval. It hadn't been helped by the Japanese invasion in the thirties, but the American messianic spirit was in vogue. Literally. Whereas we believed trade could bring prosperity to the world through our empire, the Yanks thought the word of God could achieve more. We'd been through our religious phase; the result was the Indian Mutiny and thousands dead. Lessons were learned as they always are with us, the hard way. What I'd learnt about Americans was that they didn't want to be like us, but didn't want to learn from us either. The results, like their initial disastrous losses in France in 1918 when their generals refused to heed hard-earned lessons from the British, could be stark.

'Howard's a fanatic. He's heading for the top job one day in the corporation, I'm told. And that makes him untouchable.'

I didn't mention the meeting I had with the aforementioned Ben Howard. But I was intrigued to learn that he and King would soon be in London. At least then, I would be on my own turf.

Turning to more mundane matters, I mentioned how returning to wartime Britain would be a shock after the luxuries of Washington.

'I've sent off a little box addressed to Scarborough for your kids,' he replied. 'Should arrive soon.'

'That's real decent of you, Harry.' I raised my glass.

'Wish it could be more! But on that score, I might just have the ticket for you!'

Draining my glass, I mumbled, 'What ticket?'

'That little fire-cracker of a girl, Meredith Macaulay. From what I heard an impression was left … on both sides!'

'Aye, she's a nice lassie, alright. Well, I won't be seeing *her* again.' I mourned and poured another drink.

'Really? I've heard she's on a list of State Department staff earmarked for London to bolster our headquarters over there.'

My heart started pounding. 'What are you up to, you old gossip?'

He roared with laughter. 'Ah, the romantic spirit of old Caledonia! What did Robbie Burns say? "O would some Power the gift to give us, to see ourselves as others see us!" And you should see yourself now, Jamie, old sport!'

'Stop peeing around and tell me what you know, you slavering fishwife!' My former good humour was now wearing extremely thin.

'Relax, *pardner*! I can't have an angry Jamie Melville biffing me across the table in The Willard! Christ, I'd be blackballed from every club in D.C.!'

I calmed down as my excitement settled on the prospect of seeing Meredith again. 'Alright, I'll not batter you! Just tell me. Go on. The secret's out it seems! And what do you mean anyway? You *are* blackballed by every club in D.C.!'

He continued to chuckle, and his frail body shook as he leaned over and stubbed out his cigarette.

'She wasn't on the list, originally. But she's a nice kid and deserves a break. I spoke to a friend of mine in the Department and I think I can get her on the boat. After that, you'll just have to brush up on your Highland love songs or whatever it is you guys use on the girls. Though from what I hear you have no problems on that account.'

I started rubbing my forehead. 'I'm too old for her.'

'What? Come on, Jamie! You're a war hero, you're cute lookin'.' Do you know you can easily pass for a man ten years younger? You mix with the very best and you're a real gentleman! What red-blooded American girl can resist that? And from what I've heard, Miss Macaulay certainly couldn't!'

'Rubbish! You're talking utter rubbish, Harry!' But of course, I wanted to believe it. And there was silence for a while.

'Anyway, enough about your sex life.' He picked up the original conversation again. 'Just be careful in London when our guys come calling. That's all. This thing isn't over yet. Not by a long shot. There are a lot of people in this country who are still fully-convinced isolationists, with a lot of clout. They think we should concentrate on the Japs and let the Germans go hang. MacArthur's obsessed with retaking the Philippines. That man is insane, believe me. He thinks *God* should bow down to him, never mind mere Presidents. And King will do all he can to send equipment to supply Nimitz in the Pacific rather than to Europe.'

'What a bunch!' I spluttered in disgust. 'And these are our allies? Christ, the French weren't so bad after all.'

'As I said before, have faith in Franklin. He can deal with these guys. But Winston has to help him, too. Tell Brookie to keep Churchill's great ideas down to only *one* a day.'

I knew what he meant.

That evening we stood outside the British embassy building awaiting transport to an airport in Baltimore, where we would board the *Bristol* for the flight home. There were a couple of policemen stood around, and I was chatting to Sawyers when my eye caught one uniform alone across the street gazing over at us.

Then Winston came out of the building with Brookie, and I noted the same policeman look up then reach into his pockets.

The vehicles arrived and pulled up next to the kerb, which triggered the usual kerfuffle over who goes in what car. Winston insisted I drive with him, and as I walked round to the roadside to get into the vehicle, the policeman strode forward toward me.

I then noticed that his "uniform" consisted of a scuffed pair of navy trousers and a black short-sleeved shirt. He was wearing what looked like a pair of working man's ankle boots and the badge he wore looked like something out of a cereal box. The hat on his head was a bashed sailor's cap. He looked directly at me and then to my astonishment muttered, 'Fella, see me? I'm going to kill your fucking bastard, that Churchill!' and I caught a glimpse of something brilliantly white that seemed to disappear inside his shirt. Without stopping to think, I flipped up my stick to where my hand grasped it just below the handle and snapped it forward, catching the potential assassin square on the nose.

There was a spray of red, and I could hear the thud where it connected. He raised a hand as I hit him again, his arm this time deflecting the blow onto his hat. He was still making a pulling motion with the other hand from inside his now unbuttoned shirt as I screamed, 'Here! Here! To me! To me!'

Thankfully, at last, two men in plainclothes grabbed him away from me and wrestled him to the ground.

If you're wondering where Walter, Winston's bodyguard was during all this, he was doing his job by shoving his boss back towards the embassy door whilst policemen appeared all around the cars with their pistols ready.

The man was led away and I noticed a white object lying on the road that wasn't there before. He must have been putting them on and dropped one, and I wondered why someone who was going to shoot in full view was bothering to wear gloves. It was confirmed afterwards that he had a history of mental illness, and was later incarcerated in an institution for the insane.

After receiving numerous pats on the back, we were then able to get into our designated vehicles and the convoy sped off. Walter took the front seat, while I was alone with Winston in the rear behind a glass partition.

I soon began shaking badly and leant forward with my arms wrapped tightly around my stomach to try to stop the shuddering. Winston passed me his hipflask and sat up beside me and rubbed my back to try and settle me. I thought of my girls and how potentially close I'd come to never seeing them again.

'That's the problem with crackpots, James. They don't have to worry about making a getaway!' Winston declared, now with his arm around my shoulders.

I had difficulty speaking. 'Wh … why was he w … wearing g … glove's, Colonel?'

'What can one expect from the insane, my boy? But once again, you may have saved my life. This time, it is certain not to be reported. You won't have to embarrass yourself when asked about it. I know you loathe discussing such matters, unlike me!'

I was starting to calm and the shaking began to cease. Winston's flask contained Scotch and I slugged some down. I leant back into the heavy leather upholstery.

'Good, good,' Winston soothed. 'Straight to your bunk when we board the aircraft, I think. I shall ensure Sawyers keeps his revolting eye on you. As for myself, there is much to discuss with Brooke.'

There was silence for a long while as we gazed out of the window, both of us lost in thoughts. He of the President and the discussions no doubt, and mine of near death, my daughters and Meredith. Mostly Meredith.

It was I that finally broke the silence, now more settled as the whisky began to work on my system. 'Did you get what you wanted?'

His mind was never far away from business, as I expected. 'Yes. But there shall be a price. What it will be, I know not. He is a great leader, is the President. But his mind does not work like normal men. I believe he is deceitful and to an extent, untrustworthy. This round has gone to us, but in future, as the numbers of men and material grow, the Americans will inevitably supplant us and thus our influence shall consequently diminish. But until that day arrives we must use everything we have to ensure our views are to the fore in this war.'

I was not surprised to hear this of Roosevelt. I had a feeling about him too that I couldn't quite place. He was a politician of course, but there was something more than just dissembling and artificial about him. I felt it in my guts. He was willing to put one over on his own people and I strongly suspected he'd think nothing of doing the same to us.

We arrived at the base and boarded the Clipper, which left late that night. I sat in my seat and looked outside as the plane took off, and caught the lights of the settlements below before it banked off to head towards Newfoundland where we were due to land in the morning to refuel. Sawyers brought me a snack and afterwards, as I climbed into my bunk, I thought about my little girls, Meredith, the events of the day and Winston's prophetic words, and was glad I was going home.

Chapter Fourteen

THE EVENING AFTER our return I was summoned to Downing Street, where I found Winston sitting alone in a private room. He greeted me warmly.

'Ah, my fellow transatlantic voyager! How are you after our epic journey?'

My internal clock was still adjusting to the shock it had been put through in such a short period. 'Just trying to get used to Blighty time again! Colonel, I'd like to head up to Scarborough for a few days to take up the presents I brought back for the girls, if you don't mind.'

'Of course!' he agreed heartily. 'My sweethearts must not be denied their Hershey bars and candies!'

If anyone else among his immediate staff had made such a request he would have given them short-shrift. He even expected people to work throughout Christmas Day itself. It was a signal of his affection for me that I was excluded from some of the more disagreeable aspects of his rule; mainly his, at times, extreme rudeness and lack of consideration for others.

I had noticed subtle changes in my old colonel's behaviour on my return to his service. When I first knew him, in the trenches, he was the very personification of tolerance, patience and understanding towards everyone he came across, regardless of rank. Indeed, his concern for us Jocks was marked and certainly flew against popular belief that he never felt guilt over Gallipoli. I had personal experience of knowing that was utter nonsense. I was a fifteen year old laddie who saw the very real tears in his eyes whenever that subject was brought up. It was no act; of that I was certain.

But now, over twenty years later I'd personally witnessed a number of instances of his behaving with unacceptable boorishness towards the types of people he was usually extremely kind and considerate to. On a number of occasions I'd heard him roar and bellow at secretaries, both male and female, and observed the inevitable results, blokes red-faced with embarrassment and the ladies in tears. I'd watched an elderly cleaner being screamed at for knocking over his ashtray and drivers cursed for being late or, in his lofty opinion, deeming to take a route he did not believe correct.

He did attempt to apologise to his victims afterwards; though he never actually uttered the word *sorry*. It was usually along the lines of 'I was much remiss the evening before, forgive me.' Or he would apply unnecessarily fulsome praise if someone, formerly the object of his wrath, completed a simple task on his behalf. I pondered much on this subject for on one occasion he tried it with me.

I was still finding my way around the Downing Street jungle. John Martin initially handed me tasks to complete that he believed were within my capabilities. I coped fairly well and soon moved on to more complex work. I often wondered what he thought of me. We were from different worlds entirely. He was slightly younger than I, classically educated and a high flyer within the civil service. But being a mystery does have its plus side and though he did know what I *wasn't*, he didn't know for certain what I really *was*. Mind you, neither did I. Being surrounded by an air of mystery can be glamorous but also damned confusing.

I'd typed up a memo and made the mistake of not letting a secretary screen it first. When I took it through to hand to Winston personally he was prowling round his office with a note in his hand, barely aware I was there. I dropped it on his desk and left him; I was just sitting back down when I heard an almighty holler.

'Who in the name of *Christ* scribbled this illiterate nonsense? I demand to know!'

I then saw him standing in the corridor furiously waving a sheet of paper, his face apoplectic with rage. No one was brave enough to approach him. I sighed, got up from my chair and walked over. He started smacking the fingers of his free hand childishly against the offending article as I approached.

'I want to know which ill-educated and incompetent cretin typed this up!'

'Can I have a look, Colonel?'

He pushed the paper towards me. I took it and saw that it was the memo I had placed on his desk moments before.

'Oh, this is mine.' I looked over it again to find what, if any, errors it contained.

I glanced away momentarily from the paper and fixed him directly in the eye. He then pulled a face as if stung by an electric prod and seemed to take a step backwards.

'Would you like to go over the paper with me?' I asked deadpan, still looking at him intently.

His expression then adopted a countenance that was as close as I'd ever witnessed of him to mortification. Speaking not a word, he slowly turned and went back to his office, his shoulders sunk as he shuffled off.

I returned to my desk. Everyone else was back at their own work once more, having all to a man and woman stopped to observe the scene in silent but awe-struck fascination. I noted the "error" in my memo. I'd left out a full stop at the end of a sentence.

There are undoubtedly those out there who'll recognise these types of bosses. They do exist but you would have thought with all Winston's concerns, such an omission would not be considered worth blowing his top over. But there were countless instances of this type of behaviour and it made him unapproachable unless you were tough enough to know how to deal with it. In all the years I knew him that was the closest he ever came to losing his temper with me. If it had been anyone else I'm certain they would have got at least a mouthful of spleen.

Of course for me, this was all to the good as it added to my status as someone *unusual*. People saw this and Winston's response and believed I had some sort of hold over him. There were downsides, of course, including being asked to approach him about matters that others were too afraid to raise themselves.

In truth, he was no tyrant but he had become something of a bully, which again for me was a revelation and one I found difficult to accept. Most of his staff could handle him after a fashion. He took some getting used to; they got there even though his ways of working were trying, to say the least. He spared no one. Whether a junior typist or the Chief of General Staff.

But I was still my own man and knew what I could get away with, just as I had all those years ago in Belgium. I often thought of hauling him through the coals for treating people the way he did. I knew that someday it might happen; such a clash was inevitable as we both had volcanic tempers and I had a detestation of bullying of any kind.

After a few more words about Scarborough, Winston led me out of a door into the garden of Downing Street. The June evening was balmy and dusk was beginning to settle. There were two gentlemen waiting for us. One was a Royal Marine guard standing alone a little out of earshot and the other was the man I knew only as "Uncle Claude."

Winston escorted me over to him.

'Mr Melville! I do hope you found your visit to the United States interesting?' Claude asked ingratiatingly.

'Mr Melville played a vital role for his country, I can assure you,' Winston replied testily as I instinctively tightened the grip on my stick.

If possible, Claude looked more malevolent than usual. Then he said a strange thing, 'Mr Melville, do you mind if I look at that exquisite cane you are holding?'

I handed it over, unthinking. Then to my astonishment, he gripped the cane high up the shaft and with the other hand twisted off the gold handle! He then extracted from inside his jacket what appeared to be a pair of tweezers and placing them delicately inside the top of the shaft, carefully removed a thin cylindrical-shaped object about two inches long that looked like a tiny cigar holder.

He then replaced the tweezers, screwed the handle back on and returned the cane to me.

'What's that? How...?' I asked, completely baffled.

'Something vital to the war effort, Mr Melville,' Claude answered grandiosely. 'We can't thank you enough for assisting us. Once again, you have performed a great service.'

He then said his goodnights and the guard led him out the garden towards the door of the room we had left. Winston and I stood together alone.

'I'm grateful that is over!' he announced with palpable relief.

I had endless questions running through my head. I had the mother wit to know I shouldn't ask most of them but I didn't like being used. Winston noticed this, of course.

'No, James, not here. Let us go inside.'

We returned to the same room where I had met him. The house cat, Smoky, a grey Persian, sat Sphinx-like on a settee. His eyes were closed and his displeasure at being disturbed was followed quickly by a purr of delight as Winston babied him with 'Puss, Puss, Puss!' whilst lifting him onto his lap, stroking him with further endearments.

I poured drinks and lit cigars. We both puffed away quietly for a few moments.

'Winston, there was no point at which I can remember that stick not being with me,' I announced evenly, trying to mask my concerns. In truth I was somewhat rattled. 'How on earth was that ... thing hidden inside it? How could someone have planted it?'

'Are you not more concerned with what it *is*?'

'Am I allowed to know?'

'Why would you not be?'

'You tell me. Colonel, who *is* that man, Claude? What's going on? Why was I given a warning and handed a pistol to take with me to Washington?'

Smoky stretched, kneading his paws into Winston's thighs. He then dropped off and sauntered casually to the door, sat and started to wash himself.

Winston then replied, 'James, to answer your first question, that man's name is Claude Dansey. He is a senior figure in MI6, which is another name for the secret service. I have known him since the Boer War and he is an extremely capable and experienced officer who is dedicated to the defence of this country. I speak of this to you because I...'

He stopped. He then settled and continued as I got up to open the door as Smoky left and ran up the passageway. I returned to my chair.

'There are very strong intelligence sharing relationships being built between ourselves and the Americans,' Winston continued as I settled back with my glass. 'We have excellent sources on Germany and they have equally impressive sources on Japan. But lately, the information on Japan has reduced in quality whilst ours has maintained the very highest of standards. We believe that there may be agents within the US intelligence community who are unwilling to provide us with this information, consequently we must be adept in the manner in which we communicate data to each other.

'I am unable to provide details on how we normally pass our information to the Americans but we believe it may have been compromised by these unfriendly agents, therefore we must use more imaginative methods to ensure safe receipt from time to time.'

I can be slow on the uptake but not now. It all seemed clear.

'So, I was being used to carry their stuff back.'

'Precisely. But at any time you may have been targeted, Jamie. Thus the pistol.'

'It's that serious? I might have had to shoot it out with someone?'

'Thankfully, it did not come to that. But our operatives believe you might have been approached at some point.'

'Or *seduced*. Meredith.'

'The young lady? I hardly believe you would have behaved inappropriately.'

'Maybe she didn't expect that either,' I replied, more to myself than to Winston.

'My boy, do not let this worry or concern you. It is over now. I apologise if you believe that you were used. You *were*. Dansey came to me and I explained our concerns and he created the "operation" as he called it. I pray you do not have to be used by him again.'

'But you told me on the seaplane…'

I realised now that he spoke to me that night as a guardian. But I'd been manipulated, alright. There was no real reason for me to be with the party to Washington.

'You *did* prove yourself invaluable to us, James,' he stated, reading my thoughts. 'The situation with Admiral King, a very difficult man, could have set us back months in recrimination but for your quick thinking! There was the fine impression you made on General Marshall and the President, also.'

'Aye, but surely that has no effect on strategy, Winston! I'm just a wee bloke from Gorgie!'

Winston dismissed this. 'Diplomacy is the key, James. A crisis may arise and develop beyond repair due to the fact someone fails to speak up at a certain moment. A look or nod of the head misinterpreted. A written note or a telephone conversation misunderstood! But if James Melville of Gorgie Road can turn a singular, unforeseen moment fraught with danger of the utmost gravity into a triumph of fellowship and good cheer with a rumbustious song, then the entire history of diplomacy must be rewritten!'

I laughed at this and there was now an inner glow which wasn't entirely a result of alcohol. This was a moment with the colonel, alone together. We had a similar experience on the seaplane, though that had been somewhat brief. It helped ease the pain that I felt at being duped. I did experience some respite in knowing that Winston had been worried about me all along. And the fact he bore that burden whilst trying to deal with the Americans made me feel a little less perturbed over my painfully obvious naiveté.

'I suppose I have to do my bit for the war effort. Not just type out the odd memo and learn how to fire a Bren gun!' I replied generously.

He patted my arm. 'My boy, I want you here. You are a fully paid up member of the civil service doing a vital job on my staff but you are the *only* one I will allow to come and go!'

It was late now but I didn't want the evening to end just yet. I didn't want to lose the opportunity of being alone with him because I didn't know when I'd get the chance again. I wanted him to myself for a few hours, just like the old days.

'Returning to the Americans, what happens next?' I asked.

'Oh, more horse-trading. James, the United States Navy has won a titanic battle with Japan in the Pacific. This of course, is good news but it also means that they will start planning a campaign to assault a number of islands on the way to Japan. For this endeavour, they shall require landing craft. But we need these for our attack in North Africa. We must ensure that we get them.'

He was referring to the recent Battle of Midway, in which the US Navy had sunk a number of Japanese carriers and tilted the balance back to them in the Pacific.

'Admiral King won't like that!' I declared while tapping my cigar over the ashtray.

'No, he will not,' Winston agreed.

He continued with various strands of strategy, but as he spoke my mind drifted off to my recent exertions in America. I have to confess I felt that overall I had handled myself pretty well despite the surprise I'd received. I didn't want to make a habit of it though and I was still slightly miffed at being an object of deceit. Inevitably my thoughts turned to Meredith, if indeed that's what her name was. But then again Harry Hopkins had blithely told me of her imminent arrival in this country. Was I jumping to conclusions? Circumstantial evidence they call it. I wasn't experienced enough in the *Great Game* to be certain of anything.

Winston had stopped speaking. 'You are thinking of that delightful girl?'

I wondered how he knew. 'Yes. I wished you'd seen her! She was a real sweetie!' I then told him about Harry's arranging for her to come to London.

You've probably worked out by now that I was seeking his approval. I'd already received it from my daughter a while back, of course. As for Meredith, I was now coming to terms in my own mind that she was indeed part of the whole set up, either for or against, and that at least I could feel a little better that I hadn't attempted to jump her bones. Instead, I'd provided her with a more difficult task than she'd anticipated.

'Christ almighty!' I suddenly blurted out.

'James! What is the matter? Have you burnt a hole in my furniture?'

The cigar between my fingers was dangling precariously over the edge of the arm of the exquisite Wedgwood chair as I jumped up in my seat and looked over at it.

'Colonel! She *is* a spy!' I declared breathlessly.

'What? James, you shouldn't drink sherry! It's always had an effect on you quite unlike any other liquor! I distinctly remember one evening back at the battalion where I caught you quaffing from a bottle of mine and being violently sick afterwards! Shameful! If your mother only knew, I hate to think!'

I then settled back.

'Winston, I'm not sure, but I think Meredith was there to try and get something from me. At the time I thought she might have wanted information about you. But she was … it's hard to explain. She wasn't *cut out for the task*, if that's what it was. Whoever sent her had chosen the wrong person.' He looked at me, his face expressionless.

'I wish I had more *experience* in these matters!' I continued regretfully. 'I just have to go on my gut. I think her heart wasn't in it, somehow. There *was* a moment when my cane was out of sight. But I could be wrong. Winston, I'm just so confused by it all!'

'My boy, when she arrives in this country, by all means, meet up with her,' he replied sympathetically. 'Every account points to her being who she says is. Please do not pass judgment until all facts are known.'

Until all facts are known. What did that mean? I didn't press and we then turned to other matters. But those last words nagged away at me.

I wished to hell I'd never set foot in bloody America in the first place.

My relationship with the United States was to continue further; I stood at a platform in Euston Station a month later as the senior American delegation arrived.

As the officials stepped down from their carriages, General Brooke greeted them on behalf of the Prime Minister along with US Ambassador Winant and General Eisenhower, newly installed as head of United States forces in Great Britain.

I was standing there because I'd earlier received a cryptic telegram from Harry Hopkins asking me if his package arrived and to expect another imminently.

The "parcel" he had prepared for the girls had turned up and was the American equivalent of a tea-chest in size. To squeals of delight, I'm told, it revealed luxuries including the latest dolls and board games, sweets, chocolate and a couple of bottles of excellent bourbon for their old man. I generously offered one of them to good old Uncle Tom, who like me, was never the same afterwards. But I hoped fervently that another kind of doll was arriving from the States. One sent especially for me.

Impatient, I cursed Harry inwardly for his meddling and scheming as I stood waiting anxiously; viewing first General Marshall and then Admiral King close in around Brookie. The desire to strangle Hopkins became even more extreme when suddenly the man himself appeared looking, if possible, more haggard and gaunt than usual. I moved forward towards him as he caught my eye.

'Hey, fella!' he then seemed to slouch wearily and leant back precariously between carriages. I dashed forward and grabbed an arm and jerked him forward as he then appeared to awaken to his surroundings.

'Take it easy, Harry,' I said and eased him over to a bench where he sat down and reached up to loosen his tie.

'This travelling sure beats the hell out of a guy!'

'Just rest for a moment. Do you want a drink of water?'

'Need something stronger!' He croaked and reached for a cigarette. I then heard another American voice.

'Mr Melville?' I looked up at an officer in the uniform of the United States Navy.

'I see you've made it to London, Commander Howard.' It was my acquaintance from the White House dinner.

'Is Mr Hopkins well enough to continue?' he asked. There was impatience and a barely concealed undertone of tetchiness in his manner.

Harry then eased himself up with some difficulty. I rose with him and put a hand under his arm.

'You see that, Commander?' Hopkins gestured to Howard. 'Hands across the sea.'

We followed the uniformed man as he joined up with the group towards the exit, Howard striding ahead joining up with King. I walked slowly with Harry. After a few steps he stopped.

'Are you sure you can you manage?' I asked, now extremely concerned.

166

He turned around to look back at the train standing at the platform.

'I'm just … *there!*'

'Harry, are you alright?' mystified, I looked back and then I saw her.

Meredith Macaulay was standing on the platform speaking to an American military official holding a clipboard. He was rattling intently through sheets of paper trying to find something. In a quandary, I looked at her and then Harry, who broke into a tired but happy grin.

'Your package has arrived, pal!'

Commander Howard then appeared beside us again. 'Mr Hopkins?'

'That's quite alright, Commander!' Harry pushed away the arm that was offered.

They both then joined up with the entourage to their motor vehicles as I was left alone, unsure of myself. To see her standing there, here in London, was what I'd longed for since I'd returned from Washington. But now that she was here, the moment that I had wanted and so not wanted was now upon me.

I felt Gemma's presence stronger than ever. Scenarios, excuses, longings, terrors all flashed through my mind but the overriding emotion was an inability to *decide.* There was that hot flash of desire similar to when I'd wanted to kiss her that last night in Washington. This time though, it was an almost uncontrollable urge to turn around and limp out the station as fast as I could in order not to have to make such a choice.

Run away. Retreat into the comfortable emptiness again. I thought of making my way to Kings Cross and going home, to my girls and never again to return. *Do it, just do it.* I spoke the words out loud to myself. *I want to go home. I don't need this.*

The military police had now re-opened the main entrance for the public as travellers started making their way in to the station. I moved slowly around them as I headed towards the exit, in misery. I stopped and made to look around but my view of the train now was obscured. I walked on further then turned around again. There was no sign of her as I winced to myself and made for the concourse outside, bright and welcoming after the gloom of the station.

I stood in the street, feeling desolate despite the pleasant July sunshine. I couldn't even decide on whether to walk or hail a taxi.

'Jamie? Jamie *Melville*?'

I looked up and she stood before me. She wore a light overcoat that covered her knees. Her hair was braided, her cheeks flushed and there was a slight dab of moisture around her lips and under her eyes as though she had been exerting herself. She looked lovely.

'I must have missed you in the rush! Harry told me you'd be here!' she said excitedly.

'I didn't know.' I was at a loss for a moment, before I gathered myself. 'But it's nice to see you again!'

'Are you alright, Jamie?' A flicker of concern crossed her face. 'Is that all you can say?' Then she laughed. 'Boy, what a trip! I got off the ship at Green Knock and stayed in a poky little hotel that was so quaint! God, the food was terrible! But I was rescued by Harry who arranged for me to meet up with him at Presswitch!'

I'd later work out she meant Greenock and Prestwick but I was happy to let her prattle on. I really didn't know what to say and as long as she was talking, I didn't have to. She seemed genuinely effervescent and joyful. It may just have been her new surroundings but I hoped it was more than just that.

'Where are you staying?' I managed to ask as she caught her breath.

'Oh!' she then looked at a piece of paper she was holding. 'I'm to make my way to the embassy.'

'Are you in a hurry?'

She looked at me. Her blue eyes sparkled and her freckles never looked cuter.

'Gonna buy me breakfast?'

Chapter Fifteen

THERE WAS A small outdoor cafeteria near Clive Steps that I knew well because of its proximity to the War Rooms. Its speciality was fresh eggs. The girls that ran it were from a farm in Sussex, they brought back their produce after trips home on the weekend.

They had their favourite customers and I was fortunate to be one, often being handed a sly egg or a few potatoes to take back to North Street. I introduced them to Meredith and they asked her how she liked her eggs. "Over easy" was the response. By now the girls were becoming used to Americanisms and the look of ecstasy on Meredith's face as she guzzled them down was testament to their skills with war-time rationing. I'd eaten earlier and only nibbled at mine but Meredith noting this, had the temerity to ask if I wanted them.

I pushed the plate towards her.

'You're such a sweetheart, Jamie!' she tucked in and they were gone in no time.

We sat at the little table on the pavement beside the bar and looked over St James's Park. Meredith lit a cigarette after she finished eating. 'Those were good! Oh, Jamie, you don't think I'm a pig do you?'

'Not at all! Just a hungry wee lassie!'

She laughed out loud, as though remembering an old joke that amused her greatly and reminded her of former happy times. Then my heart skipped a beat as she stretched out her free hand and held mine as it rested on the table.

She looked into my eyes. 'I missed you when you left. I … well; I thought I'd never see you again.'

She was like someone relieved of a terrible burden or released from a dreadful sentence. Able to run freely, to breathe fresh, clean, invigorating air. To be what she wanted to be again. Her transformation from how she had been in Washington was remarkable. She then released me and sat up in her seat.

'I had no idea I was being sent here! I still can't believe it. I'm so happy to get out of the States! It's been such an adventure! Oh, God! On the boat I had to side-step about three thousand G.I.s! It was a troop ship and I had to share a cabin with two girls. There were nine of us in total. We were in first class but those guys still found us! I have to say the enlisted men were nicer than those officers! Some of them thought we were just there to service them.' She lit up and blew smoke.

'Better sticking with Lance-Corporals like me!' I declared. 'They're the boys!' She rocked in her chair, laughing joyfully.

We chatted and time passed pleasantly. She had been told to board the ship in New York as she was to report to Grosvenor Square in London where the Yanks had their joint embassy and military headquarters. She didn't know her role yet, or where she'd be living but all would be revealed later.

The other girls were designated for American headquarters in Northern Ireland and the new General Supply Division in Cheltenham. On arrival in Greenock she received a telegram from Washington telling her to make her way to Prestwick airport in Ayrshire where she met American officials and after a wait of two days was driven under military escort to the railway station. She remained there until late that night and joined up with a party amongst whom was Harry Hopkins, who she had been ordered to report to.

Like her, I wondered about the subterfuge at first but then thought that Harry had probably laid on the surprise for me as a thank you present for what he felt were my efforts in Washington. He was matchmaking, undoubtedly, but I still wasn't sure whether to be grateful or not.

'Well, I'd better be going to the embassy,' she said finally. 'Jamie, could you be a dear and please show me the way?' I was happy to and grabbed one of her bags as we left the café. It was a lovely morning.

'Is it far to walk? I'd like to stroll with you,' she asked.

'It's not too far, but we're carrying your cases, Meredith…' It was a bit too far, I thought. If we didn't have luggage it would have been fine.

Noticing my discomfort, she let me off the hook. 'Jamie, I'm sorry. I forgot.'

I waved away her concern. 'I know what we'll do. We'll put you in a taxi and you can make your way to the embassy and I'll see you there for lunch. Say about one o'clock? That'll give you time to settle in.'

She agreed and we found a taxi. As the driver loaded up her bags she grabbed my arm and kissed me on the side of the mouth – then she drove away.

I was only aware of what she'd done as I turned to head back to Downing Street. I didn't put my hand to my face because I wanted the wonderful tingle and sweet scent to remain there.

Forever.

That same day Winston flew into a terrible rage.

The Prime Minister had wanted the Chief of Imperial Staff to bring Harry Hopkins, General Marshall and the others directly to Chequers, the retreat in Buckinghamshire where Winston was awaiting. He wanted them there to gauge their thoughts before they had time to settle in and be debriefed by Eisenhower in London. This was sheer craftiness on Winston's part but Marshall was wise to it and when I left them at Euston they were making their way to Claridge's where they had booked a large number of rooms for their stay.

Instead, that evening the British Chiefs headed to Chequers themselves and when they arrived Winston let rip at General Brooke.

It has to be said that Winston often behaved like an absolute swine towards that man. I really don't know how Brookie put up with it. The General always portrayed himself publicly as the iron soldier; somewhat unapproachable, almost *frightening*, and people felt they were well-matched. But I knew Winston, and I was beginning to know Brookie. To me the austere Ulsterman was always very kind and considerate. For the first time in our long relationship together, I began to develop not exactly dislike, I could never feel that, but certainly *disgust* at some of Winston's antics towards people.

Of course, it was the terrible strain. The man was tired. He was sixty-seven and literally had the weight of the world on his rounded shoulders. I asked myself, what can I do? I knew I had been a success in America which, as Winston had told me, had removed a lot of pressure from him. I fervently hoped that some of the burden could be removed from him entirely and then he might be able to return to his old self. The *true* self I knew. The kind and generous colonel of old.

After knocking off for lunch, I made my way to Grosvenor Square for my date. I showed my pass to the military guard as I asked for Miss Macaulay.

The guard looked at it carefully, asked if he could shake my hand and let me in. I found myself standing around a bank of desks where typists were sat, none of them my girl. I heard a commotion and turned to see who it was.

'Mr Melville?' It was General Eisenhower with a couple of junior officers. 'How are you, friend?' he asked, pumping my hand. The Yanks seemed to want to do that a lot lately, I'd noticed.

'Oh, General! Fine, just fine. I was looking for one of your new members of staff! I was to meet her for lunch.'

He flashed that charming grin of his. 'Doing a bit of *poaching*, Jamie?' he winked.

Then Meredith appeared. She was wearing spectacles and carrying a file as she walked towards us. She looked up, smiled and removed her glasses.

'Hi, Jamie!'

'Ready for lunch?' I asked.

She looked a little uncertain. 'Oh, I don't know if...'

'I think the Allied cause can allow the lady time off for a spot of lunch with our Scottish Fusilier!' declared Ike, standing with his hands on his hips, still smiling.

'You're a gentleman, General Eisenhower!' I declared genially.

'Remember we have that bridge date, Jamie! Don't forget!' he reminded me.

This was a particular compliment to me because the General was notoriously unwilling to involve himself in any social events arranged for him as Commander of US forces. He felt all the dinners, speeches, invitations to tea etcetera, though well-meaning, took up too much of his time. He was an amiable man but had an undoubted steeliness and an explosive temper that he kept hidden just beneath the surface.

Gemma had taught me bridge years before and we used to play regularly with friends. When she died I stopped completely. Ike had told me in Washington that he had become an expert in both bridge and poker as the latter was used to supplement the terrible pay that officers in the US army received in the inter-war years. He'd become good at it out of necessity. I'd offered to be his partner should he ever make it to England. But only at bridge. No way was I getting involved in a poker school.

I acknowledged his invitation and he hurried off with the two officers (who also wanted to shake my hand – it was just about dropping off at this point) and I was left with Meredith and the other typists who were pretending not to notice us.

She held the file close to her and walked up to me poking the corner of it in my chest a few times, smiling artfully. 'Where exactly *are* we going, Lance-Corporal Melville?'

I smiled back at her. She knew the answer to that question better than I.

We lunched at The Corner House in the Strand. Eddie Marsh had known the owner years before and we'd dined often together there. It was in different hands now but the menu still offered slightly better fare than was available elsewhere. We ordered and began to chat as we awaited our meals.

Meredith had that decidedly American manner of speaking directly, wanting to know everything about me but I didn't find it intrusive. I was content to reveal myself to her.

I *wanted* a girl in my life again; to talk of the things you do on first acquaintance, sounding each other out, listening, flirting, eager to learn about each other. But I seemed to be doing most of the revealing, very little was reciprocated.

She asked me about my leg. I told her about the blast that nearly killed me at Plugstreet, about being sent to the hospital in London and about Gemma.

'You weren't much more than a child. Jamie, I had no idea you were so young.'

'Young and daft!' I replied, wistfully.

'You've lived an amazing life. You're blessed, Jamie.'

'What about you, Meredith? I don't really know much about you. I've been gibbering on about myself all this time.'

She reached out and took my hand. 'I like to listen to you.'

Just then the waiter came to take away our plates. I asked her if I could smoke. She smiled. 'You don't have to ask me.'

'Ach, I'm just old-fashioned!'

'Utterly charming and so sweet.' Our heads were bowed down close as she looked into my eyes.

I took out a cigar as I needed to control my emotions. My hand shook but she took hold of the lighter and lit me. 'Have you found out where you're going to be living?'

'I'm sharing an apartment with a couple of girls close-by.'

'You're in England, now. You have to say *flat*.'

She lit a cigarette. 'There's a lot I'll have to get used to.'

I paid the bill and we left. I thought *to hell with it, I'm friends with a general* and took her for a wander round Trafalgar Square. We found a bench and sat together.

'Well, what do you think so far, kid?' I asked.

She looked ahead towards the Column. 'Jamie, I couldn't be happier right now. No, really.'

She then leant her head against my shoulder. I put my arm around her and we gazed at the scene before us, at the panel that had amongst its figures the negro sailor. It was the only one that wasn't covered in an advertisement. The reliefs were based on real people and I had often sat and contemplated it years before, wondering about the lives they had led.

We were quiet for a moment, lost in our own thoughts and then Meredith snuggled into my shoulder, turned and reached towards me as our lips met softly. The kiss was short but long enough to matter.

I pulled back slowly. 'Come on, we better not keep your new bosses waiting *too* long.'

She smiled lazily as we stood up together, my arm now around her waist.

'Can't we just *walk* back?' she pleaded, dreamily.

I was perfectly happy to this time.

After seeing Meredith off at Grosvenor Square, I wandered slowly back towards Whitehall. I had free time as I was under no official constraint. Winston was at Chequers, though he had hinted that he wanted me there. The American delegation's deft sidestep had knocked his timetable somewhat. I laughed to myself, good for the Yanks.

I had come to like them immensely. Harry was a real treasure and Marshall was everything they said he was. Eisenhower appeared competent, inspiring confidence. King was just an old stick in the mud. The one I couldn't fathom was Howard.

There was something innately troubling about him and I just couldn't put my finger on what it was. For a start, he didn't look right at King's side. To me, he was no disciple; rather he seemed a fellow traveller and an equal. I remembered Harry saying he was destined for greater things. I'd been charmed by his sincerity that day at the Lincoln

Memorial. He believed in his ideals but I felt he wasn't the fanatic Hopkins described him to be.

He'd told me that he longed to see London. Maybe I should offer to be his guide for the time that he'd be here. On my own ground I could try to find something out about him. He was educated at Yale, I would discover, and I left school in Gorgie Road when I was barely fourteen but I was willing to give it a try, trusting to the old Melville charm.

I strolled off towards Great George Street. I didn't want to go to No. 10 as I was trying to avoid Tommy Thompson wherever possible. There had been another incident with him when the Marine guard who I'd befriended after he approached me about collecting Winston's cigars got himself into trouble. He'd allowed staff who'd forgot their passes into the War Rooms and on one occasion Tommy spotted him, gave the Bootneck a severe roasting and had him transferred.

The Marine approached me to tell me what happened and I collared Thompson and pleaded with him to give the lad a break.

'Mr Melville,' He never called me anything else. 'That guard allowed individuals to pass without correct authorisation. By rights he should be court-martialled. I'm sparing him that by having him transferred. *Pour encourager les autres.*' We were alone and out of earshot on the stairwell inside Downing Street.

'Leave off the Latin, you weasel. Just tell me where he's been transferred to.'

'French, actually, Mr Melville,' he corrected. 'I hardly think it's any of your concern where he's being sent.'

'Look Tommy, that bloke's from London and his family were bombed out. He has to live in the city.'

'I'm very busy and besides, the paperwork's already gone through. Good-day.'

He passed me on the stairs and I had an urge to grab him but let it pass. I stored it away, though. We Melvilles never forget a bad turn.

There was a chiefs of staff meeting being held. I usually went to my own room and had a smoke or a read if I was at a loose end. If John Martin was about I'd ask for work but he wasn't to be found. Possibly he was with Winston at Chequers. I was chatting to Enid, the typist who'd asked me out (and harboured no hard feelings for being refused) when the meeting broke up.

I then spotted Pug. 'Jamie! The man himself! General Brooke's looking for you.'

General Ismay walked me along the corridor where we found Brookie filing away papers. He turned to me as I entered the Joint Planning Staff meeting room.

'Ah, Jamie! The very fellow! Now, what about this birdwatch we spoke about?' He sat down and I pulled up a chair next to him.

'General, I've had a think about that! The truth is I just don't believe my leg could take lying prone for hours!'

He chuckled. I could see he was now in his relaxed mood, which was completely opposed to his dour professional demeanour.

'I was concerned about that, I admit! If not that, then how about a spot of fishing?'

This sounded much more to my liking. Tom and I had done a bit of fly-fishing back home so the General and I discussed that, and a pleasant time was passed in the smoky bunker.

When we'd finished I decided to broach a more serious subject as I needed some advice.

'General, the American delegation. Commander Howard is with them.'

He nodded. 'Yes, Admiral King's staffer.'

'Do you think that's *all* he is?'

Brookie clasped his hands and laid them on the desk. He spoke deliberately. 'What do *you* think he is?'

I stretched back in my seat. I told him of the meeting I'd had alone with Howard in Washington.

'And you haven't told Winston about this?' He asked when I'd finished.

'No.'

'But you're telling me. You must be concerned, Jamie.'

'I am. That's why I thought that as Howard is in London right now maybe I could stick close to him and see what he's about.'

'Well, he would not be party to our discussions. Obviously, I expect Admiral King to discuss the results afterwards. Though Howard doesn't exactly strike me as some subservient acolyte either,' he said, agreeing with a point I'd made.

'No, and I'm glad you think that too,' I replied, somewhat relieved. 'I felt in Washington I was being suborned by him somehow.'

The General then looked at me directly. 'Jamie, I urge extreme caution in any approach you adopt. You are not a soldier. No one has command over you. My advice is to tread carefully. If you believe this man may be some kind of threat, by all means pump him all you can. Though I strongly suspect a sophisticate like that will see through any such subterfuge.'

He may well have been right and I was grateful for his concern. I was unsure whether I should get involved. But Brookie hadn't said *don't*.

We were just getting up to leave the room when an officer walked in and handed the General a note. He looked at it and cursed.

'Damn it all!'

'What's wrong?' I asked.

'Bloody P.M. wants us all up to Chequers right away!'

I saw an evening with Meredith fast disappearing. 'Surely he doesn't want me around? Please, no!'

Brookie then adopted a mischievous grin and looked again at the paper. 'Mm, "James Melville" it says. Haven't seen the chap anywhere. I wonder where he could be...'

'You're on for that fishing trip, General!' I pronounced as I scarpered out of the door.

I was due to meet Meredith late that afternoon but on arriving at the embassy there was a flap on and every member of staff was required. I received a quick peck on the cheek and an address in Marylebone where she was boarding. As I was leaving the main entrance, Commander Howard was making his way in my direction.

'Mr Melville? How are you?'

'You Yanks owe me a night out!' I shook his hand. 'I was just about to take a beautiful lady out for dinner but the war got in the way.'

'You have a girl here?' He looked surprised. 'That's what I call close allied co-operation!' We stopped outside. 'I've been allowed some free time as the jawing doesn't begin for real till the day after tomorrow,' he confided.

'How about dinner then, Commander? I know a place in Regent Street, it's a nice night and I can give you a wee tour of the town.'

'How can I say no?' he flashed his attractive smile at me. 'It'll be a pleasure.'

I'd booked a table for two at the Budapest originally for Meredith. Restaurants could be tricky places to grab a seat in back then but dropping my brother's name got me in the door. I wanted her to meet him. It might help thaw out relations between us brothers. And I wanted her to see that I'd nothing to hide and was who I said I was. I'd mentioned Tom and Arthur to her but left some detail out.

As we wandered along, I noted Howard's interest in his new surroundings. He stopped and gazed at some of the more heavily bomb-damaged buildings and looked over them with barely concealed expressions of sadness and regret, as if viewing a noble animal lying dead, it's great, powerful body desecrated by the unimaginable force that had destroyed it. Shaking his head slightly, he moved on again with me.

We walked along Brook Street, past Hanover Square and down into Lower Regent Street where we came to the

Budapest. I asked if Arthur was in and was told his shift began later and we were led to our table.

'It has to be goulash, Commander. Don't even bother with the menu!' I joked.

'Okay, goulash it is.' He smiled agreeably. 'But on one condition.'

I looked at him blankly.

'You call me Ben.'

I smiled, relieved. 'In that case you'll have to call me Jamie.'

'Fine,' he said easily. 'No problem.'

We chatted for a while. I told him not to expect great things food-wise, but they could always dig out a nice bottle of wine.

'One thing,' he asked. 'Aren't Hungarians our enemies?'

'Not these blokes. They're all either refugees or Jews. The problem with this restaurant is keeping their staff – they all want to join up! But I'll let you into a secret: only the chef and the zither player are Magyars!'

He laughed and again I found it entrancing. He didn't smoke but I lit up as our wine arrived.

He sipped at it. 'You're right. It's not bad.'

'So, how is Claridge's these days?' I asked.

'Pretty neat. I'm impressed! The war hasn't affected everything in London. We're booked into around twenty rooms!'

'Have you always been in the Navy?' I asked.

'I worked in the Foreign Service before the war. Out of the US Consul in Hankow, then Shanghai. Made my way up to third secretary.'

'And then?'

'I was told I wouldn't get any higher. Came back to the States.'

It was a conversation killer and I couldn't work out why he'd told me. I just couldn't fathom him. I felt a bit out of kilter at that point.

'I spent three years in the Navy back in the early thirties,' he then continued, unexpectedly. 'I was in the Reserve so

I had no problem signing up again. But they grabbed me and put me in an office! Luckily someone spoke to King and mentioned me and I was transferred to his staff.'

'That must be fun,' I chided, mischievously.

He looked up at the ceiling and smiled wryly. 'I'll say!'

The food arrived. Hot and steaming, but sadly, that's all it was. Howard was a good sport and didn't pass comment. He chewed slowly, using his fork. I wolfed mine as usual, and was finished well before him. I emptied the bottle into our glasses.

'That ordeal's over!' I laughed.

He raised his eyebrows humorously. 'We'll just have to ensure the war is ended quickly so you folks can start eating real food again!'

I raised my glass to that and then caught Arthur heading towards our table.

'Here he comes!' I said to Howard.

'Jamie, nice to see you.' Arthur was in full get up, tails and dicky-bow.

'Late night shift?' I asked him.

'Yes, worse luck. Long lie-in in the morning, though.'

'That's the stuff! Oh, this is Commander Howard of the United States Navy.'

Ben reached over and shook Arthur's hand as I introduced him.

'Pleased to meet you, sir. I hope my brother is taking good care of you?' Arthur asked.

'Couldn't be in better hands.'

Arthur then said he had to start work and I joked that he'd missed a decent tip. He pulled a pretend face which made Howard laugh and I asked him for another bottle.

He gave me a pained look. 'No chance, Jamie.'

Instead we had tea served. Howard said he preferred it to coffee. I told him how I'd revelled in that brew whilst in the States and he countered that if he knew he would have brought some over for me.

'Is there a Mrs Howard?' I then asked.

'There was. Not anymore. That old American tradition: two families push their kids together and out of politeness they get married. Result? You can guess.'

'Sorry to hear it.'

'She was a nice girl. I hope the best for her.'

'No kids?' He shook his head.

I puffed on my Tom Thumb. 'Anywhere in London you particularly want to see?'

'So many places but I doubt I'll have the time. The Portrait Gallery I *will* visit. Even if I have to throttle King.'

I didn't want to tell him that most of the treasures of the National Gallery had been hidden away in Wales since the outbreak of the war. Instead, I told him how I used to spend time there years ago with my old boss.

'Edward Marsh?' His eyes flickered with interest. '*The* Edward Marsh?'

'The very man.'

He then bombarded me with questions about the Georgian Group, Rupert Brooke and others. I told him about Isaac Rosenberg. He seemed enraptured and wanted to know every detail about my brief encounter with that enigmatic soul. I told him of meeting Siegfried Sassoon at Gray's Inn and of once telling Robert Ross, the great friend and defender of Oscar Wilde, to take his hand off my knee or I'd *batter fuck oot o' him*, a la Jock Paterson.

He roared with laughter at this final anecdote. 'Colourful characters, all! You've led a fascinating life, Jamie. How I envy you.'

I then couldn't resist telling him of Lady Pamela and Diana Manners and of that naked model I nearly sat on in Denmark Street. Of Violet Asquith calling me 'a bonnie wee laddie' and all the other beauties I'd come across.

'Jamie, I do believe you're just showing off now!' he joked.

We laughed uproariously together and in all I hadn't

enjoyed a night out so much for a long time. It certainly compensated for the loss of not being with Meredith. I'd also seen another side of my new acquaintance. There was more to him than met the eye, undoubtedly, but on this occasion, I tried to be content and enjoy the unexpected surprise of his good fellowship. I even remember wondering if he was in the Craft.

It was getting late. I'd done all the talking whilst he'd revealed little of note about himself.

But he'd told me enough.

'Jamie, you've been terrific but I think I'd better call it a night. I'm bushed!' He wanted to walk and we slowly made our way to the corner of Brook and Davies Street and stood outside the hotel.

'That was a great evening, Jamie. We have to meet up again before I leave.'

'That's a date! You know where to find me!' We shook hands and I left him. I made my way to North Street and as I walked happily on alone I thought about the events of a euphoric day. Meeting Meredith and *kissing* her; my feelings towards her now surely reciprocated. I wondered if it was all real.

Then nagging doubts about Howard and other matters reclaimed me, bitter in their depressing intrusion on my all too brief moment of happiness.

Chapter Sixteen

THE FOLLOWING DAY was a Sunday. I've never been one to loll about in bed all morning so I left North Street early for a wander, beckoned by a lovely late July day.

I'd had a restless night. Meredith, Howard; everything was moving too quickly for me. I've always believed that if your gut is telling you something isn't right, then it isn't right. But you have to decide if the reasons you're telling yourself that something isn't right are the correct ones or you can end up making a serious mistake. It was no use afterwards blaming it on your tummy.

I'd spent my life acting responsibly; from as far back as a child growing up in Edinburgh, caring for and earning money to ensure my sisters were fed and clothed, leading mum to her bed in many a drunken stupor, making certain she lay on her side so as to not choke on her own vomit (and cleaning up after). I'd not been allowed the luxury of letting events take their course. I had to influence them because, as I had learned from an early age, you rarely get a second chance; you can't go back and change things later.

I was conditioned to strive for an error-free existence, to be the one in control. It was either that or starvation, destitution, possibly even death. Only as I grew older and discussed with my grown children those times was I able to take cognisance of it from the point of view of others. I was never one to remind my own kids of my poor background. Now and again I'd make mention of the differences between my childhood and theirs. But of course, with children, that sort of thing goes over their heads.

What did I really want? Was I deliberately trying to back

away from Meredith? American women were more preda-
tory than British females. She had practically thrown herself
at me. But it didn't frighten or cause me to lose any attraction I felt for her. It was a cultural difference. I'd have to get
used to it. I consoled myself that I'd been out of the game
too long and maybe there was truth in the talk that I was a
catch. Though the very thought still remained absurd to me;
a fishmonger from Yorkshire.

There was nothing on for me that day. Winston's entourage
would not be back till the Monday. I was again at a loose
end. It would strike me that due to the paucity of acquaintances I had in London, I faced the prospect of the day alone.
Apart from the Whitehall staff, I knew no one; certainly no
one to socialise with. Gemma's brother David was in North
Africa. Heading home to Scarborough was too much bother.
There was only one option available to me.

When in doubt young man, go west. Or in this case, to
Grosvenor Square.

It may have been a Sunday but it was all hands at American
H.Q. I got chatting to a typist who told me that there would
be little rest for anyone over the coming weeks as the United
States H.Q. in Britain geared up its presence in London. Of
course, she would not have known much about the talks going on at that time but it looked like dates with my girl were
going to be at a premium. At least I knew why.

An army corporal shook my hand and led me through to
a corridor where Meredith sat with another girl. They were
on a coffee break. I was able only to offer a brief 'hello' and
receive a wink in return when I was hustled by the corporal
further on into the building to a poky side office occupied by
two naval officers, one of them being Commander Howard.

Ben greeted me with an effusive smile. 'You don't seem
to be having much luck seeing your girl, Jamie!' he ribbed
jocularly.

'You Yanks are in too much of a hurry to win the war!' I

joshed back. 'You should spend a little more time on developing inter-allied relationships.'

The other officer rose from his chair. 'Gotta go, Ben!' he declared, resignedly. 'I've got a lot of work to do myself. Nice to meet you, Mr Melville.' His hand was out and after I shook it he left us both together. Howard motioned to the vacated chair.

'That was real fun last night, Jamie. Once again, thanks.'

'No bother. I would appreciate you using your influence to allow a darling wee typist of yours time off for lunch though. Can you help me, Ben?'

'Sure! But first try this coffee.' The delicious aroma of coffee had distracted me since I'd entered the office. A fresh pot was steaming on his desk and he was obviously an accomplished mind-reader. He poured it into a mug and miraculously sugar appeared, he dropped not one but two lumps into the wonderful brew.

On seeing my lean and oh so hungry look, he laughed. 'To think the world's greatest empire has reached such a condition! Jamie, if I was to offer you a hundred gold dollars I still think you'd prefer a fistful of sugar cubes.'

'Ben, dollars don't taste as good as this!' It was heavenly, thick and like caramel. I sipped it slow, relishing it to the full.

'You know if a fella wanted to bribe you, Jamie...?'

'I'd happily sink into perfidy if this was on offer.' I lit a Tom Thumb, my first of the day. We chatted easily for a while about how he was settling in and then laid out my problem to him.

'The deal is this,' I said. 'You get me Meredith for lunch and I'll take you out for some more sightseeing. If a busy man like you has the time, of course.'

'You got it,' he grinned. 'Now, Meredith *who*?'

He was as good as his word and we arranged a lunchtime date. Howard wanted to go for a stroll as my part of the bargain and we headed into the centre of the city. We cut through Berkeley Square towards Piccadilly as he started happily whistling the tune about that old nightingale.

'You know? This sure is a great town. You can feel it. The people are undaunted. They go on. They *endure*. I'm so glad to be here.' He seemed in very good spirits.

We walked on into Leicester Square. We stopped for a look around then made our way towards the other one, at Trafalgar.

'Jamie, do you mind if we take a breather here for a moment?'

We sat and he gazed at the Column as I had done earlier with Meredith. Where we were situated seemed appropriate as a number of the key moments of my life had been spent there. He then got up and walked over to look at the uncovered plaque on view. I sat back, removed my coat and had a smoke.

'Well, I've now seen it!' he said contentedly as he returned to me. He wasn't the only serviceman around that morning. There were sailors and airman with their girls, groups together laughing and ribbing each other. Blokes climbing up onto the plinths, gesticulating and showing off. It was a happy scene.

'We'll have to find you an English rose while you're here,' I said, noting one Yank sucking the face of a hardly-resisting young local.

Howard was looking at the couple also. 'All in good time,' he chided dreamily.

I puffed away. 'What was China like?'

He grinned. 'You've got that lunch date, Jamie, how much time have you got?'

'I like to hear travel tales,' I shrugged.

We got up and started to walk. We made for Admiralty Arch and strolled slowly along the Mall. After some moments of silence as he gazed fixedly at buildings, he spoke. 'China. It's kind of tough. For a start it's more than a country. It's another world, unlike anything you've known. It smells so different for one thing.'

'Yes, human shit, I believe. They use that for fertiliser.' Apart from the stereotypes of the time – Chinese laundrymen, chopsticks, opium and Oriental inscrutability with a bit of *Charlie Chan* thrown in – I was as ignorant as the next man about that land.

He became serious but not to the extent that I felt I'd overstepped any kind of mark.

'We tried to export our so-called culture over there. Our modern form of civilization which we're so convinced is superior. But the fact is we failed entirely to understand that their civilization is deeply embedded.'

'You mean you behaved just like any other imperialists?'

He continued in the same vein ignoring my comment. 'The Chinese invented paper and gunpowder. Silk, porcelain and ceramics but we'd cheer as we believed we made headway in changing their culture to ours. And applaud as bit by bit that magnificent heritage was devalued.' He spoke as if lecturing a child. It was a mannerism I wasn't prepared for and it irked me.

'If you mean trying to stop them binding the feet of children and killing baby girls, then where lies the problem with that?'

He smiled. 'Like you British tried to abolish *Suttee*? Tell me, Jamie, who thanked you for that? The Chinese are a people with four thousand years of civilization. They have superstitions that encapsulate every part of their daily lives. And it starts at the top with their Emperor. He's not immune to it either.

'When they publicly behead criminals, children run up and hold coins over the spouts of blood shooting from the decapitated corpse. They hope to catch drops and then hang the coin in a chain round their necks in order to ward off evil spirits. Do you think that a crucified man is going to upset them? He was executed between two criminals, remember.

'As for the women, they are *nothing*.' He emphasised the last a little too strongly for my liking. 'They're chattel, owned first by their father or their brother and then if they're lucky, their husband. They don't even have names when they're born. They're given a number. Those who, as you said aren't drowned or strangled immediately after birth.'

'So, what's wrong with missionaries going out there to try and help to change things?' I asked.

'The Chinese people aren't interested in Jesus Christ. Since the early 1800s Americans went there and tried to bring the word of God to a people who'd rather have something to eat. Why preach about the Shepherd of the Lord to people who don't know what a sheep is and have never seen one? And of a "Devil" with horns and a tail? The Dragon is a sacred symbol of reverence in China!'

'What's the answer then?'

He looked ahead as we approached Buckingham Palace. We took a seat on a bench. He sat at the end, looking over at the King's residence.

'Not Christianity. My father wanted to go out there under the auspices of the Student Volunteer Movement. The VAM. He came from a wealthy background but he got the *Call*. He wanted to go out there but they told him he had to get married first. It wouldn't look good morally for a single man to go alone. Only problem was he couldn't find a girl to marry him on those terms. Eventually he found my mother, who did say yes. But she wouldn't marry him if he became a missionary.

'He was a frustrated man but still determined. His father had business dealings out there so he went to work in the Shanghai office. He learned to speak Chinese and on weekends he went out to villages on his own and started literacy classes for any peasants who were interested. The funny thing was, not many of the adults were but most sent their children. As for the villagers, he discussed modern agricultural methods with them. Some took them on board, most didn't.

'He told me an old missionary found out about it and collared him. He lambasted him and told him that he should be teaching them the Word of God. Could he not see their poverty? Christ was needed in their lives! There was nothing to be gained by learning to read! They were a dishonest, morally corrupt and lamentable people who only God himself could save.

'My father didn't see this old man as representative of the kind of missionary that was needed. He believed that education was the answer. Along with like-minded others, he believed that if China was to take its place at the table of leading nations of the world, a gradual influence by the Missions based on prosperity and education was the essential requirement to bring the country forward. Jesus Christ was supplemental.'

'And you?' I asked.

'I was born there. I was seven years old before my parents came back to America for their leave period. When we returned I became a day student at the American School in Shanghai. My Grandfather then insisted I go to Yale but I wanted to go to Oberlin. He got his way.' He looked at me with a melancholy smile.

'I *so* wanted Oberlin. A lot of the other kids were going there. Sons of missionaries but I didn't, and after that straight to the Academy at Annapolis and the Navy. *I* had to pay the price for my father's rebellion. But I left and joined the Foreign Service.'

'What was that like?'

His smile grew warmer in remembrance of this time of happiness and fulfilment in his life. 'That was what I really wanted. I was able to do *something* at last. We were sent to Hankow at first. People get shuffled around, Yunnan-Fu, Tsingtao, Peking, wherever. It's a small community, everyone knows each other. You take your turn in each consulate.

'In Hankow I was asked to go out and gather information on the local communists. As a political officer it was my job. I went everywhere. To all the foreign legations. Spoke to newspapermen, local party headquarters. I went to places that I shouldn't have but had to in order to find things out. I was praised by the old hands. I went where nobody else would go.'

He laughed joyfully. 'I meet Chou En-lai himself! Hankow was also where Chiang was based back then. I was making steady contacts with the communists. Whilst many believed they were a spent force I gathered evidence to prove they owned about a fifth of the country and were getting stronger.

'My argument was that in order for there to be a revolution that would succeed, unlike in 1911 and 1927, the great mass of people of China must be included. A kind of socialism, inclusive of all levels of society was the way forward. Please understand, I'm not a socialist but based on my observations, what Chou was espousing was a more realistic and encompassing vision than that of Chiang. I mean, what is Chiang? What is his *vision*? He's just the bandit with the biggest army.

'All the Kuomintang do is exploit the people. Do you know they have nearly a hundred different taxes? They even tax the kettles the peasants use to cook with. I heard a story that a warlord had a whole bunch of tyres he "liberated" from a warehouse. They were sent over from the States as aid. He made all the locals who had carts buy rubber tyres to replace the traditional wooden ones. He then taxed the tyres.'

He sighed in conclusion. 'Of course the biggest problem right now is the Japanese. They must be defeated first.'

'And then Chiang and the communists fight over the spoils?' I didn't know much about such matters but I knew enough that for all the faults of Chiang and his Nationalists, at least they were *fighting* the invaders.

'That is a problem, yes.'

'What's the answer?'

He leant back and crossed his arms. 'I don't know. But at

least I'm going to get the opportunity to go back there. I'm being transferred to General Stilwell's staff. A lot of guys I knew from the service are with him already. John Davies is in New Delhi where I'll meet up with him before we make our way to Stilwell's H.Q. in Chungking.'

"Vinegar Joe" Stilwell was the senior American General in the Far East theatre. He was notoriously irascible, anti-British and pig-headed but undoubtedly brilliant. It was said the job he'd been given was the most difficult assignment of the entire war. In effect he had to deal with Chiang Kai-shek and to make him fight the Japanese instead of his own internal enemies such as the communists. Such a delicate task required tact and diplomacy and Stilwell had none of either. It was an endeavour doomed to failure from the start.

'But he's not Navy,' I stated.

'Jamie, I'm going as a China Hand. They're short on linguists out there. I had to get on my knees and beg release from the Admiral before he gave in to me! Fortunately, King and Stilwell are on the same wavelength about Japan They're both sons of bitches, too!' he laughed. 'I'm swapping one tyrant for another! Stilwell's vision is one I share. He loves China too but he hates their leaders!'

I asked him why he left the Foreign Service. A subtle change came over him. He remained silent for a moment and then responded in a weary monotone.

'My superiors viewed my report on the communists with a mixture of disdain and awe. One of them said, "We don't need to know half of this." It was generally deemed to paint too pretty a picture of the Reds. I didn't set out to do that, believe me. But that's how it was regarded.'

'And that caused problems for you?'

He stopped. I now sensed another change of mood. He seemed to almost turn in on himself, as if he had realised that he had said too much and was thinking back on which parts to refute. At that moment, he felt entirely false and alien to me; any former liking I had for him dissipated. In what was for me a rare moment of perception, I saw him for what he truly was, a charming liar and dissembler.

For better or worse, I chose that moment to ask what I really wanted to know. 'Tell me this, what did you want from me in Washington?'

He stood up and spoke impatiently. 'You've got a date.'

I rose to my feet with him. 'There's enough time. Who is Meredith to you?'

'You know the answer to that.'

'Stop fucking me about, Howard. Is she your wife?'

He drew in a breath. 'Yes. We're separated. She's yours now, it seems. She likes you.'

His manner angered me and I grabbed him furiously. He didn't move but looked from his arm to me. 'Jamie, calm yourself,' he said mildly.

I kept a grip of his forearm. 'Listen to me. Whatever you were up to in Washington, leave that girl out of it. You tried to get her to screw me for some reason. Well, you should know, she doesn't do that. You picked the wrong girl. And I know why you met up with me at the Memorial. You wanted a second look. For what? To see if I was queer because I hadn't done the job on her?'

He then pulled away from me. He was flustered and his face coloured. I'd rattled him somewhat unexpectedly. I'm pretty good at that with people who make the mistake of underestimating me.

'I have no idea what you're referring to. Meredith? She works for the State Department. I have nothing to do with her any longer.'

'You're a liar. I don't know why exactly. Not yet anyway.' I released his arm. 'I think you've been playing me for a prick. I believe Meredith is being used. I'll warn you now, leave her alone. Keep *away* from her. Or I swear I'll give you the beating of your life.'

I shoved him away angrily and strode off leaving him by

the bench. I'd lost my temper and hadn't handled it very well. I wasn't cut out for this kind of thing but I was certain I wasn't wrong.

I was now down an American friend. I thought about Gemma as I wandered back towards Whitehall. I wanted her then so much it hurt as painfully as the pounding I was giving the concrete, which wasn't doing my leg any favours.

It was something I did a lot. I would find myself muttering her name and talking out loud as I carried out conversations in my head with her. I'd hear her reply to me in her common sense way and she would tell me what to do for the best. We even talked about Meredith. She was non-committal on that subject.

I *was* out of my depth here in London. I wanted to return to my real life again. I'd tried to be the *big man* and discovered I wasn't very good at it. I might have been wildly wrong about everything.

I scolded myself. *Rubbish*, Jamie! You know when something stinks. You've got a job to do. It could affect Winston and his security, along with the girls and even Tom's family, which were all I cared about. I decided to keep my lunch appointment but endeavour to do as Howard had advised and remain calm.

I had an hour to kill and popped into the War Rooms. I really wanted to talk to Brookie, though I knew he was not yet back from Chequers. Walter would be with Winston. I could try to find Brendan but instead I went to my room and lay on the bed.

At times like these, I would think of Gemma's grandmother. Years before, when I was a lad in London, I'd visit her from time to time. My own grandmother had left a strong impression on me and if truth be told, she was the greatest influence on my early childhood. I would run off to her home in Colinton, which was some distance away and pour my troubles out to her. She would console me and hand money and parcels of food to take away with me. She provided me with unconditional love, care and good advice; the very kind I failed to receive from her own daughter, my mother. She died when I was fourteen and her absence left a terrible void in my life.

Gemma's grandma filled that gap again somewhat. She was a marvellous woman who cared not a fig for the stuffy mores of the times she lived in. She was something of a monster but whatever she was, she saw something in me as Winston had. She became my confidant and surrogate mother for a time. I think I've always needed a woman like that in my life. When you are the one who has to carry the concerns of others, to negate your own life in consequence, it is liberating to find someone who recognises the burden you carry and is always there with patience and understanding. Gemma performed that duty, too, in her own way. God, I missed them all. Those three wonderful women I was fortunate to have in my life, none of whom was my *real* mother.

That's what I saw in Meredith. I thought of her as someone like that. She was strong and opinionated and tough, like them but also incredibly feminine and attractive. I was certain about her; I *wanted* it to be true.

There was a knock on my door. It was a secretary from Downing Street. 'Mr Melville?'

'Yes?' I rolled off the bed.

'I'm to advise you, sir, that the Prime Minister will return this evening and wishes to see you.'

I said thanks and got to my feet as the secretary closed the door. I felt instantly cheered and remembered that I was running low on cigars.

I made the lunch date with Meredith and found a small restaurant off North Audley Street. It was pretty poor fare but it was busy and noisy and suited my purposes. She was as vivacious as before, took my arm and asked me where her kiss was as we left her office.

'You Americans are so demanding! But here it comes!' and we embraced and kissed on the street.

We walked off hand in hand and arrived at the restaurant. There, she was introduced to egg and chips. I admit I felt embarrassed, but food was food to her and she tucked in with a will.

I had a form of tomato soup with a couple of slices of bread. I wasn't hungry. God, war-time food was grim. I had actually lost weight since coming down to London and was now under eleven stone. Back home there was plenty of seafood nefariously acquired to fill me up which I missed.

I'd mentioned this to her, but she palmed away my concern. 'Jamie, don't worry about that. You're gorgeous and I like you as you are! But I think we should keep an eye on you! I don't want you wasting away to nothing!'

'I'm more worried about you! You'll be a shadow in six months on London rations!'

'No, no! I'm doing something about that! I'm getting packages sent to me from the States! And we're given extra at the embassy, so don't worry about me fading away!'

'A bottle or two of bourbon included?' I asked hopefully.

She reached over and gently rubbed my face. 'I'm taking care of my boy, don't worry, honey!'

I think at that moment I nearly told her the words I believed I felt were genuine. I was as sure as I could be that she wasn't putting it on. I'd noted in Washington that she was no actress.

'Meredith? Who is Ben Howard?' I then asked instead, foolishly regarding it as the easier option.

She continued chewing her food but slower. Her face seemed to pale as a sombre look came over her. She put both hands on the table.

'I have to ask you. Please tell me,' I pleaded gently.

'Jamie, not here. Please.'

'Finish your meal. Then we have to talk.' She picked at her food which was obviously not an encouraging sign. Then she gave up and pushed the plate aside. We'd already paid the bill and got up to leave.

'Where are we going?' she asked, her entire being now seemed a fount of misery.

'Don't worry, it's not far.'

It was difficult with her. She became almost child-like and walked slowly and deliberately as if she was being led into the headmaster's office for punishment. I comforted her as we turned into Upper Brook Street and headed for Hyde Park. We found a spot and sat down, looking over at one of the anti-aircraft gun emplacements that filled its grounds.

We sat together silently. She was rigid with some deep concern and kept her head down.

'Meredith, let me say first, I don't know everything. But I have to ask you about Howard.' I took her hand and with my other held it between both.

'*Please*,' I urged desperately. 'I have to know what is going on.'

She stayed silent and then without lifting her head, she spoke in a slow, ponderous monotone.

'What's *going on* is that he wanted me to sleep with you.'

'Who? Ben?'

'He's my husband.'

I gave no indication that I already knew that. 'Why was he using you?'

She then lifted her head up and looked at me. 'Jamie, you're *real*. I was told you had lost your wife. That I only had to look at you and I'd get you into bed, as any man would. I was to stay the night with you and that's all.'

Ignoring this I asked, 'What does Ben do in the Navy?'

'Intelligence.'

I looked at her knowing I had to press on and hating myself for it.

'Don't you want to see me anymore?' she wailed distressingly before I could speak. She looked up at me, her eyes big with pleading. She looked back down at her hands. 'I wouldn't blame you. I thought I got a break, being sent to London. To get away from it all. Ben blew it on both accounts. He never for one moment thought I'd *like* you. He didn't know you were kind and sweet and *different*. Don't be put off by his charm. He has charm, but he's also ruthless and unfeeling.'

'And he wanted you to whore for him? Nice. *Very* nice.' I spoke more to myself than to her.

But she heard me, of course. 'He was so handsome. Our parents pushed us together. Well, my mother did. My mother is so foolish. Looks are everything to her. And money. He has both.'

'He told me he grew up in China.' I attempted to push the conversation on.

'I met him when he was at Annapolis. He was dazzling. The most beautiful boy I'd ever seen.' I still didn't know what her sleeping with me would achieve.

'Meredith, have you any idea what he wanted from me? Why he used you?'

'Don't be like them, Jamie. Please.'

I understood her. 'I'm not, dear. Believe me. I've been used, too. I was just a donkey to bring something back from Washington. I only found that out when I returned to London.'

'Was it in your cane?'

I nearly fell off the bench. 'How did you know?' I said trying to keep control of feelings slowly beginning to boil over.

'Ben wanted me to pass the cane over to him while you slept.'

'Christ!' I exclaimed in shock.

She became noticeably frightened.

'Sorry!' I tried to ease her obvious fears. 'It's just … oh, don't worry about that. We've both been set up good and proper! But please, Meredith, please tell me why? Why did you do this?'

Winston had told me that there was nothing in the cane when I took it to Washington. Dansey later told him that the enclosed package he'd removed in Downing Street had been what was expected and not been tampered with.

'I … I *owed* him.'

Mystified, I move closer to her. 'Owed him what?'

'Oh, please, please! No more! I'm not a whore! Oh, God, Jamie. I … I have feelings for you. Please believe me! I just want to be with *you*, now! I feel safe with you! Don't ask me anymore!'

I didn't, and held her as she sobbed on my shoulder. People passed and looked over but I ignored them and let her cry herself out.

She stopped and I lifted her head. Her face was that of desolate and pitiful child as tears ran down her cheeks. I bit back my self-loathing.

'Look,' I said. 'I'm going nowhere. We'll talk about this another time. No one is going to use you anymore. I told Ben Howard this morning to stay away from you or he'll have to deal with me. And believe, me, I'm a tough wee lad! No one messes with me!' My attempt to lighten things fell flat and my levity was soon replaced with a feeling of revulsion, with Howard, with her, with myself.

She seemed to perk up a little and a handkerchief appeared as she dabbed her eyes. 'Jamie, I just can't talk now. I think I'd better get back.'

'I'm going to see you again? Aren't I? Meredith?' I held her by her arms and looked at her imploringly.

'Yes,' she answered almost inaudibly, but I wasn't convinced. We walked back to the embassy and I left her at the entrance. She didn't kiss me.

My tally of American friends had reduced even further.

Chapter Seventeen

Sawyers handed me the box and I split the seal and removed a cigar while Winston refilled our glasses. We were left alone together in his study in the Annexe that evening. He was out of his suit and tie, having removed his collar and changed into his off-white duck trousers and slippers. We were discussing the subject of *stogies*.

'Really, James! It's about time you smoked a *proper* cigar!' Winston complained after an interminable monologue on the origin of the weed.

I'd heard him out, bored silly and allowed my exasperation to show. 'Colonel, you hardly *smoke* them yourself! At least *I* inhale mine! You chew the bloody things half the time! And leave a disgusting mess! As I know too well.'

'How dare you! I have been *smoking* them for over fifty years!' he riposted, furiously.

I reached over for some of the snacks Frank left us. 'No, you haven't,' I countered, smugly.

On his feet by the drinks table, Winston blew a huge smoke-ring that seemed to hang in the air like a floating doughnut before it slowly dissipated.

'Do that, then!' he challenged.

'No. Waste of a good *inhalation*,' I replied.

'At least you are starting to drink properly,' he granted generously.

He had finally, after more than twenty-five years, talked me into watering down my whisky with soda. But whereas he weakened his to the extent that you could hardly tell the difference, I insisted on two fingers before the soda drowned out all the goodness.

'That's both fingers to you as well,' he said after handing me my glass.

I gave him the "V" sign in return. 'Better be.'

I was obeying the summons from earlier that day. Clemmie was absent on war-work and as it was Sunday he had for once graciously allowed his usual entourage of military men, secretaries and various hangers-on the night off. They had all bolted immediately, as he often changed his mind on a whim, the selfish old bugger. I was touched but not surprised that he'd requested my company.

Still on the subject of alcohol, we then discussed Bourbon and I told him of my discovery in Washington. He was not too keen on it himself, he declared, but was willing to be a participant. We then spoke of the Americans and the talks.

'Brooke and I will tell them that there is no viable alternative to an invasion of North Africa. The Americans will have to accept it as a *fait accompli* and report back to the President. We will not back down on our position.'

'Do they know this?'

'They may suspect it, but I believe they are trying one last push for France.'

'But the President clearly wants North Africa,' I pointed out. 'Unless he's changed his mind, or *they've* changed it for him.'

'Like all military men they cannot see the bigger picture. Like all military men they believe politicians are dolts on military strategy. I am not a dolt and neither is the President. But they must be given their lead. They are servants not the master. They shall be listened to and then when we have listened, we will order them to do what is to be done.'

It all sounded a bit churlish to me. But if anyone thinks the meetings of great men are anything special, they're wrong. They argue, cajole and shout at each other and go off in the huff just like the rest of us mortals. And as often as not, they get things wrong.

I was certainly with Winston regarding strategy on invading France this year, 1942. There was nothing in the tank.

Everything we had was stretched to the limit, made worse by our new enemy: Japan.

Though we'd moved on in two years somewhat, the handing over of 150,000 men at Singapore was a serious setback. Strategically, the fall of Tobruk was far less problematic in comparison. All that did was extend Rommel's already precarious supply lines, which was the Achilles heel of both armies in the Western Desert. With the exception of India, we'd been kicked out of our Asian empire and even the Jewel itself was now in a precarious position after we were hounded from Burma.

That's why to attempt a dicey invasion into France with nowhere near the amount of basic shipping required, no control of the air and a far from beaten foe to face was lunacy at that stage. Even the Yanks admitted themselves it would take two years to build the necessary vessels required for the task. They were being too impatient and recalling the conduct of some of their generals in 1918, they should have been grateful to the Prime Minister for his wisdom in the matter rather than try to force the issue.

Winston was content to let the Soviets soak up the losses. And why shouldn't he? The Russians were Hitler's bosom buddies not so long before, carving up Poland between them and supplying them with millions of tons of raw material for their war effort against us up to the very day before the German invasion. People forget that these days. At one point we nearly fought the Russians ourselves in Finland, before the operation to attack was called off.

That's not to say he was sanguine about Soviet losses. I knew he wasn't. But he was realistic about the limitations of citizen armies and what they could and could not achieve. The early reversals of the war profoundly shocked him. He was a Victorian and with few exceptions was used to the British Tommy being able to endure and overcome any hardship despite poor leadership. But now, it seemed even that was failing; and it frightened him to his very core.

I was considering all this and voiced a question that had been worrying me.

'But what about the time when the Americans have overtaken us in men and material? What kind of say will we have then?'

'By that stage, we will have squeezed Hitler from all sides to such an extent, weakening him fatally, that we will be able to freely sail across the channel and complete our mission.'

That was the strategy that won us the Empire, of course. Whenever an upstart in Europe tried to upset the delicate balance of power we'd form an alliance with everyone else and attack on all fronts, together. It invariably worked. Except when we were the upstart, fighting the Americans for their "independence" and the rest of Europe had seen their chance and done for us.

This time, we had no allies in Europe except the Russians and they were almost on their knees. Stalingrad, the great victory that turned the tide was over six months away. It was still touch and go whether the Soviets could continue battling on as the Germans launched their tremendous Operation Blue which initially swept all aside as they swung away from Moscow for the Caucasus and the oilfields. There was the very real danger that we'd be evicted from North Africa and the Germans would meet up in the Middle East. If they did, the war was lost.

There could be no risky all or nothing invasion at this present time. But something had to be done to relieve pressure on the Soviet Union. There were over a quarter of a million Axis soldiers in North Africa. They were being held at present – only just. Winston was determined that North Africa was where we should strike the first serious blow of the war. Practically speaking, it was the only place anyway.

It required a delicate balancing act from the President also. He fully concurred with North Africa, Winston believed, but still had to contend with the Japan First lobby. From my experience, I wasn't sure how he could achieve this.

'He is a politician of consummate artistry, James,' Winston pronounced on my voicing the question. 'He shall find a way.'

I left it at that and filled him in on my last few days. I went into every detail of my confrontations with Howard and Meredith. He was my one true friend and I held nothing back. I knew that leaving out any detail was impossible anyway as he always asked me so many questions that he would have got the truth out sooner or later. I was used to him being my confessor and felt completely uninhibited.

'You have acted correctly though, as always, James. Your heart will out before your head but you always come through in the end. That angel of yours watches over you with a careful eye!'

We had a private joke between us about that. I'd told him earnestly years ago as a laddie at the 6th that I believed in such things and that one looked after me. It might not have been as fanciful as you think, considering the scrapes I'd got into in my life.

'I feel as though I've mucked things up, Winston,' I fretted. 'Especially with Meredith.'

'I sense the depth of your feeling towards this young lady, James. Clemmie and I have spoken many times of our concerns for you. She has made suggestions to me on finding suitable appointments into the Melville household on a number of occasions! And Diana and Sarah have done the rounds on your behalf also!'

'What? You're kidding me on!' I was genuinely surprised to hear such a revelation.

'Naturally you would not think of such matters,' he grinned. 'But that is you! You never stop to think that there may be others who care for you and are concerned for your welfare.'

I drained my glass and got up for a refill. He handed me his and I topped it up. I wondered who some of these ladies were…

'And some particular beauties, I can tell you!' he chuckled, reading my thoughts. He then mentioned a couple of names which I won't divulge and I nearly choked on my drink when I returned to my chair.

'Really? Away with yourself! Lady ------?' (I spoke the name of a certain highborn stunner I'd met once at Chartwell.)

'She practically drooled whenever your name was mentioned.' He was enjoying himself, the *auld wifie.*

'I wish I knew more in order to be sure, about Howard, I mean,' I said, returning to more serious matters. 'By diving in head-first today I might have looked like a fool. Maybe I've got the wrong end of things with Meredith. Maybe I expected her to want to tell me everything far too quickly.'

Winston stretched over and patted my hand in sympathy.

'Oh, well,' I sighed. 'Ships that pass in the night, eh?'

Next morning I made my way to Downing Street where John Martin handed me some tasks to perform in light of the imminent talks with the American delegation.

I plugged away till lunch time. I was glad of the work as it helped to take my mind of Meredith. Maybe it was all a case of wishful thinking. She was a visitor in town, I was the only person she knew and I was jumping to conclusions. I'd shown her kindness; though to me, it was just ordinary decency. But I couldn't escape the fact that she was involved in treasonous activities during war-time and I'd nearly come a cropper through her deceit.

But I still thought of her. I've never been one of those types who falls for wrong 'uns. I still felt a residue of respect if not liking for Howard, too. After all, what was his crime? America was still polarised regarding the war. Not to the extent it was prior to December 7th 1941, now it was mainly about who was the real enemy and for many, it was Japan. The anti-British feeling was still rampant; *why should America fight to get back Britain's empire?* was a constant theme among many Americans.

Howard and his cronies were acting where others merely shouted loudly and printed columns in newspapers. Admiral King was of the same point of view and so was General MacArthur. I was not that naïve however. I understood that it was damaging to us and had to be dealt with. We were guilty of doing our utmost to bring America into the war ourselves before Pearl Harbour and had an espionage network set up in Washington dedicated to achieving that goal.

My only post-Gemma romance, if you could even describe it as that, had proven a disaster. I wondered if I liked Meredith so much because I was *desperate* to. I just didn't know for sure. But I still thought of her. She was a poor soul from what I now knew about her. Though in reality, I didn't know that much at all. I promised myself that, if there were a next time, I'd avoid lame ducks. They're too much like hard work.

At noon I told John I was off to get some lunch at the nearby Lyons Tea Room but on leaving the building I was approached by Walter Thompson, who informed me that Winston wanted me round to his place for lunch. Walter raised his eyebrows even as he told me and I also gave him a look, as Winston was not known for such generosity during the working day towards his staff. Then again, I wasn't exactly a normal member of his inner circle.

We both made the short walk to the Annexe and on entering his study where I'd spoken with him the evening before, through the tobacco fumes I made out Winston seated, peering over a document. On my entering the room he dropped the paper onto a small table. He wasn't wearing his coat but his waistcoat was bulging at the seams and his bow tie was undone with one end longer than the other, hanging around his collar. Harry Hopkins, in rolled up shirt sleeves and tie loosened, sat in the chair I sat on previously looking over a paper of his own.

After leaving him at Euston Station, I hadn't seen much of Harry. I was happy to renew our acquaintance as his pleasant demeanour always cheered me.

He looked up from his reading. 'Well! Lover boy! How's it goin'?'

'How dare you describe James Melville as such? He is first and foremost a warrior, Heart of Midlothian Football Club supporter, *then* a great lover, in that order!' Winston declared humorously.

I shook Harry's hand and plumped down on the settee next to Winston.

'Please, Colonel! Not at this time!' I moaned loudly as he had risen to make drinks and we settled after some debate on tonic water. Sawyers entered with a plate of sandwiches which he handed to me and then left, muttering to himself about "mucky pups."

'We've eaten, at least I have!' Winston explained about the plates, empty cups, crumbs and crusts that lay about the room. What a pair of slobs they were. 'How this stringy American remains breathing is one of the great mysteries of life,' he added playfully.

'A diet of good Scotch and tobacco is all a man requires,' Harry answered amiably. It was a prophetic statement as one or both would assist in killing him one day.

I munched on the sandwiches, sat back and relaxed. Winston and Harry spoke about the upcoming talks. From where I was sitting I could just make out the document that was on the table that Winston had laid down.

I stood up and walked over to the chair where Sawyers laid my coat and removed a cigar. I advanced to where I stood directly behind Winston and made slow work of lighting up.

The letter bore the header:

THE WHITE HOUSE
WASHINGTON

It was addressed to "Winston" but what was mystifying was that it was hand written and not typed. It comprised only a few lines. I made out some words including "Gymnast a real goer," whatever that meant, and it was signed by "Franklin."

'Jamie, I insist you have a whisky. In fact, as your commanding officer, I order it!' Winston was in terrific mood and I could see that refusing a second offer was not an option.

He handed me an industrial-sized glassful. 'Oh, the ice! Sawyers!' he roared and the blast caught me in the side of the face.

'Steady, Colonel! You nearly deafened me there!'

'My boy! I do so apologise. But that man knew you were coming and forgot the most important ingredient of the Melville brew!'

'You're very happy today, Winston!' I pointed out, chewing away on my sandwich after returning to the settee.

'Indeed I am! Our allies are here, we are no longer alone and we have the opportunity now to plan real action! Of course it is a happy day!'

I took him at face value but I knew him well enough. On entering the room and seeing him alone with Hopkins, it had given even me pause. And I'm not exactly in the Machiavellian mould as you'll have noted by now. Something was up.

I let it pass over my head. I'd had enough of double-dealings. In fact, I wanted no more. The work I'd done that morning for John was enough for me. I was entrusted with viewing important documents and doing something worthwhile, even if it was just glorified office work. I also knew in being close to Winston there would always be the chance of something out of the ordinary rearing its unwelcome head. I think at that moment, at the age of forty-one, I accepted I was getting old.

'Just what I want to hear, Colonel,' I replied as positively as I could.

'Now, Harry here is at a loose end today and I want you to take him out for drinks and then to dinner later,' Winston ordered.

'I suppose I could do that,' I replied, 'but you better square it away with John Martin as he has work for me this afternoon.'

He suddenly became irritated and angrily dismissive. 'Oh, to hell with Martin! James, you are not here solely to push paper around!'

I felt like asking what the devil *was* I here for, but an afternoon in Harry's company was probably what I needed after the last couple of days.

I always loved July in London – the way, as a child, I used to like the month of August in Edinburgh best. I say 'like' because I have never felt any love for my home town. Many people are like that; I don't believe I'm alone in this. Why should anyone feel compelled to admit affection for the place where fate gave them their beginning? To please the petty and jealous minds of some of those you left behind in all likelihood. I love Scarborough; I only *come* from Edinburgh.

But August seemed to be the one month when we always got hot, sunny weather. I used to walk to Princes Street and sit in the Gardens with a book and a bottle of pop every Sunday. I looked on it as my little holiday to myself, away from the mayhem of room and kitchen life. I'd watch the steam trains going past from Waverley Station below the Castle rocks and dream of being on one, riding away to some destination far removed from the unhappiness of reality.

That day did arrive eventually though not in the way I could ever have imagined. As I sat with Harry after we'd lunched in St James's Park, I recalled those times to him.

'You got out, Jamie. You made something of your life. My old man just wanted to bowl for a livin'! Yeah, can you believe that? That was never enough for me. They say if you do better in life than your parents then you haven't failed. You succeeded.'

I didn't want to say anything about my recent adventures but I knew he'd mention Meredith.

'I saw her,' I replied to his prompt. He didn't press further. We got up and started walking slowly through the Park.

He asked about my girls and told me he was getting married as soon as he returned to the States. I congratulated him and said that was great to hear and wished I could be there for the wedding.

'I'd love to have you there, pal. I'm pretty sure a word in the right ear could get you on the seaplane back with us.'

I took it that he was serious. He was the most generous of souls and maybe he sensed my troubled frame of mind and was trying to help.

'No, I don't think so,' I replied, a little distant. We walked on.

'Can I say something, Jamie?' he asked. I shrugged indifferently as he carried on, 'It's terribly difficult to know what to do for the best after you lose someone. For a time I just plunged into work. It helped somewhat but you can never really escape the moments when they come. Even the most mundane things remind you. And stab at you. You flinch inside and turn your head away from them in recoil.'

He'd lost his second wife to cancer. Strangely, it had been in the same year, 1937, when I lost Gemma. I listened to his soft voice as we slowly wandered along the path.

'You think of some ... betrayal. A kind of *infidelity in thought*, when the moments come and you want to throw it off you. You are angry, after all. And it can be so tiring. But because it's so much easier, you just return to it and the comfort of that very reluctance to *renew* embraces you, though you hate it and lose yourself in it all over again.'

'I can't throw off Gemma. I just don't know *how* to let go,' I responded forlornly, understanding him only too well.

We walked on silently.

'Take that little girl, Meredith,' he continued after a short time. 'I know something about her. She's someone who's been through some hard times. Oh, you'll say, "not as tough as I have, I reckon." But then she meets someone completely unlike anyone she's ever met before. She's thrown, too. Only, in an agreeable way. Alright, she may not be who she seems.

At *first*. But people are still people and is anyone what they appear to be *at first*?'

We'd stopped as we'd now walked almost the entire park. We were back at my favourite spot, the bench where I sat years before at the Horse Guards end. The bench where I used to while away the time to think and to reflect. I'd subconsciously made my way to it like some primal memory. In this case, not so ancient, but as profound as any other.

He put a hand on my shoulder. 'Just some thoughts I have. From my own experience of course. I don't want to impose. But sometimes a friend has to say *something*, I guess.'

I looked over the pleasant, bright, sunlit view. From Prince's Street Gardens to St James's Park half a lifetime later, I was still dreaming of leaving something behind.

Chapter Eighteen

THE DISCUSSIONS CONTINUED over the next three days at the War Office. Winston and Brooke listened as Marshall presented his plan and Admiral King sat seething as our side stonewalled.

The American chiefs were attempting one final throw for a small scale invasion of France that year. It still seems incredible to think that they pushed so hard for it. Their plan was to land an army in Cherbourg where they expected it to hold out for a year while a major force built up in England. That force would then thrust across the Channel and hurl itself against the Germans.

Brooke dismissed it by claiming the original contingent wouldn't see the year out before it was destroyed. King then demanded that if that was our concern then they, the Americans, would turn their attentions elsewhere, meaning the Pacific. He thumped the table but Brookie thumped back harder.

In staccato tones the Irishman explained why the US plan was doomed to failure. In that rapid voice of his he shot them down completely point by point. Marshall was humble enough to hear him out; King had to be persuaded back to his seat as he had stormed out, refusing to listen.

It was a period of terrible strain for everyone involved. They all wanted the war to end as quickly as possible with as little loss of life as was within their power. They were two morally courageous men. Marshall had never heard a shot fired in anger in all his years as a soldier. Brooke had seen what poor planning, even worse execution and the efficiency of the German foe resulted in when commanding his division of the British Expeditionary Force in France in 1940.

He had personally saved the 2nd BEF from catastrophe after it landed in France under his command in a hopeless quest to assist the beaten French army. In a furious cross-channel telephone exchange, he had shouted down Churchill and demanded that the army be returned to England, rather than have it destroyed for some chivalric but futile urge of Winston's to save a dying ally. A stunned Churchill allowed the General his way. He filed away the name of the fierce Ulsterman for the future.

Marshall and Brooke were both extraordinarily *humane* individuals who shared a deep loathing for war and all the agony it caused. They only differed on how to go about achieving their shared aim of ending it victorious.

In the middle of that week I had the pleasure of being invited to dine at Claridge's as a guest of General Marshall himself.

The British chiefs had invited their American counterparts to dinner, though it was expected to be a somewhat fraught occasion. Admiral King had been heard to mutter, 'I'm only goin' if they bring along that Jamie fella.' This remark had been jumped on eagerly by Marshall and Winston.

That evening I found myself in the chair that no one else of British origin would have dared sit in, the one next to Admiral King himself. Howard was not present; I assumed he was working late at Grosvenor Square on the results of the day's talks. I was grateful as his close proximity combined with free-flowing drink risked the potential of me being unable to keep my mouth shut.

King himself was enough to deal with, as he growled at everyone around him but was the very soul of consideration towards me. He told me about his own Lodge in Georgetown, whilst gruffly drinking a toast to allied solidarity. I did find as the night wore on that, as Howard had told me, he could be fairly sociable when circumstances permitted.

He was interested to hear of my early life and fascinated

to learn of the business in Scarborough. I achieved greatness in the eyes of my companions when something that resembled a grunt-like laugh emitted from him during tales of my legendary sea-sickness.

It may have been the drink but as the evening wore on we could be seen heads down gassing away together, and in truth he had a lot of interesting things to say. Of course, he revealed nothing of the day's talks but he was a decent conversationalist after a fashion, though overall, he was hard work.

The Admiral had just left for a visit to the head when General Marshall took the opportunity to join me. He gripped my hand. 'Mr Melville, you do have a way with difficult cases! I should like to have you on my staff!'

Winston joined him as he rubbed my shoulder. 'This laddie is our secret weapon, General! All it takes is a meeting on the *level* and our wise Solomon before us delivers his pearls!'

The General was all smiles. He then crouched down and squatted to the side of my chair.

He spoke quietly. 'Brother Melville, it's my fraternal duty to inform you that certain gentlemen here tonight, not present in Washington on a now *famous* occasion, have expressed an interest in a certain *tune* you sang that evening.'

I was half-cut by now and ready for anything.

'Gonna help me up on to the table, Brother Marshall?'

I suffered from the most terrific hangover the following morning. By some grace I'd had enough wits left in me to ensure the taxi dropped me off at North Street, thus I was able to spew my innards out undisturbed at home. The thought of waking in that condition at the War Rooms was unthinkable.

With the amount of noise I made I must have terrified the neighbours into thinking the air-raid warning was being sound. I'd made the mistake of drinking straight whisky which the chiefs poured down me after my song concluded to riotous applause. I'm told Brookie and Pug had to carry me into the taxi as they sent me on my way, very late on.

One thing about a serious sickie like that is that it takes your mind off other concerns. It was well into afternoon before I was able to crawl with painful fragility out of the sack without heaving. I drank a little water and once I was able to keep it down longer than five minutes I knew I was reaching the recovery stage. But it was a grey and gaunt Jamie Melville that left his front door for some fresh air that beautiful afternoon.

It was a Thursday. I walked towards Whitehall but I had to take it slow because when I'd been poured into the taxi the night before, my companions had forgotten my cane and I was of course too sozzled to remember to bring it with me.

I limped along, stopping to rest every now and then as my leg started to play up. I gradually reached the stage where I was now feeling the need for a dram in order to clear my head. I remembered that I kept a bottle at the War Rooms and on finally reaching my destination presented my pale self to the Bootneck at the entrance.

'Bloody 'ell, Mister Melville! Ye look like a three-day-old corpse! Can I have some o' what ye've had?'

'Piss off, Richie. Let me in quick or I'll write to your mum in that Liverpool hole you come from and tell her what you're really up to in the big city.'

He glanced at my pass and allowed me through. 'Ye'd have to drag her out the pub first! In ye go, Jamie!' He was too cheery for me, the gloating Scouse swine. My stomach, though more settled, still ached abominably as I suspected I'd tweaked a muscle or two through all that heavy duty vomiting.

The dull underground lighting was welcoming after the headache inducing glare outside. I stumbled through the smoky, echoing labyrinth, offering quick hellos to staff and various uniforms as I found my room and fell on to the bed. I lay for a short while then took out the half-bottle from the little cabinet. I slugged straight from it, rinsing the liquid round my mouth and spitting out the juice into a waste bucket. I lay down, rubbing the cool bottle along my forehead. I felt exhausted but at least I wasn't thinking of Meredith.

I must have dozed off and awoke around an hour later. I got up to look for one of the ghastly chemical toilets and then made for the canteen in desperate need of a cup of tea. I found General Brooke there, looking over a book of photography.

'Ah!' he welcomed. 'The Merry Mason!'

I dropped down beside him with my cup and saucer. I weighed up whether or not to try and attempt eating something. Though if anything was guaranteed to make me boak it was that kitchen's cuisine.

'Feeling the effects still?' he asked concernedly.

'I'm getting old, General. There is now no question of it! By the way, did anyone grab my stick last night?'

He thought for a moment. 'No, Jamie. I can't recall if anyone did. More than likely it's still awaiting collection at Claridge's. I'm sure it'll still be there.'

He began to laugh as he remembered the evening's jollity. 'By heavens! I haven't seen anyone down straight Scotch like that for a long time!'

I pulled a face. 'How are things going with you?'

'Oh, I'm just enjoying a moment of precious Winston-free time! The chiefs have been sent for by himself, in, ah!' He looked at his watch. 'About twenty minutes!'

'At the Annexe?' He nodded.

I pulled his book over towards me. It contained wonderful photographs of birds in flight, at rest, in trees, on top of houses. He was a keen amateur photographer himself, particularly of nature shots. Such a civilized pursuit, I thought.

'General, how do you reconcile such a peaceful hobby with the mayhem of war?'

'You only have twenty minutes, Jamie! Not enough time! Not enough time!' He grinned. 'But there *was* a time many years ago when I loved to hunt. I bagged many fine creatures until one day I thought: *but why?* Did they not have a right to live freely? Are they not of God's creation? If man is given all the advantages he has, why must he deliberately take away the only thing that beasts own, their very lives? And for what? The perverted desire, and it is a perversion, to kill? And yet, I still cannot resist the desire to grouse-shoot on occasion!'

'But how can you believe that and then order men to their deaths?'

He reached over and closed the book. 'That is a question which is similar to the one where it is asked, why does God allow such pain and unhappiness in the world? It cannot be answered, Jamie. General Marshall and I had such a conversation and concluded that our moral duty was to fight but to take no satisfaction from it. And if we are granted victory to then strive afterwards for a world where such wars can never happen again.'

I'd come to know him over the short time I'd been in London. He was always extremely considerate and found time for me in his manically busy schedule. I knew that he'd lost his beloved wife years before. He blamed himself for it as it was in a traffic accident where he was said to have been driving erratically.

I'd blanched before from bringing the subject up and I did again. But his words had eased me somewhat, though I have never had the slightest religious spark about me.

Then he surprised me. 'You miss her terribly, don't you, Jamie?' he said gently.

My eyes stung and tears came to me. He rubbed my arm and told me to let it all out. I didn't feel self-conscious at all but experienced a kind of release afterwards.

After a short time he rose from the table. 'I have to leave now and go to our master! Jamie, if you feel up to it, I'm having a little dinner at Westminster Gardens this evening. General Marshall shall be there and I know he never tires of your company! If you feel able, please come along. You're more than welcome.'

I thanked him and drank the tea down as he left me alone.

But something had now been taken from me. Whether I was light-headed after my earlier exertions, the queer atmosphere of the bunker together with the General's mystical words and demeanour, I felt a sense of peace for the first time in many a long while.

I didn't make it to the General's dinner. I jumped in a taxi shortly after the General left me for his meeting and made my way to Claridge's in order to retrieve my cane. I felt bad that I'd mislaid it, precious thing that it was. I knew I'd suffer the pains of self-loathing for a while if it was lost to me due to, albeit uncharacteristic, drunken behaviour.

At the entrance I approached Mr Gibbs, the genial head doorman who knew everything and everyone connected with the famous hotel and availed him of my situation. He walked over with me to the restaurant and relayed my story to the Maître d' as I provided a description of the cane. Thankfully he replied yes, one such cane had been handed in and went off to fetch it along with Mr Gibbs.

Relieved, I leaned over the edge of the desk where the guest book lay open. I swung it round and opened it at the page for the day before. We'd all signed it, laughing and joshing one after the other, even though the Yanks were staying there. There was my name of course, Marshall, King, Brooke, Winston and the others. I confess I felt a wee bit of pride swell within me to see Alexander and Nancy Melville's wee boy in such company. Probably be worth a fortune that book, one day.

Then my eyes fixed on another name above them all and I wondered why I hadn't noticed it the night before. It was signed a few hours before our party had booked in. The signature was clear to read, *Alastair Cheyne*. I turned a page back to the day before and the one before that but it appeared only once, Wednesday, 22nd July 1942. Last night.

Mr Gibbs then appeared with the cane and I thanked him and asked the Maître d' for a quiet table. A waiter approached and I ordered tea. I needed to think. Cheyne was my mother's maiden name.

No diving in head first, Jamie was the *second* thought that sprang into my mind.

I telephoned the Budapest. He'd worked the lunchtime shift and had already left.

I'd dined of a sort earlier at the War Rooms; just as well, though chips and beans were about as good as it got there, about as much as my stomach could take. I then started out on foot for Piccadilly and found myself standing outside the entrance to The Cherub.

I banged on the metal door and the letter box opened. 'Yes? What do you want?'

'Is that Dilly? I'm Arthur … Alastair Melville's brother. I'm looking for him. Do you know if he's been in today?'

'Don't know any Melville, love.' The door opened and it was the same bouncer as at the previous occasion I'd visited the club.

'Do you remember me? He calls himself Alastair. Blond, receding hair. He works at the Budapest?'

'Oh, *Alastair*,' he replied with catty disdain. 'Keeping very odd friends of late. But don't we all? Hasn't been here for over a week. Shall I tell him for you?'

'It's alright, I just wanted to say hello.'

'Shame. I do remember now. You're his nice-looking brother. He doesn't deserve you. I'll let him know you were asking. Do you fancy a drink yourself, dear?'

'No, it's alright. Thanks anyway, Dilly.'

He closed up. I thought as I walked away maybe I should have accepted the offer and tried to find out more from him.

But I wasn't sure I really wanted to.

I took a taxi to Argyle Gardens and knocked on the door of the house he roomed at. The landlady said he wasn't in. It was early and his lights were out. I asked to see for myself and she got shirty. Avoiding a scene, I returned to the waiting cab.

I considered Grosvenor Square. But the possibility of bumping into Howard made me baulk. I might just lose my stick for good; after embedding it in his skull.

I thought of someone else whose *heid* I wanted to batter. *Surely not.* Maybe it's another Alastair Cheyne. Some Jock officer on leave? No, he'd have added his rank. The signature had no title before it, just the name. Anyway that was all wishful thinking. I recognised the handwriting.

He was playing with fire. He'd been in jail already. Of course I didn't know what he got up to at the best of times. Probably ran the risk of prison constantly. But this new entanglement was dangerous. I cursed the stupid sod, roundly. But how could I be that certain he'd come to Claridge's to meet whom I suspected him to? That was wild conjecture.

No, it wasn't.

I remembered a telephone number I'd stored away some time ago. I'd been used by this particular bloke already. Now, I'll get some use out of him, I thought. I asked the driver to stop at a phone box and got out and dialled the number. It rang twice and a male voice answered.

'Speak,' was all it said.

I hesitated slightly, before steeling myself. 'I … I have to talk to Uncle Claude.'

Chapter Nineteen

I ARRIVED FOR work at No. 10 that Friday morning and found the atmosphere even more frenetic than usual. John Martin took me to one side and told me the latest.

The President had sent a cable to General Marshall confirming his acceptance of the British plan to invade North Africa. There were a few addendums, including a request for a number of aircraft originally destined for the Middle East to be transferred to the Pacific. But the main concession from the American chiefs was that there would be no invasion of Europe that year. We'd been saved from a potential disaster. Gymnast, as the operation to invade North Africa had been codenamed, was on.

'Gymnast, did you say?' I asked after Martin had finished speaking. I wanted to be certain I heard correctly.

'Yes, Gymnast.' He smiled. 'But I believe they'll come up with something else to call it in time! They're forever changing codenames. Such schoolboys!' he mocked. That "something else" was of course Operation Torch.

'Want something to do?' He asked me.

'Only for a couple of hours,' I replied. 'I might have to take the afternoon off! Winston will want to celebrate, no doubt!'

He smiled knowingly and left, returning with some paperwork for me.

I found it difficult to concentrate on my task. My mind was fixed with worrying thoughts about Arthur, Dansey, Howard and something else. The mention of that codename confused me no end. The letter I viewed in Winston's study appeared to back the North African invasion. What was FDR up to? Why send a team out with a completely different agenda when his mind was already made up? That explained Hopkins being alone with the Prime Minister and Winston's eagerness to remove Harry from the centre of things with that convenient walk around St James's Park and dinner. Something stank.

Of course I should have been elated and was indeed relieved to hear that a potentially suicidal dash across the Channel that year had been abandoned. Only a few weeks later the disastrous Dieppe raid was carried out with horrendous casualties and no end of lessons learned; mainly over the folly of attacking a heavily defended beach without adequate support in place.

My thoughts returned to that conversation with Winston as we were leaving Washington for Baltimore and the journey home. Of how he believed Roosevelt was deceitful and untrustworthy. I thought of Brooke and wondered if he was in on it. Was the stonewalling just a ploy? I wasn't party to the discussions but heard plenty of snippets after. The inference was that we had offered nothing except "no" to France and "yes" to North Africa. Why was there no middle ground offered as there normally is when sensible people reach stalemate?

There was more that did not feel right. The transfer of aircraft to the Pacific when we were about to launch an attack in the desert? I wracked my addled brains but for the life of me couldn't work out the puzzle. But I trusted my guts. I knew something was wrong but what exactly, I had no way of knowing.

Grand strategy aside, I'd more pressing personal concerns, mainly my *daftie* of a brother. Contacting Dansey alone had cost me sleep the night before. Now I was even less sure it had been the right thing to do. But if anyone could locate Arthur and scare him off, it was nice Uncle Claude. I doubted very much Arthur would pay heed to me. He never heeded any of us Melvilles in his life. At least his mistakes should have been his own, but he had a knack of placing the blame elsewhere.

I'd never understand him or his way of dealing with life. He seemed content to be solitary. At least that was the front he put up to us, his brothers. I'd always believed that he just disliked humanity generally. I would observe this first-hand on the few occasions where I viewed his behaviour in dealing with customers at the hotel in Scarborough and in the restaurant in London. He was either 'a sugar or a shite' as my grandmother used to say.

The rules of a civilised society are that you must, even in the most basic fashion, associate with your fellow human beings each and every day. Arthur disdained his fellows and as he was forced to endure this calvary, when things went wrong in his life, he could justify to himself that the root cause of his failures was down to the others he was compelled to tolerate. The shared rules that obliged him to undergo the purgatory of daily contact with lesser beings were not of his devising, therefore he was precluded from following them to begin with.

But the more I thought about it, the more desperate I became. Unable to think of him as anything less than my mother's son despite conflicting emotions, my mind raced with visions of Arthur being beaten, jailed or worse. And there was also a less prosaic reason guiltily nagging away within me, the potential for embarrassment to Winston and by definition, to me.

Walter Thompson had explicitly warned me to keep Arthur away from Downing Street. Why on earth would I bring him there anyway? But what he really meant was to keep him *at arm's length*. Period.

Who'd told him that Arthur wanted to see me that day? I'd assumed it was friends in the police. Or could it have been someone else? And why? Why care about Arthur appearing on the scene all of a sudden?

I rose from my desk and asked John Martin where Winston

was. I made an excuse that I urgently needed to see him. In truth I couldn't concentrate on the job in hand. The war effort could do without me until I sorted out a family problem. Where Winston was, Walter was. And I wanted to speak to the giant bodyguard. On his own.

Winston was in the building, making a nuisance of himself as usual, no doubt. I made my way upstairs and found Walter sitting outside the small Downing Street flat the Prime Minister sometimes used.

'Walter, have you got a minute?'

He got up and we walked off down the hall. I opened a door and looked inside a room that was empty. 'This'll do,' I motioned to the huge policeman.

'Heard the news, Jamie?' Walter asked as he entered the room.

'Yes. He got his way, then.'

'Thank God!'

'Aye, thank God indeed,' I agreed. And Franklin Delano Roosevelt.

I wasn't sure what I was going to say to Walter. We'd struck up not exactly an overtly friendly relationship, rather a good understanding. But bearing in mind that a bodyguard can never be allowed to trust anyone no matter who it is, it was always a fairly sociable one and he did occasionally confide in me.

'Come on, Jamie, or the old man will skin me!' he chivvied. Straight to the point, I asked him who spoke to him originally about Arthur wanting to see me.

'I told you. It was a mate of mine,' he replied guardedly.

'Walter, I think he's in trouble and…' I was hesitant to say it. 'I think it could involve Winston, indirectly.'

'Are you being pressured?' It was a policeman's response. I understood that and could only feel relief that he did not laugh me out of the building.

'No, I'm not. But I believe Arthur is being manipulated.

Maybe *I'm* being manipulated. I can't really say more because the truth is I just don't know for certain. But I'd be grateful if you could tell me anything you know.'

He looked at me and took a breath. 'Your brother's been part of a gang of poofters who've been hanging round big hotels soliciting and in some cases, attempting to extract hush-money from lonely American officers. He was brought in just after you came down but mentioned your name. Some checking was done and I was approached. He was let off with a warning as what he's been suspected of is difficult to prove, I'm sure you can understand why. But he was ordered to keep away from the hotels in future.'

I spent my life convincing myself that whatever I heard about Arthur Melville could never shock me as he had an uncanny ability to surprise with consummate ease. But this was beyond anything I could have ever imagined him capable of.

Walter continued. 'You know he's been inside?' I nodded miserably. 'He was blackmailing a married police officer in Whitby before he was chased out of town years ago, too.' That would have explained the night he came to my door begging for money.

'He forges cheques and has a record of petty theft. He's a right little villain, Jamie. I'm very sorry.'

I paused to gather myself. 'I think he's at it again. With Yank officers, that is.'

'Anyone we know? Jamie, if it concerns Mister Churchill, I must be informed.'

I revealed what I suspected but cautioned him it might be coincidence. Arthur may have targeted Howard at the Budapest that evening we'd dined there. If he did, what in truth could I do about it? Nature would take its course. But I still felt some respect, even sympathy for Howard and hated the thought of my brother conning him.

'My advice is to just leave it alone, Jamie,' Walter advised. 'As you say, it may be a coincidence. But the fact is he now knows about the American delegation at Claridge's and is trying his luck there. I can call the hotel staff to advise them. But that could mean your brother going to jail if caught. And if he goes there again it'll be for a long stretch, believe me.' I must have looked distressed and Walter taking pity, patted my arm.

'I'll have to call them,' he decided after a bit of thought. 'We can't risk anything happening now the talks have concluded to our satisfaction. But if he's brought in, I'll let you know and see what I can do.'

We stood up together. I was feeling light-headed and the walls of the small room seemed to be closing in on me. I wanted to go outside, into fresh air. Leaning heavily on my cane, I was barely able to comprehend anything he was now telling me.

'You did the right thing, Jamie. For everyone. It can't have been easy. But I can still pull strings here and there. Hopefully, it won't come to that. Is there anyone else you've told about this?'

I collected myself and took a deep breath. 'I'm afraid there is and I wish to God I hadn't.'

After we'd spoke, he returned to his vigil and I thought for a moment of speaking to Winston. Normally I would whenever I had a problem. But I decided not to this time. Walter could fill him in on the details if he wanted to.

I was almost bent double with shame.

I didn't feel like lunch and knew I wouldn't be able to concentrate much on the work I'd been given earlier. I told John Martin I had to rush off as something had come up. He gave me a look and asked me if I was alright. I thanked him and said I had a bit of personal trouble to sort out and he wished me good luck. He told me he'd find someone else to finish the job I'd started.

Shame was slowly being supplanted by cold and bitter

fury. I tramped along streets in the direction of the Budapest muttering away to myself in increasingly incoherent wrath. For the first time in my life, the very real desire to do *actual*, deliberate and extreme physical harm to another human being enshrouded me in a blazing cloak of endless, incandescent rage. I thought of holding him down and pounding that supercilious, lying, deceitful face of his. I tried to think of us as children together but such memories were consumed by my anger and loathing for the type of creature he'd become.

I believe something had finally run its full course within me as I listened in open-mouthed horror to Walter's account of my brothers' criminal career. When you hear from someone as inherently trustworthy and reliable as Churchill's bodyguard, himself an experienced police officer, the cold, legalistic description of what your brother is known to be by the world at large, there's no coming back from it. Thompson would have had knowledge about it all for quite some time. But he would have been less than human if he had not wondered in his own mind what I knew and what I didn't know.

I felt the guilt of association, the guilt of the *brothers*. But it would all end today if I found him. He would be warned one last time and then he was forever on his own. If that's how he wanted to live his life, I would grant him his desire and be truly damned to him. I was finished with Arthur Melville.

I was savvy enough not to telephone the restaurant. I was now of the certain belief that he was so devious that if he heard I was coming, he'd dash away. I was reducing myself to his level but was now of the conviction that only an idiot fights his battles fairly.

The lunchtime crowd was in and I entered and caught sight of Arthur leaving a table and making for the kitchen. I made my way through and grabbed his arm as he pushed at the swing door.

'You and I have to talk now! Any trouble from you and I'll tell your employers what you've been up to!'

He tried to pull away but I swung him around. 'Put away your tea-towel and come outside with me.'

He looked around him but I'd kept my voice low. I pushed and prodded him towards the exit. It might have looked comical if I wasn't so incensed.

We stepped into the street and I pressed him a few steps further before he turned to me.

'Alright! What's wrong with you? How dare you embarrass me like that?'

'Listen to me now. And listen closely. This is the last conversation we're ever going to have.'

'What...?'

'Shut up. I know about you and that American naval officer, Ben Howard. The one whose arse you're rimming at the moment? Followed by a little extortion afterwards, to pay some bills, perhaps? Well, I've got bad news for you. The police know all about your little circle of criminals and they're on to you.'

'Jamie, this is nonsense! What American? Ben Howard? I've never heard of a Ben Howard!'

'You bloody liar! I'm not interested in your cries of innocence any longer. You met him with me the other night. There's a saying, *it takes one to know one*. Well, when you have a brother who *is* one, you can soon spot others too! I'm letting you know that you better stay away from Claridge's and any other hotel because the Law are on to you. My advice is lay low and pick better friends in future.'

'This is insane! I've not been seeing anyone!' he pleaded angrily but also with a clever undertone of hurt but false incredulity. By now people passing by in the street were looking over at us, though I was oblivious to anything or anyone other than the miserable cur of a brother who was lying through his teeth before me. I did not want to listen to his protestations. I could only concentrate on keeping my temper, which was paramount.

'Where did this come from? Believe me! I'm telling the

truth,' he continued. 'The police? You know what they're like. They're the liars! Not me. I live quietly. I've given up all of that! Jamie, there's a lot I haven't told you, but believe me, that's all in the past now. I'm trying to get on with my life. I tried to join up. The Catering Corps! They wouldn't take me. I tried the Medical Corps, though I can't stand the sight of blood! Even they wouldn't have me!'

The pseudo-English accent that he'd acquired had dropped away to pure Gorgie Road.

'I said I'd do anything. Bed pans, cleaning up sick even! But no! And I know there are plenty of *queers* in the services! They do their bit. All I want is to do mine.'

It was pitiful and my heart was of stone. I'd heard it all before. He might as well fire arrows into me, I'd still not flinch. I was beyond him now.

'You're a criminal, that's why they won't take you,' I replied coolly. 'But I don't believe you anyway. You'd run a mile from a uniform but you don't mind stealing from good men who wear one.' He was a step or two in front of me as I gathered myself for the last words I'd ever say to him.

'You are never to come near me again, not that you do anyway. Stay away from Scarborough and my family. If I see you there I'll contact the police immediately. Goodbye, Arthur.'

I turned and walked away from him. I felt no release. Instead, a deep feeling of disgust of such intensity that I'd had to say what I did. I tried to think of nice things like the girls, Gemma, Tom and the lads playing football.

But my mind fixed on two very small boys holding hands tightly as the older one led them both to the bakery in Gorgie Road to buy bread. The younger one's face a mask of concentration but his little chest bursting with pride at being permitted to clutch in his hand the few precious pennies his mummy entrusted to him to carry.

The tears poured down from my face, bitter as the taste of betrayal.

Chapter Twenty

AFTER MY CONFRONTATION with Arthur I seriously considered jumping on a train heading north from Kings Cross. What good had my return to London achieved? The world was blasting itself to hell. What could a one-legged cripple do about it? I'd fought my war, this latest one wasn't mine. I scoffed as I thought about "doing my bit."

I can go home, I reasoned. There's decent trade now at Humphries and Melville Fishing Company. I'd been in London nearly five months and it had had its moments but I really couldn't see what further use I could be now. Winston had wangled the Yanks to do what he wanted and apart from the class-clown act coming in handy on occasion, I'd achieved little of note.

Meredith had been a dream. But she wasn't what she seemed and I'd made a fool of myself over her. At least not many knew about it which was consolation of a kind. But not much. I was caught in a web of self pity, indecision and uncertainty.

I wandered disconsolately back to Whitehall and was passing the Café near Clive Steps that sold those wonderful eggs. A tall bloke with his back to me was turning from being served a roll and I recognised Harry Hopkins. He smiled over a bite as the grease dripped down the sides of his mouth.

'I only come here because those girls are real cuties!' he winked. 'How are you, pal?'

It was testament to how low I felt that even his usual cheery nature couldn't assuage me. I walked on past him, childishly.

'Hey, Jamie! Stop there!' He caught up with me. 'What's wrong? Come on, it's me!'

I stopped. 'Why don't you lot just sod off back to America?' It was like hitting a defenceless child, an easy target and the behaviour of a lout and a bully.

'Jamie, what's the matter?' he gasped, incredulous.

'You got what you wanted! Screwed Marshall and King while you were at it! *Your own men!* Devious *bastard* of a politician!' I emphasised the word and filled it with bile.

I was taking it out on him. I didn't really care all that much about American politics. But I was wrathful of all forms of deceit and trickery at that moment and he was just the luckless innocent that became the recipient of my petulant broadside.

'Now just wait a minute! What's that supposed to mean?'

'You fuckin' know full well! I saw that letter from your boss! The one about the "Gymnast" being "a real goer". Conniving old swine!'

His mouth literally dropped open and his eyes widened in shock. 'You keep your goddamned mouth shut about that! Jesus Christ, Jamie! You dare spread that about and you're in serious trouble!'

I then cooled somewhat, the anger dissipating as it quickly dawned that once again my temper may have got me into bother. I was still riled, though. 'You make a move, Harry and I'll knock you on your arse!' I warned.

We stood glaring at each other. I'd thrown down the cane and my fists were clenched. We were still only a few yards from the kiosk and I could make out one of the girls looking over at us curiously.

'Jamie, we have to talk.' He bent down and picked up the stick and handed it to me. 'Come on. Let's walk?' he offered.

I didn't want to, but I knew I'd messed up and needed to do something to retrieve what my tantrum had given away. But I was still me and wasn't about to grovel to anyone. Not even him.

'Alright, but don't give me any soft soap, Harry. I'm not in the mood.'

We set off together for the park and stopped at a quiet spot. We didn't sit but stood on the edge of the grass alongside some trees.

'Jamie, I don't know exactly what's happened to you,' Harry began. 'No, hear me out. I know you're having a tough time right now. But these are serious matters and you have to rise above it all, there's too much at stake.'

'You know nothing about me.'

'I know a lot, pal. It's my job.'

'Job? You call it a job?' I guffawed mordantly. 'You're a lapdog. I'm a low class buffoon. That's what *we* are!'

'Yes,' he agreed evenly, 'you're correct. But answer me this, how else do you get things done? We nearly suffered a catastrophe in Washington until you got up and behaved, as you say, like a buffoon. But let me tell you something. *Nobody* thinks you're stupid. Far from it. Do you believe men like Marshall and King would respect someone as much as they do you if they believed you were an idiot? That's your personal inferiority complex showing through due to this country's God-awful class system. You're as a good a man as anyone, Jamie. Didn't Winston himself tell you that when you were a kid?'

He then changed tack as he noted how uncomfortable I must have looked listening to all this praise so soon after committing such a serious *faux-pas*. I felt like a complete fool, if the park opened up and swallowed me whole it would have been a blessing just then.

'Do you know that Brooke and King nearly came to blows the other day?' he confided. 'Ismay had to separate them! And then once again, as you say, soft-soap the pair of them! Thank God for old Pug!'

'Harry, it sounds to me like these people are nothing more than a lot of *prima donnas*, as *you* once described them to me.' My eyes were heavy, my leg ached damnably and my head was beginning to thump from the glare of the warm sun. Above all there was now the overwhelming desire to return to my home and to my girls. I was tired and wanted no part of London or my old colonel any longer. But I owed it to Hopkins to explain myself. He was a true friend, it was the least he deserved.

'I've been around Winston longer than you've known Roosevelt and he acts like a spoiled child most of the time. I'm wearied of being around him, Roosevelt, Tommy Thompson, King, Howard and everyone else who thinks they can just use and manipulate people and then dispense with them as soon as their services are no longer required. This isn't the real world. Not to me anyway. That's why I left Winston before and that's why I'm going to do it again.'

Harry placed a hand on my shoulder. 'I hear what you're saying, Jamie. And I understand, though I regret that you feel that way. It's my belief you *shouldn't*, but a man has to go his own way, you as much as the next. As for Winston and Roosevelt, regardless of what you think of them personally, when the doors close and the man is alone and has to act, they both step up to the plate. FDR is the best friend this country has, but he is just that, a friend. He is primarily an *American* politician. You've been there. You know the problems we have with isolationists, anti-British feeling and now this damned Japan First brigade! Do you have any conception of the problems he faces?'

'Have you any conception of what it was like here in May and June 1940?' my bitterness flared again, exacerbated by how I was feeling physically. 'We were laying tree trunks along beaches to make the Germans think they were gun emplacements! We had nothing! And still your President sat on his arse and left us to it! Lend-lease! Fuck me! A load of rotten old boats that were condemned to begin with!'

'I'm goddamn proud of the Lend-Lease legislation we passed, Mister!' he retorted angrily.

He then calmed. 'But there are still issues that need to be

dealt with. Surely you must understand that ultimately the United States will take the lead? It's just the numbers, Jamie. There's more of us and we build things in greater quantities. It's inevitable.'

'Winston's right about not invading France,' I countered wearily, feeling like a washed out rag again.

'Yes, of course he is! But FDR has to be seen to be fighting the Japs, too. He knows Germany must be the priority. But there's one matter in which he is adamant, there will be no repeat of the last war when Pershing, Foch and Haig told their elected leaders how to run things. That'll never be allowed to happen again.' We'd started walking and halted at the lake.

The little island in the middle of the water chirped with sparrows and starlings nipping the turf for worms while chasing each other around in little skirmishes. There wasn't much in the way of bread crusts these days and it was a bully's charter for the few rancid pieces that the more fortunate ducks had missed. Invariably, the sparrows lost out.

As for me, I now no longer felt any concern over the particular matter of my indiscretion. Of course, Harry understood that I'd never repeat anything. But we were in deep now so he continued.

'He has to give the generals their lead. And then *he* makes the decision. The hand is stacked, necessarily so. Let me ask you this, Jamie, did you never stop to think the surrender of Tobruk came at an opportune moment?'

I failed to comprehend fully what he was implying. 'Don't tell me Winston knew about that beforehand!'

'No, no! You misunderstand. Look, I disagree with FDR over Gymnast. I think we should be building up for France, like Marshall does. But I understand Franklin's reasons. Tobruk meant a *fait accompli*. We had to react to that. We can't afford to lose the Middle East. So, everything now fits. North Africa keeps Congress, the people, the press, the British and the Navy happy. Yes! Do you know that most of our Navy men here in London disagree with King privately? They have a more realistic idea of what it takes to land an invasion force on a lee shore in the English Channel in October!'

'Alright. But answer me this, did Brooke know?'

'Ask Winston, though I advise you not to. That's one stubborn Irishman, old Brookie! But my gut tells me Winston did tell him.'

'What gets me is what the President does next. How does he tell the Japan First crowd they're getting nothing in return?' I asked.

He stopped and looked over the water. 'Maybe they *are*.'

I looked at him, my tired brain valiantly attempting to keep up with Harry's revelations. But I had a question of my own that required an answer. 'Are you telling me that King is in on some kind of a deal? Harry, please tell me what that was all about in Washington with Meredith and Howard?'

'You need a lot less men to invade Algeria than to invade France,' he said cryptically. I was lost for a moment. 'What does that tell you?' he asked.

I paused, breathless as the result of the all scheming, subterfuge and deceit at last revealed itself before me. 'You don't need as many landing craft.'

'Right.'

I looked over as a mother with two small children attempted to retrieve a ball that had fallen into the lake. I resisted an urge to go over and assist her.

'Howard never wanted an invasion of France or North Africa,' he explained. 'So he was letting it be known that we didn't have enough craft for either. Meanwhile, what craft there were he was helping to transfer to the Pacific. With FDR's deniable approval.'

'What? You're mad!'

She'd rescued the ball and was drying it off on the grass. Both children had lost interest and were running after each other, whooping and screaming.

He ignored me and carried on. 'Then FDR declares that

we're not invading France, we're invading North Africa, Operation Gymnast. Winston is happy. Franklin then lets the chiefs know that landing craft which would have been used for France are going to the Pacific. There's enough to spare now that a smaller North African invasion is to be launched. The chiefs are happy. Everyone is happy.'

'Except General Marshall.'

'Marshall's a big man. He'll move on.'

'But who does Howard work for?'

'Himself and a few others with his misguided sense of priority. But whether King knew and tacitly approved it, well, you'll have to dig up evidence from somewhere to prove it.'

'What was to be planted on me in Washington?'

'True estimates of our levels of activity in building landing ships. Winston would use this to hit our chiefs with.'

'Then Howard's not a traitor. If the President approved…'

'He *is* a traitor in the eyes of the law. But nothing will happen to him. I told you before. He's being lined up for a top job. Washington's full of China Hands. They're our equivalent of the Masons! Only you have better songs!' he laughed.

One thing still nagged me. I remained to be convinced that Winston could be fooled by anyone.

'What you're saying is that the President was playing everyone against each other, particularly his own service chiefs. Maybe he was and quite successfully, too it now appears. But I just can't believe he was fooling Winston. I've known him nearly thirty years and he's the smartest man alive.'

'I've told you all I know. And as for Washington, you'll have to ask your secret service and our office of naval intelligence about their interest in you. But my guess is they were running turf wars of their own and using you and Meredith. 'You were an innocent in a strange town, Jamie. It was unfair on you. But go easy on Meredith. She was a *victim*.'

Mention of her name in such an enigmatic context caught me out like a splash of cold water to the face. Old feelings, former *strengths* I had deliberately suppressed or believed lost forever to me were now restored, vigorous and vitalizing in combining an iron resolve to act decisively qualified by a clarity that could no longer be dismissed as the desperate longings of a lonely human being. Harry's words revealed the plain, unadulterated truth to me. Despite everything that had happened, I wanted her still.

Harry knew it, too. Later I came to believe that he deliberately mentioned her name in order to give me the well-deserved shaking that I undoubtedly required. He leaned back against the bench and lit up, looking for all the world like he was trying to make his mind up about something. I wondered if he was regretting his candour.

His head was down as he held the cigarette in his lips. 'Hell. I might as well tell you. All of it. After I do, it's up to you to do what you want with it. I couldn't care a good goddamn.'

Chapter Twenty-One

'When I was a kid I caught the religion bug. I guess when you're in your late teens you either want to follow the drum or follow Jesus.'

He told his story freely, as if he had rehearsed it a long time. He was like some actor, relieved that opening night was finally upon him. He would stop and look over the park, light up, take a few draws then continue. He smoked incessantly.

'My old man moved around a lot. We started out in Sioux City, Iowa and for a while we lived in Chicago. One day my dad was knocked down in the street by a milk cart. He was hurt real bad, busting a leg. My pop was a sassy fella and sued the driver. He won a big pay-out and took us to Grinnell and bought a harness store. Later he sold other goods: food, drink, newspapers and such. His true love was bowling and he was good at it. He won a lot of money on side-bets and we did alright. But my mom was a Methodist lady and in them days, I took after her more than my old man.

'I had it bad for a while, the religion thing. But then I met a girl. This was just before I started college at Grinnell. She wasn't like me, she wasn't like Grinnell, Iowa neither! Pretty blond with a pert little nose. I had just got over a dose of typhoid. God alone knows what she saw in me! Probably the devilment that would surface one day once I was through my old-time religion period.

'My parents liked her. She came from decent farm stock and I liked her too. But some fellas at school were, I dunno, *jealous* or something and started making up stories about her. I believed them. Hell, I was full of God's good intentions and those guys knew what buttons to press. They were my buddies on the basketball team. I was a popular guy. They called me "Sky" 'cause I was so tall and skinny. Some pals, huh?

'I was to meet her that night at the theatre. But instead I made off to her house to have it out. She was there waiting for a ride to take her to meet me! I'd walked all the way there. She was alone as her mom and dad were out at a local union meeting.

'I sure as hell hit her with it! I told her the wrath of God would smite her for her sins! Hank Lawrence and all of them other fellas she'd known carnally were all bound for hell but this pilgrim wasn't! She just laughed her head off! I looked at her and thought, she's got a real pretty smile! I guess Beelzebub was working his black magic because in that big old farmhouse one thing led to the other and well, you can guess what happened next.

'I saw her a few times after and nothing like it happened again but I suffered the guilts bad. Jesus was working on me now. The last time I saw her we were to meet up outside my dad's store. She was real happy to see me as always but I told her the shame I felt was too much and that if anyone ever found out my parents would disown me. Truth was I didn't want to see her again. I knew now what the boys said was true. She started crying and I left her there and went home. I sure behaved like a snotty little prig.

'About a month or so later she left town to go and live with her aunt in New York City. I guess Iowa wasn't big enough for her. I knew how she felt and had a kind of hankerin' for her for a while. I didn't exactly feel bad about how I'd treated her but my attitude to the sin we'd committed had changed somewhat. I guess my religious phase was over.'

He told his tale with humour and self-deprecation. But there was the middle-aged man's wistfulness and regret over lost opportunity, and some degree of conscience. I got the feeling he still carried a torch for this girl. She was his first love and who forgets that?

'In the late twenties I became a big cheese in the New York Tuberculosis Association,' he continued. 'We did a lot of good in the area of welfare reform. One day my secretary told me a lady wanted to see me. Turns out it was my old girlfriend. Right there in my office. She'd heard about me and came looking for a job. There was nothing doing but later when FDR was Governor of New York he set up the Temporary Emergency Relief Administration. He wanted his old pal Jesse Straus to recommend someone to run it. You probably don't recognise the name but he's the fellow that owns Macy's.'

'Who are they?' I asked.

'Oh, I forgot! Department store. The most famous in New York?' He looked at me, trying to coax recognition of the name.

'Never heard of it.'

He sighed. 'You British! Anyway, Straus recommended me. I accepted and later asked Jesse to find a position in his store for my girl. Not long after he found her one on the perfumery. Nothing went on between us, please believe that. I was newly married to my second wife. I was doing all this good for strangers but wrecked my first marriage through having an affair and nearly lost my three boys over it. I didn't want to risk blowing things a second time.'

I'd heard talk that he was something of a ladies man; that he'd mucked around during his married days didn't come as too much of a surprise to me. He had charm but I didn't think he was *that* charming. He was lanky, had as much flesh on him as a butcher's pencil and was not exactly Hollywood in looks. One of the great failings I've noted in American males is their inability to keep it buttoned up. No wonder divorce rates are sky high over there.

'We did become friendly again and met up periodically for lunch,' Harry admitted. 'She lived in a little place in Brooklyn. She didn't tell me much about herself at first. But then one day she told me about her daughter. She was at school upstate and was coming home soon. I said fine, no problem, let's meet up. I had no inkling. None whatsoever. I met the girl, a gorgeous little redhead. Better looking than her mom at that age.'

'Stop right there!' I ordered.

He looked at me, his eyes wide. 'Wait a minute, Jamie! It's not what you're thinking!'

I've got a strong Calvinist streak in me and I don't care who knows it. I wasn't exactly John Knox and hadn't seen the inside of a church since Gemma died, but I didn't want the conversation going any further.

The *filthy* bugger! I must have looked a sight, red-faced and trembling, fit to commit murder. I'd put two and two together and came up with an orgiastic scenario that would have made Caligula blanch.

'You've got the wrong end of things!' Harry pleaded. 'Hear me out will you? This ain't easy for me, you know.'

I stood up and let rip in purest Edinburgh. 'I'm no' interested in hearin' any mair o' yer dirty stories! Mothers and daughters? Well, I never! Bloody degenerate! That's what ye are, Harry Hopkins! Ye'll burn forever in the fiery flames o' hell, so ye will!' I stabbed my finger at him in righteous Presbyterian anger.

He looked up at me in something akin to acute astonishment and then as it dawned, began laughing uproariously to such an extent it started an awful, hacking cough. For a moment I was concerned it was about to carry him away.

He began to settle back but still couldn't stop chortling to himself. I could only gape at his reaction which wasn't what I'd expected.

'Jesus Christ! You're the prize chump of the century! God, I love you, Jamie! No wonder Winston calls you his secret weapon! So help me, I haven't laughed so hard in years! Lord bless you, pally!'

He stood up and with further blandishments, persuaded me to sit back down. The truth was I had a terrible suspicion about what was coming next. I had stronger feelings than I realised.

'Are you okay? Can I continue? Don't worry, bud. No one will ever know about this! If I were to tell them I'd have to reveal too much about myself in order for folks to get the joke! Still pals?' he asked.

'Aye, suppose so.' I now felt a bit of an idiot. 'Sorry, Harry. I've had a rough day.'

'Sure looks like it! Anyway back to the story. You guessed it, the daughter was Meredith.'

I took a breath and controlled myself as much as I could.

'I did the math. Yes, I know what you're thinking. Her mother said it wasn't me. That's all, just that I wasn't the father.'

'How well did you "do the math?"' I asked as tactfully as possible whilst trying to mask the emotion in my voice.

He rattled off some dates and I noted that she was a little less than nine years younger than me. This in itself relieved me somewhat. There was a short silence.

'Close, Jamie. Very close,' he concluded, now sensing the lessening of tension within me. 'In truth I wasn't certain. It was possible it was a pal of mine in the team. The reason she lit out for New York is because her parents had to get her out of Grinnell, fast, of course. She then had Meredith and made the best she could. She met some guy called Macaulay and married him. He soon took off.

'The aunt and uncle brought the kid up. They were decent folks and did their best. But my old girlfriend was young and wanted a life and she stayed out a lot. The aunt paid for Meredith to go to a little boarding school to keep her out the way of the men and the good times. She did well, got a scholarship to a nice college and grew up a sweet kid.'

He looked at me with a diffidence that I thought out of character. 'I guess deep down I wanted her to be mine. My boys looked at me kind of squint and I thought I could at least try and make things up with the little girl.'

'You said you didn't think you were her father,' I said pointedly, still somewhat unconvinced.

'The way my mind was working then was different from today. I'm pretty certain now she isn't mine. I did some more checking later on. I'm not going any further into that.' An element of coolness now appeared. I put my hands up.

Noting this he became apologetic. 'Sorry, Jamie. It's not you. But I kind of think every man in that situation would want it to be so, if he wasn't lying to himself.' I thought about it later and realised he was correct.

'I found her a place with the Relief Programme. She was good at her work. Her mom was happy, she'd got herself a job and her daughter was set up so it suited everyone fine.

'Then Meredith met a boy. She fell for him like the proverbial. He was an ensign from Annapolis. Good family. Father a China freak and money from rich gramps. He also looked better than Gable. How could a girl say no?

'He graduates near the top and is given a post in Washington. They get married but the groom's parents aren't happy about the distaff side. I'm invited on to the scene as a favour to her mother and assure them she's good enough for their little boy. Grudgingly they accepted. Long faces at the wedding but Meredith's mommy can't stop smiling.

'Howard is then posted to the Philippines. Meredith falls pregnant. Ben can't keep the smile off his face. The pregnancy goes smooth as can be. Only, when the time comes, the birth is a nightmare. The baby breaches and the cack-handed naval surgeon delivers the kid but messes up sewing Meredith together again. She then gets a serious infection that nearly kills her. She pulls through only to be told no more children.'

I had my head in my hands at this point.

'Are you alright?' he asked, noticing my distress.

'Just carry on. But get it over with quick, will you?' I answered, irritably.

'Okay, nearly finished. She recovers but things are not

good and she wants to go home, to the States. They fight and argue. He has to complete his tour as it's important for his career and he needs a wife to be there. She relents.'

He stopped and lit up another cigarette. 'Only, she just made the worst mistake of her life because a meningitis outbreak hits the base.'

'Christ! No more, Harry,' I pleaded.

'You're not dumb, Jamie. Slow at times, but not stupid. Yes, the child died.'

We sat silent for a moment. I now knew what Harry had meant when he described her as a victim. But what I'd heard so far only scratched the surface.

'He now gave in to her pleas and they returned to Washington. The only unselfish thing the son of a bitch ever did for her. But he was given a lousy job as a reward. The bastards thought there was a lack of "fibre." But his grandpa had connections and found him a place in the Foreign Service. So he quit the Navy and made for Hankow, China. Thing is, he wanted to go on his own but Meredith went with him. She was his wife after all.

'This is where it gets mean, Jamie. A kind of meanness I can understand, but not you. That's because you're a decent guy. Me and the Howards of this world? We're what you British call, "proper shits."' He pronounced the term in an elegant upper class English accent and it coursed with bitterness.

'The foreign compounds in Shanghai were full of the worst kind of colonials. And the Yanks were as bad as any. The British led the way and we sure like to think we're different but we're not. A Chink is a Chink and that's all there is to it. Howard never saw it that way. They were a cultured people that needed our help.

'Pretty soon Howard was promoted. He was good at what he did but he was advised to keep his opinions to himself. Meredith buckled down but the cracks were growing. The marriage? Initially Howard saw this little girl as ideal. Poor and impressionable, wanting to rise above herself and eminently pliable. Give her a kid to take her mind off where she was living and husband pursues his career and looks for other pleasures.

'Then the plan goes out the door and he's stuck with a child he can't have and a wife he doesn't want. He's also seen in parts of the city he shouldn't be anywhere near. There's a story doing the rounds about some Chinese boy. Howard claims he's just a communist he's cultivating for information. This all coincides with a brilliant, though controversial report he writes for Washington on the future of China. It's not appreciated by his bosses. He's then told he's gone as high as he can go.

'He quits the service and on returning to the States after one last argument, Meredith finally walks. They separate.'

Try as I did I couldn't listen to him with anything other than fascination. It all seemed so outside my basic experience of life that it was difficult to absorb. It was a horror story, no question. I didn't feel any kind of desire to rush and embrace Meredith and whisper kind words. I felt completely alien to her and the entire saga. And also somewhat frightened.

'How do you know all this?' I was able to ask after a short pause.

'She tracked me down in Washington. Jamie, in her heart that little girl believes I'm her father.'

'But you're not.'

'No. I'm not. But it's hard to explain. I'm just asking you accept that things are completely genuine between us and that I care for her very much. I have my own little girl, now. Diane. But I like to believe I have *two*.' The heart is truly beyond comprehension and I knew these last words were difficult for him.

I patted his arm. 'I believe you; no one lies about things like that.'

He puffed away and stared ahead, saying nothing.

'I found her a job in the State Department. She wanted to get on with her life. But all that has to affect a person,' Harry mused. We were strolling slowly together now, the only other sound was from my cane on the path.

'After I met my second wife I started seeing a psychoanalyst,' he continued with that strange lack of inhibition Americans have when they discuss their private lives. 'I know, you British "abhor the very idea, old bean!" But I needed to understand why I was so intent on ruining the lives of those close to me. In truth, I wanted to learn why I was so horny all the time! I began to study Jung and Freud. Couldn't find an answer. But while this was going on with Meredith I was still seeing my shrink now and again. You'll have noticed that Meredith likes her food?'

It was the first opportunity I'd had to smile.

'She wasn't like that when I first met her. I asked my doc and after giving him a brief outline of her situation, he told me Meredith is now filled with self-loathing and sees food as a comfort. Deep down she wants it to make her so fat and unattractive that no man will look at her again!'

'What a load of old cobblers!' I exclaimed angrily. 'She's just a bonnie wee lassie with a healthy appetite!'

He laughed agreeably. 'You're the best, Jamie! God, if only FDR had someone like you!'

'He has. His name is Hopkins,' I replied.

It was a lot to think about but answered many questions. My pity towards Meredith now grew and so did other feelings. I suppose I'm a sucker for a sob story. That combined with the sweetest face and deadliest figure is an irresistible combination.

I wanted to learn more. I wanted to hear how Howard got his hooks in to get her involved in his espionage activities. But in truth, I knew. It didn't take a genius to work it out.

He'd worked his magic on me for a while too. But I've never believed that people are completely good or completely bad. I tried to find a reason for Howard's behaviour.

Sometimes it doesn't pay to analyse too deeply. Perhaps he was just a bastard. Life's full of them.

Harry returned to our original discussion. 'FDR's stipulation was that if the British dig in and say no to France, he could turn to Congress and say that the invasion was undoable this year but an invasion of North Africa was feasible.'

'Whilst letting them know that material was available for the Pacific,' I countered.

'In a roundabout way.'

'Some way to fight a war!'

'Franklin knows two things, Germany must be defeated first but that an invasion of France is a risky undertaking that has to be done right. He likes to make out he's an amateur on strategy. But there's never been a politician yet that thinks he knows less than his generals. We forgot that twenty-five years ago. He's determined not to repeat that mistake now.'

I thought of another politician who believed he knew better than his generals a quarter of a century before. And still did today.

'Well, that's certainly one thing they both have in common, Winston and the President,' I said wistfully.

'These talks are just window-dressing, Jamie. The decision was made last month. Howard was a useful tool when it mattered but he's had his run. Do you know a fellow told me the other day that we'll be able to build ships in less than a week pretty soon? That's what America coming into this war means.'

We passed some young nannies with their charges and I thought again of Meredith.

'Jamie, you understand this can never be discussed? I regard you as a friend. Never put yourself down. Franklin was almost slobbering in praise of you in Washington. That was a bad moment, believe me. King is a pain in the ass. You really saved us. God knows what trouble he might have caused.'

'Winston did more than I, Harry. I was just the *finale*.'

He chortled again as we'd now returned to the point we'd set out from. 'I think I'll get me another one of them buns! I'll pay for it later, but what the hell!' he announced happily.

'Harry, I'm so sorry,' I apologised.

'You can tell me all about it one day. I know my Jamie Melville. Something really painful must be hurting you. That saddens me.'

He made his way to the Café. I stood waiting for him. I still had no appetite though I'd had no lunch and it was mid-afternoon. I put it down to the growing excitement within me now that my decision had been made. Harry returned from making his purchase, munching away agreeably. I thought at that moment I was blessed to have such a friend.

'Real good! I miss this old town when I'm away! I do love it so! No goddamn Nazi or anyone else will place his jackboots on these streets while I'm around!'

I smiled. 'Everything is good now, huh?' he asked. I couldn't speak for a moment. He looked at me steadily. 'Jamie. *Meredith*. She wants to talk to you.'

I laughed off-hand. 'Harry, why are you so keen to match her up with me?'

'Matchmaker!' he laughed heartily, 'Well, I've been called a lot of things in my time!'

'You don't deny it then?' I smiled with him.

'No, I do not! She's a nice kid, you're a nice fella.'

I became serious. 'Harry, I *asked* you.'

He gave me a knowing look and said nothing.

'I'll think about it, then,' I conceded, though my mind was now made up on the matter. Irrevocably.

'She's screwy over you, buddy,' Harry confessed finally. 'But then again, Jamie Melville could never see the wood for the trees. And it was Winston who told me that.'

Chapter Twenty-Two

My spirits had lifted greatly. Harry left to return to Claridge's to go over some final points with Eisenhower and Marshall. I wanted very much to talk to Winston and made my way back to Downing Street, across Horse Guards.

When I arrived John Martin, that very decent man, asked me how matters were as he was concerned about me. I put his mind at rest and told him I'd sorted everything out satisfactorily. He was pleased and I asked him where Winston was to be found. In the Cabinet Room, he replied. I made my way through the building, knocked and entered. He was sat in his chair with Anthony Eden seated next to him.

'Oh, I'm sorry.' I apologised for disturbing them and turned to leave.

'No! No, James! Come back in here!' Winston roared.

'About four o'clock, Prime Minister?' Winston grunted a positive to Mr Eden as he gathered up some papers and made ready to leave.

'Good to see you, Mr Melville,' the Foreign secretary acknowledged as he made his way out. I sat down in the chair he'd vacated.

Winston rubbed his hands comically. 'I did it, laddie! I did it! No! *We* did it!'

'I didn't do anything, Colonel!'

Ignoring me, he continued gleefully, 'Oh, Lance-Corporal Melville! What a glorious day!'

He stood up and made for the door, opened it and barked an order.

'TOMMY! Get some bloody alcohol in here, now! And James is here so you better not bugger it up this time like you have before!' He almost danced back to his chair.

'Aren't you going to ask me?'

I had to play him along which I always hated doing. He swore me to secrecy and told me what I already knew. I raised my eyebrows at the right moments and congratulated him.

'Where in the name of suffering Christ is our whisky?' he had stopped his reverie and jumped out of his chair again. This was the liveliest I'd seen him in months. Exuberant and bouncy, full of zest. It was wonderful to see him back to his best again. And somewhat of a relief.

'I'll have a look, Colonel. Just sit yourself down.' I got up, opened the door and saw Tommy heading towards me with a tray.

'You! Monkey-features!' I pointed my finger at him. 'Where have you been with that drink? Get your arse in here, now!'

There were a couple of girls about and I shouted for effect. I knew the building would be full of the tale very quickly – one more brick was laid in the monument to James Melville.

'Thompson, you'll never make a waiter! Damnable time you've taken. *Action this day*, remember?' Winston complained as Tommy laid the tray on the table before us.

'Colonel, I'll put one of your little stickers over his mouth if you think it'll make a difference?' I added helpfully.

Between looks of stomach-churning sycophancy towards his master and cold-blooded malevolence towards me, Thompson left the room without uttering a word.

'And close the sodding door next time!' Winston stood and slammed it shut leaving us alone once more.

He made our drinks and handed me mine. I supped on it as he threw back his glassful.

'Nothing like the *Water of Life!*' he announced, joyfully.

'Nothing like it, Winston,' I agreed. 'There's nothing like the truth, either. I think you've been lying to me.'

He put his empty glass down. 'What is the matter, my boy?'

'Colonel, I know everything.'

He poured another drink. 'What do you mean?'

I pushed away my glass. 'Why did you insist that Dansey give me a gun to carry to Washington?'

'He *had* to.' He was calm and measured, the earlier bumptiousness now gone entirely.

'It was all a fraud, wasn't it?'

'Yes. Ultimately it was. Deception is a most vital weapon of war, James. Truth, the most valuable commodity and so precious that it can only be protected by a shield of lies. You were part of that deception.

'I wanted you to carry that pistol as I was concerned about your safety. You are an innocent, James. The innocent must be protected from evil intent. I knew not what awaited you in Washington for certain. There were so many imponderables. There always are. I have faith and trust in your wits but considered some signal must be given to you of the potential danger in order that you remain vigilant.

'I also had faith that you would not be deceived by anyone. You can always spot a wrong 'un! That quality I have long admired in you. But I truly did not know how they would come at you. The young lady was a cruel trick to play. On you both. Yes, I know all about Meredith Macaulay!'

He stopped and took a drink. He placed the glass back down and clasped his hands, leaning forward in his chair and looked down. From old, I recognised that he was about to tell me something revelatory.

'Others knew of Miss Macaulay, too.' He then turned to me, his head slightly lowered and consequently his eyes looking up at me. I felt uncomfortable but steeled myself to listen.

'Jamie, what I will tell you now must never be spoken of. I reveal it to you only because of the closeness of our special bond and also as a warning.'

'Don't tell me. I don't think I want to hear, Winston.' I began to rise from my chair.

'No!' he bawled. 'James Melville *runs* from nothing! Sit down, boy!'

I did as I was told, like a child admonished in a class-room. I reached over and took a sip from my glass to steady myself.

'You are here with me now once again, and I thank God for it,' he began, his temper returned to normal. 'But you have no conception of the dangers that are involved when you delve into the *secret world*.'

'Colonel, I still don't want to know.'

'I will tell you, regardless, and one day you shall thank me for it. That world I speak of is not so very different from the everyday one we all inhabit. There is pettiness, jealousy, nepotism, hypocrisy and incompetence at every level. It so happens that in this case, SIS, MI5, MI9 and others all compete with each other. But there is also a relatively new service, which I myself ordered into existence during the very worst days of 1940. The Special Operations Executive. The SOE. This organisation's existence is so secret that even its very own operatives are unaware of its true designation. Its primary purpose is to raise havoc in occupied countries. To this end, vast resources are allocated to it and this along with its perceived inexperience and remit has caused bitter-ness amongst the other fraternities.

'The brave young men and I can say proudly, *young women*, of the SOE know nothing of this internecine warfare. And it is war, believe me when I tell you. The other services, usually at each other's throats, are now united in their desire to strangle the young upstart at birth. This I shall not countenance.

'Claude Dansey is the most vocal critic of SOE and is known to actively desire its destruction. He is head of op-erations at SIS, a very fine officer with many successes. But he is living in the past and will not adopt modern methods for waging modern war. There is a place for the tried and tested, yes. But fresh ideas to meet new challenges must be allowed to develop.'

I would only comprehend much later that these "methods"

consisted of conducting electronic warfare by deciphering German signals through the breakthrough in the reading of Enigma codes. Ultimately this would prove a more efficient system of gathering intelligence and certainly a far less costly one than dropping inexperienced young men and women blind into enemy territory.

I listened but there was one overriding thought going through my head. 'Colonel, get rid of Dansey and sack the rest.'

'That cannot be done. I will not go into the reasons why,' he mumbled as he took a drink.

'What has this to do with Washington?' I asked.

'Everything. Dansey was hoping to use you as leverage in his struggle with SOE.'

'Leverage? How? And against whom?' I sat up in my chair.

'You are known to be an extremely close associate of myself, trusted implicitly and possessed of unwavering loyalty,' he explained. 'If you could be implicated in a plot, photographed, caught "red-handed" dealing with rogue elements in the American intelligence community, it would cause great embarrassment to me. It would raise the profile further of SIS and they would only have to name their price to keep the entire affair out of the public domain.'

I was unable to disguise the tone of incredulity in my voice. 'All this if I'd slept with Meredith and been photographed? Come on, Winston!'

'You did not fall for that particular trap. But you did have a meeting with Commander Howard alone, did you not?'

'Eh? What are you slavering on about! I went for a walk to see the Lincoln Memorial! He was *following* me!' Of course the words were only out of my mouth when I realised the implications of that seemingly innocent conversation.

'I know that is true, of course. But you were "set up" as the saying goes, all too readily.'

'So, I was there as a sort of pawn, to be used by both sides.

But answer me this, was there collusion between Dansey and Howard? And did you originally set me up to meet Dansey that day with Bracken?'

He looked away from me and turned his head to face the other side of the room.

'The answer is yes to both questions. I wanted Dansey to appraise you. Of course, I knew he would underestimate you.' It was a concession on his part but one that provided little solace to me.

'You've been lying to me from the start!' My voice was raised and he turned back to face me.

'Please, James. Not so loud!'

'That story you told me, the night Dansey came for my cane. That wasn't the truth, was it? It sounded good. You're good at telling stories.'

'James, one thing I have learned in all my years of dealing with the secret world is that there are always too many questions and not enough answers.'

If it wasn't for Meredith's involvement and my feelings for her now I wouldn't have pushed it. But I wanted the truth.

He remained silent for a moment. Then spoke. 'What I have told you about Dansey and his vendetta with SOE is true. What I have told you about Howard and his fanaticism is true. What I have told you about the lady is *not* entirely true. And I know this is the point of your real complaint. It is your heart that pains you, Jamie, not your pride.'

'Like you said, Colonel. I'm an innocent and so is Meredith, believe me. That's *my* truth. I know about her now. Hopkins told me her story. Enough of it anyway, I can almost fill in the rest of the pieces. But you can help me complete the picture.'

He took another drink. 'You deserve to know. I shall tell you.

'The information that Howard has been passing in place of official material has been of great use to us in our negotiations with the Americans,' Winston began. 'For, from such a source we have been able to deduce the true strength of

American capabilities at present. For example, we know that there are not nearly enough invasion barges or landing craft available, nor shall there be for quite a considerable period of time.

'The President is aware of these facts but daren't make them public as it would be politically dangerous to admit to such unpreparedness. Particularly as a sizeable and extremely vocal element within the nation is crying out for a greater effort against Japan. That is *Japan*, James, not Germany.

'The President is unmoveable in that he deems Hitler the greater and more dangerous enemy and is fully committed to his destruction first and foremost. But he must guard from making this view too public for reasons I have explained. He is also aware that we, the British are of the same mindset and cannot countenance anything other than defeat of Germany first.

'The last thing that the Japan lobby desire is the focus of attention to be on a cross-channel invasion of France this year. That is the only area in which we are in agreement with them. It is not a public agreement, nor can it even be a private one. But the Japan First supporters are happy to hear of us stonewalling the very suggestion and a few are more than pleased to provide us with the ammunition to fight our corner.'

'And Howard was the one supplying it?' I concluded.

'He was one source, yes. His ultimate aim was to discourage any attack in Europe and instead turn America's focus to the Pacific.'

'But how were we able to prove what he told us was the truth? He could have made up or manipulated facts to suit his own agenda?'

'An excellent question, but when the facts are put before the US chiefs and they are unable to refute the figures, what else are they *but* the truth? And they were the truth. The chiefs had their own agendas too, James.'

'Chiefs? You mean King and Marshall?'

'Who else? Of course, King and Marshall. King as you

know wants the Pacific to have priority. Marshall demands an invasion of France. Neither must have their way. Therefore there must be compromise, whilst keeping the various political factions satisfied at home.'

We were getting to it now. I felt more uneasy as he spoke. It seemed difficult to believe that I was somehow involved in all this, even in some minor way.

'For the talks in Washington and here in London, pressure had to be maintained. I have been aware for some time that Claude Dansey was looking for ways to destabilise SOE. So far, he has not been able to achieve that by the nefarious means at his disposal. For whenever there is infringement of the territory of my brainchild, it comes to my attention and I act swiftly to sweep it up. But I grew impatient with the time that was wasted over such petty squabbles and I decided that "action this day" was required.

'Dansey was sent for. I informed him of our mission to Washington and that information had come to my attention about Howard and his actions. I told him that you would be flying with us and that you were to be used unwittingly on the visit to transport items of vital importance back to the United Kingdom. A trap was then prepared.

'And Dansey just happened to fall into it?' I sneered cynically. 'Very convenient, Colonel.'

He looked at me directly. 'James, you do not have experience in these matters. I will only say that a man like Dansey would have been formulating a plot before he even left my presence.'

I felt somewhat mortified. 'I'm sorry, Winston. I'm not being cheeky. You're right, I don't know much.'

'That is quite alright, James. There is no shame,' he consoled kindly and continued. 'I immediately alerted a very senior official in New York City. I cannot divulge the name of this man but one day it shall be known to the world and lauded throughout. His loyalty to me is beyond question. His competence is legendary and his disdain for the infighting that goes on in London is enormous. With the assistance of this gentleman and his networks, the plan was put into place.'

I would later learn that this mysterious individual he spoke of was none other than Canada's William Stephenson, the remarkable "Man called Intrepid," head of SIS in North America. He had worked with Dansey before the war when Dansey had created the highly effective "Z" operation after faking his own public disgrace. But the legendary Canadian spymaster had grown to despise both the man and his methods. His own personal loyalty to Mr Churchill was all-encompassing and he would have been more than pleased to put one over on his detested former boss.

'At this point,' continued Winston, 'it is believed that contact was made in Washington between an individual working for Dansey but who in fact answered to my friend in New York and Commander Howard or someone close to him with similar aims. Either way, Howard was alerted of our arrival in the city which should have been known only to very few at the White House. This operative advised Howard of my intention to use you as conduit, or if you prefer a "mule" whilst there on our business. At the same time, the operative, on behalf of Dansey asked Howard to prepare a "honey-trap" and if this succeeded, he would provide inside information on the affairs of the British government which could be used by interested parties in the United States as reward.'

'Bloody hell! That's unbelievable!' I needed another drink and poured a stiff one. Winston wiggled his glass so I refilled his also.

He leaned over and placed a hand on my arm. 'James, in every operation mounted such as this there are always factors that cannot be accounted for in the planning stage. That saying about plans going awry is as appropriate in espionage as it is in battle. Human behaviour is imponderable.'

'But human beings are involved, Colonel. That's inevitable.'

'Yes, of course, but experience is then used as a major factor in the mitigation of risk. Fortunately, in this case, innocent parties, persons with no knowledge whatsoever of such matters were placed in vital roles. This was planned in your case and in that of Miss Macaulay, a quick and convenient expedient that had not been properly considered, due to the timescales involved. This combination together proved to be decisive.'

It made me feel like he was describing abstracts and not flesh and blood people. It was disconcerting and I was glad I had a drink down me.

'I am not party to the discussions or motivations behind Howard's use of his former wife,' Winston stated baldly.

I flinched as though stung.

'I perceive your discomfort, James. I respect your depth of feelings for this unfortunate young woman. I too, am aware of her sad history. It is a grubby and dirty profession and those involved think nothing of the weaknesses and inner turmoil of those they use. But Miss Macaulay was able to find an inner strength that she may not have known she possessed and her estranged husband miscalculated disastrously.

'She was told to prepare the trap for you. I will not ruminate on what may have occurred. There would have been the possibility of what the Americans call, "the badger game" enacted along with photographs taken to provide evidence.'

I choked and started coughing heavily, caught between horror and hilarity. It was the straight-faced way he spoke of it rather than the picture in my own mind that set me off.

'Good heavens, James!' he bellowed as he smacked me on the back. 'Did you swallow badly? Really! That Scotch is excellent!' He leaned over the table and sniffed at the decanter. 'Nothing wrong with it!'

'Aye, Colonel. It went down the wrong hole!' I spurted out, unable to get the image out of my mind of my bare bum in the air and Howard bursting into the room, crying 'Stop, you cad! That's my wife!'

'Are you quite better? Really, James, I'm becoming gravely concerned over your level of alcohol intake recently!' The kettle crying the pot black indeed.

I mumbled I was alright now and please continue.

'Very well, then. But no more than two fingers per glass!' he ordered. I pushed my glass aside, cleared my throat again and continued to listen.

'Of course, we know now that you foiled their plan. Both of you did, by all accounts. But on leaving you that first evening, Howard reproached her and demanded she carry out her orders. What methods he used we can only guess. She met you for a second time and your conduct once again was happily beyond reproach.

'It was then that once more, due to the use of amateurs, the plan took an unexpected but welcome turn. Meredith approached someone known to me in Washington and poured her heart out to him.'

I knew who that would have been.

'Yes, James. I can see from your reaction that you are aware of the identity of this mysterious figure. He listened to her and offered his advice. He then told her how to proceed.

'James, what I will tell you now may seem beyond belief, but it *did* occur. Meredith then visited you at your hotel room?'

'Yes, she did.' I recalled the occasion in every detail.

'You left your room to go to dinner with her?'

'Aye.'

'You left behind your cane?'

'Winston! We've been through all this!'

'James, it was then that Commander Howard entered the room and inserted the capsule containing secret information into your walking stick!'

'Never!' I wailed, despairingly. Part of me remained unwilling to accept that she could have conned me. But it was the losing part. I still tried to defend her. 'She wouldn't, Colonel! Believe me, you're wrong.'

'James, it is true. She was advised by our mutual friend to do just that. You see, the information she placed contained nothing more incriminating than negatives from photographs taken of you and Howard strolling in Washington the day you met together. That was all that Howard had to offer Dansey.'

I tried to work out in my mind again how things went that night at the hotel. Surely, she hadn't planned it...

'It was so ... natural, Winston. I could have easily have just gone back and grabbed the stick and there's the end of it.'

'But you didn't. I would say that the young lady spotted the opportunity and took it. It happened, and that is an end to it. By such small margins, great successes are achieved.'

There you go. She *had* done a kind of job on me. But she'd been working for the angels at the time, so it was alright. But it wasn't. I'd been diddled.

He read my thoughts. 'James. I beg of you not to remain in judgement of Meredith. Nor should that glow you have when you think of her be any less than bright and warm! She is just an ordinary human being and did what she had to do. And in doing so, she executed the decisive move in the game!'

'What bloody game? Colonel, what was the point of all this?' I replied sullenly.

'James, that *look* on your face has appeared!' he laughed, slapped the table and leaned back in his chair, his thumbs hooked inside his waistcoat. 'I have known it nearly thirty years! You were always a sore loser! I sometimes wish I had never taught you backgammon! Really! The sulks you pulled when you invariably lost!'

That was back at Plugstreet. We played for raisins and he usually won. I'd strop about and dance around Laurence Farm in a fury, cursing my ill luck, his cheating, etc. He'd calm me down with a biscuit or piece of chocolate. He was almost insanely patient with me. I smiled at the recollection.

'Ah, halcyon days!' he reminisced wistfully. 'How I miss my lads! But back to the present. The task was now complete and the package ready to be delivered.'

'But Winston, *what* package? Surely when Dansey took it from me, he would have seen the information and negatives! He would have used them! Alright, they weren't pictures of me and Meredith up to *haughmagandie*, but why give them to him in the first place if you were worried he might use them?'

Then a look came over *his* face. I knew it well, too. It was the impish grin of sheer mischief and cunning that was only one of many reasons why I adored him so.

'Lance-Corporal Melville, do you take your old colonel for a *beginner*?'

'I don't know what's coming, Winston but I feel sure it calls for a celebration!' I poured into both glasses and we clinked them together and drank.

Winston then placed his glass down. 'James Melville. Have I ever told you how badly you snore after imbibing?'

'What? Eh? You can saw logs yourself, Colonel! I know!'

'On the seaplane, returning from America that evening, remember how after that vile creature Sawyers served your supper, you went to bed at my express order?'

'I must be drunk! What are you on about, man?'

'I entered your cabin whilst you were asleep, removed your cane, took out the package planted there and inserted one of my own.'

I just looked at him. For the life of me I didn't know what to say.

'I must confess I was in a sweat the evening we met Dansey at Downing Street!' he was enjoying himself now. 'I was worried he'd open the capsule and have a look! But that pleasure was left to him on his return to his office. How dearly I would love to have seen his face!'

I now found my voice again after the stunning revelation.

'Winston, if you don't tell me what was in it, I'll never forgive you!'

'There were negatives, yes. Scenes of Washington that any traveller would take snapshots of.'

'Is that all?'

'There was some microdots containing nothing of relevance. Supplied by my friend in New York.'

I was still lost. I couldn't see what all this achieved. 'Of *what*, for Christ's sake?'

'I believe they consisted of statistical information on the rise of venereal disease in the United States Armed Forces since the President's declaration of war!'

I burst out laughing. I would have given a year's wages to have seen Dansey's malevolent mug, too.

'James. Dansey failed and a message was sent to him to that effect,' Winston concluded. 'That no matter what, he was but a servant, answerable to *my* will. That no matter how devious he believes himself to be, he is just another number, as you would say. This I told him personally and advised that he would be removed if his conduct did not reflect this new state of affairs. With regard to Howard? He has his wish. There will be renewed focus on the Pacific. And we have *our* wish.'

'Dansey was the main target in all this, then?'

'Not necessarily. For we now have names of individuals who Howard was in cahoots with. The trap that Dansey attempted to spring was merely turned on *his* head.'

'A man like that won't take it lying down,' I declared ominously.

'Yes,' Winston agreed, 'nothing short of shooting will. He has been warned off for now. But I have no doubt he will be spoiling for revenge.'

'But you used me. Are you not like Dansey?'

He stirred in his chair. 'As I said, there are too many questions. I will say no more on the subject. Except this, I reiterate what I have told you before. Claude Dansey is an evil man and you are to be wary of him. Do not underestimate him. He failed this time. He will try harder the next and he never forgets a slight. If ever you see or hear from him again you are to advise me immediately. He has his uses but never believe you can get the better of him by yourself alone.'

I waved this away, irritably. 'I'm not bothered anymore about all that! It's done! Winston, I don't know if I can stay part of all this anymore. I'm feeling like I did back in 1918 again. Out of my depth.'

'The times I played out our last conversations back then in my head! If only you knew!' he declared regretfully. 'I longed for it not to be as it was. But I understood. I would never stop you. But I did hope that as you grew older, you would hunger to be part of this world again. Your talents are suited here, James. Truly. Honest men *are* required! And you are one.

'I know that you do not relish many of the things you are forced to contend with. But you will persist in succeeding in them so admirably! Nothing is beyond you! I saw it all back then. In Belgium. I always listened to you, more carefully than you realise. As you know, it is something of an accomplishment for me to listen to anyone other than myself! Your mind was keen and you wanted to better yourself. Yet you were torn with devotion to your loved ones. I understood your dilemma. Only one as selfish as myself could!

'If you decide to remain with me, I cannot in truth say that you would not be placed in such a position again. But I can promise this, I would never knowingly put you in a situation that I believed beyond your capabilities or place you in unnecessary danger. I hold you dear as a son. I always have and always shall.'

There it was, all laid out. I could no longer argue with any of it. There was also the weight off my mind that Winston had somehow been deceived. Of course he hadn't. My world would truly have caved in on me if he had been. But I knew all along, deep down he wouldn't be outsmarted by

Roosevelt, Hopkins, Howard or even Dansey. He was the puppeteer, alright. I was one of his puppets too but I'd happily dance a jig for him. *This time.*

'Jamie, very soon I shall be journeying to meet Marshall Stalin in Moscow. I will tell you now, to the depths of my very soul, I believe he is a monster as wholly evil as Hitler himself. Consequently we cannot allow ourselves to weaken as a foe to Germany and as importantly, an ally of Russia. They are both sides of the same coin. We must not spend our strength too quickly on hurried and improperly prepared endeavours. Small pin-pricks are enough for now, whilst the full potential of the mighty United States is built up.'

'What frightens you about Stalin?' I asked somewhat surprised at his disarming candour. 'He's our ally, isn't he? And he's losing.'

'What frightens me is that he is not a czar. What frightens me is his *potential*. Russia, if properly led, can become a giant. All through history, this has been the concern though it has never been realised. But now in this mechanical and scientific age, I truly fear it bearing fruition at last. And when Hitler is beaten, as he surely will be, our relationship with Russia will be the deciding one for the future of the world.

'At this moment, that is not a concern of the President. But in time it shall be. I intend to ensure that it is. Now is only the beginning. He must deal with his enemies within and he has now crushed them. The ends have justified the means.'

'The "means" including Howard and me,' I noted.

'But you met a charming young lady who I believe you care for deeply and that feeling is entirely reciprocated?'

I swung round to him. 'Alright, Colonel! As everyone is so bloody keen on marrying off Jamie Melville! What a bunch! You, Harry. *Sweetiewives!* The lot of you!'

The atmosphere now reverted to our old routine as the drink flowed hard and we laughed and reminisced together. After a while he stopped and asked me directly. 'And your decision?'

I was unsure what he referred to. 'Meredith, you mean?'

'That too, yes. But is it to head north again? And leave behind your old commanding officer?'

I was feeling a lot better than I had earlier. Harry's words. Winston and his whisky. They'd allowed me to see that the world was not so bad a place. Brothers, dead wives, little girls. They all had their place. But friendship was a healer. I'd regenerated my affections for Winston and had again felt the glow of his. And I might have lost a brother but on coming to London and meeting Hopkins, I had truly found a new friend. And best of all, there was Meredith.

'Oh, I'll have a wee think about that!'

'About *both*?' He asked slyly.

'Stop shit-stirring, Colonel! And by the way, it's your turn to pour!'

Winston had to leave to prepare for the chiefs of staff meeting Eden had mentioned earlier. The President had cabled back his approval of the results of the talks. There would be an invasion of French North Africa this year, probably towards its end.

Marshall and King were forced to accept that their British allies were intractable on the subject of invading France in 1942. I heard that King took it pretty well in the end. Maybe he did know something.

Marshall had to accept that all the plans he'd worked for had come to nothing. But Roosevelt knew his man. He was no Black Jack Pershing or Douglas MacArthur. He would not go whining to the press behaving like a petulant child. Instead, he picked himself up and readied himself for the task ahead. And no man on earth but he would have achieved what he accomplished, turning an army of 115,000 men into a vast force of twelve million by the war's end, only four years later.

But the genie had been let out the bottle. America had *arrived*. They'd learnt from their defeat and prepared properly for the battles ahead. We'd get our way for another year, including the invasion of Italy, which they were vehemently against. But after that, there was only one nation running the show. And it wasn't Great Britain.

Only at the very end, with Roosevelt dead, would a new President fully recognise Winston's prophetic words about Joseph Stalin.

Chapter Twenty-Three

IT WAS NOW early evening and my appetite had returned with a vengeance. Normally when I soak up drink on an empty stomach the results are fearful. Thankfully, Winston had ordered in some snacks and I believe those helped to take the edge of the amount of booze consumed.

There was a feeling somewhat akin to mild exultation within me. A combination of the events of the day and the alcohol had brought it about – I was now determined to start my life again from this moment on. Imbued with confidence, enthusiasm and belief in the future along with a certain element of liberation, I decided to treat myself to a slap up dinner to celebrate my new beginning.

I didn't mind eating alone. I had a lot to think about and considered contacting Meredith there and then, I had reason to now. She would be busy at the embassy, working on the American delegations paperwork. But I decided to leave it for this evening. Instead, I made my way towards The Causerie at Claridge's, limping along as briskly as I could to try to burn some of the drink out of me.

I wasn't drunk, just a little unsteady. A good feed would round off a pretty satisfactory day. I confess that I now had a strong feeling of relief that I had finally closed the door in my life that was Arthur. And I had come to a decision about opening another.

As I entered the restaurant there was an early Friday evening crowd beginning to build up but the Maître d' recognised me and found a fairly quiet little table to myself. They were experimenting with what would today be called a *buffet*, in an attempt to make war-time fare a little more appetising. It was a Scandinavian-inspired spread mainly involving herring, dried-up pickles and even thirstier looking lettuce. Uninspired, I asked for the waiter's recommendation from the set menu. He tried to talk me into ordering their latest variation on the Woolton Pie, the very mention of which nearly ruined my appetite. Good humouredly, I smiled away his sales-pitch and chose a concoction involving chicken wings and scallops followed by a blackcurrant tart soaked in a greyish-yellow custard that contained all the consistency of water. War truly is hell.

Still, it filled a wee hole as we say in Scotland and my good terms with the staff paid off when I was poured a glass of wine and told to keep the rest of the bottle on the house. They remembered me fondly from a few evenings before.

I asked for the cork and stuck it in the bottle to take back to Downing Street to have a night cap with Winston. He'd appreciate that and I felt a glow of deep affection when I thought of him. And Harry, too. God, I was a lucky man to have such friends. Maybe I'll stick it out down here in London after all. See it through. I'll certainly never have such a chance again to be at the centre of great events.

I began to dwell on Winston's mortality. He was nearly seventy and beginning to show it. Like the feelings that slowly come to you as you grow older and your own parents age with you, you prepare a way ahead in your mind to deal with the inevitable loss that is now so much closer. I say this because I never truly felt this way for my then still living mother. With her, I'd parted the way long, long before. And now that she was in her sixties, I only thought of the material side of her passing. The arrangements and the funeral. I felt nothing for her other than that. The scars of childhood had been reignited by my own experience of parenthood and though I still felt some affection for her, she was now beyond any real call on me.

With Winston, it was the dread of loss of a truly beloved parent. I couldn't help noticing how old and done he appeared to be at times. He was desperately in need of a long rest, that was clear to anyone. But I wanted him to announce to the world, 'Enough! I am leaving it to you all! I have prepared the way, you must carry on till the end!' with great emphasis and flourish then leave the stage forever for a well-earned retirement in which to paint and write to his heart's content at Chartwell.

But he wouldn't and no one could do it for him. Afterall, who would replace him? I heard talk that General Smuts, the great South African leader had been approached and advised that should Winston resign, fall ill, or die in office, he would be offered the position of Prime Minister. This was a secret of course but I'd rather have had him than Winston's personal choice, Anthony Eden. He later proved a failure in the role as is well known.

Smuts would have been a fine choice. He took nonsense from no one but was universally admired and was about the only person living (apart from Clemmie and me) who could shut Winston up. His strategic vision was exemplary and he also, like Winston, mistrusted Stalin.

I pondered on these thoughts over dinner and they dampened my feelings a little. But all in all the day had ended better than expected. It had been a long day, but it wasn't over yet.

I asked for the bill and stuck the bottle in the inside pocket of my coat. It was the lovely grey lightweight suit I'd bought in Washington with Meredith. Thinking of her made me return to my earlier happiness.

I grabbed my stick and sauntered along back towards Whitehall. It was now around seven p.m. One of those beautiful July evenings in London where to stroll was one of life's privileges. No bombing had occurred for a time and it seemed a semblance of pre-war life was returning.

I dropped some coins into an old accordion player's hat outside a theatre as I turned into the West End. I liked to mix up the routes I walked and saw the sign for Cockspur Street and cut through Theatreland.

My thoughts were of Gemma. Where I was at this moment resonated of her in times gone by. We would often wander around together here, taking in a show, shopping, having a meal. I walked with a smile of gratitude. The heat and light of the summer evening infused me with carefree memories of love and happiness. The drink helped of course.

I'd lived a blessed life. I was fortunate enough to know her and consequently she would always be with me. I now knew I was permitted to love again because that original love was beyond dissolution. Her presence was physical each time I was with my daughters and her spirit was everywhere I wandered.

Arriving at Great George Street, I showed my pass and went to my room. I wanted to change my shirt before meeting Winston with my bottle.

'Mr Melville?' I turned towards the door, my shirt unbuttoned.

It was one of the secretaries. 'There's a telephone call for you, sir.'

I buttoned up rapidly as I followed the secretary along the corridor, wondering who on earth wanted to speak to me and how they knew I was here.

I picked up the receiver. 'Yes?'

'James Melville?' the voice asked.

'Aye, this is Jamie Melville.'

'Jamie, this is Uncle Claude. Please make your way to Argyle Gardens immediately.' The phone then went dead. I immediately felt a cold clamp of fear and dread deep down in my stomach.

I'd put out of my mind my call to him the night before. The talks with Winston had soothed away my concerns. But now on hearing Claude's voice again, those fears re-ignited and I renewed my self-reproaches at jumping the gun and contacting Dansey in the first place.

I returned to my room and picked up my coat. The bottle was still inside the pocket. I thought for a second but then took it out and placed it on top of the small cabinet beside my bunk.

The pistol was lying in a suitcase under the bed in North Street. I looked around me, not finding what I was searching for and then made for the canteen. On the way I passed some desks, their occupants momentarily absent from them. There was a glass paperweight about the size of a cricket ball resting on some papers. No one was around. I pocketed it.

Striding on into the canteen, I noted a couple of girls sitting over cups of tea while smoking and chatting together. I looked over the unused tables and picked up a set of food-encrusted cutlery lying over a plate that had been left by a diner. The knife would have had trouble slicing through air, never mind butter and I laid it back down on the table. I could at best only threaten any possible assailants with food-poisoning with one of those. I left the canteen and made my way to the secretaries' typing pool.

'Get me a taxi!' I shouted over to a girl named Margery. By God's grace I was able to apologise as she was visibly startled. But in those minutes my mind was racing in every direction. I thought about Walter and how much I could use his assistance now.

Then my old pal Commander Thompson appeared, attracted no doubt by my loud Scots voice. 'Mr Melville! What's going on? How dare you abuse *my* secretary?'

'Where's Winston tonight, Tommy?' I spoke impatiently and with intensity. My fuse was ready to blow and he was the last person I wanted near me.

'You mean *you* don't know where he is?' he sneered.

I was in no mood for any of this pipsqueak's nonsense. 'Listen, Thompson. I'll batter the shit out of you if you don't answer me.'

'Oh, don't be so melo...' Before the words were out I'd grabbed him around the throat and forced him back so he was almost lying over a desk with me leaning hard over him.

'Where is Mr Churchill?' Any remaining effect from my earlier intake of alcohol had by now completely dissipated. I was now thinking very straight. But squeezing too hard. I felt something warm and wet come into contact with me. He had pissed himself.

'The Prime Minister's attending a ... a dinner at the Admiralty! At Greenwich!' he coughed out.

I released him and in sheer frustration, punched him unforgivably hard in the stomach. He rolled around the desk, heaving and spluttering as I pushed him over onto the floor in my fury. Where Winston was, so was Walter. I had no backup and would have to go on alone.

The secretary I'd bawled at stood with her hand over her mouth, looking down at Thompson, who was now retching and sobbing.

'Margery, is that taxi here yet?' I asked her in a measured voice.

Whatever she may have thought of Thompson, she'd witnessed the shock of violence and was momentarily unable to answer me.

I grabbed her by the arms. 'The taxi?'

'It's ... it's outside waiting, sir.'

I released her, darted outside passing the Marine guard and got into the cab, telling the driver to head for Kings Cross. I removed one of my socks and dropped the paperweight inside and placed it in my right pocket.

If you know where to look, weapons are everywhere. Walter Thompson taught me that when we were together at the ranges months before.

I attempted to imagine what was about to confront me. The possible scenarios were varied and I knew that I could be leaping to false conclusions. In my mind I prepared for the worst.

I told the driver to let me off at the station forecourt, paid him and got out. I didn't want to announce my arrival to Dansey, preferring to do a reconnaissance of the area first.

Argyle Gardens was barely a minute's walk away across Euston Road. It was a Victorian residential street built around a tree filled square of greenery. The metal rails and gates had been removed long before and a few motor cars nestled together in newly created parking spaces.

Crossing over the road, I stepped onto the pavement and walked along towards Arthur's address. There was a man standing solitary in the space where the former front gate of the property stood. I approached him.

He tossed away the cigarette he was smoking. 'Mr Melville?'

I flicked my cane up into my hand, holding it tight around the handle. I was face to face with the young driver who had met me at Kings Cross the day I arrived in London to be welcomed by Brendan Bracken.

'Please come this way, sir.'

I said nothing and followed him along the path. He opened the door and we entered the property. In the dank hallway, standing by the communal stairwell was the landlady I'd spoken to earlier regarding Arthur. Next to her was a middle-aged working man wearing a stained, collarless shirt with his braces hanging by his sides.

There was a third individual, standing on a small landing half-way up the stairwell, leaning against the wall. He had a moustache and his hands were in the pockets of a camel-hair overcoat with a trilby pushed back over his forehead. He would have been in his thirties.

'He was here yesterday!' The landlady declared on seeing me. 'Wanted to talk to *him*!'

'Quiet, will you!' The man on the landing snapped.

The driver left me to return to his post outside as the man in the trilby gestured me to follow him up.

'Go in, sir. Straight ahead,' he directed and walked back down to the landing. I stepped through the doorway into Arthur's room. Before me stood Claude Dansey.

'Jamie. Thank you for coming.'

I looked at him. 'What's going on, Dansey?' my cane was now in my left hand and I had the right by my side.

The room was dark and I noted a pair of black-out drapes pulled together. It was an incongruous scene, as it was still light outside.

It was a warm evening, yet Dansey wore a long overcoat. His penetrative eyes behind spectacles were fixed intently on me as I walked forward towards him.

'If you'll allow me, Jamie.'

He brushed passed my left side. I had an urge to swing at him but the room then lit up as he turned a switch.

Before me on a double bed was the body of a naked man lying face up. His left arm lay across his chest covering what looked like an entry wound from a gunshot. Blood lay blackening all around the corpse soaking what was already a fairly grubby and crinkled white bed sheet. His legs were crossed at the ankles and pulled up towards him in a bow shape and his right arm lay over the side of the bed.

'Do you recognise this man?' asked Dansey, now standing alongside me.

'You know as well as I do who it is.' I'd not witnessed anyone who'd suffered a violent death in over twenty-five years.

'Can you explain what might have happened?'

I turned to him. 'No, I can't. Why aren't the police here?'

'Commander Howard was under surveillance. We have no powers of arrest. They'll be here presently.'

I turned from the bed and looked away from Dansey. The room was well furnished, probably out of Arthur's pocket. There was a dressing table with a mirror, a half-sized, well stocked book case and an elegant mahogany single easy chair he may have picked up from a bomb-site. The walls were covered in a stock lime green, flower-patterned wallpaper. A three-quarter sized polished dark wood wardrobe finished off the interior.

'Where's my brother?' I asked. 'Look, Dansey, you better tell me. If you've harmed him, believe me – I'll kill you.'

His face remained impassive. 'The owner of this property heard what she believed to be a pistol shot and contacted the police. As this location is on our watch list they advised us immediately. We arrived less than an hour ago. What you see now is what we discovered and nothing else, I assure you.'

Ben Howard died here. I was sure of that from the evidence of the blood. It had soaked through the mattress and was still dripping in places along the wooden edge of the bed-frame. I looked behind me and there was nothing to be seen leading to the door. I had an urge to check the soles of my shoes but fought it down. I noted a Browning automatic pistol lying on the floor by the right side of the bed.

'Watch list?' I enquired. My mind was sharp and I was thinking clearly. I was unsurprised at how little effect the sight of the body had on me.

'Your brother is a known associate of the deceased. As you confirmed last night in your telephone call to me.'

'I confirmed nothing. I only advised you of my suspicions. Howard has only been here a week. You're pretty thorough.'

'We are, Jamie.' He then walked over to a side table by the bed where a lamp rested and picked up a small item.

'This is Commander Howard's wallet. There is no cash inside it.' He held it open for me to view.

I looked at it and back to him. 'Turn out your pockets, Dansey.'

A faint smile came over him. 'Come now, Jamie, that's quite unfair. It does not prove that your brother fired the shot. Only that he has been here at some point.'

'Does it hell!' I snapped impatiently. 'You can try and prove what you like! That miserable old bitch of a landlady could have taken the money! No way did Arthur do this. He's a ponce and a thief but no killer.'

'Your brother may have found himself in a most disagreeable situation.' Dansey spoke equably, ignoring my testiness. 'There may have been a quarrel. He stormed out, leaving the Commander alone having no idea what would follow. The landlady's telephone call? Maybe he entered the room just after the shot was fired. He panicked. Looked for the wallet and emptied it for necessary funds and took off. "Disappearing" is a particular habit of his. Possibly that is the solution. Then again, your brother may have fired the shot himself after a squabble. Howard may have discovered a plan to blackmail him. For this type of criminality, your brother is known to the authorities.'

'Maybe Arthur gave him the key,' I reasoned. 'Maybe he hasn't even been here. Did anyone hear a row? Arguing? You've got it sewn up already, congratulations. Well, thanks for calling me. I'll hang around until the police arrive.' It wasn't Arthur lying there dead, after all, and I thanked God for it.

My eye then focused on the easy chair and to the clothing resting on it. A light grey suit and cream coloured shirt with a collar. The coat and shirt were laid neatly over the back and the pair of folded trousers hung over an arm. The buckle end of the belt rested against one of the legs of the chair. I saw that the belt had missed a loop and from the angle I noted the loop would have been the one immediately below the wearer's lower back. Someone hadn't been careful enough. There were no items of naval uniform visible to me.

'Remember, Mr Melville, you've been associating with both parties over the last few days.'

'I've told you about that,' I replied brusquely. He was waiting for me to talk. I knew that I didn't have to say anything to him and stalled for time.

'Why don't you phone the police again? I think they're the ones I should speak to. Not you.'

His temporary façade of composure cracked as his irritation with my stonewalling burst through. 'Oh, come, Mr Melville! Enough of this! Stop wasting my time! You saw your brother earlier today! You met Howard a few days ago! You don't know anything? You called asking *me* to look for Arthur. What were you arguing quite publicly with your brother about outside the Budapest? You were acquainted with Howard in Washington were you not?'

I smiled gleefully. 'It's over, Dansey. Winston's outsmarted you. And so did the Yanks. You lost. He had you playing silly buggers in Washington while the real package was already signed and delivered! Just leave it now, eh? Some you win and some you lose. I'm tired and I'll give it five more minutes then I'm telephoning the police myself. Now go and crawl back under your stone before I forget you're an elderly man.'

His former passivity returned but it remained edged with scorn. 'If you believe all this is about two sodomites and their revolting practices, you're even more naïve than I took you for, Mr Melville.'

It was my turn to react angrily. 'That's my brother you're talking about!' Where the hell were the police? I began to feel even less sure of things and started to make for the door.

I could sense the deepening exasperation and aggression in him as he now spoke with an almost reptilian hiss. *'Where are you going?'*

'Like you said, you've no powers of arrest. I'm going home.'

'No, you are not!' he grabbed me by the shoulder and I shoved him back.

'Piss off, Dansey!' I swore as he stood glaring furiously at me.

'And as for *sodomites* as you call them, I knew another one, long ago when I was just a young lad. He was an associate of some famous men of the time. Men who themselves had interesting tastes. He told me a story about a lonely little schoolboy he befriended, years before. Of course, there were rumours about the friendship. Scandalous rumours. It was never proven, luckily for them both. But he told me that this same little chap grew up to live quite an adventurous life.

'He fought the Matabeles in Rhodesia as part of the British South Africa Police. He became a friend of Mr Churchill and served with him during the Boer War. He then found adventure fighting tribesmen in Borneo and Somaliland, helping defeat the *Mad Mullah*. After that he left to go to America where he became acquainted with powerful and influential men and came to the attention of the security services in England, mysteriously disappearing into that other *secret* world. My queer friend told me I reminded him of this boy and that I was as sweet to him as his little *Claude* had been.'

He uttered not a sound as his face reddened deeply and his eyes narrowed to pinpoints of rage. His hands were now fists and one seemed to be boring a hole into the chest of drawers it was resting on.

'Do I have to say his name?' I asked him directly.

'You *dare* say it!' he spat out in warning.

'*Robert Ross*.'

He stepped forward and made a furious back-handed swipe at me with his right hand. I was just able to step back from it as I felt the rush of air bypass my nose with the blow missing completely. Then I was on him, driving forward, both hands out, shoving him backwards. I winced inwardly as I jolted my knee and stopped as he steadied on his feet. I threw out a right hand that smacked off the side of his head and he stumbled back against the chest of drawers as I fell forward and then righted myself. There was a pause as he laboured heavily, trying to catch his breath. I reached into my right pocket and took out the sock and wrapped it round my fist. I took a step back and swung the heavy end threateningly.

'Keep away or I swear I'll smash your skull in,' I cautioned.

I then felt myself being dragged backwards and drove my elbow behind me but failed to make any contact, instead suffering a terrific crack in my leg that shot up into my cranium. Don't let anyone tell you never to lose your temper in a fight, rage along with pain gives you strength and keeps you alive. I knew from what I'd heard from Winston about

Dansey that I was now fighting for my life and the explosion of Melville passion within was all I had to see me through.

The man in the trilby had grabbed me round the chest with both arms but I swung him around, broke free and battered the sock off an arm. He yelped and I dove in with my left foot and caught him flush on the knee.

He still came on. I swung again with the sock but his hands caught it and pulled me towards him. We grappled and I managed to push him back against the window ledge. My right hand still clasping the sock went round his throat, my face close to his.

'Give it up! Give it up!' I roared.

From behind me I was now grabbed around the throat, the driver trying to drag me off. But as I was pulled backwards I swung the sock which connected with Trilby, smashing down off the side of his face with an awful *thunk*. Senseless, he crashed to the floor, dead to the world.

Trying to right myself, I felt punches in my lower back then caught a glance from the side of Dansey as he closed in towards me. I turned and kicked out with my right foot, I shrieked louder than he did as an almighty shock ran up my body.

I managed to release the driver and threw away the sock, now an encumbrance, which crashed off a wall knocking down the room's sole adornment, a faded picture of the *Blue Boy*. I turned to see where Claude was but I could only scream as I felt a horrific, unimaginable pain engulf my right side. I looked in astonishment at the sudden red effusion. As Dansey stepped back I saw the wooden handle of a knife sticking out of my body.

'*You fuckin' auld bastard!*' Losing all thought other than absolute blind, unthinking hatred, I dived forward, screaming and swinging both fists down on Dansey, his hands covering his head. I must have stumbled and fell crashing to the floor, kicking desperately to try get back up on to my feet. Just then other figures came into view.

I was starting to go in and out of consciousness as dizziness and pain began to shroud me. I was awake just long enough to catch Walter Thompson swing his huge hand and connect with the driver's face hard enough to lift him off his feet. I then watched as Richie, the Royal Marine guard, dressed in a suit of civilian clothes, punched and kicked Dansey to the floor. It was then that I blacked out completely.

I awoke to Walter sitting with me in the back of a motor car. I could hear his voice urging, 'Try to stay awake, Jamie! Try to stay awake!' And Richie who was driving, yapping away in thick Scouse, 'Yer alright, mate! We're off to the hospital! You can sure scrap! I'd not mess with ya! Yer goin' to be alright!' and other examples of what seemed to me, mindless drivel.

I thought well, so this is how it all ends. At least I went out fighting and no one beat me. Then Joanne spoke to me and asked if I could help her with her sums. She wasn't too good at division and Tom wanted me to hand him the garden shears, which were dripping red with blood, because if he didn't cut down the hedge then no one else would. He told me to clean them with a cloth after use in future as that's what all good tradesmen do. I then caught a dull light in my eyes from a fluorescent tube and looked around at grey and green walls and felt cool air rushing past me as I lay prone.

I was now sitting in Trafalgar Square with Gemma. Duncan, Jock, Davie and Tommy were with me. They were in uniform but bareheaded and all four completely encrusted in wet, cloying mud. Tommy and Davie sat together on a bench playing cards. Duncan and Jock were standing, passing a bottle to each other to swig from. I was talking to Gemma but she stood up and said she was off to see the King. Duncan and Jock took her arm in arm and the three began to walk off together. I stood up but the ache in my leg was nothing compared to the agony that encompassed my entire body. It hurt unbearably and I had to sit back down again. Gemma turned and said, *don't worry, it's alright Jamie, my* darling, you don't have to come with us. You stay here, we'll see you another time. I turned from her to Davie and Tommy in desperation but they were gone too.

I was left alone with relentless waves of pain passing over me. I burst into tears as I watched them saunter off amongst the crowds of people. No one left in the Square seemed to notice. They were all too busy celebrating.

EXTRACTS FROM THE WAR JOURNAL
OF GENERAL ALAN BROOKE

24 July 1942: *Just about to leave for the Admiralty banquet when Winston burst into my office at WO and told me awful news about James Melville. He was in a very bad way with tears rolling down his cheeks and repeating, 'My Boy! My Boy! All my fault! All my fault!' Quite extraordinary. He'd just returned from Westminster Hospital and said the situation with Jamie was very sticky. His daughter, who works for Bracken has been informed and taken to his side. The doctor said the next day or so would be decisive as it is suspected his lung was punctured. We both arrived in Greenwich very down and of course told no one. It seemed rather pointless.*

Simply cannot bear the thought of never speaking with that extremely pleasant chap again. In the motorcar home tonight I recalled the many enjoyable conversations with him which were a wonderful release from the burden I carry each day. The fellow always seemed to be around at the right moment and offered himself quite freely. He should be top of everyone's dinner party guest list! And his manner in dealing with Winston is peerless! There were times when I envied his wonderful ability to shut the PM up! Will pray for his recovery as I believe he has very young ones living in Yorkshire.

26 July 1942: ...*received news by telephone from Pug who informed me that Melville has pulled through! Absolutely wonderful! Pug was ever so pleased and said Winston cried with joy on being told. Pug then told me in amusing detail that as a military guard was to be placed at Jamie's door, there were no end of volunteers amongst the Royal Marine contingent and two of them came to blows over the honour! Tommy jumped in to try and separate them and received a most marvellous black eye when he caught a flailing elbow from one of the quarrelling Bootnecks! Priceless! Pug said his own diplomatic skills were brought to bear when, on visiting Jamie himself on the PM's behalf, he was involved in an altercation between the ward matron and a small but extremely pushy young American! She claimed to be a friend of the patient but the matron insisted only close family and those with requisite identification i.e. Downing Street passes were allowed admittance. Happily, Pug was able to resolve the situation to the satisfaction of all concerned!*

Jamie still very dopey but able to pass on greetings with the words, 'Tell the boys ah'm daein' fine!' Pug then left the young lady alone with her Lance-Corporal. I am so grateful that my prayers were answered. Jamie has lived the most fascinating of lives and is a delightfully unprepossessing soul though he has suffered a great loss which I am convinced he has yet to recover fully from. My fervent prayers now are that he himself is as fortunate as I was, my darling to find someone like you who brought me such peace and happiness in order to return to the living again in joyfulness and with all that strengthens me each and every day of my life.

Chapter Twenty-Four

THE EXPECTED TAP came and the girls shrieked as they fought one another to be first down the stairs to reach the door. I heard the trample of bare little feet pounding on the hallway floor as they both squabbled over who'd answer the knock.

'One of you! For God's sake!' I bawled in a slightly nervy voice, probably a little *too* loud. I heard the door opening and female voices speaking.

'Dad!'

I rose from my chair in the sitting room. 'Well, let the lady in then, you wee toerags!'

They giggled together at the last. They'd always found that term hilarious for some reason known only to themselves. Then the reality of the situation dawned on them as they both moved to stand behind me.

'My! What a welcome!' Meredith walked through and stood in the hallway, a suitcase in either hand.

'You can hang your coat there.' Alison pointed to the coat-hooks.

'Why, thank you very much! You're Alison, right? And you're Claire? I'm Meredith!' she put her hand out. After their initial exuberance the girls had now resorted to painful shyness. Then Claire coyly reached out her hand. She was always a crawler.

'Right you two, upstairs!' I ordered after introductions were concluded. 'Miss Macaulay and I need to have a wee chat together!'

They both then raced each other back up, a door slammed shut and excited jumping up and down began on a badly-creaking bed.

'You'll put your feet through that mattress! Get off that bed now!' I roared from the foot of the stairwell. I hadn't yet quite come to grip with my nerves.

'Nothing wrong with the voice!' Meredith laughed.

'Come on through,' I motioned to her.

'What kind of welcome is that, Jamie?' We embraced. She turned her head towards me. Our lips came together and slowly we released each other. Leaving her luggage in the hallway, I led her through to the sitting room.

'You're so thin, Jamie! I've brought things sent from the States. The best – all of it!'

I had visions of her humping boxes full of Spam and peanut butter but it was, in fact, a package that was being delivered later that day from the railway station.

'Always thinking of your belly!' I joked.

'No! Yours! I don't want my guy fading away now I'm here!'

We sat down together on the settee as she held my hand. I was grateful for that as it eased my trembling somewhat. She had evidently noticed.

'I'm nervous, too, darling!' She whispered then turned from me and looked around the room. 'I hope I'm not being a fool. Your girls are gorgeous! Like their Daddy!'

I thought of when she'd first visited me in hospital. I'd been barely conscious and full of morphine. I don't know what I said to her exactly. Gobble-de-gook, no doubt. I think I told her I loved her. I was pretty certain she said the same to me. I couldn't for the life of me remember in what order we pronounced our feelings for each other.

'Was the journey up alright?' I asked.

'Yes! How lovely England is in the fall!

'It's the *autumn*,' I replied. 'You'll have to start calling it that from now on.'

She smiled. 'The cabbie took me through Scarborough. The town's getting itself together again after the bombing,' he told me. It looks a beautiful place. You'll show it to me properly, won't you?'

'I guarantee you'll fall in love with it and not want to leave. Ever.' My eyes followed her as she stood up and walked over to the side-board that contained photographs, mementoes and ornaments. I knew she wanted to know what Gemma looked like. She picked up our wedding photo.

'Your wife was so beautiful,' she said, then replaced it reverentially.

I didn't speak. There was nothing I could say. She then looked at other photographs. The girls, me. Tom, Irene and the lads.

'My God!' She picked up one of Winston and me together, taken when we were at the battalion, long ago.

She put it back and held her hand to her face and began to sob. I walked over to her and led her back to the settee.

'It makes me feel like that too, sometimes.' I consoled her gently and clasped her to me.

'It's … it's just such a shock to see how young you were. A child amongst all that horror. Innocence, you know? You had the face of *innocence*.'

It was the first moment of intimacy between us since a tearful visit to my hospital bedside, days after the episode with Dansey at Arthur's lodgings. Her later visits would be more guarded after that as we slowly revealed ourselves to each other.

After my release and return home to Scarborough, we wrote and when at last I felt up to it I invited her up. We both knew what that meant for us.

'Winston protected me. He protected all of us. We were a happy bunch and we adored him. He gave me everything I have today.' We embraced again and held each other tightly. I blanched slightly. The wound hadn't fully healed yet.

She broke away and looked at me. 'Oh, I'm sorry, was that painful?'

'You'll have to take it easy with me! That's the part I'm looking forward to most.' Relieved, her smile returned and she stepped back.

'It's just … to be *here*, with you in this lovely home. With those little girls, it's a little overwhelming for me. I've wanted it so much these last months. The truth is I've thought of little else.'

I stepped towards her. 'You're here. I want you here. I *need* you here.' I spoke the words heavily and had to look away after.

There was further rumpus from upstairs to interrupt the moment, though I was relieved as it had broken some of the tension between us. Kids can be useful at times.

'Pair of wee monkeys!' I groaned, theatrically. 'Are you ready for lunch because I think my little darlings are trying to tell me they want to be fed.'

She smiled. 'Oh, yeah. I'm *ready*.'

I'd dined in swank restaurants in Washington and London but this was Scarborough and though it was autumn, early October can be a benign month, particularly on the coast. So we went to an establishment on the harbour that I knew well. We all sat outside eating our fish teas. The proprietor was a long-standing customer of mine, friend and fellow angler and we chatted over everyday matters as he pulled up a chair to join us.

No doubt Meredith had difficulty understanding Wilf's Yorkshire accent. I had trouble understanding him at times. He'd served years on the fishing boats and saved enough to buy the little place in the town that narrowly missed destruction during the bombing of March 1941. The girls knew it well and it was always a starting point before a day's donkey rides, Peasholm Park and trips to the shops resulting in me being fleeced by the two little grasping devils.

Wilf gathered up our plates after we'd finished and the girls ran off excitedly with far more than their usual allotment of pennies to spend. Meredith then lit up.

'I don't want the girls to see me smoking!' she explained. 'I think I can give up food but not cigarettes!' She'd finished off the fish but left most of her chips and peas.

'Whatever makes you happy!' I remembered Harry's theory about her.

'I never used to eat much.' She looked over the harbour to the North Sea beyond. 'When I was a little girl, there wasn't much around at times. I learned to go without.'

I looked over at the view. To the right, the South Bay and the majestic sight of the great Victorian hotel perched like an eagle upon its eyrie. So similar to Edinburgh and one of my favourite spots in the town, rich in memories of Gemma. It didn't feel so very different now with Meredith. Maybe I had moved on, finally.

'How was London?' I asked. There had been a pause which needed to be filled.

'I'm too busy to notice! God, they work us real hard! It's kind of fun flirting with everyone, though!' She laughed at my comically raised eyebrow. 'Aww, it's alright, honey! You've no *serious* competition to concern yourself over! There's a lot of gossip about I must say! Who's seeing who, just normal stuff, really. That's what I like about it. It's not the same without you there.'

'We've had ... an *unusual* beginning!' I stated with mock levity.

She laughed that lovely little girl's giggle. 'We sure did! But hey, look! We're at the beach now!'

We were indeed after leaving our table, having walked arm in arm down the steps leading off the harbour path onto the sands.

'The girls?' she asked.

'They know the routine. I usually walk along to just below The Grand and then turn back. By that time their money is usually spent!' Meredith chuckled heartily.

We walked slowly, savouring the warm comfortable feeling of her arm in mine. We paced along a few steps and she stopped, embraced me and kissed me slowly holding me tightly against her.

'That's what I've needed.' She looked up at me. Her lipstick smudged and its flavour tingled around my mouth. 'Jamie, I love you. You know that, don't you?' I looked at her as she placed her fingers delicately over my lips.

'Say nothing, darling,' she whispered. 'You'll have enough time, later.'

We carried on and she smiled ironically. 'I'm always meeting guys who live by the sea! I must be a born sailor's girl! God, the places I've been! I used to dream about all that. Being swept away by some handsome rogue and ravished on a desert island. And not being too worried by the ravishing part either!'

'I think this girl has hidden depths! What am I letting myself in for?' I hooted.

She laughed out loud. 'That's exactly what Ben told me once! If only he'd known I'd prefer a quiet life. I'd wanted him and all that came with him but the day we left on the boat for the Philippines, in my heart, I wanted to get off and return home.'

'Why did you feel like that?'

'It was too perfect. *He* was too perfect. He was incredibly considerate and kind to me at first. I knew then, I think, that it wasn't real. He never argued over anything.'

'You were newly-weds. He was getting to know you, probably.'

'Yes,' she agreed. 'At first that's what I thought it was. I admit it did infuriate me at times. He would just say I want you to be happy and let me have my way. I know now it was because he didn't know a thing about women and wasn't interested in finding out.'

'Many young fellows are like that, it can be down to how they've been brought up,' I suggested, though I knew the truth as much as she did.

'Jamie, he was homosexual,' she stated firmly.

We walked on. We were now arriving at areas of her life I wanted to learn about and would have to discuss. My experience is that there are few women who won't reveal every detail of a past relationship to their new love. It's a form of exorcism, perhaps.

'He would change his shirt, two, three times a day and there were other little things a woman notices,' she continued as if offering an explanation. If only she knew, I thought. 'I figured at first it was a sign of vanity. Maybe it was. It began to annoy me. I didn't know a thing. I was twenty-one and *virgin intacto*. Our wedding night was a disaster.'

She stopped, bent down and sifted some sand through her fingers. 'But I knew he could have given me more, even as inexperienced as I was. I was left wondering, what was the point of all that beauty if I couldn't have it all alone to myself to make love to? But it was married life and one of the great mysteries. I thought it would work out over time.' We walked on past a few dog-walkers but we had the beach mainly to ourselves.

She stopped. 'You were lucky, Jamie. You and Gemma. You were children who grew together into the kind of love most of us can only dream of.'

'There were problems for us too, Meredith,' I explained. 'I was marrying way beyond my class. It took a lot for Gemma to do that, even with the grandmother she had. There were times when I felt guilty and feared that the love may not be real, that it may not *last*. That I was fooling myself and worse, her. Like you said, over time it worked out. Thank God, I had that time.'

I felt free and able to talk, to reminisce, to recall past moments of great love and memories so precious that to impart them to another in this way was like a deep cleansing of all the pain of loss that clouded me in solitary moments over the years. I was left completely guiltless at last and without any reproach for the providence that had brought me to this moment.

I turned to her after looking out across the sea. 'I can say it now, if I haven't said it to you before.'

'You can say it when you want to, darling. I know. ' She said quietly.

'I love you, Meredith. I love you so very much.' My arm was around her shoulder as I pressed her close. We walked on till we were beneath St. Nicholas Cliff and the elegance of The Grand Hotel above us.

'I'll have to show you my hometown one day,' I said as we gazed up at the edifice. 'It's got a castle there, too. But it's in a lot better condition!' Scarborough's ruined medieval fortress, high on the North Cliff, sprawled long and convoluted in comparison with old Edina's proud rock. It still provided both an evocative scene and vital artery to the heart of the town.

'I can't wait to see it. A *real-life* castle.' There was a deep longing in her voice that seemed to harp back to another time in her life. A time of innocence where childlike desires long ago suppressed, cast off, had now reawakened and were renewed with a vitality that shook me a little.

'You said something to me once,' I recalled. 'You said that "you owed him." What did you mean by that?'

'I was wrong. I didn't owe him anything. But when I was with him, even after the separation, he would work on me. I don't know what it was. I still felt such a pull of physical attraction for him. He was *that* beautiful. I also saw his gentleness. He was surprisingly feminine in his instincts but he wasn't *effeminate*. God, it was strange! Jamie, you don't know how it feels for me to have someone like you who is so simple to understand!

'He *was* excited when I fell pregnant. I wanted a child much sooner. I … I won't go into detail about that side of things. Bed … and all that, I mean. I feel I have some loyalty never to impart that to anyone. But it eventually happened. We were nearly through our time in Subic Bay.'

I stopped her. 'Meredith, there's no need to go any further. I don't want you bringing up painful memories. I'm sorry. I only want to know about Washington.'

'You don't think that's a painful memory too?'

I felt awkward and wanted to move away from the subject now. 'Meredith, I'm…'

'No, darling. You're right. I only have memories but those little girls nearly lost their father because of me.'

'Not because of you. You were used. I just want to know; to get it out of the way so we can move on from it.'

She paused before she continued. 'His own life wasn't easy. He had a strange upbringing in China. He was left with his mother who hated it there. The poor woman had no release from it all. She had an affair with a French official but he was sent home. He had his fun. Then she tried to kill herself.

'His father was obsessed with the country and disappearing all of the time. He passed that onto Ben, the only thing he did and it had to be something like *that*. I used to think my mother a frivolous and stupid woman. But she has *character*. There's always been *life* in her. Ben's parents were frightened of revealing anything of themselves. Ben was like that too, of course.

'His grandfather was a strong influence on him. They never met till he was seven but carried out a remarkable correspondence in letters. I read some of them when I was alone in Subic Bay. It was quite beautiful. This love they had from a distance for each other. I believe that was the strongest connection he ever had with another human being.

'His only son, Ben's father was considered a disappointment. But the old man wasn't a monster by any means. I grew to love him too. He tried so hard to keep us together. He was so kind to me after we parted.'

'When did you separate?'

'When we came back from China. Ben…' she paused momentarily, 'he didn't care anymore. He felt he'd been betrayed. He was doing well but wasn't happy with US policy. He wasn't alone. Many others felt the same way he did. America was backing the wrong horse. We should now be reaching out to Chou and Mao as well as Chiang. He thought

Stilwell would do that. That's why he wanted on his staff.'

She was very knowledgeable. I felt a little distant from her as these recollections from a past life were recalled. It was strange and I felt as I had when I'd spoken to Harry about it, like an outsider.

She continued. 'Ben wrote a report stating that the Reds should at least be given equal status. Chiang was no more than a glorified war-lord. That at least the communists had an idea for the future of China. All Chiang wanted was to make money for himself.

'Ben was so brave over there. When we were in Shanghai, everyone, even foreigners had to tip their hats to the Japanese or risk a beating. He refused to do it to a group of soldiers one day and stared them down. From then on, he never wore a hat again.'

Those with similar attitudes that Ben Howard worked with in China would all later be denounced by the State Department and Senator McCarthy as those who lost China to the communists in 1949. Remarkable men like John Davies, John Stewart Service, Oliver Edmund Clubb, and John Carter Vincent. All would be accused of being Red sympathisers or worse and made scapegoats. Their mistake was in reporting the truth about Chiang, how corrupt he was, how he cared only for how much he could squeeze out of Uncle Sam and paid the price.

They would end up in lowly jobs in the Foreign Service, ambassadorships to the worst places on earth for those who were fortunate enough. Others would be hounded out of their jobs. One who left could only find work as a furniture salesman.

'And they kicked him out the Service for that?' I said.

'No. They're more subtle. There was another reason.' I could guess and it was what Harry Hopkins had alluded to.

'I ... had an affair. He was a naval attaché.' My jaw must have dropped. The story had taken another turn where I'd assumed wrongly.

We were seated now. We had climbed up the steps just below The Grand where there was a tea-shop, and ordered two cups.

'He was married and a lot older than me. I sometimes think I did it to see if I was capable of doing something like that. Really, I did it for the excitement, the *sex*. I was completely bored and so unhappy. That's how basic it was. I wanted *closeness* with someone. In my mind I could imagine that it was what married life should have been like. I'd never believed myself capable of doing something like that before. I was so down-trodden, I blamed myself. But the guy was fun to be with and really sweet to me.'

'Did you love him?' I felt I had the right to ask.

She paused. 'No. The problem was he fell in love with me! God, can you believe it. *Femme Fatale*, me. Right?' She smiled ironically.

'He wanted to leave his wife and we had a big scene. I told him I couldn't leave my husband. I desperately wanted *not* to have to tell him I didn't love him. I cared for him too much to hurt him that way. Of course, he asked me straight out if I did.'

I lit a Tom Thumb and looked over to The Grand. A group of young Royal Air Force officers were standing in the grounds laughing together. The hotel was now a temporary base for trainee aircrew.

She would not tell me her response. 'I broke it off but Ben found out about it. God! It was happening everywhere! People were sleeping with everyone. There was nothing else to do. Ben was a very cold person. Sometimes I just wished he'd hit me. Of course, he wouldn't do that.

'He was censored for the report he'd written. He was also told that his wife's behaviour was the talk of the foreign compounds and that it wasn't going to be tolerated. The matter of his other habits wasn't discussed, he told me. Yes, I knew about him by then. A really terrific marriage, was it not? And the result of it all: his promotion was not confirmed that year.'

I held her hand as we sat at the table. 'Jamie. It's so lovely here. So peaceful. I love you. I love you so very much.'

I couldn't speak. She was indeed exorcising her past life. She'd married a completely unsuitable man, was then left virtually alone and childless with little prospect of having another in a foreign land and turned for comfort to someone who fell for her completely. She still couldn't bring herself to discuss the most painful aspect of her story. But I understood it all. She didn't give her heart easily. When she did, I truly believed it was all encompassing and without equivocation.

'When did you know you loved *me*?' I asked.

'When I met you at the station, in London,' she answered, without hesitation. 'When you stood in the street and turned round and looked at me. You've got the most beautiful eyes I've ever seen, Jamie. More so than Ben's ever were. There was never any softness in his. They were empty. But in yours I saw fear and hope and some dread. I saw someone who was so easy to fall in love with that if I didn't act fast someone else would find you. Women *like* you, Jamie. You just can't see it.' She smiled. 'That's *why* they like you.'

'And when you came back to America?' I continued for her.

'I left him. On the ship back we hardly spoke. It was just awful. The bastard had been screwing little Chinese boys but I was the one who'd wronged *him*.' Bitterness had crept in.

'I told him I was leaving, he accepted without demur. He made no attempt to try to save our marriage. No pleas, nothing. He seemed *beaten*, no longer caring. I moved back to New York and got a job and tried to carry on with my life. Saw a few men, nothing special. Ben called me from time to time and we talked and healed things to an extent. He was just freewheeling, doing nothing in particular. He didn't even appear interested in China. It was then I realised how down he was and we became friends again.'

It would have been just before Pearl Harbour, she said. He came to visit her in New York.

'I still hadn't started any divorce proceedings and neither had he. He asked me if I would hold off a little longer. He told me he was going back into the Navy and it would look better for him if he was still married.

'He was quite excited about it. He knew war was coming and wanted to be in on it and hoped he'd be sent to the Far East. Then came December 7th and he was kept in Washington. Admiral Stark was removed and King took his place. King knew of him and wanted him on his staff.'

'His past was forgotten as easily as all that?'

'Russia was our ally now. He managed to convince them he wasn't a Red but saw them as the lesser of two evils. The report was looked at again. They saw the passion in it. He retracted a lot of what was written. His record was expunged as a reward. King didn't seem to care. He backs the view that we should use the communists to fight the Japanese. Ben was an excellent officer who shared his own beliefs about defeating Japan. He also saw someone who looked good and could charm anyone. King knows he's unattractive and abrasive. Ben was there to smooth things over. I imagine his transfer to Stilwell's staff thrilled him more than anything.'

'What were you doing in those days?'

'Harry got me the job in Washington. He was seeing my mother again. It wasn't anything big, just meeting for lunches whenever he was in the city. His wife had died. They'd been very happy together. He found peace with her.'

It was all coming together slowly. On listening I still had to stop at times and ask what I had to do with it all. I was past the point of wanting to retreat as I may have tended to before. I was *part* of her story now.

'I moved there and he helped me settle in. God, he was so ill! In and out of the Naval Hospital. I nursed him a lot. He was such a worry to me. That's where he met Louise, his new wife.'

I knew how she felt about Harry being a concern. We had left the tea room and taken the long set of steps back down to the beach. We did not speak again till we found ourselves back on the sand.

Her manner now changed subtly. She did not look at me, instead she stopped and gazed out at the water. 'Harry came to me and told me he had a big secret. There were some very important visitors arriving from England to meet the President. There was one who needed a guide for a few days to show him around town. Harry was sweet and nice as always and said he'd arrange with my bosses for some time off. It would be fun, at government expense and that you were cute.'

The day had begun bright and clear but an autumnal squall wasn't far away. We stopped and watched the tide rolling up off the sands. A bloke with bare feet and his trouser legs rolled up was standing in the water, looking out absently as little waves washed against him.

'He said it was up to me to decide but to tell no one. He told me you were a widower with small children. He made it sound off-hand and I didn't know why he said that. I know now.' She squeezed my arm.

'I said, no problem, sounds like fun. I wanted to return a favour, I guess. I know now there was no way I wouldn't do it. It was no big deal. Take some fella round museums for a couple of days.

'The next day Ben called wanting to talk to me. I thought nothing of it. We'd do it from time to time. He came over to the house that night.

'We were alone. He seemed to always know when the other girls went out or worked late. He told me that important members of the British High Command were due in Washington for talks. There was one of them that he wanted me to meet. He then told me straight out what he wanted me to do.'

She spoke in forthright tones. I realised later that it was the only way she could without the emotion overwhelming her. At the time, I thought she was fairly cold about it all.

'He said this man was a widower but would be looking for opportunities while alone in the city. He was a danger to the American cause as he had a baleful influence on decision making in London.'

'Jesus Christ! Don't tell me you believed such tripe!' I was aghast to hear that two seemingly intelligent people could come together with such a plot in mind just to ensnare Jamie Melville of Gorgie Road.

'Why, Meredith? Why not kick him out the house? Or tell Harry right away? The whole thing is insane!' I was becoming heated and frankly a little exasperated.

'Why? Because I didn't think I would go through with it anyway. If I did go to Harry, Ben would have been arrested. I felt I'd done enough to him.'

'What had you done, for God's sake? Had an affair? You lost your child because of him!'

'Don't say that, please!'

I cursed inwardly at my temper. 'Please, Meredith, we don't have to talk anymore. This should be a happy time. I'm just trying to understand it! That's all. Don't get upset, sweetie. I couldn't bear it!'

She was still dry eyed as we looked out towards a heavy bank of cloud heading landward.

'You want to understand. Of course you want to. I thought I could play him along. He told me that I had to get the cane out of your sight for a while. I had to use any method I saw fit. We were also to be photographed.'

'Photographed? Where?'

'He told me there are ways of doing it. The negatives are then used to pressure you. They don't have to catch you in the act. Inference is enough. That along with other evidence they put together, I gathered it was to be a long-term thing.'

'God almighty!'

'I said, okay. I just wanted him out the house so I could think. I considered calling Harry but I was becoming paranoid that maybe I was being watched.'

'Let's walk back now.' I took her arm as we turned towards the harbour.

'I met you that first day at the embassy. I just acted mechanically. Tried to look *through* you, as if you weren't really there. I didn't do it too well, I'm no actress.'

I'd thought that too and agreed with her.

'When we were walking around Arlington, I told myself I wasn't going to sleep with you or do anything like that. I saw that you were nice and not some skirt-chaser on the prowl. I'd been lied to about that. No matter what Ben thought, I was out of it. Harry called me that night and asked how it went. I told him I was still happy to meet you the next day. I'd decided in my own mind now.' That was the day we went shopping in Georgetown.

'I was enjoying myself picking out shirts and a suit for you. I'd never done that much with Ben. It was little things like that I remembered doing for old boyfriends in the past. Presents at Christmas and stuff. When you came out of the changing room to ask my opinion, I thought that Harry was right. You *were* cute. Very cute. But I tried not to think like that.

'I wasn't thinking of you as anything other than a stranger I was told to spend time with. Then I realised I'd missed the point. I'd forgotten that it was Harry's idea originally and it was supposed to be just a few pleasant days together. I'd allowed Ben once again to take control of my life and I determined that I wouldn't any longer.

'He called me that night in a fury. I'd let him down. I was supposed to be with you at your hotel. What was I playing at? I was messing around with some very serious people.

'He'd gone too far. It was like I was no longer the same person. I changed when my little boy died, of course I did but in those few days I finally threw off Ben Howard forever. He was just a voice on the telephone to me now. He no longer had any hold over me. I could see him as he was. I also had Harry. I always did but usually balked from asking him for help. Now I knew I'd grown up, I no longer worried

299

about that. I contacted him and a cab arrived outside the door in minutes. He was in the back and looked terrible. We drove on and got out and spoke.'

'Weren't you worried about being watched?'

'No, because I knew that Harry's boss was bigger than anyone else's. I would be safe with him.'

'What happened?

'We drove off towards the White House and were led thought the gates. The cab stopped and we got out and walked to a little spot on the lawn. I told him everything. He listened and when I finished I was crying, begging him to help me. He said I was not to worry – I had to meet you again and do this one thing.'

'Did you feel he knew more than he was letting on?'

'I didn't care if he did. I only knew he would help me. He told me to meet you once more at your hotel at a certain time. I was to get the cane from you somehow, *anyhow* and leave it in the bedroom whilst we went to dinner. He also told me you liked me.'

'He was right! As always!' The atmosphere had lifted a little and her smile returned.

'He said I had to go home and call Ben or leave a message. I would see you again and do what Harry had told me to do. After that it would be over and I'd never have any kind of relationship with him again, he assured me. I realise now that he had helped arrange for Ben to go back to China.

'Ben came round to the house the next morning. You agreed I wasn't a very good actress, now I didn't have to be one any longer. I was someone else instead. I was who I was before I'd known him but older and stronger. I'd become Meredith Macaulay again.

'He thanked me and left. Nothing more, which suited me fine. I knew now that he meant nothing to me and could no longer make me feel any obligation. Though later, when I heard he'd died – I cried. I guess I'm not that tough after all.'

I defended her. 'Not tough, or hard or anything else like

that. Just an ordinary person under difficult circumstances. Who knows how any of us will react?'

'The afternoon I met you at the hotel, it was as *me* again. Do you understand that night was our *first date*? When we left the room together I hadn't noticed you'd left the cane. Please believe me. What I said to you was genuine. It was only afterwards I realised what had happened. Maybe my mind was working subconsciously but when I told you to just leave it, I would have said that to anyone. It was when we had dinner that Ben got into the room and did what he had to do. Jamie, I so loved that evening with you but I thought it would be our last.'

'He inserted a wee capsule full of microfilm and negatives,' I informed her.

'What happened to them?'

'Let's just say that they reached the people they were meant to! Darling, it was all arranged by Winston. He was pulling the strings. Howard walked into his trap. He was out of his depth and had no right to involve you. It ended alright for us, if not for him. If you ask me whether I have any sympathy for him – I don't. I'm tired of mixing with people who just use others for their own ends.'

'But isn't that what Mr Churchill did to you, if what you're saying is correct?'

'It is correct and yes, he did. But he's the exception. The only one I'll allow.'

We were nearing the restaurant. I could see the girls seated at a table with glasses of juice in front of them. Courtesy of Wilf.

'What do you really think happened to Ben?' she asked finally.

I'd thought long and hard about that whilst lying in hospital. I could not decide between two scenarios, suicide or that he was murdered by Dansey out of revenge or to use his death as a form of blackmail. The third alternative, shot by Arthur, I thought too simple. But it was always a possibility. I never would find out the truth.

I replied that I just didn't know for certain.

'I'm sad his life is over,' she concluded regretfully. 'Harry ensured I was in another carriage on the train down when I got off the ship in Scotland. I knew Ben was in London but I had no desire to see him and hoped I wouldn't bump into him in Grosvenor Square. He deserved happiness as much as anyone and I don't see his death as some form of release. I've looked into myself and know that I left him behind long before. I have that truth in me.'

We were now with the girls. 'Dad! How *long* were you taking! It's freezing!' moaned Claire.

'What a whinger!' I retorted in my "Daddy" voice. 'And in front of Miss Macaulay, too! Let's find a taxi, then.' They both began walking over to the nearby stand where a motorcar stood idling.

Meredith laughed. 'Tell me, Jamie, do you really need *another* girl in your life?'

'The more the merrier!' I sighed wearily.

She smiled and then became serious. 'Can ... can I ask you if you've forgiven me? I have to know.'

I hadn't expected that. In all the time since I'd known how I'd truly felt about her, such a thing had never occurred to me.

'There's nothing to forgive. You're here now. Our life together begins *today*.'

We were married just before the year's end. My mother and sisters came down from Edinburgh, Tom dusted off his best man's speech and Harry Hopkins sent a telegram to congratulate us, wishing all the best for his girl and me. We held the ceremony at St Mary's.

All my girls were present.

Chapter Twenty-Five

I was in hospital over a month recovering.

The knife wound could have been worse I was told. It was only a small blade and was stopped from puncturing my right lung deeper by cracking a rib on its way in. The doctors felt with rest and proper care I'd return to full strength.

Walter Thompson had officially been granted the night off. This was unusual as the Prime Minister had an official engagement, but a relief was found to replace him as both were concerned about me. Winston had ordered Walter to keep an eye out after the bodyguard related to his master the conversation we'd had earlier that day. The call from Dansey to the War Rooms was logged and when I stupidly rushed off to my near-fatal rendezvous, Walter was already in Downing Street. I'd been followed back expertly from Claridge's by young Richie the Bootneck. This surprised me no end when I heard about it later as I had no idea I was being shadowed. Walter had requested a Marine from the guard detachment and chose well.

They nearly lost me in traffic but Walter deduced correctly that I was making for Kings Cross. He already knew Arthur's address. They had to hang around well out of sight when they arrived as they weren't sure how many people Dansey had brought with him. When Richie spotted the driver disappear quickly from the doorway shortly after I'd entered both he and Walter were in the building within seconds. I've no doubt to this day that I'd be dead if they hadn't.

I made the decision in the hospital that I'd be going home after I was released.

Winston had spent that period on a jaunt to North Africa where he relieved the senior British commanders who'd been fought to a standstill by Rommel. He then made another potentially disastrous error of judgment. Gott, the officer chosen to replace the dismissed Commander General Auchinleck, was a tired man and quite as unsuitable as all the Prime Minister's previous choices had been. Only days later the aircraft Gott was travelling in was shot down. The new commander of the 8th army and the entire crew were burned to death.

Brooke's original preference had been for a protégé of his, a certain Bernard Law Montgomery. That confident and clever little man who looked nothing like Winston's idea of a general was now sent for, and we never looked back.

The next stage of his foreign journey was on to Moscow to deliver the painful news that there would be no Second Front in Europe that year. By all accounts the meetings went well, though I later heard from Brookie that the amounts of alcohol consumed at the dinners and receptions for the Prime Minister would have sunk the Royal Navy. The Soviets could match Winston for late night follies, but they never out-drank him.

On his return, Winston visited me in hospital. I told him there and then I was going home to rest and to think things over. Despite his assurances of my safety, I believed it for the best. I wanted no more of the high life. I'd be looking over my shoulder most of the time. At least in Scarborough, I was on my own patch. I never truly believed Dansey would exact revenge – I was certain Winston's "assurances" involved threatening the spy-master with sudden death should anything befall me or any of my family.

There was also the question of the circumstances surrounding myself and a homosexual scandal involving my brother and a dead body. If it got out questions would be asked that might result in the government, i.e. Winston, being scrutinised. In a way that made my decision easier and

I could be seen as doing my bit to spare certain people embarrassment by removing myself from the scene. I wanted a return to normality again. And I had something to look forward to. Winston became a little upset but was ultimately forced to accept my decision. Once again.

For the record, Howard's body was shipped home and his family were informed he'd died in a bombing raid.

Dansey remained in his job and was knighted a year later. He was reputed to have been involved in the destruction of the notorious Prosper network run by the SOE in France in 1943. It was rumoured that Winston had a hand in that too, but I believe that to be nonsense. It could never be proved of course, but Dansey was said to have grinned triumphantly when he heard the news that the group had been pulled apart by the Germans. Hundreds were arrested and many died terrible deaths in concentration camps including the famous Indian Princess, Noor Inayat Khan. Dansey himself died in 1947. At least, I hope he did.

Harry Hopkins carried on in his capacity as the devoted fixer for President Roosevelt. His health deteriorated until he suffered a complete collapse at the end of 1944. The added blow of the death of his youngest son in the Pacific came about at the same time.

With his new wife, Louise, he moved out of the White House and into a new home in Georgetown. But he was only able to work a few hours a day. He did travel with FDR to the Yalta conference in February 1945 but when the President himself passed way in April of that year, Harry was heard by people to say that his life's work was over. His own condition then became a matter of grave concern.

The new President, Harry S. Truman, still required the services of the *White House Rasputin*, as his enemies referred to him. With incredible resolve and courage he travelled at the President's request to Moscow in an attempt to iron out differences with Stalin and prepare the agenda for the three-way Potsdam Conference in July 1945.

The meeting was a success but on his return his body finally gave out. The botched surgery performed ten years previously weakened his system, left him in constant pain and, on a number of occasions, very close to death. He also had financial worries and no private wealth other than what he had earned as a government servant. The final two months of his life were spent in hospital, where he died in January 1946 of liver failure.

Winston Churchill said of him: *Among all those in the Grand Alliance, warriors or statesmen who struck deadly blows at the enemy and brought peace nearer, [Harry L. Hopkins] will ever hold an honoured place.*

As for Arthur, I was reminded of Winston's other words about there always being more questions than answers. The next I heard of him was when I received a letter in the early 1970s informing me of his death from someone he lived with for a time. The relationship had ended before my brother passed away.

He was found alone in a high rise flat in Leeds. He'd been lying there for days before the door was broken down due to the smell.

The letter I received was from a woman.

I voted Labour in 1945 and told Winston why. It wasn't exactly an *et tu Brute* moment and I didn't regard it as any kind of betrayal. Winston said he didn't either, but I'm not sure I believed him.

I saw him a few times after the war. We were invited to Chartwell during the summer every year up until he became Prime Minister again in 1951.

After that we saw less of him. He should have taken it easy then. Clemmie and the family wanted him to, but the Tory party never had the guts to bin him after all the trouble he'd caused them over the years. There's irony for you. Mind you, there was no-one else.

So he went on. Doddering into his eighties and even

suffering another heart attack in office. Eden champed at the bit mostly through his own inability to stick the knife in. Too much of a gent was our Anthony. It could have been worse, that little appeaser Rab Butler might have succeeded him.

When he finally left office, Winston spent a lot of time on cruises and holidays provided by rich friends. People criticised him for this, though he had grown increasingly feeble. He was entitled to his place in the sun of his beloved south of France. After all, he'd only saved western civilisation. That should count towards *something*.

The business did well through the post war years well up into the 1960s. We eventually sold the company in 1970. Tom's boys had moved out of Scarborough as none of them wanted to stay around fish for the rest of their lives. One joined the Royal Air Force and worked his way up to Wing-Commander.

Meredith got a job with the local council and rose up to a fairly high position in the planning department. She never lost her accent and never lost her love for her new home. She showed no desire to ever return to the United States. We were unable to have any children.

My daughter Joanne ended up living in Folkestone married to a Civil Engineer she'd met during the war whilst he was serving in the RNVR. He was the only one of my three daughter's husbands I had any time for.

Alison and Claire both married lemons. One of them I threw out the house once for making a remark about Scotland. The other ran off with a work colleague. Claire didn't seem to bother too much. She became a physical education teacher, remained single and had no children. I often wondered about her.

As for me, I looked after the business up till we sold it. We were pretty well off and I could afford to become a gentleman of leisure somewhat and took on help. Tom got involved in the local football scene as a coach of a boys club and one of his own lads had a trial with York City. I took up fishing in a big way and joined the local angling club.

Meredith and I enjoyed holidays to Europe. We liked Paris best and went there regularly. We had our ups and downs like everyone else. I discovered she had a temper as bad as my own and had to learn to duck at times. It was strange to have two wives who were so different. But we never spent a night apart in all our years together. I was indeed a lucky man to have found her.

Chapter Twenty-Six

THE CALL CAME just after New Year. His private secretary informed me that he had suffered a massive stroke and his doctors believed this time the game was up.

He was being visited regularly but no one was sure he knew what was going on around him. He showed signs of life around Randolph, Sarah and Mary (poor Diane having died the year before), but he was in and out of consciousness and the end was now expected.

I spoke to Meredith who told me to go. I'd never live with myself if I didn't.

I travelled down the next day and made my way to the house. He'd spent most of his retirement years living at Hyde Park Gate. Word had leaked out and the press had gathered along with the usual rubber-neckers who are attracted by such events. As the house was at the end of a cul-de-sac, the crowds had begun to affect the daily movements of the other residents. A plea from Clementine had resulted in the interlopers moving away a respectful distance to the top of the street.

I was allowed entry where Mary and Clemmie welcomed me. I was then left with one of the staff who was employed to care for him. The nurse, an efficient looking woman in her forties, gave me the prognosis.

'He's asleep mostly. When he's awake he seems lucid. If you speak he may move his lips but we don't know if he is aware of any presence there with him. He seems to respond to his children, we're not so sure the grandchildren are noticed. Still, that is to be expected, especially in cases where there are so many *kinds* of visitors.'

'I think I'll be alright,' I assured her.

The nurse looked me over with a weary smile. She must have offered the same spiel countless times over the last days. This was just one more.

'After all, I know the magic word,' I explained.

She must have thought she had an imbecile on her hands but opened the bedroom door for me and left me alone with him.

The room was on the ground level and had been his private secretary's office. The curtains of the window that faced onto the street were half closed. Fresh flowers sat in a vase on a table beside him. He was lying in bed, propped up on his pillows. His cat lay curled up beside him.

His eyes were closed. His head seemed huge. It was completely bald and his face was smooth though goo dribbled from his lips. His pallor was better than I'd expected. There wasn't the ghastly yellow-grey precursor of death but fresh white creaminess akin to a healthy baby. One hand rested near the cat and the other on top of the bedding across his chest.

'Have you been up to your old tricks again?' I knew he was extremely deaf but I spoke slowly and clearly.

There appeared to be no response. I moved round the right side of the bed, leant over and spoke directly into his ear.

'I said, have you been causing bother, *Colonel*?'

The eyes flickered and his body began to shake slightly. His lips parted.

'You know your old batman, don't you? Jamie, Jamie Melville?'

I looked over him as stared up at me and I knew there was recognition. He moved his lips again.

'I've got something to show you, Colonel.' I slipped my hand inside my coat and brought out a photograph.

'Two fine lads, eh! Remember when this was taken?'

I placed it in his hand which lay across his chest, arranging the picture so that it was very near for him to see. He was staring at it.

His hand shook somewhat but I steadied him by gripping it softly with my own. He stared fixedly at the image. His lips moved more keenly but nothing comprehensible came from them. Then a twitch of a smile appeared, finally.

'Aye, you know! That's us two! Way back in the day! A right wee laddie I was, eh? And you knowing what you knew at the time! If I did, I wouldn't have looked so miserable!'

It was the image that had upset Meredith the day she arrived in Scarborough, taken by Archie Sinclair the day before Winston relinquished command of the battalion. He was leaving to return to London to try and fight his way back into the government.

We were standing in the courtyard at Laurence Farm. He'd just had pictures taken with the officers while I had been hiding away on my own in the farmhouse trying not to let anyone see me cry. Up till that moment I thought I was off to join Archie's regiment as his batman and feeling desolate, believing I would never see Winston again.

'James Melville, where are you!' I heard him bellow.

I wiped my face the best I could and walked out into the courtyard. Blokes were running around daft, clearing away stores and equipment as the battalion prepared to head for Moolenacker to join up with the unit we were amalgamating with over the next few days.

'Jamie, fancy a picture?' Archie asked kindly. I didn't but I walked over to where Winston was talking to another officer.

'Here he is!' he exclaimed turning to me. 'Why, James! Are you ill? Have you been sick again?'

'Ah dinnae feel well, Colonel! Ah've got an awfy sair stomach!' I wailed piteously. I thought that sounded better than admitting I'd been *greeting*.

'Oh, dear!' he commiserated and put a hand on my shoulder, scrutinising me closely. 'We shall have to investigate! The finest doctors in the British army must be summoned to solve this medical conundrum! What shall they discover?

Overindulgence in Dundee cake followed by too large a helping of rice pudding? James, you must never mix your desserts!'

The other officer, Captain Ramsay, laughed and shook hands with Winston before walking off.

'Now, Mr Sinclair,' Winston turned to Archie. 'The battalion's most important member has arrived and is now prepared to be launched into posterity!'

Archie held up his box brownie. 'Closer together, lads,' he ordered.

Winston moved to his left and placed an arm round my shoulder.

'That's the one!' cried Archie.

The picture would reveal Winston Churchill peering intently down the lens, wearing his famous Poilu steel helmet and next to him, a child of fifteen in uniform wearing a Glengarry with a backdrop of the courtyard and an open stable door behind them. The distorted figures of a few others behind them are in view. The boy's face is pale and as severe as his colonel's stare only that intensity is due to how hard he is trying to keep from sobbing.

Meanwhile, a sniffing sound came from Winston that I recognised as a kind of laughter.

'You've been kidding them on all along? Old devil that you are!' We stayed like that for a time. I spoke of our days in the battalion.

After a while he began to fade and was clearly tiring. The most difficult moment of my life, since I'd told my little girls their mummy wasn't coming home from hospital, had arrived.

'Well, Colonel. I have to leave now. Got to catch the train! I'll leave the photo. I've got another one like it at home. That's *your* one.'

Then, as I removed my hands from his, from some reservoir of strength that still remained within him, he brought the photograph close to his lips in what was undoubtedly a kiss. His hand then shook uncontrollably but his determined fingers clung steadfast to the picture.

The shadows were gathering and he was now finally beyond mastering events. I was having difficulty controlling myself. All that remained was my farewell.

I held his hand in mine again and leaned over and kissed his cheek and slowly pulled back.

'I've never thanked you before, Winston. Thank you for my life. Thank you for each and every day of it. I love you and always will. Goodbye, Colonel Churchill.'

A few days later, he passed away.

I was invited to the funeral service at St Paul's, but I called Mary to tell her I couldn't make it as I was feeling under the weather. We chatted for a while and I said I would carry out my own private memorial.

I read about the route the funeral cortege would take in the newspapers and made it down to London again on my own. I stood in Cannon Street in the City near the entrance to the station that had been destroyed in the Blitz. That entire area of the capital had been devastated in 1941 and was undergoing a renewal. Its regeneration alone was testimony to the man we'd come to do honour.

It was a bitterly cold January day and I was wrapped up to the nines. Meredith insisted I wear something on my head. I've never been a hat type and the only one I felt comfortable wearing was the one that was fortunately, most appropriate for the occasion.

I stood next to an old Seaforth Highlander and we started talking. He noted my Glengarry and cap badge and asked me. I answered, yes. I was one of his lads.

It was getting colder, just standing there waiting. People were going off to buy tea and hot drinks and returning to their spots. I daren't as my bladder had almost given way over the years and anything would have passed through me in that chill. I was sixty-four at the time.

Then we heard bells peeling, the faint but slowly strengthening sound of music, the drill of boot heels and the clopping from horses as the Life Guards passed before us followed by the bands of the Guards and Royal Marines. Sounds from the wheels and chains of the gun carriage pulled by the naval guard of honour echoed around, taking us back to another age.

The procession had left the service at the Cathedral and began the stage towards Tower Pier and the waiting launch by the Thames. His body would travel along the river before being taken to the train at Waterloo where Winston would leave the splendours of London forever, to make the final journey to the tranquil surroundings and lasting peace of Bladon, near Blenheim Palace.

I was standing in front, on the edge of the pavement, next to my old Seaforth as the sailors marched by and as it passed us he saluted the flag-draped coffin. I stood still, thought for a second and then saluted too.

There were tears and voices crying their salutations: 'Bye, Winnie,' 'Thank you, Mr Churchill,' 'God bless you, Winston.' Others, less than decorous were hushed down. We stood, some mesmerised by the spectacle and some merely chilled. Others like me, lost in memories as the procession, marching to sombre refrains made its way slowly along Cannon Street. I didn't hang about long after that and caught a connection for Kings Cross and home.

I'd stood where I wanted to stand, amongst my people, not mingling with our so called-betters. To share my gratitude and to say goodbye as one of *them*, those who bore the brunt of the pain and shock of it all.

Listening to his words around the wireless, their children evacuated and taken from them, some forever in sunken ships in frozen oceans. Huddling together in precarious and insecure refuges under the ground, coming up afterwards praying that their homes were intact. Experiencing the awful finality of receiving telegrams in brown envelopes and the crushing of dreams forever. I stood for them all.

The people who'd been exhausted, bled and bereaved, but never beaten.

> *So Churchill sleeps, yet surely wakes*
> *old warrior where the morning breaks*
> *on sunlit uplands. But the heart aches*
> *at Bladon.*

Chapter Twenty-Seven

I'M ON THE move again.

At the age of eighty-six I've another adventure ahead of me. I'm saying goodbye to this old house. The Legion found me a lovely rest home in the town and I have to admit I'm looking forward to it. I can't get upstairs any longer and that bloody electric lift contraption I paid a fortune for broke down once too often. One morning it left me half way up the stairs before the home-help arrived and heard me shouting. That decided matters for me.

My two youngest were furious. They expected me to leave the house to them but I had to sell it to pay for my new ac-commodation. That's what I told them. It's not true but the look on their faces was worth it. They both stormed out the house saying they'd washed their hands of me.

Joanne has been very helpful as always. She wanted me down in Folkestone and showed me around a nice place there. I was tempted, believe me as I love Kent. But I've two wives and a dear brother lying in St Mary's churchyard and couldn't leave them.

Meredith passed away in the late 1970s. I'd given up years before but her own heavy smoking caught up with her and lung cancer saw her off. A few of the old girls who'd been eyeing me at the tea-dances joked that I'm too risky to get close to. I have a habit of out-living spouses. They want to know my secret.

I have a friend, Vivian, whose husband I knew and she became my companion after he died. We went on coach holidays together to places like Blackpool, Skegness, Mar-gate and the south coast for a few years but eventually the journeys became too much for me. I spent the holiday in the hotel room recuperating from the bus trip there and preparing for the ordeal of the return journey home.

She stuck it out with me though and along with my grandchildren, ensures that I'm not neglected. I've got five of them, three boys and two girls. Two of the boys and a girl are here in Yorkshire. The boys assure me that Hearts are their second favourite team.

My granddaughter visits me once a week. We always have a lot to talk about. She just graduated from university in York and has plans for the future. I'm afraid she may move away soon. I hope it's not too far. She has rows with her mother about me. Alison was always easily led and Claire's a right little bossy boots. But Julie can shut both of them up. She's like me that way and in many others she reminds me so much of Gemma.

I told Julie I'd written something. I said I would tell her the full story over her next few visits. She laughed and said, 'Granddad, don't be so desperate. I don't need a reason to come and see you.'

I gave her what I'd written and she went away and telephoned me the next evening. She was stunned and had no idea. Mum had told her nothing except about holidays to Chartwell years ago. I said I didn't expect them to as I'd never told her much – as she was never interested anyway. Her Auntie Jo knew a lot, though.

Julie said it has to be published. People must know about it. I made her promise to wait till I was gone and whatever money was made from it could go half to her and the boys and the rest to the Legion to help old and not-so-old warriors like me. She agreed. She's a sensible girl.

Some of her pals have offered to help me move. Julie sometimes brings them when she visits. The girls have pink hair and earrings through their lips and noses and the boys have skinheads and are fascinated to hear my stories. They're very nice and they always do justice to my hospitality. I miss them when they leave.

One of them wants to join the army as he can't find a job. I advised him to join a regiment where he can learn a trade. 'Don't become an infantryman,' I said, 'all you learn is how to kill.' He listened carefully and said thanks, it sounded like good advice. Sad that young lads are still forced to enlist as there's no work. Some things never change.

I'll miss this house. So many memories. The people who have bought it seem decent types. They've moving up here from Driffield. They said I can come over anytime. I don't think I will, somehow.

I'm pretty sure I'll enjoy my new surroundings. It over-looks the South Bay, by the Spa and near The Grand. I have a room to myself with a lovely view of the sea. I have my own television and I'm bringing a lot of my old knick-knacks with me. The most important one is my video recorder. I don't know where I'd be without it. It still amazes me how I can watch the football on one channel and record something else on another at the same time to watch later. I like films best but not war films. I love Westerns. John Wayne, James Stewart and Robert Mitchum are my favourites.

I do have trouble understanding how to use it and Julie and her friends have to assist me. I know a few of the residents at the home and a couple of the staff are pretty knowl-edgeable and have promised to show me how to work it. My nephews in Edinburgh send me tapes of Hearts matches and that's always something to look forward to. My old team went through a bad patch for a few years but are now back and doing well. They have some really good young players like Robertson, Mackay, Colquhoun and Levein. I can see those boys playing for Scotland one day.

The down side of living on the South Shore is that St Mary's is at the other end of town. I go there regularly to put flowers on the graves of my girls and Tom. I might not be able to for that much longer, but where there's a will there's always a way, as the old saying goes.

I was at the doctor the other day. He told me that I had the heart and lungs of a man forty years younger. My bloods are good and everything else, kidneys and liver are in fine shape. The arthritis and rheumatics won't kill me but will continue to affect my quality of life. I have slightly high blood pressure and I must take my pills, exercise the best I can and see him regularly so he can keep an eye on me. He said he has no doubt I'll receive my telegram from the Queen.

I feel good. I've got a new life ahead of me. I've got Vivian, I won't be alone and I've got my video. Best of all, I have my grandchildren. The staff in the Home arrange bingo nights and sing-songs and there's a weekly trip to the Pictures and Legion for dominoes and other games. Not a bad life, I'd say.

It's not been a bad life altogether. I've been blessed, no doubt about it. But there's nothing more to tell. I'm riding off into the sunset like one of my beloved cowboys. And to think it all began with a stolen ten shilling note, and a wee Edinburgh boy who ran away from home to help his family.

A poor but resolute young lad, who found himself fortunate enough to journey through life walking proudly at the side of a great man.

THE END